During and after the last war Ted Allbeury served as an officer in the Intelligence Corps, working on counter-intelligence duties. Since then he has been a director of an advertising agency, a farmer, managing director of a pirate radio station and a PR consultant. He now lives in Lamberhurst, Kent, with his family.

By the same author

# TED ALLBEURY

# All Our Tomorrows

**GRANADA**
London Toronto Sydney New York

Published in paperback by Granada Publishing Limited in 1983

ISBN 0 583 13606 0

First published in Great Britain by
Granada Publishing 1982
Copyright © Ted Allbeury 1982

Granada Publishing Limited
Frogmore, St Albans, Herts AL2 2NF
and
36 Golden Square, London W1R 4AH
515 Madison Avenue, New York, NY 10022, USA
117 York Street, Sydney, NSW 2000, Australia
60 International Boulevard, Rexdale, Ontario R9W 6J2, Canada
61 Beach Road, Auckland, New Zealand

Printed and bound in Great Britain by
Collins, Glasgow.
Set in Monophoto Times

This one is for
Alewyn Birch

Few people can be happy unless they hate some other person, nation or creed.

Bertrand Russell

British Communists should, if necessary, use every kind of trick, cunning, illegal means, concealment of the truth or prevarication in order to get into and stay in the trades unions. They should learn to support the Labour Party leaders by their votes 'as the rope supports the hanged man'.

Lenin

# 1

A long spur of elms extended from the south-east corner of the woods, down the slope of the meadow to a few yards short of the bridge that led to the farm-buildings. The pale yellow early-morning sun of March cast long shadows in front of the cattle as they made their way slowly across the bridge to the meadow on the near side of the stream. There was a grey coating of frost on the grass and the breath of the two men following the herd hung in the air.

The two Germans standing just inside the woods had woollen scarves across their lower faces. They watched the movement of the cows and the two farm-labourers. As the herd slowly made its way up to the edge of the woods the taller of the two herdsmen walked alongside the leading animals. Five minutes later he was inside the woods following the white painted blobs on the trunks of the trees.

As he approached the Germans, he said *'Dobry den.'* The taller of the two men held out his hand, *'Tag.'*

An hour later they were in the big house on the outskirts of Brunswick that was used as a safe-house by the West German intelligence service, the BfV. Five hours later, after the man had bathed and they had started his de-briefing, one of them left the room and called an unlisted telephone number in Bonn.

By the early evening there were six men interrogating the man. Not aggressively but carefully and meticulously, with the calm assurance that comes from knowing that their time and effort had not been wasted.

The man they were interrogating was a major in the KGB. A liaison officer between the KGB and the Soviet military intelligence organisation, the GRU. He had contacted them four months earlier and they had gone through the usual cautious processes of testing applied to all potential defectors. Motives, information offered and pay-off required. He had been reluctant to tell them what his motives were and would go no further on what he had to offer other than to say that it was vitally important. They already knew of him and were aware that he could provide top-grade information if he so chose. But it meant taking chances to let him come over with so little. He could be a KGB plant. He could be no more than a con-man hoping to sell routine stuff for a flat and a pension, and they already had half a dozen of those. But there was something about him that made them eventually take the risk and arrange his crossing a few miles south of the Helmstedt check-point.

The photographic section had already enlarged the microdots he had concealed on the back of his upper dentures. That information alone would have justified their decision, But there was far more. He was talking freely, answering their questions, and his motives were clear. He was scared by what was going to happen. And they were scared too. It had always been a possibility but because it never happened it had gradually been dismissed as an unlikely scenario.

One of the interrogators drove back through the night to Bonn, and another took the late plane to Berlin. A girl was waiting for him at Tegel. A French girl, who sat drinking coffee with him in the airport restaurant, the plain brown envelope folded to fit her handbag. She knew nothing of the information contained in the envelope which she delivered at noon the following day to a man in a flat over a fishmonger's shop in the rue Monge in Paris.

The information that the defector had brought with him, and its time-scale, might possibly have allowed the NATO forces or the United Nations to prevent an aggressive plan being turned into bloody reality. Instead, it became a catalyst that worked its chemistry on centuries of rivalry and hatred, between England and France, stretching back through the battle of Agincourt, to 1066; and forward to farmers bickering over Golden Delicious apples and the import of chickens and turkeys. Those ancient rivalries, and the underlying hatreds, provided the excuse for a weak but ruthless and ambitious politician to turn a potentially grave incident into a certain disaster. A disaster that would affect the lives of millions of people.

# 2

He nodded his acknowledgement brusquely as the mess sergeant put the drink beside him on the table. When he had finished leafing slowly through the television pages of the *Radio Times* and then through the *TV Times*, he tossed them both onto the seat of the nearest armchair. He reached for the glass and held it to the light, then sipped his drink cautiously. There were only two real danger spots so far as he could see.

Colonel Harry Andrews checked the TV drama offerings whenever he was likely to be at home for most of a week. Not that he was interested in drama. Far from it. He loathed drama, whether it was on the stage or in real life. And he included in his loathing playwrights, actors and particularly actresses, and all those hangers-on who earned money from any form of drama. Most of all he loathed his wife. Not because she was connected in any way with the stage but because of the effect it had on her.

The Sunday film on BBC-1 was about the gradual decline of a once beautiful woman, a Hollywood star, and her neglect by old friends, her husband, her lovers, when at last her fortune has been frittered away and her beautiful body is no longer desirable. For five days Paula would play that part in their married quarters. Tears would brim over her eyelids, while she repeated the same banal phrases of reproach from the film. Paula Andrews identified immediately with all down-trodden, hard-done-by women, from Delilah to Erin Pizzey's battered wives. You didn't *have* to end up neurotic just because you were breathtakingly beautiful when you were 17; but being that beautiful certainly helped if you were determined to make neurosis your career. And if that beauty was allied to a natural acting talent, and the kind of vivid, if distorted, imagination that all psychopathic liars rely on, then you could enjoy making the lives of your nearest and dearest a living hell.

He knew she would play the fallen star for only five days because on the Friday following there was Lauren Bacall and Humphrey Bogart in *To Have and Have Not*. That would change her in ten minutes into the lovely, wise-cracking woman of the world – amateurishly lighting and smoking a cigarette, eyes half-closed as she looked at him, despising him for his weakness. Or was that Bette Davis in *The Scapegoat*?

Harry Andrews treated his reading of the *Radio Times* as one of his special SAS groups would treat a routine reconnaissance. As the army said: 'Time spent in reconnaissance is seldom wasted.' Forewarned is forearmed, and all that. The colonel took his wife's idiosyncrasies in his stride. He had coped with them for fifteen years and you don't get to be a colonel in the SAS by dwelling on minor details. Way back he had made out a list of things he could do to alleviate his wife's condition and his own situation. He had tried several GPs, four psychiatrists, energetic sex, paternalism, and had finally settled on indifference as the lifeboat for both of them. He had watched the psychiatrists and other experts settle down to their various therapies. They never admitted defeat. But they were always defeated. She was a psychopathic personality, would always lie, always be totally unreliable, and her apologies and contrition would inevitably be spurious. They told *him* this, not her. She was too beautiful to be told such damning facts. And once she was off their lists as a patient they could set about getting her into bed. It took no great planning to do this. She knew that they knew what she was, and letting them sleep with her was proof that she had won.

Andrews walked back to his office in the old vicarage, unlocked his office door and separated one key from the others on the ring before he sat down at the metal desk.

It was the afternoon of an early spring Saturday and only the men on guard-duty were around. Most of them were playing or watching cricket, in nearby Tunbridge Wells. Harry Andrews had been a cricket Blue and had played for one of the minor counties, but from the day he had been promoted to captain, hobbies and sports to him became solely a means of occupying the minds and energies of troops who might otherwise get bored – to a point where they became a nuisance to the general public and the police. Andrews loved them all as if they were his sons. But he was a cool, tough father who expected a look from his pale brown eyes to make words unnecessary.

He unlocked the bottom right-hand drawer in the desk and took out the two files. The thicker file was labelled 'Joint Intelligence Committee Reports 1980–1984' and the second file had, hand-written on its cover, the title 'Cromwell – Critical Path Analysis'. He opened the thick file and read slowly through the latest monthly report dated January 1984. Twenty minutes later he reached for the telephone without looking up, still reading, and asked the duty officer to get him an Edinburgh number.

Despite the clear blue sky there was a thin scattering of snow on the hillside and small drifts where the wind had swept it against the outcrops of stone. The thin black and white collie was crouched on her belly watching the sheep, inching forward to stop them from crossing the shallow stream. Cautious and controlled so that the flock didn't panic, because it was the last week in February and the rams had been put in with them, as usual, on Guy Fawkes' night. Those that had lambed already were down by the barn, but the rest had been left up on the hills. The flurries of snow had made him decide to be cautious and bring them down nearer the farm buildings. They were mainly small, hardy, Welsh Mountain, but there were thirty or so that had been served by a Swaledale ram to improve the fleeces. Their rumps had a blue patch instead of the usual red and they looked heavier in lamb than the rest.

As the flock of over three hundred streamed down the valley he looked across to the mountains. A buzzard hung in the air above the spur of the hill, on the look-out for new-born lambs, and where the tree-line ended the rockfaces were purple away from the fading sun. The man, Glyn Thomas, was a poet as well as a farmer, and he smiled to himself as he realised that his mind was half on the beauty of the hills and half on his lambing figures, which were reasonable but not good. An average of 1.5 still made him thankful for the Hill Farm Subsidy.

Looking down to the foot of the hill he saw the smoke from the stone chimney curling up straight until it met the wind as it came off the hill. The farmhouse was long and narrow. Stone, with a slate roof, it had been built in 1820, and the L-shaped barn a few years later. The bigger open barn, and the stables block, had been added by his father, and the small milking parlour for the twenty-five Friesians was only five years old. It had been an experiment and had not yet proved its worth. In the one mild winter he had made a good profit but in the other years he had barely broken even. Four generations of his family had farmed the same hills and valleys. But it looked as if he would be the last. Meg was 34 now; the gynaecologist in Cardiff had gone over the tests with them and suggested with a smile that all he could advise was that they went on trying. Their machinery was in good working order. Both of them. Glyn Thomas smiled again as his father's oft repeated words echoed in his mind: 'Maybe the Good Lord is sending you a message.'

As the massive ladle swung on its chain Joe Langley watched them working, noting the surge of scum as the ladle tilted forward to fill the two hand-held ladles. The two men walked to the lines of moulding boxes and as they moved from one to another, pouring, he got that old familiar smell of oil and sand.

He waited until they had re-filled the ladles and poured until all the moulds were filled and steaming. Then he walked over to the two moulders and the young labourer.

'How long you been working here, lad?'

'This is my third week, Mr Langley.'

Langley pointed to the rake in the youth's hand. 'Has anyone shown you how to use that?'

'Yes, sir.'

'Well why didn't you use it, then. You're just letting the slag flow over into the first ladle. That means two castings for the scrap-heap. Pulls down your piece-work rates and wastes the company's money.'

The youth stood silent and embarrassed. Langley looked at him for a moment or so then nodded and walked away.

In his wooden shack of an office he dumped the pile of computer print-outs onto the side table and sat down at his desk. Even the scrap figures were on the computer now, up-dated hourly, and broken down into locations and teams. If he took action on every flaw thrown up by the figures they might just as well close down. The equipment was out of date, but some Ministry man had said that their work was vital. They were producing spares for army tanks that had long been obsolete. But they provided statistics that helped the Ministry of Defence justify their spending on Trident and Matador. Not that it kept the others in NATO happy. Just four Emergency strike groups were left in Germany. Fifteen thousand men. And three years still to go before Trident was operational.

The phone rang as he was reaching for it. It was the gateman letting him know that the night shift foreman was on the premises so he was free to clock off.

At 48 Joe Langley was a stocky broad-shouldered man who had spent all his working life since the army in iron and steel foundries. Despite the unhealthy working conditions he was as healthy and energetic as he was when he had first started work. He no longer played football for the works team, but he was a much respected off-spinner for the local cricket club in Aston. Born a Catholic he had abandoned his faith early on, out of distaste for the troubles in Belfast. He missed the singing and the element of showbiz but most of all he missed the consolation of attributing the world's evils to the limitless wisdom of an unseen God. With an instinct to belong, he had briefly considered the virtues of the Quakers, the Salvation Army and the Congregational Church, and had finally decided that, uncomfortable though it might be, he would go it alone. In fact, without realising it, he had found his religion: the Amalgamated Union of Engineering Workers, Foundry Section. Before that it had been No. 2 Squadron, the SAS Regiment.

It was an old-fashioned office, with the walls lined with mahogany, and a large walnut book-case behind the antique partners desk. Despite the tall windows, the heavy curtains kept out most of the light. The whole room spoke of generations of solid success. In the waiting room outside hung the traditional portraits of past High Court judges but in the office itself the paintings were of Scottish landscapes – none of them by well-known artists but all of more than mere competence.

The man at the desk was in his mid-thirties, neatly dressed in a light grey suit. Neatness was characteristic. He was neatly featured and neatly built. While in the Army he had played rugby for Scotland. Good looking and lightly built, he had set many female hearts a-flutter when, as full-back, he waited calmly for the ball as opposing forwards pounded towards him.

After his clerk had knocked on the door and opened it for a tall, gaunt, elderly man, he stood up and took his client's bony hand.

'I'm sorry I had to drag you down here, sir, but the document has to be signed in my office. It's a legal requirement but it has some sense to it.'

'And what sense might that be, may I ask?'

'Do sit down, sir.' He moved back behind his desk as the old man made himself comfortable. 'It was originally to prevent beneficiaries from taking advantage of sickness or senility, and in the end it was modified so that lawyers themselves were reminded of their own responsibilities.'

The old man bared his yellow teeth in a grin. 'So just you be reminded, Jamie Boyle. And how is that busy father of yours?'

'Down in Westminster, pressing the case for an independent Scotland, as usual.'

'And that pretty wife?'

. 'She's resting at the moment. They've just come back from a Scandinavian tour and they're all exhausted. She swears she never wants to see a pair of ballet shoes again.'

'You know I never had the slightest interest in ballet until your parents took me to see her dance just after you were married. I had always loved the music, and admired all those pretty bottoms, but that was all. But your Jeanie ... I thought at first she was on wires or something. I'm still not convinced it isn't some mechanical trickery. She seems to float in the air before she decides to come down. I'm a fan, I tell you. I never miss a couple of visits when they're here and she's dancing.'

16

Jamie Boyle smiled. 'I'll tell her that. She'll lap it up.' He picked up the two pages stapled together and pushed them across his desk. 'You have to read them first, sir.'

'Did you draw them up yourself?'

'Every word.'

'Then I don't need to read 'em.'

'I want you to. It's part of me being responsible.'

The old man grunted, took out his glasses from his top pocket and picked up the papers. He read them through twice and then reached into his pocket for an old-fashioned fountain pen. After he had signed, half-way down the second page, he leaned back in his chair, took off his glasses and stuffed them back in his pocket together with the pen. For a moment he sat there in silence. Then, sighing, he said, 'It's a funny world, Jamie. Here I am, arranging to dispose of what I've accumulated in a life-time. But as I walked up here from the club I wondered why I was bothering.'

'In what way, sir?'

'It looks to me like the world I know is coming to an end. Not when I die, but long before. Whatever happened to us? Maybe we never really recovered from World War II. But why us? Why only us? The Germans, the French, even the Italians all recovered. They have their ups and downs but by and large they carry on. But we're beginning to be the leper colony of Europe. There's all this talk that we are going to pull out of the EEC and NATO but it's no longer a threat to them. They *want* us to pull out. They've had enough of us. We're a burden. Financially, economically, militarily, we are a burden. And a complaining, disagreeable burden at that. How did we get like this?'

Boyle looked at the old man for a moment, then he shrugged. 'We let things drift. We let the criminals get away with it. We let the thugs take over. What was unbelievable became the norm. Rioting, looting, hooliganism, were excused as being caused by racialism, and an acceptable response to the police doing their legal duty. Nobody liked it, nobody wanted it. But nobody wanted to do anything about it. They said it would be putting the clock back, giving in to revenge. The time was never right to take action. So it paid to be a thug.'

'Who's they?'

'You, me, the politicians, all of us. We are scared of being labelled Fascists or reactionaries. It's nice to be soft. And liked. And in the end it could get you votes. The thugs and militants are the most militant constituency so you advocate tolerance and rehabilitation, instead of just punishment.'

'Is that all it is?'

'More or less. We've become moral cowards and now we have to pretend that it's right. My father tells me that the Canadian and Australian governments are going to ban all immigration from Britain. It's not just the thugs they're refusing but the victims too. They say they don't want Britain's middle-class lack of morale and guts imported into their communities. We didn't value what we'd got. And now it's gone. Freedom, tolerance, democracy . . . we threw them away.'

'And nobody's going to do anything to stop all this?'

'It's too late, Mr MacKay. It's too late now. We can only deal with what happens, when it happens.'

'What's going to happen, Jamie?' MacKay said softly.

Boyle opened his mouth to speak, hesitated and then closed his mouth. There was no point in frightening the old man any further. He shrugged again. 'Maybe nothing will happen. Maybe it'll all settle down again.'

The old man stood up unsteadily, resting his hand on the desk to retain his balance. He sighed heavily as he left the room without speaking, waving his hand vaguely towards the young man behind the desk.

The big clumsy-looking youth leaned with his elbows

on the counter, looking at the Indian checking invoices.

'They gonna do you, Sanji.'

The Indian looked up at the boy. 'Why would they want to do that, Freddie?'

'Becos' you're a Paki. That's why.'

'I'm an Indian, Freddie, not a Pakistani.'

'Well it's all the same, in'it?'

'If being English is the same as being German then they're the same. They're two different countries. Two different nations. In no way connected. In fact you could say that at the moment they are enemies.'

'But you're all blacks.'

'We're all Asians. If that's what you mean.'

'You gonna board the shop up Sad'dy night?'

'I board it up every night, Freddie.'

'They say you're the ringleader.'

'Of what?'

'The resistance.'

'Who are we resisting then?'

'The skinheads. The NF. The Whites.'

'Why are you telling me all this?'

'I like you, Sanji. I don't want you to get beat up.'

'They won't beat me up, Freddie. I'm not scared of them. We know how to deal with them now.'

'They're coming from all over. They've hired coaches.'

Sanjiva Singh smiled. 'They're going to be disappointed, Freddie.'

'How's that, Sanji?'

'You'll read it in the Sunday papers.'

'My old man says you're the leader of all the local blacks.'

'I'm going to shut up now, Freddie. D'you want to help me?'

'How's Indi?'

'She's fine, Freddie.'

'When you gonna let me take her to the cinema?'

'She prefers Indian films, Freddie.'

'OK. I'll take her to one of the Indian places.'

'They're all in Hindi, Freddie. No sub-titles even.'

'Doesn't matter Sanji.'

The Indian looked at the ungainly youth, his deep brown eyes not unsympathetic. 'We'll talk about it one day, you and me. I'll explain things to you.'

'You don't want 'er going out with white fellas, is that it?'

'Not entirely. Like I said ... we'll talk about it.'

The youth moved towards the door and pointed at the Indian behind the counter. 'If you want help at the weekend you just send for me, Sanji. Don't you forget.'

The Indian nodded. 'I won't forget, Freddie. You're a good boy. Take care of yourself.'

Sanjiva Singh put up the boards on the windows, double locked and barred the shop and set the security alarm, and then went into the small store behind the shop, nodding to the four men silently waiting there. They followed him down the corridor and up the stairs to the room on the first floor.

On the wall were large scale maps of various districts in London where there was a sizeable population of Asians. At a long table a young Sikh, his head turbaned despite the earphones clamped to his head, sat operating a Yaesu FT-101ZD transceiver. A cassette recorder was plugged into the set and a scanner was flickering a red digital display of frequencies being monitored on a Bearcat 200.

The four men sat round the trestle table in the centre of the room and Sanjiva Singh sat at the head of the table. They all spoke Hindi, and two also spoke Gujarati, but at their meeting they spoke in English. A thin man next to Singh said, 'Was he threatening trouble, Sanjiva?'

'No. On the contrary, he was warning me and offering his protection.' He smiled. 'He has a soft spot for my daughter Indira. He wants to create a good impression.' He raised his eyebrows. 'To work, my friends. There is much to be done.'

An old man with a beard said softly, 'Has it worked, Sanjiva? Has it worked?'

Singh smiled and nodded. 'As from Wednesday last we have thirty sources of information. Straight from the horse's mouth.' He smiled at the English slang and went on, 'It has cost us 25,000 new pounds, but it is well worth it and will save us ten, twenty times that amount. And save us blood and humiliation too. Twelve phones are permanently tapped and twenty rooms and meeting places are bugged. We know every move they plan and what is even better we know their doubts and fears.' He paused. 'And they have many doubts and fears, my friend. I will play you some of the tapes. They will lift your hearts. However ...' he lifted his hands gracefully, '... there is bad news too. There is no doubt that they are being advised by men at the Soviet Embassy. One of them is the man who has offered to help us. Who tells us that the Soviet Union is our mother and father. The protector of the down-trodden, the disadvantaged.'

'And what do we do with what we know, my friend?'

A man in a khaki shirt and slacks interrupted quietly, 'We kill them. The ones who matter.'

The old man sighed. 'You kill one dog and the master buys another.'

Singh waited to see if the others had anything to say but nobody else spoke. He said softly. 'I have already made the arrangements. I have given the orders. They were all volunteers. All of them, strong, resourceful and determined. Five of them were in the army.'

'Who were they?' the man in khaki asked.

Singh smiled. 'I just call them the "young lions". They will have no other names.'

The old man smiled and looked at the others to see if

they had noticed the significance of the name. In Hindu, 'Singh' is the word for 'lion'.

They talked for a few minutes, embarrassed by the decisiveness of Singh, and then three of them left. Only Singh and the old man still sat there. The old man lit a thin cheroot and blew out the smoke. 'What are you going to do about the Russian, Sanji? Do we kill him too, to teach them a lesson?'

'No. We teach them another way. By tomorrow night there will be twelve of them dead. Publicly they are not connected. They are the men behind the scenes. Slowly, slowly the newspapers will put the pieces together. The police will know but they won't care too much. A few token raids but all this ...' he waved his hand around the room '... will be gone two hours from now. The Russians will know. They will offer their help again. And we shall take it.'

'Why? Why should we do that?'

'Because they are more on our side than anyone else. They play games with the others to cause the breakdown of society here. The more street fighting, the more looting and arson, the harsher the reaction by the police and the government. Soon there will be civil war. But we shall stand to one side. The communists will win in the end. One more year, maybe two, and the English will pay for twenty years of humiliation. That is all I want. All that I have planned for. Always they had a scapegoat. The Irish, the Jews, then us ... the West Indians, the Pakistanis, the blacks they call us. The blacks. Remember that, old man. And thank the Russians for helping us.'

'Why should they help us?'

'Because we help them get what they want.'

'Are you a Communist, Sanji?'

Singh smiled. 'Old man, I am first a Hindu, second an Indian from Calcutta, and third a husband and father. Beyond that nobody should know or care what I am.'

22

The old man stood up slowly and walked to the door. 'You know where I am if you want me, Sanji ...' he paused, '... remember the man who rode on the back of the tiger, my friend.'

Singh's brown eyes were hard as stones. 'I am the tiger, old man. Remember that.'

# 3

He drove the car over the river bridge, down the main street and on until the old buildings gave way to open countryside. He generally counted the churches as he went through the town. There were nine not counting the convent.

It was about twenty minutes before he parked his car in the official parking lot and the man gave him his plastic card. He looked up as he started down the main street. There were blue patches of sky but the clouds were moving so fast from the high winds that he felt for a moment as if the ground was moving under his feet. For a second he closed his eyes, and when he opened them he looked towards the shop windows. It was a typical small-town high street, with the usual complement of chain stores. Woolworths, Tesco, Boots, Marks and Spencer and a dozen or so small retailers. A café, a radio shop, a greengrocer's, a news-agent's and on the corner the entrance to a small cinema.

Although it was all typically English it wasn't English. It was almost 200 kilometres north-east of Moscow. Not far from the ancient town of Suzdal. The town that Lev Aleksander Savalev had driven through.

Suzdal on the River Kamenka is one of the oldest and most historic towns in the Soviet Union. Documents still exist chronicling its existence in 1024, but Prince Vladimir of Kiev had sent a missionary bishop to build a church there long before. Visitors admired its ancient buildings, but Lev

24

Savalev loathed the place. After four years in New York and six years in London he longed for the bright lights and the embassy parties that had been his daily routine. The transfer had meant promotion, however, and Savalev was driven by ambition. Whether it was at Moscow University or on a dozen KGB courses he had attended, Savalev was always the top man.

The training centre had been built in 1979 and hundreds of men and women had passed through the gates in the high perimeter wall. Men and women who came from a score of different backgrounds. Lawyers, administrators, engineers, managers, police, the Red Army and Air Force, and workers from the major industries. All had two things in common. They already spoke some English, and their backgrounds and skills met the requirements of a computer program that had been designed and written in 1975.

In 1975 the program had been no more than a serious exercise. It concerned an unlikely eventuality. But KGB resources of money, time and manpower are vast, and it came to be evaluated as interesting and worthwhile. The courses lasted six months and included intensive language training. Students lived as if they were in England, using English currency in the shops to buy English goods. Because the instruction was so concentrated, the course was reckoned to be the equivalent of eighteen months actually spent in England.

Major Lev Savalev was Commandant of Training School 405. After the first two courses he had found the job intensely boring, but he was too experienced and sophisticated a KGB man to let it show. There were usually several pretty students who helped relieve the boredom.

Savalev had never married. He had seen too often how a wife and family could hinder a man or make him vulnerable to pressures that he could otherwise have resisted. His superiors had tacitly approved his determination not to be emotionally entangled. And they turned a blind eye to his compulsion to head for Moscow at weekends without reasonable excuses.

There were two or three hundred men in the Soviet Union whose lives and careers from an early age were shaped and guided towards some specific rôle of which they were completely unaware. Savalev was one of them. He was vaguely aware of protection from above, but attributed it to luck and personality rather than design. It was accepted by those who arranged such things that probably fewer than twenty or so of these men would ever fulfil their designated rôles. They were there as the insurance that if certain events took place, if some evaluation team's forecast turned out to be true, the right man would be available. There was a special section at Dzerzhinski Square primed for forward thinking, divided into groups whose whole time was devoted to thinking solely about the needs of the KGB in the future.

There was a smoked-salmon sandwich and a half-bottle of white wine at the side of his desk. In front of him were the usual two days' old copies of *The Times*, the *Daily Telegraph* and the *Guardian*. He pushed the other two newspapers aside and slowly leafed through the *Guardian* as he ate the sandwich.

Ten minutes later he reached for the thick red marker and outlined three items for the research people to cut out and put on file. He read all three items again as he sipped the wine.


### ARMED STUDENTS HUNTED NF RIVALS

A lecturer and eight students formed a Left-wing 'hit squad' and armed with a 'fearsome array of weapons', used a polytechnic college's van to look for Right-wing rivals, a court heard yesterday.

Their weapons included a nail-studded wooden batten, a sledgehammer and a length of iron tubing, said Mr Anthony Hammond, prosecuting at Manchester Crown Court.

'It is quite clear they intended, if they found any National Front members, to use these weapons with whatever consequences might follow,' he said.

All nine were Trotskyists and members or supporters of the Socialist Workers' Party, said Mr Hammond.

In the dock were John Penney, aged 28, a sociology lecturer of Riverside Park, Northwich, and students Stephen Tilzey, aged 23, of Brooklands Road, Sale; Brian Broadley, aged 21, of Blenheim Road, Bolton; Michael Butroyd, aged 31, of Churchill Street, Stockport; Robert Piatt, aged 27, of Belmont Street, Stockport.

Stephen Cooper, aged 24, of Foxland Walk, Wythenshawe, Manchester; Mark Kent, aged 22, of Blakelaw Road, Macclesfield; Paul Hallatt, aged 20, of John Nash Crescent, Hulme, Manchester, and David Smith, aged 23, of Robert Adam Crescent, Hulme, Manchester.

They will be sentenced today.

## TWELVE YEARS FOR HELL'S ANGEL WHO KILLED BOY

One of the leaders of a London Hell's Angels group called Satan's Breed was gaoled for 12 years at the Old Bailey yesterday for stabbing a schoolboy to death.

Stephen Baker, aged 21, the group's vice-president, used a knife bought the previous day to kill Tony Marsh, 15, in a row over a 13-year-old girl, said Miss Ann Curnow, prosecuting.

The judge said: 'The background in this case is quite horrifying,' he said. '... You start an organisation dedicated to violence, you take drink and drugs, you attract young people into your organisation, and it ends with an epileptic boy of 15 being killed.'

A plea by Baker, of Armoury Way, Wandsworth, of not guilty to murdering the youth at a squat in Princes Way, Wimbledon, on 22 May but guilty to manslaughter, was accepted by the prosecution.

Miss Curnow said that the president of Satan's Breed, Stephen Cook, was serving six years imprisonment for other offences.

Mr Stuart Shields, QC, defending, said although Baker had a previous conviction for manslaughter, he was neither a vicious killer nor a vicious criminal.

## ANDERTON PAYS TRIBUTE TO HIS FORCE

Greater Manchester's Chief Constable, Mr James Anderton, yesterday published a post-Scarman commendation of his force for the way it handled the summer riots on Moss Side Manchester, and Toxteth, Liverpool.

Mr Anderton's commendation, copies of which will be framed and hung in police stations, reads:

'The Chief Constable has commended the Greater Manchester Police force for outstanding police service in connection with the steadfast devotion to duty, the most distinguished professional competence, enormous bravery, great fortitude, and loyalty to their calling and public trust displayed magnificently by all police officers, civilian staff and special constables of the force in quelling the riotous disorderly and criminal behaviour widespread in Toxteth, Moss Side, and elsewhere in July 1981, and in effectively and speedily restoring the Queen's Peace throughout the county of Greater Manchester for the benefit and protection of all its citizens.'

The chief constable explained there was no other way he could adequately express his personal gratitude to his force for 'their exceptional courage and impressive achievements in a time of serious civil unrest when the disciplined strength and integrity of the police stood between freedom and anarchy'.

Pushing the newspapers to one side he reached for the internal phone and dialled the number for Central Registry. Five minutes later he signed the docket for the three files.

He opened the thickest one. The red diagonal stripe from corner to corner emphasised its confidentiality, and its title was explicit. 'Political infiltration in UK. Current Quarter. Part I, Labour Party.' The two other files covered 'Part II, the Trades Unions', and what was referred to as 'Part III, General'. A pasted-on index listed: press, TV, radio, local authorities, armed forces, the arts, miscellaneous.

# 4

The canteen looked much the same as it had twenty years before when it was built. Concrete floor, breeze-block walls painted white every other year. Long wooden tables, the older ones covered with dark brown linoleum, the newer ones with formica tops and metal edging. Wooden folding chairs for the foremen, and stackable tubular chairs for the rest of them. At the far end the metal shutters where the food was dished out were closed and padlocked, but the smell of fried fish and chips still lingered from their lunch-time meal.

There were six chairs behind two tables placed end to end and in front of the tables were a dozen rows of chairs. The other eating tables had been stacked in the corners of the room.

Joe Langley rapped on the table with a spanner as he stood up, and the chatter gradually subsided.

'Good evening, brothers. You all know what we're here for tonight. Mr Mercer from the union headquarters is here as an observer. We only have one item on the agenda. Is it the wish of this meeting to make the unofficial strike official. Whatever we decide, the union will make up its own mind. But they want to know what we want on the shop-floor.'

As Joe Langley paused to collect his thoughts several voices shouted. 'Have a bloody vote now. Cut the cackle.'

Langley nodded to acknowledge the comment. 'We'll vote

when we've heard the facts, brothers. So I call on Arthur Macfarlane to give the views of the unofficial strike committee. As you all know, he's the committee chairman.' Langley nodded to a youngish man with a plaid shirt and a thin sallow face.

'Comrades,' he started, and the Glasgow accent was not only unmistakable but exaggerated. 'Comrades. Our Chairman has described the strike as unofficial. In a comment to the local press he described it as a wild-cat strike not wanted by the men. Let me tell you right now that my committee have received one hundred per cent support from the men in the fettling shop from day one. The issue is clear. It is Labour Party policy that the capitalist weapon known as the neutron bomb should not be stationed in this country. We believe that castings are being produced here for the chassis of launchers for that bomb. We will play no part in the manufacture of these castings. We have told the management so. We were given two days ... forty-eight hours, to carry on production or we should be locked out. We have asked the union to make our strike official but they haven't had the guts to give us an answer.' He pointed his finger towards the rows of men. 'Are you going to be party to making weapons that are designed to kill people and preserve buildings? They admit that's what this bomb is designed to do. The Labour Party says they are infamous weapons. The resolution was passed by an overwhelming vote at the last two conferences. Are you going to defy that vote just to earn a few more coppers for the capitalist murderers who are the lackeys of the American military-industrial dictatorship?'

As he sat down dramatically there was a roar of applause from a particular group of men, a stamping of feet, and shouts of 'Bombs out, bombs out'. The group of men went on shouting as Joe Langley got to his feet but they gradually fell silent as men near them rounded on them.

'Brothers,' Joe Langley paused. 'And I say brothers. Comrades belong in another party even if they try to kid us and call themselves Labour. First of all the castings concerned have been made here for the last eight years. They are used on several British Army armoured vehicles. The management have assured me that so far as they know they are not parts of the launchers for any new weapon.

'Secondly. There is no such thing as a neutron bomb. It is a shell. An artillery shell to be used against tanks. The Soviet Forces have five times as many tanks on the frontiers of NATO countries as the Allies have. The shells kill tank crews not civilians. The Russians have mounted an extremely successful campaign against this shell because it neutralises their vast numbers of tanks. The Red Army's SS20s are several hundred times more destructive of civilian life than the neutron weapon. And of course the Russians have the neutron shell themselves. They just don't talk about it.

'But all that is not what we are dealing with in these works. A weapon that has been discussed by Parliament and voted on is a legitimate part of our defence system. If we strike against making some casting which may or may not be associated with that weapon we are indulging in a political strike. I've no need to remind you that the Industrial Relations Act 1982 makes such a strike not only illegal but makes the union concerned subject to fines that would exhaust our funds completely. What brother Macfarlane has started, and is trying to persuade you to support, is both illegal, and would cripple our union if it is continued.'

As he sat down there were cries of 'rubbish' and 'scab', until a man stood up at the back of the hall.

'Does that mean Brother Langley is asking us to defy the democratic vote of the Labour Party Conferences?'

Langley half stood. 'Brother, I was a delegate at both those conferences. I voted against the neutron weapon as the representative of the local party committee. But unfortunately votes at Labour Party Conferences are not necessarily government policy or the policy as voted in Parliament. Unlike some of my colleagues I believe in democracy. I may not like some laws, I may try to get them changed, but I respect the law of the land as decided by Parliament.'

Macfarlane stood up, his face flushed with anger. 'Comrades we came here to vote, I move we vote.'

Langley half-smiled. 'Put forward your resolution then.'

'I propose that this meeting demands that the union declare the strike official and takes steps to encourage other unions to support our stand.'

Several voices called out, 'Seconded.'

Langley, still sitting, said, 'That's a two-part resolution. Not allowed at shop-floor level. If you keep to the first part you can put the second part if the first part is voted successfully. Is that what you want?'

Macfarlane stood up again. 'I propose the union makes this strike official immediately.'

There were more voices seconding the proposal and as they died away Langley said, 'I propose an amendment to the proposal. I propose that it is left to the union leadership to decide whether this strike should be made official or called off.'

Two or three older men stood and seconded the amendment. The secretary called for a show of hands on the amendment and it was narrowly carried. The union representative was howled down as he stood up and tried to speak. Langley let the furore run for several minutes before he banged the spanner on the table and declared the meeting closed.

Back at his home Joe Langley sat in his armchair eating

a bacon sandwich with an enamelled mug of strong tea on the floor beside him. He had told his wife what had gone on at the meeting.

'What do you think the union will do, Joe?'

He shrugged. 'If they make the strike official they'll go bankrupt. The government are just waiting for a chance to show they mean business. A small union like ours, without any clout, is an ideal target. If they make the strikers go back every official of the union knows he's a marked man. The militants will work like beavers to oust them, and revoke their pensions.'

'It's terrible that a few men can do that.'

'The Union leaders should have stood up to them long ago. Everybody knew what the perishers were up to. They let them run the show. Nobody spoke up. Nobody said the emperor had no clothes on. The Party was just the same. Callaghan was trying to be another Wilson ... the man who could hold the Party together ... but he wasn't a Wilson ... they fixed him with "the winter of discontent" ... by the time Foot was the leader there was nothing left to lead ... he should have stuck to writing books.'

'How's it all going to end, Joe?'

'God knows, love. I keep saying to myself that we're too sensible a nation to let it go on ... but I'm beginning to wonder. But I tell you one thing, girl ... I'm glad we never had children. We thought it was a tragedy, and in a way it was. But, my God, I'm glad there's no hostages to fate from us.'

She looked at him with sad, worried eyes. She had never heard him talk so cynically before.

He said, 'Go on up. I'll lock up, and I've got a phone call to make.'

'Don't be long.'

'I won't.'

When he was alone he looked at the number that was

written, with the digits reversed, on the blank page of his driving licence. He dialled it slowly and it rang for several seconds before he heard the voice he recognised. He took a deep breath and said, 'It's Joe Langley. You can count me in.'

They had parked the stolen Jaguar broadside across the road on the south side of Sloane Square, and when the driver of the number 14 bus had climbed down, protesting, from his cab, Louden had struck him across the back of the neck with the police truncheon, and the rest of them had dragged the passengers off the bus.

There were forty of them, a few blacks but mainly white youths. They had assembled outside the Oval cricket ground an hour earlier and had rampaged along Meadow Road throwing bricks and stones through windows until they came on the Jaguar in Dorset Road. They had stolen the truck from a builder's yard. It was Martin Louden who had roused them to hi-jacking a bus. They had turned them over and burned them in the street riots, but they had never actually hi-jacked one.

Louden told Carr to drive the bus and he'd got it into bottom gear, nosing the Jaguar aside as he headed for King's Road. He stopped at the Markham Arms and the gang poured out. Shouting and chanting 'You'll never walk alone' they smashed window after window of every shop back to Sloane Square, throwing goods from the shops into the street, looting anything they fancied that was portable.

Martin Louden stood watching them, he wasn't interested in loot himself. As they came straggling back to the bus he passed the word round that they were going over the river, down to Croydon to give the 'posh bastards' a taste of what was coming to them.

By the time they were all back in the bus he had another

inspiration. He had once been on a road-mending crew employed on contract by a local council in the Croydon area and they'd worked in a place called Sanderstead. It consisted of road after road of posh middle-class houses, with a small row of shops at the top of the hill. The place was so phoney that there was some local law against pubs and there wasn't a single one in the whole of Sanderstead.

Two hours later he stood at the top of Sanderstead Hill, tense with excitement as the houses burned and the people ran screaming in all directions, beaten and savaged by his gang. They had used parked cars to stop the fire-engines getting through, and the fires were spreading rapidly. He saw Harper shoot down a man in pyjamas with his shotgun and there had been several other shots further down the hill. He went back to where the bus was parked and there were four or five of them taking their turns with a pretty young blonde. Despite the blood running from her nose you could tell that she was pretty. She had given up screaming and struggling. He gave them another twenty minutes and then he blew the whistle.

They drove back to London and dumped the bus in Stockwell, walking the mile or so to Kennington, Lambeth and Brixton. It was the first time that houses had been attacked as well as shops.

Just under a hundred houses had been completely burnt down, while a further hundred and fifty were rendered uninhabitable. Three men had been killed and forty-seven people severely injured. Nine girls or women had been victims of multiple rapes. The damage was officially estimated at twelve million pounds but that was only the first rough estimate.

Over the next two weeks similar attacks on houses rather than shops took place in the quieter middle-class suburbs of a dozen major cities.

ITV took its courage in both hands and planned a one hour documentary on the causes of the riots.

It was one of those tatty TV studio-sets so often used for discussion programmes. A cobbled-up desk for presenter and panellists. A cubist semi-circle of chipboard sprayed with dark brown paint, harshly lit by spots to add dramatic impact and hide the rest of the studio floor. The station logo pasted on the front. A low-budget producer's delight, and a caring director's nightmare. But caring TV directors were getting fewer and literally far between; most of them had moved to Canada, America, and South Africa while there were still immigration quotas for Britons.

George Foster was the host, chosen for his reputation for keeping a 'balance' between mortal enemies and even between feuding members of the various Labour party schisms. His ability to keep a 'balance' came from weakness rather than strength, ignorance rather than knowledge. He genuinely didn't give a damn about politics, either domestic or international, and this allowed him to look amazed and hurt when the insults flew. After he was billed as 'the man of the grass roots', politicians stepped carefully in his presence. You could be treading on millions of dreams and as many votes when you brought that look of shock to George Foster's face in tight close-up. Not a word of criticism but the effect was the same.

The other members of the panel were the usual self-publicising MPs. One Labour of the militant Left, and one Tory who had moved from a rather academic Enoch Powellist approach to what had been described by his detractors as 'Fascism with a human face'. They were the protagonists, and were accompanied by Mrs Patsy Greenhalgh and Debbie Lane representing the general public; and finally Dr Marvin Slanski, a practising psychiatrist who had moved from San Francisco when London began to look as if it might provide a better market for a specialist in 'Behaviourism as an element of social protest'.

Mrs Patsy Greenhalgh had eased her way into the public eye with her Society for the Protection of British Trees. She had known nothing about trees when she started, and a filmed interview from the early days, when she waved majestically towards a stand of ancient elms and invoked the nation's protection for 'these magnificent oaks, the trees that built the ships that beat the Spanish Armada', had been destroyed quite recently as a gesture of goodwill by the BBC's Deputy Head of TV Features. But she was a quick learner, and from trees she moved to conservation in general, without actually realising that by 1981 conservation would be as much part of the furniture of politics as adultery or monetarism. She had built up an image as the woman of common-sense, not afraid to speak her mind or even to display her ignorance. From the rural tree she had moved on to give newspaper readers and TV viewers the benefit of her rough-cast views on single-parent families, Milton Friedman and the International Monetary Fund.

Crispin Partridge had been an academic moron and a non-participator in all sports at Eton, but had achieved some minor notoriety as what masters called a troublemaker, and his friends called a radical. He spent his energy and his father's money on complaining in the media about the food, the accommodation, and the standard of teaching at the school. Finding that what started as popularity amongst his contemporaries slowly turned to an amusement that made him the butt of their schoolboy jokes he became rather spiteful, and remained spiteful for the rest of his life. As an MP he was able to indulge his taste for perpetual criticism. Abuse of parliamentary privilege allowed him to slander those he disliked, and no peccadillo by an Opposition MP was too petty to escape his indignant exposure. A regular and much publicised church-goer, he paraded a self-righteousness that only added weight to his campaign of revelation. Despite his thrusting ambition, self-publicising and considerable inherited wealth, he had never held office at even the most junior level. The self-styled gadfly of the government back benches was seen more as a clumsy may-fly by his seniors in the party.

Albert Laidlaw MP was the voice of the militant Left. A whining, complaining voice that came from the throat, and words that came from the gall-bladder. Having failed to become the leader of the Miners' Union he turned to politics and could find sound reasons for blaming the Tories for the weather, the increase in crime, strikes, abortions; and the media for the fact that he hadn't become leader of the miners. He was most heartily despised by most Labour MPs but not all Tories, some of whom considered that they owed 5% of their votes to his belligerent personality.

Debbie Lane was 27. A cool young woman who had achieved fame by refusing the prize money on a quiz show, saying that a child of eight could have answered the questions. She had been a prominent member of the Students' Union at Sussex University and was now the darling of both the media and the public for her tart responses to media interviewers. She had become a sort of gauge of a chat show's seriousness. If a producer had the courage to include her on a panel he knew he was not giving his interviewer or panel chairman an easy ride. She was very pretty and she wasn't rude, merely candid in her responses.

In the hospitality room George Foster stood with his clip-board and notes in one hand, a cigar in the other. On camera, of course, he always had an unlit pipe. Men who smoke pipes are men who can be trusted, Prime Ministers Baldwin and Wilson had shown the way.

'Patsy, you'll be on my immediate left, and Crispin will be on your left. Marvin I want you on my right, and Albert you'll be playing outside right. Don't try and follow the cameras, they'll follow you. All the signs are that we're going to get a big audience tonight. We've had a good advance press and I want us to present our views calmly and amiably.' He smiled. 'Especially our two politicians. Not too much of the old ding-dong stuff, and I'll keep pressing you for facts to back up your claims, so you've been warned.' He looked at his watch. 'Now Lydia will take you down to make-up and bring you back to the studio. Best of luck all of you. Make it a good programme.'

The camera had come in on Foster's face as he turned from introducing the panel. Reading from the Teleprompter he began his introduction.

'Tonight we want to discuss the causes of the spate of violence in the streets that has been a feature of the front pages of our newspapers for the last few weeks. Does it spring from racialism, despair on the part of the unemployed, a response to harassment by the police or is it perhaps deliberately stirred up by subversives for their own ends? So let me start the ball rolling with Albert Laidlaw. Albert.'

The ferrety face of Laidlaw came up on the monitors, eyebrows raised, mouth set in disdain.

'Well. We have all read what the media have to say about it. According to them it's an attack on society by militant left-wingers. Of course that's a load of old rubbish. What we are seeing is young people without jobs, without hope, and driven to desperation by the pressures of an uncaring and steel-hearted government. This government has deliberately provoked the working people of this country and are using the police as their shock troops to smash the will of the poor, the old and the sick. And the courts have lent themselves to a fascist government to oppress the trades unions. There is no doubt in my mind that . . .'

Foster interrupted. 'Right we'll come back to you again

Albert. Let's hear what Crispin Partridge has to say. Crispin.'

'We've heard all the usual left-wing jargon from our friend Albert Laidlaw. If you take what he says seriously, which I don't of course, it means that we go back to the days when trades-unionists left us with our dead unburied, threats to cut off power and water unless they were given even more money for the lowest productivity in the western world. The Trades Unions ran this country by leave of the last Labour government. And why shouldn't they? They pay the money that keeps the Labour Party going. So why shouldn't the piper call the tune? And what Albert Laidlaw is saying is that if you are unemployed you are free to attack the police, loot shops, rape and murder, destroy property and get away with it. If you're arrested with a looted TV set in your arms it's harassment by the police, and if you're sent to jail it's because our judges are crooked. It won't wash, Albert. The people aren't all fools.'

Foster nodded and pointed. 'Patsy Greenhalgh. Let's have the woman's point of view.'

Patsy Greenhalgh had one of those little-girl-lost voices that appealed to men and was seen as spurious by most women.

'Well, George. I don't know about the woman's point of view. I can only speak for myself, and I'd like to ask Crispin a question. If you and your colleagues in the government are aware of the situation, as you appear to be, why on earth don't you do something about it?'

Crispin Partridge put on his sincere face and spoke slowly as if to a child.

'My dear Patsy, we *are* doing something about it. That's what Albert Laidlaw is complaining about. He wants us to take the police off the streets and let the hooligans take over. He wants the courts to ignore the evidence and set the looters and bully boys free. And ...' he wagged a monitory finger, looking over the top of his glasses, '... anyone who agrees with Albert Laidlaw is not only against the maintenance of law and order but is actually supporting an attempt to destroy democracy in this country.'

'You should ...'

Foster waved Laidlaw down. 'Let us hear what our psychiatrist has to say. Marvin Slanski.'

'Well, as an American who chose to live in this fine country of yours, I tend to see the present situation as the product of social pressures. When I was still at Berkeley I published a paper on a whole series of experiments we carried out on rats who were kept on half rations in overcrowded conditions, and I see many features of that behaviour in the present situation over here. Over-crowding coupled with unemployment can lead to disturbed behaviour in all mammals. Man, I am afraid, is no exception.'

Laidlaw came in quickly. 'That's exactly what I've been saying, if you ...'

Crispin Partridge shouted him down. 'What rubbish. How can you try to deceive the country with that nonsense. These hooligans are not unemployed, most of them. They don't murder people and beat people up because they need food or money, they do it because they enjoy it. And the Trots, the Marxists, the Maoists, the Militant Tendency and all the other rag-tag and bobtail incite them to do it. If they're broke where do they get the money to buy CB radios to organise the street fighting? This country is riddled with subversives. Riddled with them.'

Laidlaw came in smiling. 'It's the old Reds under the beds story all over again. Blame everything on Moscow. Blame anyone you fancy except the Tory government.'

Foster intervened. 'Debbie. You've heard what's been said by the politicians. What do you think of it?'

41

Debbie Lane smiled. An amiable, deceiving smile. 'I don't think we need bother too much about what the politicians say. All politicians are liars, in office and out of it.

'Albert Laidlaw and his party want to oust the government and have their turn in the corridors of power. They can't get it from the voters in an election so they're seeing if they can frighten the public into giving them what they want.

'Crispin Partridge represents a political party that stands for law and order but is scared to take the necessary steps to achieve it because the unions and the subversives might bring industry and the country to a grinding halt.'

Foster smiled patronisingly. 'So what do you suggest is the solution?'

Debbie grinned. 'There are two things we could try. An all woman parliament because women have more common sense than men. Or have only a token central government. Not even regional government. County government, maybe local communities can manage their own affairs better than London. The Federal Government can be responsible for defence and diplomacy. The rest can be local.'

Foster shrugged. 'Sounds like Communism.'

'No way, darling. Maybe with a small "c".'

'What do you think we shall actually do?'

'Nothing. Sweet fuck-all as usual.'

Foster nodded at Partridge.

'The government is considering a Bill that will give new and additional powers to the police, a building programme for new prisons has already been approved. But in the end the responsibility lies with the people. All of us. If we want to end the present vicious lawlessness we must get the ringleaders, the evil men who cash in on . . .'

And at that moment TV screens tuned to ITV went blank all over the country. The fault was not traced and put right until two minutes before News at Ten was ready to roll.

The blatant, overt act of sabotage was obvious to everyone, but it caused little stir. The country was used to militants who disrupted the printing of newspapers; who claimed that it was a union's right to censor unfavourable comment about the Left; who were prepared to cut off essential supplies in order to force through a wage claim; all of this while union leaders on TV shed crocodile tears over their not wanting to damage the public by their actions – which were specifically designed and timed to do exactly that.

# 5

They started off as a group of fifteen, but after the first ten miles they were in straggling groups of twos and threes. They had clambered down from the lorry just after dark, had been given a map reference to memorise, and after two minutes with an ordnance survey map in the lorry's headlights, they were sent on their way.

The mist was already rolling along the east side of the mountains and there was almost no light from the moon as the clouds moved relentlessly across the night sky. After nine months of SAS training they still didn't know their fates. There were only two alternatives. They would be conditionally accepted or RTU'd. Returned to their original units. Squadron officers made clear that being RTU'd by the SAS was no disgrace. Any man who survived nine nonths without being sent back would certainly be promoted when he got back to his old unit. There had been a time when it was SAS policy to discourage volunteers by submitting them to harassment, exhaustion, and demands of dedication so consuming that few could provide them. Then the seventies had increased the need for SAS men, but the volunteers now came from a society so supportive that recruits were easily discouraged. The SAS realised that they must train their volunteers in adversity before they could be put to any test of loyalty or fortitude. The night's exercises were just part of that training.

They had eight hours of darkness in which to get to the

map-reference which, even ignoring the contours of the map, was almost thirty miles across country. They had neither food nor water and they had already carried out a normal day's army duties. If you arrived after the given time or fell by the wayside you would be RTU'd. There were no excuses. Twisted ankles, broken bones, exhaustion, losing your way, none of this was acceptable. For in the kind of duties the SAS performed you had to be where you were needed when you were needed. And ready to go into action. The Regular Army was full of competent soldiers; to be a member of SAS competence was taken for granted. As a starting point, not an achievement.

On that particular night four men decided that the SAS was not for them; six were found unsuitable by the SAS training and evaluation staff for a variety of reasons unconnected with the night exercise; while acceptance of two men who had to be treated in hospital for exhaustion was made conditional on medical reports. The three others were provisionally accepted, conditional on their performance in the final eight months' training programme.

Unlike the media and public image of the SAS its members did not look either like all-in wrestlers or like John Wayne. They tended to be of average height, lean rather than stolid, and of average appearance. Their only visible idiosyncrasy was a tendency to the type of exaggerated moustache worn by World War II fighter pilots. Loners instinctively and by training, they were loyal to small groups of their fellows rather than to humanity in general. Like that of policemen, their attitude to the rest of the world was jaundiced by bitter experience.

On this particular night-exercise one man walked alone right from the start. With his back-pack loaded with the regulation 55 pounds of bricks he didn't take the short-cut that was obvious on the survey map, but kept to the narrow path that wound back and forth along the contours of the rocky slopes. As the night wore on he watched for the breaks in the clouds that provided a few moments of moonlight, then, using his issue compass, he took bearings on his estimate of his target in the valley. It was of only marginal help because there were few features on the terrain and the more obvious ones had been eliminated on the map which had been specially printed for the SAS training staff.

But in the hour before dawn he stood quite still, his eyes closed, his head bent, and he heard it. The soft splash of water as it gushed over a rock to the pool a few feet below. He walked on slowly until the thin stream was at his feet, following it down through the rocks to the soft tussocky foothills until he came to the gorse and the bracken. An hour later he saw the light in the farmhouse below. There had been no farmhouse shown on the map, no buildings at all, but that was the map reference he had been given.

As he walked past the barn across the yard, a door opened and a path of yellow light flooded across the cobblestones. Two men were standing at the door. One he recognised with surprise, and the other was a stranger.

He wiped the sweat from his face with a damp face-cloth, slid the pack from his shoulders and leaned panting against the doorpost.

'How are you feeling, Sergeant?'

'Knackered, sir.'

The man laughed softly. 'Come on in.'

Lieutenant-Colonel Andrews looked out of place in the stone farmhouse and its old-fashioned kitchen. The sergeant was used to seeing him in uniform, not in an old tweed jacket and drill trousers. Sergeant Cameron Davies wondered what new trap was being set to test his thinking or endurance. Maybe it was going to be one of those sudden unannounced mock interrogations that were as near to the real thing as no matter.

Andrews introduced the other man as Glyn, and Glyn poured him a plate of thick porridge from a cast-iron pot on the black cooking range. When he had finished eating Andrews said quietly, 'I want you to do something for me, Davies. Something special. Something important.'

Cameron Davies nodded. 'Anything you say, Colonel.'

'I want you to apply for your discharge from the Army.' Andrews paused to see if there was any reaction but Davies didn't even blink. 'I've got a special job I want you to do. You'll be paid more than you get in the SAS. A better pension and some civilian perks like a car, a house and so on.' He paused. 'How d'you feel about that?'

'Anything you say, sir.'

'This isn't some test, Sergeant. It's for real. I mean what I say.'

'Like I said, sir. Whatever you say.'

'You haven't asked what you'll be doing.'

'I'll do whatever you say, sir.'

'You'll be working with Glyn, here. Glyn Thomas. And you'll be responsible for training groups of men, civilians, in basic SAS techniques. You won't discuss this with anyone. And you won't discuss one group with another. As far as they are concerned they are the only group in existence. You won't discuss with them the reasons for the training because you won't know the reasons until I need to tell you. Understand?'

'Permission to ask a question, sir.'

'Carry on.'

'Is this part of the army, sir?'

'No. You'll be a civilian.'

'Is it official or unofficial?'

'Unofficial, but approved by me ... and others.'

'When do you want me to start?'

Andrews reached inside his jacket pocket, pulled out a

folded paper and spread it flat on the table. It was a buff official form, an application for discharge.

'Fill it in now, Sergeant, with yesterday's date.' He handed Davies a ball-point and Glyn Thomas and he sat in silence as the sergeant filled in the details line by line.

When he came to the last section Davies looked up at the colonel. 'What reasons do I give, sir?'

'Religious convictions. Conscientious objections to serving in the armed forces.'

For a moment the sergeant hesitated then he filled in the last section and signed at the foot of the form. Andrews picked it up and read it through carefully, then he pulled a buff envelope from his jacket and handed it to the soldier. It was addressed to Sergeant C. Davies. 1093556. 'A' Troop, Special Air Service Regiment, The Depôt, Hereford.

'Open it.'

It was on A5 size War Office paper. The date was two days ahead. It granted his application for discharge with immediate effect. It gave brief details of documentation that would be sent to him, details of pay owing, and confirmed that his discharge was automatically a dishonourable one. When he looked up at Andrews, Davies shrugged, slowly nodding his head as he put the letter and the buff envelope inside his battledress blouse.

'I'd better get back, sir.'

'You won't be going back, lad. The stuff from your locker and your room are upstairs. You'll be staying here for a couple of weeks being briefed by Glyn.' He pushed a slip of paper across the table. 'That's a telephone number where you can contact me. You only use it in emergencies.' Andrews stood up. 'Your cooperation and loyalty won't be forgotten. I can assure you of that.'

'Thank you, sir.' Davies instinctively stood to attention as the colonel nodded to them both in turn before walking to the kitchen door and letting himself out. The early morning sun was already pushing aside the mist on the slopes of the valley.

One TV camera was facing the desk, the second was positioned for semi-profile, and the third was covering a photograph of Big Ben with an overlay which said simply 'The Prime Minister'. The producer was checking his notes for the last time and the floor manager was looking at his stop watch.

'Four minutes thirty seconds to go and . . .'

He broke off as the Director-General of the BBC held the door open for the Prime Minister and the Foreign Secretary to walk through.

'Four minutes fifteen.'

The producer walked over to check the radio microphone clipped to the PM's tie.

'Can you give me a few words, sir . . . we just want to check the level.'

The PM looked nonplussed and the producer said quickly, 'What did you have for breakfast, sir?'

'What . . . oh I see . . . porridge . . . bacon and eggs . . . toast and coffee . . . is that enough?'

The producer turned to check with the sound engineer who nodded.

'That's fine, sir. There will be fifteen seconds on the caption and then I'll count you down from ten seconds. The red light over the centre camera will be on and when I get to zero I'll nod and then the camera will be on you, and we'll be live on air.'

The Prime Minister nodded and looked disturbed as the D-G and the Foreign Secretary left the room.

'Quiet please . . . everybody quiet. One minute ten seconds to caption . . . one minute . . . thirty seconds . . . ten . . . five, four, three, two, one . . . on air . . . sound tape.'

49

The monitor showed Big Ben and the caption, and then came the last few strokes of the hour chimes.

'Right, sir ... ten ... nine ... eight ... seven ... six ... five ... four ... three ... two ... one,' and he pointed at the PM.

The Prime Minister faced the central TV camera squarely.

'I want to tell you all tonight, of a decision that the government has made after long discussions and the most careful consideration.

'You will remember that almost three months ago the government decided that it would not be possible, or indeed wise, for us to continue with our arrangements with the government of the United States to proceed with the purchase of the Trident missile system. It was a difficult decision to make and you will know that there has been much criticism from both our European partners and the United States. Indeed, there has been criticism in this country too. However, as I explained at the time, it was a decision forced on us by the country's economic situation. We bore in mind, too, the mounting criticism of our continuing the Trident programme in this country.

'As you may have heard and read in the media, certain of our European allies have gone beyond mere critical comment, reacting in a way which the government considers intolerable between friendly nations. I refer, of course, to the French government's action in banning all imports from the United Kingdom. And to the decision by the Federal German government to withdraw all their funding of the British military presence in West Germany. A presence which I must point out is there to defend West Germany itself. Our ambassadors in Paris and Bonn were instructed to make the strongest protests against these unilateral actions. Since then, both the Foreign Secretary and I have visited the leaders of France and West Germany to explain to them again our reasons for the decision and to apprise them of our strong resentment of their actions and their attitudes. These meetings were not successful.

'I came back last night and called a cabinet meeting to discuss the situation. I have come straight from that meeting, which has gone on all day, and the Foreign Secretary is informing the House of Commons of our decision at this moment.

'You will understand my bitter regret in having to tell you that as from midnight tonight the United Kingdom will no longer remain as a member country of the EEC. Furthermore we have notified our allies in NATO that also at midnight tonight our membership of that organisation is terminated. Our commanders in Europe are being issued orders to return their men and *matériel* to this country as soon as circumstances allow.

'There have been voices raised in the past years for both of these moves to be made. France herself has not been a member of NATO since 1966. It has been recognised that we have been struggling under a financial burden which meant that we, a country with many economic problems, have been subsidising with millions of pounds the richer members of the European Economic Community. For many years we have carried this burden in the hope that our sacrifice might contribute to the spirit of community. We have seen in the past few months that that sacrifice has been in vain.

'There was another time when this country stood alone. Winston Churchill described it as our finest hour. This time there is no fighting, but there is a war. A war against economic disaster which every country in the civilised world is waging. We have had long dark years and now we must go back to the spirit of Dunkirk. A time when workers and management, the armed forces and the civilians, and politicians of all parties, joined together for the common good.

'Let me assure you now that we have nothing to fear, we

have the resources and the resolve to overcome our problems. In the coming months we shall see who are our friends, and I know that many of you will feel that the sacrifices of the past years have not been in vain if we have won back our independence from the burdens placed on us by others.

'I ask that in the coming days there may be a spirit engendered in this proud nation of ours that shall make other nations envious of our strength and resolution.

'Good night to you all.'

The Prime Minister faced the camera, his face stern but handsome, until the red light went out and the producer walked forward to unfasten the microphone.

'Did that go out on the commercial channels at the same time?'

'Yes, sir. All except Satellite One. They'll be taking it an hour from now to catch the afternoon bulletins in the United States.'

The Director-General came in to escort the PM to his car. When the two men had left, the producer hurried to the telephone and dialled a Hereford number. When it responded he said softly, 'Yes, both,' and then he hung up.

British Airways Flight 139 to Paris, Le Bourget, was just leaving London Central Zone Outward when the call came through ordering them to return to Heathrow. The pilot asked the reason and was told merely that there were no safety factors involved.

In the Channel twenty-four vessels were responding to Dover coastguards' instructions to turn about and return to Dover or the Medway or they ran the risk of their vessels being impounded by the French customs authorities.

The mid-morning BBC radio programmes had been interrupted by news-flashes: the French Government had announced that in retaliation for the British withdrawal from the EEC all trade and communications with the United Kingdom had been temporarily suspended.

On the one o'clock news a number of politicians and public figures were asked their reactions to the news. The Foreign Secretary described it as 'an unfortunate misunderstanding', the Director of the CBI called it 'another piece of French chauvinism ... the kind of action that has finally made Britain decide to leave the EEC', and the *Evening Standard*'s Paris correspondent, who happened to be in London, pointed out that the ban was described as temporary.

The French Ambassador was called to the Foreign Office and given a dressing down by the Foreign Secretary himself. It was an embarrassing situation for them both, as they had been fellow students at the Lycée in Lyons and later at Balliol. When the official part of the interview was over, Claude Hollis, the Foreign Secretary, said, 'What on earth are your people up to, Henri?'

'God knows. They didn't consult me. The first I heard of it was a phone call this morning, only an hour before it was on the BBC.'

'It isn't temporary, is it? They'll keep it going, won't they?'

'They're in a nasty mood, Claude. And you know what Becque is like. The Germans are unstable until the elections are over and it looks as if Becque is going to make his big play for the leadership.'

'God. He must hate us.'

'He does. But it's more than that. He could lose next time round and he knows it. He's a nasty little toad and he probably thinks that being nasty to the English will get him some votes. He's probably right too.'

'In trade he's going to be the loser. We buy more from you than you do from us. No more arguments about Golden Delicious and bloody chickens and turkeys.'

'It'll put your food prices up, my friend. The farmers may like it, but the housewives won't.'

'We've still got the Australians and New Zealand.'

'You know that's not true, Claude. They've spent time and money finding new markets for their products and they're not going to change that in a hurry.' He paused for a moment. 'You'd better be prepared for the worst you know. Becque will bring pressure on the rest of the EEC to do the same.'

'I don't see any of them rushing in to do us dirt just for the love of Becque.'

The Frenchman sighed for what he wasn't allowed to say. He just said softly, 'There's a hell of a lot of pressure on Europe right now, Claude. You ought to be looking below the surface. There have been ominous signs that I think your people haven't noticed. Or if they have, they've interpreted them wrongly.'

'Such as?'

'The West Germans' visits to Moscow. Their contract for natural gas on very favourable terms. Too favourable, to my way of thinking. The Belgian suggestion to explore some sort of arrangement between EEC and Comecon. The communists in Italy supporting a shaky right-wing coalition.' He paused then said, 'And your own position is so desperate, Claude. You've got to act quickly.'

Hollis stubbed out his cigarette and said softly, 'Do you mean this seriously, Henri?'

'I do. Very seriously.'

'You think it's deliberate? Orchestrated by Becque?'

'You must draw your own conclusions.'

'What is there in it for France?'

'D'you remember long long ago when we were both at the Lycée we had to give a *discours* on a theme we chose ourselves?'

'No.' Hollis sighed and smiled. 'It seems a long time ago.'

'It is. But I remember your theme. It was on a quotation from La Rochefoucauld ... *"Dans l'adversité de nos meilleurs amis, nous trouvons quelque chose qui ne nous déplaît pas."'*

Hollis smiled and said softly, ' "In the misfortune of our best friends, we find something which is not displeasing to us." You couldn't say Paris and London have been best friends for a long time.'

'Enough to enjoy the misfortunes.' The Frenchman stood up. 'I will pass on your comments, Minister, to my government, and no doubt they will give you a full explanation.'

The Frenchman stood there, holding out his hand. Hollis took it and the Frenchman looked at his face. 'It makes me very sad all this, my friend. Remember, if the deluge comes, there is a place in France for you and yours ... my place.'

# 6

As programme researchers and assistant producers phoned the obvious political spokesmen and communicators for comment they were surprised that for once there were no takers of any weight. Men and women who normally leapt at any chance of an interview were strangely reluctant. Some claimed that they needed time to consider the PM's announcement, others more honestly, but cynically, said they weren't going to handle the government's hot potato until it had had time to cool down.

In the end it came down to interviewing the standard handful of political commentators from the newspapers. They cautiously pre-echoed the next day's headlines in their own journals. The *Daily Express* said, 'PM says we go it alone'. *The Times* headline was, 'PM says enough to Europe'. The *Morning Star* didn't seem to be able to make up its mind and the speech was only mentioned in a single-column box with a tagline – 'PM talks to nation'.

It was almost as if there was a ban on discussion. Nobody seemed to know what attitude to adopt. Nobody wanted to be the first herald of discord, nor the unwise protagonist of a policy that might spell disaster. For the first time in broadcasting history nobody wanted to comment on a major political decision. The reference to the Dunkirk spirit, despite its banality and cheap appeal, seemed to have worked so far as the general public was concerned. The left-wingers couldn't complain because they had been advocating both withdrawals for a decade, and the political right had loathed having to take the snubs and insults of the French and Germans for the last six months. Britain was on her own, not by her own choice, but because Europe no longer wanted her. Old debts and old antagonisms were being resurrected and indulged in on both sides of the Channel.

In the cosy room off the main hall at Chequers the Leader of HM Official Opposition sat puffing at his pipe in the leather armchair, listening to what the Prime Minister was saying.

'... I don't know how you can adopt that attitude, Arthur. Like all your party's statements it's totally spurious. I can remember way back in the early 'eighties when the pound was strong your people said that it was bringing the country to ruin because our exports were being priced out of the world market. When it fell in 1981 or 1982, whenever, it was your people who were bleating that the country was being bankrupted because the cost of imported materials was so high.

'For years your conferences and MPs have been screaming that we should pull out of the EEC, and now we've done it you won't support us. Your extreme-left lunatics all shouted for unilateral disarmament but now we've done most of what they want we're jeopardising the country's security, according to you. Why don't you make your bloody minds up what you do want?'

Arthur Drury smiled his well-known patronising smile. 'A wonderful performance, Freddie. But it won't wash with me. You didn't do these things to please my party. You didn't even do it to please your own party. You did it because you had no choice. What I'm concerned with now is what effect it will have on the country.'

'What effect did you think it would have when you were advocating it?'

'They were different days, Freddie. Different pressures and different circumstances. We weren't at the end of the road. We are now. I assume even you would concede that. Disraeli said ...'

'Bugger what Disraeli said. What are *you* saying?'

'I'm here to listen, Freddie. Not to say.'

The Prime Minister's protruding, blood-shot eyes looked with anger at his companion's face. He hated having to say what he knew he had to say.

'I'll offer you a coalition, Arthur. You'd be my deputy, and you could have the Home Office or Defence. We can work out the details to suit both sides.'

'No way, Freddie. This is going to be all yours. We don't want any part of it.'

'The public won't like your refusal.'

'Don't tell them then.'


The Prime Minister declared a State of Emergency the following day and his press officer leaked the refusal of the opposition to form a coalition government.

By six o'clock there were crowds thronging Downing Street to watch the comings and goings of well-known politicians, but the mood of the crowd was subdued, as if they recognised that there was a crisis but weren't quite sure what it was all about.

The later editions of the evening papers carried brief details of new regulations. All strikes were illegal, and if they occurred swingeing fines would be levied on union funds. All foreign currency holdings had to be declared in the next forty-eight hours and imprisonment faced dodgers and any-one who was caught trying to transfer gold, currency, or valuables overseas. No person was allowed to leave his present job without the agreement of the Ministry and the unemployed would be directed to jobs. Married women were banned from work to alleviate unemployment among male workers. All immigration of whites or blacks was temporarily suspended with no exceptions. The Riot Act was being revised and the police had already been given virtual carte-blanche to deal with 'troublemakers'.

TV interviewers roamed the streets for 'grass-roots' reactions and the usual response was low-key. If the government thought it was necessary then it had to be done. Most people seemed to assume that the State of Emergency had been declared because of the mounting inflation and high unemployment. A few mentioned the looting and vandalism in the big cities as contributory causes. Politicians avoided the media, and broadcasters had been warned by the Prime Minister's office to play it cool. Unspecified threats were hinted at rather than spelled-out. But the hints were taken. Current affairs programmes were cancelled and old comedy series were screened instead. Almost imperceptibly the country settled back into an uneasy acceptance of the new conditions.

It wasn't just an amiable gesture towards the newly revived Franco-German detente that found Charles Becque in the State box for the performance of *Der Rosenkavalier*. No connoisseur of music, he nevertheless genuinely loved all the lush operettas from *The Merry Widow* to *The Gypsy Princess*, and tonight's performance was the crown jewel of the season. Haitink and the Berlin Philharmonic. They had asked him nine months before if they could bill it as a Presidential evening and he had agreed after a few days' delay for the sake of protocol.

He had barely settled down after the first Act interval when a note was passed to him by one of his aides. He opened it as quietly as possible despite his annoyance at the interruption. It asked him to return to the Elysée Palace immediately. It was signed by Thibaudet, his Foreign Minister. He beckoned to his aide and told him to have his car ready for the second interval. He wished that he didn't know what it was going to be about. Almost certainly they must have had confirmation about the East Germans. They wouldn't want him in such a hurry if it was good news.

He closed his eyes for a moment to wash away his thoughts and then concentrated on the stage. Those swooning waltzes made him want to waltz himself, or at least wave his arms in time to the music. But he sat calmly until the interval, then told his wife that he was leaving. Fifteen minutes later the big black Citroën was sweeping through the Elysée gates. He never ceased to admire the beauty of the place and all the panoply and power that went with it. But these late-night emergencies irritated him; there was always the possibility that some Minister was just trying to draw attention to his function by exaggerating a minor emergency. When they were new it often happened, though usually after a year or so they valued their evenings too much. But Thibaudet wasn't a panic merchant. If he thought it was urgent it would be so.

Becque walked up the broad stairway, along the corridor to the farthest room. Thibaudet was waiting for him and Regnier was with him. Both men stood, and he waved them back to their seats, walking round his ornate desk to sit in the big damask-covered chair.

'Tell me your good news, Thibaudet. They have just notified us that they were combined manoeuvres, yes?'

'I'm afraid not, Monsieur le Président. A Soviet officer defected yesterday. Walked across near the Helmstedt check-point. The East Germans, with Soviet advisers, are going to invade the Federal Republic.'

Becque sighed and reached for a glass paper-weight. 'If he walked across he's surely a plant?'

'I'm afraid not. He has been in touch with the West

German intelligence people for several months. He carried micro-dots of operational orders and Soviet documents outlining the plan and their intentions.'

'And their intentions are what?'

'They intend to guarantee they will not cross the Rhine but they will occupy West Germany.'

'When?'

'In ten days' time. The fourteenth.'

'Has Bonn told London or Washington?'

'No. Only us. On Helmut Bayer's personal instructions.'

'Are you satisfied that the documents are authentic?'

'Absolutely. There's no doubt about them.'

'And what are Bonn going to do about it?'

'They are going to ask for a special session of the Security Council the day after tomorrow. They are assembling the documents and Bayer himself will head their delegation.'

Becque stood up, nodding at the two men. 'Thank you, Thibaudet. I'll let you know my views tomorrow. Meantime, do nothing. Understood?'

'Understood, Monsieur le Président.'

When they had gone Becque picked up the red telephone and pressed two buttons one after the other. Thirty seconds later he was on the line to Helmut Bayer in Bonn. They had talked for almost an hour before he replaced the receiver. For several minutes Becque sat there with his eyes closed, his lips moving as he rehearsed exactly what he would say. Twice he reached for the red phone again, and twice his hand drew back. He wrote a few words on the pad beside the phone, scoring through one word and substituting an alternative. Then he picked up the red phone again, pressed the button for the operator and asked her to get President Yevgeni Orlov on the line.

The big Zil swept from Leningradsky Prospekt under the tunnel to Volokolamskoye Chaussée and then forked left to

Petrovo-Dalniye Chaussée and on until the river lay to their left.

The park at Arkhangelskoye was roughly 16 kilometres from Moscow. The car drove across the park to a villa over-looking the River Moskva, and as Becque reached for the car door a servant opened it for him and bowed as he got out. He said politely and in good French, 'Please follow me, sir.'

Becque was shown to a suite of rooms on the first floor and his single bag was brought in, followed by a young man who smiled as he bowed. 'The Ministers are on their way here, Your Excellency. They are expected any minute.'

Becque nodded. The young man was still smiling. 'Is there anything you want, Excellency? A drink, food perhaps?'

'No. Let me know when they are here.'

It was ten minutes before Fomenko knocked and walked in. They had met many times at conferences when Becque was Foreign Minister and they had got on well together.

'Monsieur le Président, how nice to see you. A good journey, I hope.'

'No. A ghastly journey. And by God it's cold for May in this grey country of yours.'

Fomenko smiled. He knew Becque's foibles of old. 'When we've finished the talking maybe we can get you warmed up. Let's go on down. They're waiting.'

'Who's there?'

Fomenko shrugged. 'Just as you asked. President Orlov, myself. And an interpreter.'

'Fine. Let's go.'

Orlov was a large man with a big, typically Russian face, but he had an element of clumsy charm when he chose. After some banal chatter he waved Becque to one of the tapestry armchairs.

'Let us be completely informal.' He smiled. 'And off the record. Do you agree?'

Becque nodded. 'Can I be frank as well?'

'Of course.'

'One of your officers defected to West Germany three days ago. You know that, of course.'

Orlov glanced at Fomenko who nodded, then he looked back at Becque. 'Go on please.'

'He took with him a mass of documents regarding Operation Igor. They were on micro-dots.' Becque saw the muscles at the sides of Orlov's mouth stiffen. 'Bonn intend asking the UN for an urgent meeting of the Security Council.'

Orlov sat silently and Becque said, 'I came here, Mr President, to suggest an alternative but I need to know that it would be considered.'

Orlov said slowly, 'Maybe you should just continue.'

'I am assuming that Moscow intends this move as a decisive blow against the United States. In my opinion it would not only be highly dangerous but to the disadvantage of the Soviet Union, not only in the short run but for many years to come. West Germany is stable and genuinely neutral. No pretext for such action would be acceptable to the Americans or the rest of Europe. Unless you have a motive that I have not perceived the prize is too small and far too expensive.' Becque's grey eyes looked at Orlov's face. 'It would be seen as no more than an adventure to cover your problems in the Soviet Union and a blow at the Americans ... there is an alternative that has real advantages for you and which would be more tolerable to Europe and others.'

'Tell me more, Mr President.'

Becque shook his head. 'Orlov, I'm not here as a supplicant, I am here both as an interested party and as President of a country which has no love for the Americans and considerable respect for the Soviet Union. I am here for a discussion not a monologue.'

Orlov sighed deeply. 'Maybe there is nothing useful we can discuss.'

Becque shrugged. 'OK. If you can arrange a car to take me to the airport I'll get on my way.'

Orlov half-smiled. 'You French are always so touchy.'

'And you Russians are always so stupid.'

Orlov raised his eyebrows. 'Tell me about us being stupid.'

'Surely you already know. You've been making mistakes for years.'

'So tell me.'

'Afghanistan. You lost all your friends in the Islamic world. You sent the Gulf States hurrying to America for protection. In Vietnam you financed the invasion of Cambodia and made Russia's name stink all over south-east Asia. China and Japan settled their differences and moved closer to the United States. In Poland you made new enemies and confirmed old ones. For what? They were all disasters. Expensive disasters in resources and prestige.' Becque leaned forward, his voice low. 'All you did was work off the Politburo's frustrations with the Americans. You got nothing in return. And now you're going to do it again. More enemies, more confirmation that you *are* aggressive. Aggressive not for real reasons but for display. Making a rude sign at Washington.' Becque leaned back in his chair shaking his head.

Orlov sat silently for several minutes and then, taking a deep breath, he said, 'We are tired of the Americans in Europe. What business have they with troops and missiles, sixty, seventy miles from our borders? Spying on us, threatening us, encouraging others to threaten us. Testing our will to resist, day after day. Any NATO country can provoke us because it knows that if we make a move against them the Americans will pour troops in ... if we so much as lift a finger in anger. We've had enough, Becque. We're going to call their bluff.'

'And if they call yours?'

Saliva bubbled and flew as Orlov's anger welled out. 'It's no bluff, Mr President, I swear to you. Any move by any country to stop us and we shall go straight on to the English Channel and there will be no more games.'

'Do you really mean that?' Becque said softly.

'By God I mean it. I swear to you we mean it.'

'Why pay so big a price?'

'What does that mean?'

'It means that there is a far better way that you could go, and you could drive the Americans out of Europe without making any enemies. Maybe even make some friends.'

'How?'

'What is your assessment of the position in Britain at the moment?'

'They're finished. A decadent people without leadership. A ship without rudder or sails. They have no future. They are ciphers.'

'Except for one thing. Those islands command the North Atlantic. Without Britain as an ally and a base, the Americans could never supply NATO in a war. Without Britain the Americans would pull out of Europe.'

For only a moment Orlov's eyes glanced towards Fomenko.

'What are you suggesting?'

'If the British government asked for the help of the Soviet Union to free them from American domination ... to make Britain neutral territory.' Becque smiled. 'Finlandisation would be the catch-word. In return the class-war stops. Your advisers in London help them to full employment. Law and order is restored. Who can complain if you respond favourably to such a call for help?'

'Can you imagine them doing that, Becque?'

'Not today. But in one month, two at most, the country will be a shambles. They are already fighting one another. The government is powerless. Nobody obeys anybody any longer. They will do anything to stop anarchy being total. Especially if the call for help came from the workers as well.' He smiled. 'A delegation from the Trades Unions to Moscow. Begging for help.'

'They have no authority.'

'Of course not. They are just the excuse. You invite the British Prime Minister to Moscow. You give him the choice. He invites your help or he gets it anyway. With blood instead of fraternal love.'

'And who would support the Prime Minister?'

Becque laughed. 'Maybe nobody. But nobody supports him now. When he has signed an appropriate document you've got all you need.' He shrugged. 'It is that or the deluge. The Americans would move for the West Germans, but not for the British. And the whole of Europe is sick of them. They are a mill-stone round our necks.'

Fomenko leaned forward in his chair. 'Who have you discussed this with, Monsieur le Président?'

'Not a soul, Fomenko. Not a soul.'

Orlov stood up. 'How long can you stay, my friend?'

'I need to be back in Paris tomorrow night, or it will cause comment that I'm away.'

As Orlov stood at the door he turned to look back at the Frenchman. 'What are you looking for out of this?'

Becque smiled and shrugged. 'To settle some old debts with the English.'

Orlov left without thanks or comment but Fomenko stayed. They dined together and Fomenko phoned Moscow just before ten o'clock. He waited with Becque until the two pretty KGB girls arrived by car. When it was obvious which one the Frenchman preferred, he rode back to Moscow with the other girl.

The next morning Becque received a package and a note from Orlov. The package contained a Fabergé cigarette case in gold with a ruby clasp. Inside the lip was engraved the crest of the Romanovs. The note was typed in French, a quote from Descartes – 'It is not enough to have a good mind; the main thing is to use it well.' Orlov's signature was florid but unmistakably genuine.

Fomenko phoned around eleven o'clock. An announcement was being made that evening that a French company had been successful in tendering for a billion dollar computer installation to be installed over the next six years in a steel making and manufacturing complex in Siberia. No mention was made of the previous day's conversation. Arrangements had been made for a private Aeroflot plane to fly him to Brussels where a French military plane would be waiting to fly him to Paris. The text of the press release concerning the computer order would await him at the airport at Sheremetyevo.

# 7

For two nights and a day Lev Savalev faced the questions of the special committee: two from the Red Army, one from the Navy, three from the Airforce, a GRU man, two senior KGB men, the KGB liaison man from the Politburo and three dour-faced men whose rank or function were never explained.

The video-tape of the British Prime Minister's speech had been played repeatedly. The original text in English and two differing translations into Russian were in the clear plastic files in front of each man. Again and again Savalev had been asked for every possible meaning of particular phrases from the speech, and his interpretations had been taped, transcribed and circulated to other groups and committees.

He was finally released from the questioning at three in the morning. There was an inch or two of snow in the Moscow streets. It had stopped snowing but a cold wind gusted across the squares as he walked towards the apartment block on the river. She would be asleep at this hour, but to hell with her, he wanted some relief from those grinding questions and the ignorance of men who neither spoke any English nor had ever even been in England. Despite his rank they had treated him more as if he were a prisoner of war under interrogation than a senior officer in the KGB.

He stamped the snow from his shoes as he walked up the granite steps and through the double doors. Her room was on the fourth floor and there was no lift. At her door he pressed the bell and leaned against the wall, waiting. She was the prettiest girl in the Bolshoi reserve ballet group and was his second or third favourite among the Moscow girls he slept with.

He raised his head as he heard her footsteps. He saw the surprise and shock on her face as she opened the door. She was wearing his bathrobe. As he opened his mouth to speak she put her fingers to her lips, shaking her head.

'What is it?' he whispered.

'There's somebody here. I can't let you in.'

'Who is it?'

'Don't ask.'

'Don't be stupid, Tania, who is it?'

She whispered a name and he cursed quietly. It was the General in charge of Moscow's missile sites. For a moment he hesitated and she said, 'I'm sorry, Lev. He's a real pig but ...' She shrugged and pouted. 'Come and see me tomorrow.'

'I won't be here tomorrow, you stupid bitch.'

She smiled. 'What was it you wanted, anyway?'

'You know bloody well what I wanted.'

She laughed softly. 'Go to Natasha, she's in apartment seventy-four.'

'I don't know her.'

'You do. She's the blonde girl you fancied at the party at Simenov's.'

'Does she play?'

'Of course she does. She will for you, anyway.'

He turned and walked away without speaking. Angry and frustrated, he used his KGB card to get a room at the Rossiya. As he undressed, half-asleep, he remembered that May was always an unlucky month for him. Nothing really bad, but full of irritations. The only really bad May was when he and the others were thrown out of London by

Prime Minister Heath. But in two days' time it would be June.

When he reported back to Dzerzhinski Square the next morning he was handed an envelope by the security guard. He read it as he waited for the lift. He was promoted lieutenant-colonel with effect from 27 May and was posted to a new assignment. He would still be based at Suzdal but with new and different responsibilities. He would report forthwith to Room 7094.

The US ambassador's car swept through the Kremlin gates and headed for the Palace of Congresses. The man who stepped out when it came to a stop was not the ambassador, but a man who had flown to Moscow from Paris the previous evening. Sam Slaney had not discussed his mission with the ambassador. His briefing and the parameters of the discussions had been given him by the Secretary of State himself, in a meeting at a Washington hotel.

Igor Fomenko was waiting for him in the small but ornate room at the end of a corridor on the ground floor.

'Welcome, Mr Slaney. A good journey I hope.'

'Not bad, not bad.'

The American looked around expectantly and Fomenko smiled. 'He'll be here in a few moments. He's signing State documents. It's not a snub.'

Slaney nodded. 'I'm sure it isn't. You'd be wasting a snub on me, comrade. I'm not important enough to even notice.'

'And how is President Wheeler these days?'

'Fine. Over-worked, but I guess that's par for the course.'

When President Orlov walked into the room, all smiles and affability, Slaney guessed in that moment that his mission was doomed. He had negotiated too often with the Russians not to recognise the moves. When you got the glad-hand treatment before you started it was to compensate for what was coming later.

'Welcome to Moscow. How is your President?'

'He's very well, Your Excellency. He sends you his sincere good wishes.' He paused and reached into his jacket pocket, pulling out a small package. 'He also sent you this.'

Orlov smiled as he took the package. 'May I look now?'

'Of course.'

Orlov pulled off the wrapping paper and opened the leather box, looking at it for several minutes. On the blue velvet lay a gold wrist-watch with two faces side by side. One face showed Moscow time, the other, Washington time, and over each of the two circular faces was engraved the appropriate symbol. The hammer and sickle over the Moscow face and the American eagle over the other. Orlov looked at Slaney.

'A very beautiful gift. I much appreciate it. I shall ask my fellow Ministers if I may keep it myself. It's very beautiful and very ...' He looked at Fomenko and said something in Russian. Fomenko said, 'Creative.' Orlov nodded. 'Yes, very creative.' He pointed at the armchairs. 'Shall we all sit down.'

When they were all seated Orlov said quietly, 'The message said that President Wheeler was sending a special envoy to see me personally. So, what can I do for you?'

Slaney leaned forward in his chair. 'I come from the President himself, Your Excellency. Not on behalf of the government or Congress. It is entirely personal, and the President asks that whatever the outcome, my meeting with you should not be publicised in any way. We, of course, will do the same.'

'No problem, Mr Slaney. No problem at all.'

Slaney abandoned his rehearsed opening words. They hadn't been all that good but they were at least sincere. But sincerity wasn't going to get him anywhere now.

'Mr President. I was sent here in the hope that we could reduce the tensions that are arising, and arising faster every

71

day, between the United States and the USSR.' He paused for a response but there was none so he went on. 'Recent developments appear to the White House as deliberate attempts to provoke the United States into strong action against the Soviet Union. We very much regret this situation. Before taking such action we felt, the President felt, that it would be wise to try and ascertain if these recent moves on the part of the Soviet Union were intended to be provocative.'

Orlov held up his hand. 'I can assure you right away, Mr Slaney, that the Soviet government has no intention of provoking the United States in any way. Unless, of course, you would consider the defence of our national security and the security of friendly neighbours as being provocative.'

'Mr President. I'm not a diplomat. I'm not trained to weigh my words, but I recognise that what you are saying has more than one meaning. You say you have no intention of provoking the United States in any way,' Slaney smiled grimly. 'But you will surely recognise that, intention or no intention, you are doing just that. Provoking us. Day after day.'

'Give me an example.'

Slaney shrugged. 'That's not really my rôle, Mr President. I came to talk in general terms not horse-trade about particular actions.'

'That's up to you, Mr Slaney. But please go on.'

'I don't need to go on, Mr President. The reason for me being sent here is simple. So that you should know that President Wheeler is forming the opinion that many of your recent actions are not only against the interests of the United States but deliberately intended so to be.'

Orlov raised his eyebrows. 'You surely won't be surprised if I say that Soviet foreign policy is hardly decided on whether or not it will please the United States government.'

'I'm glad to hear you say that, Mr President. It was beginning to look like Soviet foreign policy was based solely on *antagonising* the US government.'

Orlov glanced at Fomenko, then looked back at Slaney. He spoke quietly and clearly. 'Let me say quite frankly, Mr Slaney, that in formulating our foreign policy the days when we took into consideration the United States' likes and dislikes have long since gone. If the United States wants confrontation that is your decision not ours. And the world will see it as such. You have never had any justification for keeping your armies and weapons in Europe. You used the pretext that those countries wanted you there. Your tanks, your missiles, your aircraft, your nuclear submarines are there. Just the other side of our borders. But that didn't seem like provocation to you. And now, those countries have learned what price they have to pay for harbouring you, and it seems that they have had enough. They are sending you packing. But you shouldn't consider that as a defeat requiring retaliation. You should never have been there in the first place.'

'And that is the message you want me to take back to the President?'

Orlov stood up slowly, patting down his jacket. 'Your President doesn't need a message from me, Mr Slaney. He's been getting my message for the last three or four months. The United States is no longer the world's policeman. You have enough troubles at home. Stay in your own backyard and there need be no confrontation.' He glanced at Fomenko and then back at Slaney. 'We should be happy to accommodate you tonight or we can notify the airport to ready your plane back to Paris or wherever you want to go.'

Slaney gave a quick bow. 'I'll be going back to Paris if you could have them alerted.'

Orlov nodded and, half-smiling at Fomenko, he walked

from the room without a handshake or a goodbye. The President's gift and its wrapping were still lying on the marble-topped table.

The papers had held the presses for the final details of the State of Emergency and the next day the streets were empty except for the determined agitators – the usual bunch of extreme left-wingers with a sprinkling of MPs and students, and a handful of Trades Union leaders. By the evening the mood had changed as organised rioting and looting erupted in the centres of the big cities. CS gas, rubber bullets and water cannon had not been enough; troops were called in under the Riot Act and live bullets were fired to disperse the crowds.

The following day a TUC delegation had called on the Prime Minister. They demanded an emergency meeting of the House or they would recommend to their membership a General Strike. When he refused to react to such overt blackmail the power supplies were cut to the whole of the country south of the Midlands. Panic buying of food and fuel came near to looting as harassed shops tried to deal with the demands.

The French added fuel to the fire by closing their embassy and ostentatiously withdrawing their ambassador and his staff, leaving their diplomatic affairs in the hands of the Swiss Embassy. At midnight that day there had been the call from the Soviet Ambassador demanding an immediate meeting.

He had only recently arrived and had not even presented his credentials to the Court of St James. Overnight he had replaced the previous ambassador, a charming academic diplomat, without any of the diplomatic niceties being observed. The new man had already been declared *persona non grata* by the Foreign Office but he had ignored the statement. Meetings of the militants had been held openly at the

Soviet Embassy and press conferences assembled outside the embassy at which the government was accused of class-warfare and 'declaring war on the trades unions and the working-class'.

Ambassador Gorsky looked like a hoodlum, and in diplomatic terms he behaved like one. When he had been shown into the Prime Minister's office at 10 Downing Street he had stormed in as if he were the cohort of some invading army. And that, as it turned out, was virtually what he was. He had stood there reading out the *démarche* from the Union of Soviet Socialist Republics. He spoke in harsh execrable English but the threat and the meaning were clear. The Soviet Union could no longer stand by and see innocent people being attacked by the police and the armed services, when they were protesting amongst other things against the stationing of US nuclear missiles on British soil and allowing the country to be used as a base for American aggression and espionage against the peace-loving peoples of the Soviet Union. Only a meeting in Moscow between the British Prime Minister and the leaders of the Soviet Union could prevent the Soviet government from taking immediate and forceful steps to bring this provocative situation to an end. There had been the usual Soviet jargon phrases on capitalism and the freedom-loving countries of the Warsaw Pact, and that had been that. Gorsky sat there as the Prime Minister told the operator to get him the Leader of the Opposition. Half an hour's frantic telephoning had not made contact. Then the Commissioner of Police reported that Arthur Drury was believed to be on a plane to Warsaw, using a false name and passport. He had been recognised by a journalist and an airport security man at Manston Airport late that afternoon, before boarding a chartered plane whose destination was given as Rotterdam. The plane had not landed in Holland but had changed its destination to Warsaw before entering West German airspace.

The P.M. turned to look at Gorsky.

'Are your people threatening invasion, Mr Ambassador?'

'They ask for a meeting with you, Prime Minister.'

'I know that. But it doesn't answer my question. Are they threatening an attack on this country?'

'I am in no position to answer that question, such things are beyond my responsibility.'

'But you don't deny the threat?'

'I neither deny nor confirm, Prime Minister.'

'I will arrange to fly to Moscow tomorrow afternoon. The RAF will liaise with your people on the time and route.'

Gorsky stood up, unappeased, still relentless. 'We will give them their instructions.'

For seven hours the staff at Number 10 had attempted to call in leading politicians and public figures. None were available. Some had gone to ground deliberately. Several were under siege by mobs in their own homes and others were stranded by the transport strike. Many others were genuinely out of contact because of the power strike. Two were under arrest and in custody.

The P.M. had slept for two hours as his valet packed his bags for the trip. There was going to be no help, not even consultation, from either colleagues or the Opposition. It had gone too far. If he applied any more pressure from the police or the armed forces the whole country would explode into civil war. From the information flooding into his office it looked as if a state of virtual civil war might already exist. The military commanders all had their instructions as to what to do in such an eventuality and he had no doubt that they would carry out their orders to the best of their ability.

They ordered the RAF plane to land at Schönefeld-Berlin and there was no point in refusing to cooperate. And minor points of diplomatic protocol had long gone by the board.

As he stood alone on the tarmac, his quiff of grey hair lifting in the breeze, he watched the Red Air Force officers crowding round the alien plane. The RAF pilot and navigator were laughing and chatting to their opposite numbers. They were in the same business despite their different nationalities. No doubt they talked flying technicalities with the same enthusiasm that he talked about gardening.

It was already getting dark, and he shivered as he looked across the runway to the terminal buildings. No doubt his landing ungreeted, to stand solitarily beside his plane, was all part of their programme to humiliate him. He wondered if Chamberlain had felt like he felt now when he made his trips to Godesburg and Munich. Beneš, the wretched Czech, would have felt the same pressures. There were some lines from a Housman poem. Something about – 'The signal fires of warning, They blaze but none regard; and on through night to morning the world runs ruinward.' His chest lifted to sigh and he stopped. Somebody would be watching him, the Prime Minister of Great Britain, standing alone at the Russian airport in Berlin, sighing. That would never do. It had been an incredible twenty-four hours since the Soviet Ambassador had demanded to see him. At first the vague hints, then the implications and finally the outright threats. They were not bluffing, he was certain of that. They meant every word of it. They even meant words they hadn't uttered. And then, without thinking, he sighed deeply.

When Chamberlain had come back from Munich they had cheered him, all of them. But a few months later they had heard him announce the declaration of war. And not long afterwards an angry House of Commons had sent him packing, to oblivion. Nobody would cheer *him* when he arrived back in London. Maybe the Russians wouldn't even let him go back. All they talked about, all they wanted, was his signature on some wretched document. They always had been sticklers for signatures on papers to prove that what they wanted was legal tender. If the top man wouldn't sign, there was always his deputy. Or the deputy's deputy. Somewhere down the line they would find a collaborator, greedy enough, or scared enough, to comply.

Then the Aeroflot ground hostess was walking towards him with a bunch of red roses in her hand, a tall handsome Russian in a well-cut suit a few paces behind her. When she stopped in front of Sir Frederick the tall man took over. He spoke perfect English with no trace of a foreign accent.

'Sir Frederick. My apologies for keeping you waiting but I was talking to Moscow. We are flying straight on, you and I, and I am instructed to see that you are well looked after.'

The Prime Minister nodded but didn't reply. The Russian half-smiled and pointed to a medium-sized plane with Aeroflot markings that was being towed onto the main runway. They walked to the plane together and waited until the boarding steps were clamped into place. Then the Russian led him up the steps.

The interior was incredible, the decor from some pre-war Orient Express. Maple and mahogany panelling, ornate candelabra, velvet curtains at the portholes and small silver vases stuffed with sweet-peas and daisies. The furniture was upholstered in plush dark red velour, with two ornate armchairs clamped side by side. The tall Russian sat himself down and pointed to the other chair. There was a bottle of whisky and a glass beside his chair on a marquetry table. He noticed that the whisky was Glen Livet. The bastards had checked everything.

'Sir Frederick, my name is Lev Savalev. I shall be acting as your adviser and interpreter during your visit. I hope that I can be of real help to you on this historic occasion.'

Cooper turned to look at the Russian, the contempt in his eyes undisguised.

'If I was in need of advice, Mr Savalev, I shouldn't be needing it from you.'

Savalev smiled. 'Of course not, Sir Frederick. Perhaps advice was the wrong word. Perhaps explanation would be nearer the mark.'

The Prime Minister leaned forward and poured himself half a glass of neat whisky as the plane picked up speed. He could hear radio talk in Russian coming from behind the blue velvet curtains that marked off the crew's compartment. He put the empty glass back on the pretty table, stretched out his legs, closing his eyes as he rested his head against the lace antimacassar on the back of the chair.

He breathed deeply and evenly as his tired but restless mind went over the events of the last few weeks. Surely there had never been scenes like those in the House of Commons in the long history of the nation. Not even Cromwell and Charles had let things go that far. It had come to a head with that fool Dawson accusing the Leader of the Opposition of being a traitor in the pay of the Soviet Union, screaming out a long list of alleged traitorous contacts above the surging roar of the opposite benches. Then one of the militant left-wingers started using a loud-hailer he had smuggled into the House, deliberately inciting the government benches, calling them 'the scum of the earth' and 'the jackals of capitalist oppression'. It was those last Marxist jargon words that had lit the flame. They were meant to of course. What followed should have seemed incredible. But it wasn't. The incredible had become the norm and it had ended with the relay of ambulances and two hundred police clearing the Palace of Westminster, two dead and 75 in hospital and Parliament suspended by the Speaker, troops from the Guards regiments surrounding the buildings, and machine guns covering the whole of Parliament Square. The Household Brigade had taken over all guard duties at Buckingham Palace.

It was raining heavily when they landed at Sheremetyevo and a uniformed policeman opened a large umbrella as the Prime Minister and Savalev went down the passenger steps to the tarmac and across to the terminal buildings.

They were led away from the main reception area to where a man with a trolley was already loading Cooper's two bags into the boot of a black Volga saloon. A short stout man got out of the back of the car and held out his hand. 'Azimov, Prime Minister, Foreign Ministry. Welcome to the Soviet Union.' Cooper barely touched the proffered hand but the Russian smiled amiably. 'We have put aside a pleasant house for you.' He broke off and spoke in Russian to Savalev who listened and nodded as he turned to Cooper. 'There will be a short meeting with senior officials in two hours time. It will give you time to freshen up.'

The house appeared to be in some kind of park but surrounded by a high stone wall. Soldiers opened the big gates as the car drove inside. There were well-kept lawns, planted with silver birches and willows. At least a dozen soldiers in uniform were stationed at various points, but there were none at the main entrance.

It was a beautiful house. A wide staircase and four or five doors led off the large pine-floored hall. Savalev, and a soldier carrying Cooper's bag, went ahead of him up the stairs and along a corridor to a suite of rooms that might have been furnished out of a museum. Bergère chairs and gilt tables, Meissen figures, and an ornate ormolu clock on the mantel of a wide marble fireplace.

'This was the villa of one of the Tsar's favourites, Prime Minister. It has been preserved and kept only for special visitors.'

Cooper turned to look at the Russian. 'Has our ambassador been told that I'm here?'

'No, sir. We thought it best that the meeting should be

kept entirely confidential until the transactions were satisfactorily completed.'

Cooper's eyebrows went up. 'Transactions? I came for discussions not transactions, my friend.'

'Of course, Prime Minister, forgive my poor English.'

But Savalev's smile was knowing, as between conspirators who wanted to preserve some outward show of normality.

There was yet another bottle of whisky and a crystal jug with water and ice-cubes floating just below the surface. 'My God,' Cooper thought, 'they must think I'm an alcoholic.' For a few moments he stood with his hands in his trouser pockets to take away the tension. 'Who is coming to the meeting, this evening?'

'Our deputy Prime Minister, two members of the Politburo, Belinkov and Sloboda, and some senior officers from the armed forces.'

'And tomorrow?'

'Tomorrow you will be meeting the full Politburo. All except one who is in hospital at the moment.' Savalev smiled. 'The average age of our Politburo has always been in the sixties, which means that sometimes the pressures are too much. He has a heart condition. What would you like to do, Prime Minister?'

'I'd like to have a bath and change, if that's possible.'

Savalev smiled. 'Oh yes that's possible, even in the days of the Tsar we Russians had baths.'

'That wasn't what I . . .'

Savalev held up his hand. 'I know, Sir Frederick. A poor joke on my part.'

The bathroom and the bath itself were of marble, and the gold-plated taps were shaped as dolphins. As Cooper lay back in the warm soapy water he wondered which of the ornate light fittings held the microphone and which gilt mirror housed the video camera.

His bags had already been unpacked when he went into the huge bedroom, and he had laid out his shaving gear on the marble shelf above the hand-basin in the bathroom.

The sitting room was empty when he walked back in. There was one place at the round walnut table laid with a bowl of strawberries, and a silver jug of cream with an old-fashioned sugar caster. They certainly knew his predilections. He helped himself to both strawberries and cream, and ate them standing by the big windows.

The garden at the back was just lawns and a few beds of chrysanthemums and dahlias. Peaceful enough if you ignored the soldiers and the half-track vehicle with its red star insignia, and the machine gun on its traverse. Did they imagine he was going to try to escape or did they visualise some desperate group of loyal parachutists rescuing him from his fate. And the word 'fate' brought back his depression. Life went on, inexorably, history had to have its day. Ten or twenty years from now his name would be in the world's history books. A name that would go alongside that of Chamberlain and Quisling. A synonym for cowardice, for an act of treason. The MC and bar would count for nothing.

Those screaming voices from the opposition benches had used the words 'coward and traitor' before he had even started speaking. He had stayed at his post as long as he dared. Longer than he should have. Maybe only one day too long. But that had been enough. The whole country had gone mad. There was no longer a silent majority. There were a dozen raucous, ravaging minorities that covered every social class in the country: the left-wing militants scenting victory out of chaos; the long-suffering middle-classes beginning to fight back, angry at the rioting and looting as it moved from the High Streets to their homes. The politicians, overwhelmed by the sudden ferocity of the rioting, had given up in despair. There was no solution short of declaring that a Civil War existed and using the troops. But who did you use the troops against? The few hundred militants could be picked off but that wouldn't stop it. They had worked for years to make it happen but they had never stopped to imagine how it would end. They wanted to bring down the legal government and take over themselves, but there was nothing left now for a mob to take over. The machinery had not just stopped, it had disintegrated. The machinery of government no longer existed. All that was left of legal government was Frederick Ansell Cooper.

Nobody had said that it all depended on him. Nobody had said anything. Nobody was listening any more to anybody. They were slugging it out on the streets or defending their homes. They were throwing it all away, and they didn't even realise it. Magna Carta, Cromwell, all those hard-won freedoms were pouring through the hole in the dam. All he could do was to keep them alive. Stop them from being the first Europeans to know what it was like to be atomised. There must be a lesson to be learned out of the shambles. There was only one that came to mind – democracy didn't work. It was too vulnerable. You couldn't just stand by and watch evil people destroy a whole society, a whole nation, just because saying what you liked was part of the fabric of democracy. Do lies *have* to be given the same freedom as truth?

Then Savalev came into the room followed by several other men, some in uniform, and Cooper was aware that he was standing holding the empty dish and spoon like some guilty schoolboy caught raiding the larder.

He made no attempt to remember their names as Savalev introduced them. One or two were familiar to him but he found Russian names were much of a muchness. The officers were all of high rank and only they were courteous enough to give a brief nodding bow as they were introduced. The civilians had faces straight from a Giles cartoon. Only one of them looked human, a tall slim man in his fifties with reddish hair, a beard and gold-rimmed glasses. It was he who led them into an adjoining room and arrayed them round an oval table, being very precise about who sat where. And it was he who led the proceedings. He spoke good English in a quiet but decisive voice, sometimes looking at Savalev in search of a word.

Maps and charts were spread out on the table. Great Britain, the North Sea, the North Atlantic, Scandinavia, and a separate map of the Norwegian-Finnish border area around Murmansk.

Sheets of clear talc were laid over the maps and charts, with chinagraph markings – figures scrawled in red and blue, and long, curving, sweeping arrows that all ended in some part of Britain.

The short explanations and their translations had obviously been well rehearsed. He listened half-heartedly to the torrent of code-names, acronyms, aircraft and Red Army units. He had got the message when they were laying out the maps and he had guessed more or less what it would be before he left London. Unless he did whatever they wanted, Britain would be invaded by massive Soviet forces assisted by thousands of sympathisers on the ground ready to cut off power, water, gas and communications. All he wanted to know was what they wanted in return for not invading. When he asked, it was Savalev who became the spokesman.

'Prime Minister, the sole object of this present meeting is to show you that there is no element of bluff or deception on the part of the Soviet government. What you have been shown are the "Top Secret" documents of Operation Reka.'

'I understand that, Mr Savalev. What I am asking is why they have been shown to me?'

Savalev shrugged. 'So that you are fully briefed for the meetings tomorrow. So that there is no doubt in your mind about our intentions and our capability in carrying them out.'

'Mr Savalev, I have been pointing out your capabilities in this area to Parliament for the last fifteen years. And you will be aware that I have suggested that when it suited Moscow you would attack one or all of your neighbours in Europe. I don't need to see this stuff or hear the military details to believe that you plan aggression. You know this as well as I do. Why this charade?'

Savalev hesitated then looked at the man with the gold-rimmed glasses and spoke in Russian, an edge of anger in his voice. When Savalev finished the man nodded and stood up, speaking quietly to the others who, looking surprised, also stood up and filed out of the room. At least two of the generals glanced at Cooper's face – as people sometimes did in London, wondering if it was the Prime Minister or not, before they asked for his autograph and the Special Branch man sent them on their way.

As the door closed behind the last of the men, Savalev turned impatiently to look at Cooper. 'Mr Prime Minister, I told you that I was appointed as your adviser during your visit. That was not a form of words. That is exactly what I have been ordered to do. I think I should make that clear.'

'And on what subject do you propose to advise me?'

'The negotiations here in Moscow.'

'I assume that you're a KGB officer, Savalev.'

'My status doesn't matter.'

'That's where you're wrong, Savalev. I don't need advice from the aggressors as to how to react to their threats. You should be advising your countrymen, not me.'

'It would be very unwise for you to adopt that attitude, Prime Minister.'

Cooper smiled a grim smile that the Leader of the Opposition would have recognised. He said softly, 'It would be very unwise for me not to, Savalev. If you've got nothing more to add, I'd like to get some sleep. No doubt it will be a long day tomorrow.'

Cooper, for some irrational reason, was pleased to see the anger in Savalev's eyes and the taut muscles around his mouth.

'As you please, Prime Minister. Ring if you need anything.' And Savalev left the room in obvious anger.

As Cooper undressed he reflected that it was almost the first time in twelve years that he had been able to speak his mind. To say exactly what he thought without weighing all the pros and cons. Nothing he said would make any difference to the outcome of these events. A little trimming here and there maybe, but nothing that really mattered. They wanted him because he could make whatever they planned look legal. The Soviets liked their legalities even if they were phoney. Even without the legality they would go ahead; it would merely be more difficult to combat world criticism of yet one more act of aggression. But in this particular case the world would not shed many tears. Protests to suit governments' own lines with Moscow, but nothing more. Half of them would be delighted to see Britain finally humbled, once and for all.

He slept soundly that night for the first time in years. Reality was a pleasant change from the Alice in Wonderland world of British politics in the last ten years.

# 8

Orlov and Fomenko sat together on the opposite side of the highly polished table. Savalev sat next to Cooper, translating as Orlov spoke, glancing from time to time at what Cooper guessed was the script of the prepared speech. The first five minutes had been the Soviet version of the relationship between Britain and the Soviet Union since 1917. A picture of hostility and provocation on the part of successive British governments and friendly gestures by the peace-loving people of the Soviet Union brushed to one side in the interests of the capitalist 'bourgeoisie'.

Cooper found his mind being diverted by the jargon. He had never been sure who the 'bourgeoisie' were. The 'workers' were obviously not just people who worked. There was some other seal of approval that made you a 'worker'. He got the impression that the pretty secretaries at Number Ten, who did a ten-hour day seven days a week were not 'workers'. But the part-time cleaning ladies almost certainly were. You had to be rather drab to be a real worker, and if you were British you had to be in a state of permanent discontent or you could easily become a hanger-on of the 'bourgeoisie'. He tried desperately to keep his mind on the boring rigmarole in case he missed the start of the real stuff. It was half an hour before it came.

'. . . no more than a base for the American war-mongers. Nuclear weapons on land and at sea vectored onto Soviet cities . . . the sole aim to destroy innocent civilians . . . hatred

87

of the men of peace in the Kremlin ... destruction of the Soviet way of life ... the CIA monitoring-establishments ... espionage ... subversion ... no longer tolerable ... the workers of Britain could no longer tolerate the Fascist yoke or stand idly by and witness the mounting aggression against their fellow workers in the Soviet motherland ... a delegation representing the workers had already arrived in Moscow demanding the help of their fellow workers ... the Politburo had unanimously decided that to avoid bloodshed and to put an end to the intolerable provocation by the war-mongers of the United States using the British Isles as their war base that the time had now come to restore peace to Europe ... the Soviet Union had no territorial ambitions in Europe or elsewhere but was prepared to assist Great Britain in returning to the community of peace-loving nations if asked to do so by the British government ... because of the present situation in Great Britain the only acceptable representative of the British government was the Prime Minister ... they would respond immediately to a request for assistance from him.'

Orlov sat with his cunning eyes on Cooper's face as Savalev finished translating.

Cooper said, without looking at Savalev, 'Is President Orlov expecting me to ask the Soviet Union to invade my country?'

Orlov obviously knew enough English to understand what Cooper had said. He held up his podgy hand to cut short the translation. He ordered Savalev in Russian to tell the Britisher the facts of life.

'President Orlov requires me to expand on the Soviet reaction to the present situation. The appropriate Soviet forces have been on Red Alert for ten days. If a necessity arose for the problem to be solved by force it is estimated that the operation would be completed in no more than three days. There would be patches of activity for maybe two or three weeks, but the country as a whole would be neutralised. Our military commanders calculate that apart from large scale destruction of buildings casualties would be in the order of one hundred and fifty to two hundred thousand killed or severely injured. Our own casualties could be as high as seven thousand.'

Cooper looked at Orlov. 'So when do you start the invasion?'

Orlov nodded to Savalev who continued. 'President Orlov has no wish to give such an order and asks that you consider an alternative.'

Cooper smiled grimly and folded his arms as he leaned back in his chair. 'What is the alternative?'

'The alternative is that you invite the economic, administrative and practical assistance of the Soviet Union in solving Britain's overwhelming difficulties.'

Cooper sighed impatiently. 'Let's cut out the jargon, for Christ's sake. What is it you're asking for?'

'A document has been prepared for you to sign that sets out the conditions on which the Soviet Union would respond favourably to your official request for assistance.' Savalev pointed to a red file cover. 'It is there for you to read. Russian and English texts.'

'Maybe I'd better read it.'

Orlov spoke for several minutes then Savalev translated. 'The President suggests that they leave you for a couple of hours to study the document.' He waved towards a phalanx of telephones. 'The priority telephones are available for your use if you wish to contact your colleagues at home or your opposite numbers in Europe. The operators all speak excellent English.'

Orlov and Fomenko were already standing, Orlov's peasant face intent on Cooper's, trying to gauge his reaction. As the two Russians walked to the door Savalev reached for the red file and handed it to Cooper. As Cooper took the file Savalev said, 'Would you like me to stay, Prime Minister, in case anything needs explaining?'

'If they've ordered you to stay, stay. It's a matter of indifference to me.'

Savalev settled down in his chair as Cooper opened the file.

The title page said simply: THE TREATY OF NEUTRALITY AND COOPERATION BETWEEN THE GOVERNMENTS OF THE UNION OF SOVIET SOCIALIST REPUBLICS AND THE UNITED KINGDOM.

As he turned the page he saw that the English text was on the right-hand page, the Russian on the left.

### PREAMBLE

THE GOVERNMENT OF THE UNITED KINGDOM REQUESTS THE HELP OF THE SOVIET UNION IN RESTORING LAW AND ORDER AND PEACE AND PROSPERITY TO ITS PEOPLES. IT RECOGNISES THAT THE INFLUENCE OF THE UNITED STATES GOVERNMENT AND ITS AGENCIES HAVE BEEN A PRIME FACTOR IN CREATING THE PRESENT SERIOUS SITUATION. IT ALSO RECOGNISES THAT THE COOPERATION OF THE USSR WOULD OVERCOME THE PRESENT DIFFICULTIES BEING EXPERIENCED IN THE UNITED KINGDOM. TO THAT END THE FOLLOWING HEADS OF AGREEMENT SHALL BE SIGNED BY BOTH GOVERNMENTS AND SHALL BE KNOWN AS 'THE ANGLO-SOVIET TREATY OF NEUTRALITY AND COOPERATION'. THE PARTIES AGREE AS OUTLINED IN THE FOLLOWING TEXT.

1. THE UNITED KINGDOM SHALL IMMEDIATELY ABROGATE ALL TREATIES WITH FOREIGN POWERS CONCERNING ECONOMIC, FINANCIAL OR MILITARY COOPERATION.
2. FOR A PERIOD OF FIVE YEARS THE LAWS OF THE USSR SHALL BE THE LAWS OF THE UNITED KINGDOM.
3. THE GOVERNMENT AND ADMINISTRATION OF THE UNITED KINGDOM SHALL BE SUBJECT TO THE ADVICE OF THE DULY APPOINTED SOVIET ADVISERS.

4. THE FOREIGN POLICY AND ECONOMIC POLICY OF THE UNITED KINGDOM SHALL BE AS REQUIRED BY ITS MEMBERSHIP OF COMECON.

5. THE RUSSIAN TEXT OF THIS TREATY IS DEFINITIVE.

6. THE GOVERNMENT OF THE USSR WILL UNDERTAKE THE DEFENCE OF THE NEUTRALITY OF THE UNITED KINGDOM AND MAY TAKE WHATEVER STEPS IT DEEMS NECESSARY TO CARRY OUT THIS OBLIGATION.

7. THE GOVERNMENT OF THE USSR WILL ASSIST THE GOVERNMENT OF THE UNITED KINGDOM IN ACHIEVING FULL EMPLOYMENT, THE MAINTENANCE OF LAW AND ORDER, AND EQUAL OPPORTUNITY FOR ALL CITIZENS.

8. A SEPARATE AGREEMENT SHALL COVER THE EXCHANGE OF TRADE AND TECHNOLOGY BETWEEN THE TWO PARTIES.

9. THE UNITED KINGDOM SHALL NOT BECOME A MEMBER STATE OF THE USSR NOR A MEMBER OF THE WARSAW PACT UNLESS AT THE END OF THE FIRST FIVE YEAR PERIOD THE GOVERNMENT OF THE UNITED KINGDOM SHALL REQUEST CONSIDERATION OF SUCH MEMBERSHIP BY THE GOVERNMENT OF THE USSR.

10. THE TREATY SHALL BE OPERATIVE FOR A PERIOD OF FIVE YEARS, RENEWABLE ON REQUEST FOR FURTHER PERIODS OF FIVE YEARS AND SHALL COMMENCE ON THE DATE OF SIGNING OF THE AFOREMENTIONED TREATY.

Cooper sighed deeply as he finished reading the document and then turned back to the beginning and started reading it again. Finally he threw the file back onto the table. Savalev reached over and set it neatly into place.

Cooper raised his eyebrows. 'How long have your people been planning all this?'

Savalev shrugged. 'What's happening in Britain is your doing, not ours.'

'If you believe that, my friend, you'd believe anything.'

'Is there anything I can clarify?'

'Do they really intend to invade if I don't sign this piece of paper?'

'Why should you doubt that?'

Cooper turned in his seat to look at the Russian. 'What do you think the other European countries are going to do? Just let you get away with it?'

Savalev nodded towards the telephones. 'Phone them and check it out. We can get you any Head of State you'd like to talk to.'

'OK. Get me Bonn. I'll talk to the Chancellor.'

'You do it, sir. Just tell the operator.'

Five minutes later the message came back. The Chancellor of the Federal German Republic was not available and the Foreign Minister was in Quebec. From Paris the message came back that the President was not available and the Foreign Secretary was on holiday in the Seychelles. Cooper had not really expected more than a few trite words of support, but the deliberate snubs made him realise that they already knew and accepted the facts. For a moment he considered calling Washington but he guessed that they already knew and that they would settle their score with Moscow their own way, on their own chosen battlefield. They were defending America now, not the free world. As always, with hindsight, the writing had been on the wall ever since the Falkland Islands business. The Americans trying to have their cake and eat it and the EEC making sure that they didn't miss a dollar's-worth of trade with the *junta*. And, as always, the bloody Irish ready to stab the British in the back the moment they got the chance. And the spectacle in the House of Commons of politicians trying desperately to bet both ways and hoping that the public didn't notice.

Savalev's brown eyes were looking at him. For a moment

he even thought there was sympathy on the man's face.

'Where did you learn to speak such good English?'

Savalev shrugged. 'At school, at Moscow University, in New York and in London.' He smiled. 'I was one of those at our embassy whom Prime Minister Heath threw out.'

'You must have been KGB.'

'I was then, but not now.' Savalev paused. 'What do you think of the treaty. It's got some good points, you know.'

'I didn't see any.'

'Full employment?'

Cooper smiled wryly. 'Compulsory employment. Working where you are told to work for wages that aren't negotiable. Striking illegal and severely punished.' Cooper shrugged. 'I wonder where you've got in mind for our Gulag?'

The brown eyes held no trace of sympathy as the Russian said, 'Ours is big enough to take your people too.'

'You've actually got it already worked out?'

'Of course.'

'What were the other good points?'

'You know them as well as I do, Prime Minister.'

'They expect me to sign this?' Cooper pointed at the red file.

'Of course they do. Like you, they know that you have no choice. It's sign on the dotted line or your country will go down in flames. The loss of life will be your responsibility not ours. We are giving you the choice. A chance to avoid a war you can't win. You haven't got the arms, the men or the planes. And you haven't got the will to fight.'

'And if I sign?'

'Then there is no war, and our experts will sort out the shambles for you.'

'And me personally?'

'You would remain Prime Minister for the moment. You would be flown back to London in a few days' time.'

'Can you imagine what the Leader of Her Majesty's Opposition is going to say?'

'There is no Her Majesty's Opposition. The Royal Family landed in Canada two hours ago. And the Leader of the Opposition is already in Moscow. He will not be returning to London for some time.'

'What else has been happening?'

'They've started burning down houses after they've looted them. The South-East and the Midlands are getting the worst of it. The army have been called in and there was a curfew announced this morning. From seven at night for twelve hours. It's worked rather patchily but . . .'

Cooper held up his hand. 'I don't need any more.'

'A week from now it will all be over. Just a piece of unpleasant history. The storm before the calm.'

'Do you want to tell them I'm ready?'

'They're at a reception at the Ethiopian Embassy.' He looked at his watch then at Cooper's face. 'They'll be ready in about twenty minutes.'

Cooper felt his first real sense of anger and humiliation. The rulers of the Soviet Union who intended the occupation of his country were not eager enough for his signature to forgo a quarter of an hour of a party at some clapped-out African embassy. They were obviously very sure of themselves. Then he realised that Savalev was speaking again.

'. . . the full Politburo. It will be treated with all diplomatic niceties observed. No attitudes indicating victory or surrender . . . a sensible collaboration between two friendly countries . . . there is no intention of humiliating you or your country.'

Cooper sighed deeply and closed his eyes. He was not a religious man but he started to say in his mind the words of the Lord's Prayer then couldn't remember them beyond 'Give us this day our daily bread'. There was a tear at the corner of one eye as he stood up, walking slowly towards the large painting on the far wall. It was one of those dreadful realist paintings, with Lenin in the foreground as always, pointing towards a factory behind him. The usual Amazonian women workers and hollow-eyed men in tattered clothes were standing around – spellbound by their God's exhortations.

An officer in uniform brought a note for Savalev and when he had read it he turned to Cooper. 'They've sent a car for us. You're getting the full treatment. TV, radio, the Politburo and the Great Palace. Are you ready?'

Cooper nodded. They really had worked out the odds and decided that he wouldn't have the guts or foolishness to refuse.

He caught sight of his face in a mirror and was shocked. His eyes were red-rimmed with fatigue, his cheeks hollow and his lips tight across his mouth, exposing his teeth as if he were some wild animal snarling at a rival.

As they swept through the Kremlin gates the guards presented arms and when they stopped at the entrance to the Great Palace he saw the Union Jack and the Soviet flag caught in the floodlights, and for a moment the enormity of what he was about to do overwhelmed him. It was incredible, impossible, that it should have come to this.

Six months ago, even five months, there had been some unrest but not much more than usual and then the whole country had started its Gadarene rush to ultimate disaster. The Cabinet had been warned by the security services of more determined moves by the subversives. Industry, the essential services, the Labour Party, the Trades Unions, had been penetrated to an incredible extent according to the reports, and were now virtually controlled by groups of left-wing activists.

Similar reports had flowed across Ministers' desks for ten years or more, but despite the fact that the current reports were more pressing, more substantial, little had been done. The old cry of 'Reds under the beds' had been raised as usual. And as usual it had played its part in deflecting the urgency of the reports. With the security services themselves being attacked by the left-wing's stooges in the House, the SPG disbanded, the independence of the police themselves under constant attack, it was easier to avoid action when it was obvious, even to the public, that the law of the land could no longer be enforced.

A military band was playing one of their anthems and he stood to attention with the Russian. He wasn't sure whether it was the Red Flag or the Internationale. It must be the Internationale – the Red Flag was the one they always sang at the end of the Labour Party Conferences. He had seen them all too often on the TV broadcasts. All holding hands, trying not to catch each other's eyes. Those creeps like Wilson and Callaghan, Benn and Foot. Well they'd have their Red Flag flying now, all right.

Then Savalev was leading him inside, through a huge hall, down long carpeted corridors. Now Orlov was seizing his hand. Thank God there was none of that hugging and kissing they went in for. One by one Orlov introduced the men around the table. And one by one they bowed briefly in his direction. A TV crew with several cameras, bathed the centre of the long table in their glaring lights. As Cooper took his place and sat down he saw the leather-bound originals of the Treaty documents in front of himself and Orlov.

To a round of applause Orlov stood up, confident, patting his pockets surreptitiously, like a self-satisfied second-hand car salesman who has just completed a good sale and can't believe his luck. Smiling benignly from time to time, gesturing in Cooper's direction. Eventually the Russian put on his glasses and picked up two typed sheets of thick cream paper. And in sometimes halting English he said his piece.

'For our friends, comrades, in Britain, we send a sincere message of brotherly love. Over the last few years we have seen a proud nation lose its way. With the signing of this Treaty we pledge our full resources of the Soviet Union to bringing back stability, full employment and respect for the Law. With goodwill on both sides we shall succeed together in our endeavours.' Orlov glanced slowly towards the camera facing him. 'Let no man and no nation venture to destroy our efforts. They would be dealt with severely should they try. A great Russian – Leo Tolstoy – said in his novel *Anna Karenina* – "There are no conditions to which a man cannot become accustomed, especially if he sees that all around him live in the same way." To our viewers in Great Britain I say this – think quietly tonight in your homes. Changes will have to be made. Changes to bring you full employment, law and order in your towns and cities, and a future filled with hope, not despair. From the Great Palace in the Kremlin I send you the fraternal greetings of every man, woman and child in the Soviet Union. Goodnight to you all.'

Pens were exchanged and the documents signed. Orlov stood up and walked towards the door, followed by the others until only Cooper, Savalev and a clerk collecting up papers were left. The party was over.

# 9

The Novosty Press Agency had already telephoned TV stations in every European country to notify them of an important and significant relay from Moscow. Some stations had put it straight into their evening schedules, others had merely monitored it and then broken into their scheduled programmes when they realised what was going on. The bar in the Press Club was full. From natural causes, rather than because of any relay from Moscow.

When Orlov stood up in front of the cameras there was no particular interest. Then the English translation came on as sub-titles, and as he moved into his speech the bar fell silent and members stood watching the screen, glasses in hand and cigarettes unlit. There was a murmur of disbelief as the computer characters gave the translation, and impatient hushing noises when he started to speak in English. Then as the image faded and the major film of the evening continued there was a short silence before the hubbub broke out. Journalists raced for phones and taxis, but a dozen or so off-duty men stayed on.

'What the hell does he mean?' The *Daily Express* man enquired as he looked around his group. 'He must be off his bloody head.'

'Has anyone phoned the *Morning Star* for a comment?'

'No. I'll go and try them now. We'll share it.'

He was back in six minutes with shorthand notes on the back of an envelope. He read out the notes slowly.

'Sir Frederick Cooper, Prime Minister, has signed a Treaty of something or other with the Soviet Union. The Soviet Union will be providing experts in defence, economics, administration etcetera, etcetera, to help the British government to bring back peace and prosperity.' He looked up, frowning. 'What the bloody hell does that mean?'

The man from *The Times* laughed. 'It means our Freddie had the choice of fighting off a full-scale invasion by the Red Army or calling it a day.'

'What d'you mean ... calling it a day?'

'Inviting the Reds to come out from under the beds.'

'To do what?'

'To take us over. To run the country.'

'For Christ's sake they don't imagine we'd just take it lying down. The army wouldn't stand for it for a start.'

The *Guardian* man said quietly. 'Come off it, Martin. The army and the police can't even cope with the looters and yobboes, let alone a full-scale invasion.'

'I'd better get back to the office. Maybe it's one of those bloody hoaxes like that Orson Welles thing in the States.'

The *Guardian* man smiled. 'You'd better go through your files old love and check what you've been writing about the Russkis these last few years.'

There was an influx of members who had put their pieces on the computers and were taking a break. Hoping that the Press Club customers somehow knew more than they did. But it was the Lobby correspondent of Thomson Regionals who had the first hard facts. He had spoken to Moscow, Paris and the Tass Office in Gough Square.

'The embassy in Moscow don't know a damn thing. They weren't even told that the broadcast was going out. They don't know where Cooper is, and they didn't know he was in Moscow.'

'What did the Tass boys say?'

The Thomson man grinned. 'They're as caught short as

we are but they've had a general directive in the last hour from Moscow. The general line is that with Soviet help it's gonna be like Christmas every day. The family walking hand in hand towards the sunset stuff. But at the back of all this I sense that they're a bit worried.'

'What about?'

'Reaction. Here and the rest of the world. Especially Washington.'

Somebody commented that it was like General Election night, waiting up for the results to come in, and the computer forecasts. From time to time new snippets of news were brought in by a newcomer. The provincial cities were strangely quiet. No looting, the streets mainly deserted. The Buckingham Palace press office was making no comment on anything. There were rumours that the American air bases were flying out embassy files and personnel around the clock. The usually well-informed and knowledgeable journalists found themselves knowing no more than their readers. Even by the early hours of the morning there was a considerable body of experienced opinion who thought that it was no more than some kind of try-on by the Russians.

For the next two days there was little fresh news from any source. The hoax theory gained ground mainly because there was no evidence to the contrary. Media sources in Europe and the United States were equally bereft of news and hard fact. A Japanese radio and TV station claimed they had evidence that the telecast had in fact, been a cable leakage from a drama studio rehearsing a TV play. Moscow sources claimed that they were overloaded with enquiries and requested written queries by teleprinter or correspondence. Meantime they confirmed that the programme had been genuine but could add no further details.

The first real blow fell in the early hours of the following day when an agency report from Ottawa claimed that the Royal family had been seen on an estate near Kingston, Ontario. The estate was owned by a member of the Canadian Liberal Party, a member of one of Trudeau's earlier cabinets. The information had been officially denied by a government spokesman in Ottawa and derided as a rumour. Gossip columnists and diary editors started checking on royal appointments and it was obvious in a matter of hours that something was going on. Not even minor royals had carried out their engagements in the previous two days.

Oddly enough, that news had more effect on the general public than the Moscow telecast. It was not just that the Royal family had left but that they had left without letting the people know. It brought a depression, an apprehension, out of all proportion to the fact. At nine o'clock that evening it was announced that the Prime Minister was back in the country and would be making various announcements in the next forty-eight hours. Previously considered a non-entity, Cooper suddenly became a saviour. The one man who knew what was going on, who would tell them what was really happening. The man who had seemingly gone to Moscow in the hope that that would bring back peace to the country.

For twenty-four hours the media had been playing it by ear. Avoiding hard comment in a genuine attempt not to make things worse. But with the announcement that the Prime Minister was back they sharpened their editorials. It was time to tell the nation the truth was the general theme. The sharpest comment was from the *Daily Telegraph* leader which made direct comparisons with Munich and asked if the nation had really decided that it was 'better Red than dead'. Or was this the decision of a small group of weak men who had lacked the guts to seize the nettle for the last two years and were now ready to surrender to those same pressures that they themselves had once held out to be subversive and undemocratic? Was this, in fact, the end of democracy in Great Britain? The dawn of the New Ice Age?

The senior Air Controller at Heathrow sat in his shirt-sleeves, his glasses pushed up onto his forehead as he dialled the unlisted number of the control tower at Gatwick. The voice at the other end that responded sounded calm and controlled.

'Collins, Gatwick control.'

'Christ, Percy, you sound like you're about to give out the hymn numbers. What's happening at your end?'

'We've given up, Charlie. All our frequencies are being used indiscriminately by every Tom, Dick and Harry. 119.45 went two hours ago. London Control Zone have thrown the switches. Biggin gave up 129.4 because it was hopeless to carry on. It's the same all over the south-east. Headcorn, Lydd, Manston, Southend. Even the bloody Volmet frequency is being used. How about you?'

'I'm still holding but it's not doing any good. Pilots are just ignoring instructions and the bloody runways look like taxi ranks. There are private planes just using the grass. There's going to be a terrible disaster if somebody doesn't do something soon.'

'Like who?'

'The CAA, the Home Office, even the Ministry of Defence.'

'None of those are even answering the phone, Charlie. Everybody's used to saying that "they" should do something and at long last they have. "They" have buggered off, and left us to it.'

'Any sign of the Russkis?'

'Yeah, we had nine Ilyushins in during the night, before the news got out and the panic started. I gather the US air-bases have got thousands of US citizens being ferried to

Shannon. Dublin and Shannon are screaming their heads off and nobody's taking a blind bit of notice. The lemmings are on their way and nobody's going to stop them. There are private pilots and company pilots making £100,000 a trip to Cork, Shannon and Dublin.'

'What are you going to do yourself?'

'Me. I'm married with three kids. I ain't got no choice. I'll just wait around and see what happens. If you're not married I should get the hell out of it.'

'You know, I can't believe it's happening. Not just overnight like this.'

'Don't let's kid ourselves, mate. It's been on its way for nearly ten years. We just looked the other way. The wise guys shipped their money overseas when Maggie took off exchange controls. Just look what's happened to Kruger-rands in the last three months. World gold price for one troy ounce – 380 quid. Last week's price for a Krugerrand in London ... 1200 quid. Somebody saw it coming, mate. I've got to go. We're having a last bash in the canteen before we see them coming in with the snow on their boots.'

'Let me know if ...'

The phone went dead and so did all the telephones in London and the Home Counties as polite Russians gave their instructions to the engineers at central exchanges.

Despite aircraft swarming like flying ants, without control, and ignoring flight paths, there were only seven reported crashes, with fifty-four casualties. The RAF and the Royal Navy had collaborated efficiently. Aircraft carriers were pulled in to take aircraft that they were not designed to take, and when it was possible planes had flown in convoy to Gibraltar and Cyprus. One Harrier was lost, but otherwise the withdrawal was without casualties.

The coastguard stations gave up logging departures early on. The Channel reminded old-timers of Dunkirk as boats small and large headed across the Channel to France,

Belgium and Holland. Enterprising men assembled convoys of light craft to make the more testing journey across the Lower North Sea area.

At French Channel ports there were a number of outbreaks of fighting between the British refugees and French port officials. But the real desperation of the illegal entrants made it a one-sided battle. Scores would be settled in the following weeks: for three days the French authorities gave up any resistance and sat fuming in their offices on instructions from the government which in turn had been threatened by Washington that all French assets in the USA would be frozen and, if necessary, confiscated, if the fleeing Britishers were not given at least temporary refuge.

# 10

The Aeroflot plane brought Cooper back to Lydd, a small airport on the Kent coast, and a Wessex helicopter took him to London. It touched down on Horse Guards' Parade and Cooper was surprised to find Savalev waiting for him with a group of half a dozen men. He was introduced to them individually. They were all Russians and they all spoke excellent English. Savalev suggested that they walk back together to Downing Street.

Nothing seemed to have changed at Number Ten. Except the staff. They too were English-speaking Russians, and Cooper noticed that the girls were just as pretty as the English girls had been. Savalev took him into the Cabinet Room alone.

'Yuri Smetana has asked me to put you in the picture, Sir Frederick.'

'Who is Yuri Smetana?'

'He is the Soviet Commissioner.'

'And what might that mean?'

'He is the man charged with the reconstruction programme. He will be Moscow's top man in the UK. You'll like him. He speaks good English. Has lived in the United States for many years. Has been trained and groomed especially for this appointment. Highly efficient and an energetic organiser.'

'And you?'

'I'm Smetana's adviser, because I've had more experience

of this country than he has. Why don't we sit down, and I'll tell you how we plan the reorganisation.'

Cooper shrugged and sat down in the nearest chair.

'Smetana will be going on TV tonight to outline the new approach. But you can hear that when he broadcasts. The legislation has been drawn up already. It's essentially our own Soviet law code but there is a bridging authority that we want you to authorise. It covers the appointment of a Soviet adviser for all towns with a population of 25,000 and over. They will have a trained staff of their own who will cover the local administration of industry, finance, and law and order. They will also administer the Soviet Reconstruction Loan.'

'What's that?'

'The first part will be roughly a 100 million rouble loan for retraining programmes.'

The telephone rang and Savalev reached for it, nodding as he listened and then hung up.

'Smetana would like to meet you now. He will be using Number Ten and you will be next door in Number Eleven.' Savalev stood up. 'He's upstairs in the private office.'

Smetana was nothing like what Cooper had expected. He was in his early fifties, well dressed and looked more like an alumnus of Harvard Business School than a Soviet party man. He stood up smiling, his hand held out.

'The British don't seem to provide well for their Prime Ministers, Sir Frederick. History before comfort.' He pointed to an armchair. 'Do sit.'

When Cooper had sat down Smetana perched on the edge of the old mahogany desk, one leg swinging confidently.

'We have some problems with local authorities accepting the appearance of our Town Commissioners. In some cases we want you to visit the area and straighten things out. We're trying to do it smoothly but it takes time for people to get used to new ways. I'm hoping my broadcast will help. But

I wanted the chance to tell you my general approach. It's going to be positive and urgent. I shall not be looking for trouble, but trouble-makers will be dealt with severely under Soviet law. I shall only ask from a Britisher what I would ask from a Soviet citizen. They will have the same rights and the same penalties. And the same obligations to the state. Hard work and loyalty will be honoured and rewarded. Slackers and trouble-makers will be treated just as they would be in the Soviet Union.'

'I think your first problem will be the House of Commons.'

Smetana smiled and stood up. 'I don't think so, Sir Frederick, I don't think so. It will not be recalled.' He smiled. 'I shall be holding a reception at our embassy this evening, I hope that you'll come along.' Smetana turned to Savalev, smiling. 'Make him come, Lev.'

Smetana's broadcast was on all TV channels and all radio stations. As Cooper sat watching the TV set with Savalev he wondered what the music was as they showed the caption. It wasn't the Red Flag but Cooper was not musically inclined. For a moment he thought he recognised an old tune called 'Wagon Wheels'. Smetana had chosen the introductory music himself. It was a melodious extract from Dvorak's 9th Symphony – 'The New World'. The caption said, simply – The Soviet Commissioner for Great Britain.

The caption faded and there was Smetana in a blue suit, dark red tie and white shirt, looking even more like a top man from IBM. His hands were clasped on the desk in front of him and there was the Karsh portrait of Churchill just visible on the wall behind.

'Good evening. In the last few days the media and other sections of society have been speculating about the plans for the reconstruction programme. Some have suggested a scenario that sounds like an old Welsh sermon – hell-fire and brimstone. Others have painted a more cheerful picture. Tonight I want to put your minds at rest.

'This is a country ... a nation ... with a long history of courage and progress ... the government of the Soviet Union have instructed me to guide this country back to its former greatness. Not in ten years time, not five years, but in months rather than years. That may sound impossible, but I assure you it is not. It will mean changes in attitudes and way of life. But I believe that the vast majority of people will welcome these changes.

'Let me outline for you some of the problems and the way we shall tackle them together.

'Unemployment is a crime against the people. Nothing can excuse it. Every citizen ... man or woman ... has a right, a duty, to work. My Town Commissioners have already been given instructions that all unemployed people are to be found work within twenty-one days. Wages and rewards in all walks of life will be exactly the same as those for equivalent jobs in the Soviet Union. Training will be given at once for those whose skills need to be changed. This includes those at present in the armed forces who will not be needed in the foreseeable future. There are soldiers, sailors and airmen whose considerable skills will be more use to the nation in commerce and industry than in lonely barracks in Germany or elsewhere.

'I come next to law and order. Every household will receive in the next few days their own copy of an explanation of Soviet law. What your rights are, what your obligations are, and the things that are not allowed. Criminal elements, hooligans and trouble-makers will be severely dealt with, as they would be if they lived in Moscow or Leningrad. The days of the law-breakers are over.

'The newspaper writers have speculated on Soviet intentions. The description Finlandisation has been used – referring to our close cooperation with our Finnish neighbours.

Others have suggested that Great Britain will be incorporated into the Soviet Union. Neither of these speculations apply. The Soviet Union has been pilloried in the Western and American media as a nation of war-mongers intent on extending its borders in every direction. In World War Two, 20 million Russians were killed by the Fascists. My whole family was among the victims. They were not just names on a list for me. They were people I loved. My background. My life. Am I likely to be a war-monger? Is any Soviet leader likely to want to be the one who leads the Soviet people into another Armageddon? I leave it to you to decide. We could no longer accept this constant antagonism from the Americans. In these islands they mounted their espionage against us. And it was these islands they saw as their European base for the next war. For many years the Soviet Union tolerated the provocation for the sake of world peace. But a line has to be drawn. So far and no farther. Trident, cruise-missiles, the air-bases and naval bases went too far. In your heart you knew this, but you were given no choice. When your Prime Minister asked us to help put things right we knew that it was our duty to do so.

'When a new society is being established, new methods, new thinking has to be applied. Let me tell you of some of those changes.

'In a modern society Lords, Earls, Barons, Knights have no place. From now on all such titles are void. Politicians have not served this country well. They have been divisive not constructive, seeking privileges for themselves and their sponsors. Therefore there will be no political parties in this country for the next five years. Not even our friends who are members of the Communist Party of Great Britain. Political parties are banned.

'I have one last announcement to make. I have given orders for the revival of something that you did here after the war. It was called the Festival of Britain and showed the world your inventiveness and creativity. I have instructed my staff that a Festival of Britain shall be mounted within two months.

'Think about what I have said tonight, and I feel that you will agree with me that the changes were inevitable and will be for the good of all of us. Goodnight.'

Savalev leaned forward and switched off the set. He turned to look at Cooper.

'What did you think of it?'

Cooper raised his eyebrows. 'Very shrewd. Very surprising.'

'What was surprising?'

'The tone. The attitude.'

Savalev nodded. 'But you don't believe we mean it?'

'Of course I don't. You don't give a damn for this country. You'll bleed us dry like you've done in every country you've taken over.'

'You're wrong. Quite wrong. We're determined to show the world what can be done with communism in an advanced country. In the Soviet Union we have had to pull ourselves out of centuries of serfdom and backwardness. We've made the sacrifices, God knows we have, and in due time we'll be getting our rewards. But in this country we can show the world the benefits of our system in months not decades.'

'You sound like a Madison Avenue advertising agency selling a new fertiliser.'

Savalev smiled, shaking his head. 'Wait and see, my friend. You're going to be surprised. It's what you and your people should have done years ago. You let this country disintegrate, and you didn't lift a finger to stop it or prevent it.'

It took a few weeks before the population absorbed what their new masters expected of them. Most of the Soviet administrators wore rather old-fashioned civilian clothes but were otherwise not all that identifiable. The more apprehensive had feared violence and perhaps looting in the early days but there was none.

At their places of work they were told what they were expected to do. Companies employing more than 50 people were being absorbed into larger groups which themselves were to become sections of the major State-owned conglomerates. The new wage-rates and conditions were posted up in all places of employment.

The old Job Centres became local offices of the Ministry of Labour and all those registered were sent to work in local companies or for conversion training at the new centres. There was no longer unemployment pay because it was illegal to be unemployed and there were no longer any Social Security benefits.

Prices for all goods were fixed and only the smallest margins were available to private retailers. They were not encouraged to continue but they were able to survive by selling their businesses for a nominal sum to the State retail monopoly that allowed them to continue as wage-earners.

The manufacture of goods considered socially unjustified was terminated and alternative more routine products could be made according to the plant and skills available.

There was no attempt to interfere with the owning of houses but it was illegal to own any property other than a permanent home. All other property including land was transferred to State ownership. The landed gentry were the only group to be treated demonstrably badly. If they were cooperative a cottage or small lodge would be made available but the rest of what they owned was taken over by the State. The bureaucracy involved was simple and not concerned with any niceties of the law. It was dealt with in a matter of hours. Ruthlessly and effectively.

The Archbishop of Canterbury and the Roman Catholic

Primate had been warned that if the church indulged in political comment or activities it would be severely dealt with. Otherwise the churches could continue. Their activities would be subject to surveillance by both the KGB and the Ministry of Social Services. Churches of all denominations were crowded from the first Sunday of the new regime, and the Roman Catholic priests were having great difficulty in handling the induction of new converts.

Travel was restricted to within the county of residence but permits for regional travel were available where acceptable reasons could be established. Petrol was rationed but supplementary coupons were reasonably easy to obtain from local tribunals administered by British staff. Telephone facilities were available for restricted categories of users but existing installations could be used between 6 p.m. and 7 p.m. on three specified days a week.

All rents of houses were slashed to five per cent of the family's joint earnings whether the property had previously been privately owned or owned by a local authority.

At least a dozen so-called Protective Custody Camps had been identified in various places in the UK. They were frequently ex-army barracks and camps in the remoter areas of the country. Much effort was put into trying to establish what categories were represented by the inmates who numbered many tens of thousands. Active Trades Unionists, Trotskyites, writers and broadcasters, ex-Labour Party functionaries, ex-Labour and Liberal MPs and a variety of university lecturers and historians were soon identified but there seemed no rhyme or reason for the detention of the many thousands of unknowns. What provided the other main talking point was the Soviet authorities' attitude to well-known Tories who seemed to have been left to find some niche in industry or commerce.

All the banks, the big five and the merchant banks with the Building Societies and Trustee Savings Banks were taken over by the State at the same time as the insurance companies. The Stock Exchange had been unceremoniously closed in the first week.

For those who cared one way or another it was obvious that what was happening had been planned for a long time. All the operations were dealt with quickly and ruthlessly. The previous laws of the land played no part and no compensation was paid no matter what was involved.

Within the first two weeks eight-page questionnaires were issued to every household with several hundred questions which had to be answered within four days. The questions covered family details for three generations, education, employment, assets in the UK and abroad and political affiliations. Failure to hand in the reports meant that the whole family was unable to apply for the plastic registration card that allowed the purchase of food and registration for work. False information rendered the signatory liable to five years forced-labour in the USSR.

President Wheeler had a liking for breakfast meetings that was not shared by several of his top advisers, particularly Secretary of State Brodsky. Wheeler, now sixty-two, had been in politics all his life and loved every minute of it. Brodsky was fifty-five and frequently wished that he was back at Amherst.

'Let's talk about London, Joe,' the President said. 'What's the latest news?'

'The Red Air Force are using our old bases in East Anglia. The embassy has been taken over by them and is now the Museum of Soviet Culture. They've taken over ICL, the British computer company. And so it goes on.'

'How are the Britishers taking it?'

'They're lapping it up. You can walk the streets without getting mugged. There's almost full employment. The old right-wingers are delighted that the unions have lost all their clout. The old left-wingers are delighted that the Lords and Barons have been done down. The blacks can't get used to equality but are enjoying trying. There're goodies for everyone. Not real goodies, negative ones. Seeing your old enemy get his come-uppance.'

'They're really winning the propaganda war. They haven't put a foot wrong.'

'Propaganda's one thing, Mr President. Real life's something else.'

'Now you're being profound, Joe. What's all that mean?'

'It means that when you're dying of thirst in the desert you pray for water and swear that you'll never leave a tap dripping for the rest of your life. After they've rescued you you're filling the bathtub six months later without a second's thought.'

'I don't see the relevance.'

'The British were in a hell of a mess. They're so occupied with getting out of the mess that they've no time for anything else. When things are a bit better they'll start thinking and then we'll know the answer.'

'The answer to what?'

'The answer to whether freedom and democracy are worth a damn. Or are just words that sound good.'

Wheeler looked at Brodsky in silence. Then he said softly, 'And how far were we responsible for all this? What could we have done that we didn't do?'

'Very little, in my opinion. Maybe we were trying to solve too many problems in too many places all at the same time. Sout-east Asia, the Panama canal, the Middle East, Libya and Gadaffi, half of South America. You name it and we were there. Europe was a problem area that we knew of old. The British problem was home-made.' He shook his head, thinking. 'Their workers wanted too much money for too little effort, the politicians just let it all drift and the mobs took over. The Russians had been working at them for years but nobody believed it could happen in dear old England. And it did.'

'I guess you're right. Tell me about the Israeli thing.'

Jamie Boyle sat on the edge of the big mahogany desk in his office, listening to the Soviet Commissioner's speech on the portable radio. When it ended he leaned forward and switched off the set. For several minutes he sat there with his eyes closed, one leg swinging slowly as he gathered together his thoughts.

A dozen times he had gone over what he would do when the crisis came but now that it was here the plans suddenly seemed too drastic. Too final. This wasn't the crisis they had had in mind, he and Harry Andrews and the others. Planning things sitting in the garden on a sunny day was a lot different from actually carrying it all out. It was like talking about life assurance, not about actually dying.

What they had imagined happening was nothing like this. Less definite, not involving the whole population, and dealing with the kind of villains they all understood. Home-grown villains. But this was far beyond their thinking.

As his hand reached for the telephone it rang and he picked it up.

'Boyle, MacNay and Fowler.'

'Is that you, Jamie?'

'Yes, Harry.'

'You heard the speech?'

'I did. But it hasn't really sunk in yet. I don't quite believe it.'

'They're already here. Heathrow and Gatwick have been cleared of all other traffic. The runways are crowded with Aeroflot planes. The estimate is over two thousand Russian administrators already here. Are you still with us?'

'You're still going ahead as planned?'

'Oh yes. Now more than ever.'

'OK. Then I'm with you.'

'How long will you need to clear up?'

'Can I have a week?'

'Sure. You'll come down to the place as soon as you're free?'

'Yes.'

'You're the last call on my list, Jamie. Nobody's reneged. But there's far more to do now than we previously envisaged.'

'I'll be there, Harry. Ready to do my stuff.'

'Thanks. See you.'

As Jamie Boyle looked around his office he wondered what his grandfather would have thought of it all coming to an end. And such an end. The old man had seen the law as sacrosanct. To be obeyed and administered to the letter. The Church of Scotland, the Lord President of the Court of Session and Robbie Burns, were the pillars of the old boy's life. He wouldn't have believed what had gone on in the country in the last five years. The excuses for criminal behaviour, the concern for criminals but not for their victims. He would have said that right now they were only reaping what they had sown. But who *were* 'they', the people who had wanted this to happen? Very few of the politicians, that was certain. No matter which of the two ruling parties they belonged to. Not the general public, they had always been indignant about the laxity. A few hundred left-wing militants? They hadn't the power or the public support. So who was it who had always put the brake on decisive action to maintain the law? Who was it who claimed that the guilt was society's?

Boyle shook his head and sat down at his desk, pulling out a drawer and reaching for a few sheets of the practice's notepaper. He wrote decisively and without corrections hoping that they would read between the lines. He left the practice to his sole partner and the managing clerk, and said that by the time they read the note he would have left the country. As he sealed the envelope he remembered that he had moved £75,000 to New York when it looked those years ago as if Benn might become leader of the disintegrating Labour Party. And it was still there. It hadn't been needed and he had left it there earning good interest.

He took a dozen or so files from the shelves and placed them on his desk. When he had locked the drawers he took two keys off the ring and put the rest beside his letter. As he carried the last of the files to his car he pulled the door to behind him and he didn't look back.

Jeanie was waiting for him, two glasses of malt already on the low glass table. He had warned her over a year before that when the time came, if it came, they would just leave the house and everything in it, and go.

She had heard the Soviet Commissioner's speech and had already packed two cases for them. The house at Cramond had been their home for seven years and he knew that she hated leaving it. He burned all but two of the files in the back garden, pounding the ashes to powder with a garden fork.

It was beginning to get light as they drove through Grangehill and headed towards the beach until the road turned back on itself around the promontory jutting out to the sea. Ten minutes later they were under the archway of trees covering the drive to the old stone house.

Despite the early hour old MacKay was waiting for them. Wearing his Black Watch plaid and a plain blue jacket he looked every inch a laird. Which he was not. The stone house and its grounds were all that he owned, and he lived frugally off a family trust fund that paid him enough to maintain a reasonable standard as a single man.

The old man put his arm around Jeanie and kissed her cheek.

'You look lovely, my dear. Let's go inside where it's

warmer.' He turned to look at Jamie Boyle. 'Your father's here already, laddie. He'll be pleased to see you safe and sound.'

They had slept until mid-afternoon and then Robert Boyle had taken his son out onto the lawn, guiding him towards the wooden bench under an old magnolia tree. When they were seated his father turned to look at him.

'You look worried, boy. Are you?'

Jamie smiled. 'Concerned, father, not worried.'

'Who wouldn't be. You've heard that they've recessed both Houses until further notice. And that means for as long as they're here.'

'I hadn't heard that. They're not wasting any time.'

'I'm not going to ask you what you're up to, boy, but I want to warn you that these people aren't just tough. They're ruthless. More ruthless even than the Nazis. So please, please take care. You and Jeanie are all I've got left.'

'I'll take care, father, don't fret about me. And Jeanie will be here now permanently.'

'Is all this to do with the man you introduced me to way back? Colonel Andrews?'

Jamie smiled and touched the back of his father's hand. 'Don't ask me, father, then you won't be involved. They'll be keeping an eye on MPs and their contacts.'

'You did what we agreed about the practice?'

'Yes.'

'I've arranged to cover Jock MacKay's outgoings while you and Jeanie are based here, so don't feel you're putting a financial strain on him. I think he's relieved, and glad of some company. He's very fond of your Jeanie and he'll take good care of her while you're off gallivanting. I'll stay on at Corstorphine and you can always contact me there if you need me.'

He slapped his knee as he stood up. A gesture of confidence that was far from his real feelings.

Jamie Boyle left that night, just after midnight.

They sat on the hillside in a rough circle. Glyn Thomas, Sanjiva Singh, Jamie Boyle, Cameron Davies, Meg Thomas, Joe Langley, and Harry Andrews. The sky was cloudless but the distant mountains looked blue from the heat mist rising from the valley. There was no sound except the bleating of sheep higher up the hill, the faint sound of birds, and the soft splashing of the stream cascading over the rocks.

Andrews had idly picked a stem of red clover, rolling it between his finger and thumb as he surveyed the ground between his brown walking boots. Then he looked at each one of them in turn.

'We agreed what we agreed a long time ago. Almost a year. What we talked about has happened. Not the way we expected and sooner than we expected. Maybe one of you, or even all of you, may feel that we were dreaming dreams when it didn't seem likely that we should have to put our plans into action. If any of you has changed his mind and wants to withdraw, now is the time to do it.' He looked from one serious face to another. 'Let me say that I would have just as much respect for someone who decided to drop out as for someone who stayed. A person without deep conviction could cost the lives of hundreds of people. And this is a very different exercise from the one we had in mind originally. Very, very different.'

He waited in silence for several minutes but nobody spoke.

'When we were planning originally we were expecting to have to deal with our own people. Right- or left-wing extremists in such numbers that the police and even the army couldn't control them. Our great advantages would have been our training, our experience in guerrilla operations and

119

street fighting, our organisation and discipline, our anonymity and ... putting it crudely ... the fact that we were prepared to operate outside the regulations that apply to the police and the army.

'What we are now faced with is fighting trained soldiers, not just vicious thugs. So ... do we have to think again?' He paused, waiting for a response. When none came he went on. 'I think that we still have most of those advantages. It will be far tougher against trained troops but let us remember that they are troops who don't speak or read our language. They are in a strange country and they don't know their way around.' He paused. 'However, we have one disadvantage that we didn't allow for. Whatever they say in public, at the moment they are an occupying power. They have no feelings for the people. They will take hostages and maybe kill in retaliation against our operations. Innocent people's lives will be at stake. So what we do has to be carefully planned. There's no room for playing cowboys or Robin Hood.

'Over the past six months we have built up a formidable force. Thirty groups. Twenty-one men to a group, in teams of three. And we shall gain more as the Russians blunder around and people come to see them for what they are ... an occupying army. And behind our groups we have built up lists of several thousand sympathisers in strategic positions who will help us in passive ways.'

Andrews saw Jamie Boyle's hand go up.

'Yes, Jamie?'

'Can we really still rely on these sympathisers now the scenario is so different?'

Andrews shrugged. 'Not all of them. We shall have to sort the sheep from the goats all over again. And we shall have to assure them that their help to us will never, never, be revealed. A solemn promise. And remember that time is on our side, not theirs. I don't want to rush into any operation until I have a lot more information about them. And there's bound to be a honeymoon period when they're on their best behaviour. It will take time for the public to grasp what they're really up to.'

'What are they really up to, Colonel?' Cameron Davies still automatically give him his rank despite all the warnings.

Andrews smiled. 'You heard what the Soviet Commissioner said in his speech. Well they're not here for any of that. Strategically they're here to control the North Atlantic. Politically they're here because it killed NATO, and to remove the Americans from Europe if they can. I think they will succeed. And economically they're here to bleed us white. As soon as they feel safe they'll turn the screws so hard that we'll be just a slave-workers' colony. Without food, goods or even a shred of freedom.' He paused for a moment. 'But don't let us kid ourselves. Some are going to like it. The cooperators, the Quislings. And they will be one of our targets.' Andrews nodded to Joe Langley. 'Yes, Joe?'

'Can even the most dedicated guerrilla force bring down an occupying army?'

'They did it in Vietnam, Joe. The Afghans are doing it. The IRA damn near did it.' Andrews stood up slowly. 'Let's eat and then you can get back to your bases.'

To Harry Andrews that other night in Pen-y-Fan seemed a long time ago. But there had been no way out. It was only three days after the Russians had come and she'd had one of her outbursts. She had seen him burning his army clothes in the orchard and loading stuff into the car, and she seemed to realise that he must have something to hide. She had guessed it must be something he wanted to hide from the Russians and had gone straight into a Bette Davies part, he couldn't remember its title, but the star had walked around in riding breeches slapping her leg with a riding crop as she denounced the man who was cheating her father. Paula, eyes blazing and hands on hips, had screamed that she would denounce him to the Russians.

The journey to Wales had been a nightmare, with the virago in the passenger seat and road blocks every few miles. It had taken ten hours and he was exhausted when he arrived at the farm. She had been all smiles and flirtation with Glyn who hadn't responded because he had seen it all so many times before.

As they sat down late that night he had told Glyn of her threat, conscious that his eyes were burning with tiredness and strain as the quiet man looked calmly back at him.

'Do you want me to do it, Harry, or you?'

'I couldn't do it, Glyn. I couldn't do it.'

'There isn't any choice, you know that. There's scores of lives at stake.'

'I know.'

'I'll use the syringe, she won't know a thing, I promise.'

Andrews had closed his eyes to pray and then shaken his head to brush away the cowardice.

'OK, Glyn. You do it.'

Glyn had insisted that he took a sleeping tablet and he hadn't woken until mid-evening the next day. Nothing had been said but all her things had gone and he had tried not to think about her too often. He had no longer loved her, that had ended long ago, and maybe it never had been more than infatuation magnified by lust, but it had gone on a long time.

After they had all left the following day Andrews walked up the stairs of the farm-house to the landing, and after waiting for a moment, listening, he reached out to touch the centre stud on the old iron horse-shoe hanging between the two willow pattern plates on the white wall. Only the soft gasp of compressed air marked the descent of the aluminium ladder from the ceiling. In the attic he pressed one of the touch switches on a panel and the ladder came up slowly, softly clamping itself into place.

There was no window up here but a video screen showed a pattern of light and shade, which slowly came into focus on the barn and the lane beyond the fence. Andrews moved the dial so that the video camera turned through 180° to show the yard at the back, the pond, and the edge of the small orchard.

On a long bench were two Revox tape-recorders and a neat black transceiver, whose aerial led to the base of what looked like a periscope tube. On a centre panel fastened to the wall behind the equipment were charts showing radio reception conditions in Europe, Canada and the United States for each week of the year. There were various metal-cased instruments including a voltage stabiliser, an FC-841 frequency counter, a Bearcat 220 scanner, a quartz controlled clock showing Greenwich Mean Time to a hundredth of a second. Set on the wall were three digital read-out panels showing time differentials in four unnamed places. A VDU and a word-processor were on a separate metal trolley.

The room was lined with tongue-and-grooved pine planks and looked Swedish. There was an ex-army camp bed at the far end, a tattered armchair, and in the corner was a cooking ring and electric kettle at the side of a small enamelled sink with a water heater and a cold tap. The floor was covered completely with grey foam-backed carpet.

Andrews pulled open the folding wooden chair and sat down at the long bench, reaching for the pad and pencil. He filled three pages with neat writing, then read them through, underlining various phrases. Going through them again, he crossed out a word here and there. Then he took the remaining text over to the word-processor and slowly tapped the keys until the whole text came up on the VDU screen. There were about four hundred words and a few figures. Roughly eleven hundred characters. After he had checked them twice he pressed two of the control keys one after the other. The first key separated the text into five character groups and the second key put the groups into code.

He plugged the coaxial cable into the rear of the VDU and into a small grey metal box with a meter on its face. From the box he plugged in a second lead to one of the tape-recorders. Ten minutes later the tape played back the message in Morse at roughly 35 words a minute. With these transferred from one recorder to another the whole message was compressed into a time of seven seconds. Unrecognis-able as Morse, and in a random, virtually unbreakable code that was electronically changed every hour.

He ate half a tin of cold baked beans on a piece of toast and waited until the satellite controlled clock showed GMT as 24.00.000. Then he stood up and walked over to the bench. When the clock showed 24.03.000, he pressed the recorder button marked playback and watched the signal meter flickering on the transceiver. He did it again exactly 23 minutes later because it was the twenty-third day of the month.

Leaving the light still burning, Andrews undressed slowly and lay down on the camp bed, pulling the old grey army blanket first over his shoulders and then over his face. His mind went over the events of the last two days. It had turned out better than he had expected.

On the steps of Birmingham Town Hall the burly KGB man pushed the two men to one side. The City Commis-sioner Anatoli Lewinski was already in a bad mood. He had asked what the hell was the difference between a town and a city and nobody on his staff could tell him. He wouldn't let them ask one of the locals and he had barked and snarled his way through the short daily-report meeting and was now on his way back to the office.

One of the two men had shuffled round the KGB man and held out a bunch of red roses. The Commissioner brushed them aside. 'What do you want?'

'I'm Rory Maguire and this ...' he pointed at his companion, '... this is Coulthard.'

'What do you want,' Lewinski shouted. 'Explain what you want.'

'We are your people in Birmingham.'

'Oh for God's sake. What does that mean?'

'Comrade Maguire is chairman of the Birmingham branch of the Communist Party of Great Britain. I am the local candidate. We want to assist you, comrade, in your essential work.'

Lewinski turned to the KGB man and spoke angrily in Russian, saliva spraying from his lips. The KGB man nodded and pointed to two of his men and then at the two Britishers.

The two men were seized and bundled into the black limousine parked at the side of the Town Hall steps. Twenty minutes later they had been stripped and were in separate cells in Winson Green prison. Four days later they had been paraded, still naked, in the visitor's room. The KGB man was already there. They looked relieved, as if they knew that with a man so close to the City Commissioner all would be put right. The thin man, Coulthard, managed a weak smile.

'I teach sociology, comrade, at Aston University. I took on the chairmanship when our friend ...'

He hesitated as he saw the anger in the KGB man's eyes. He blundered on '... our membership is small but extremely active and we await ...'

'Silence.' The word echoed around the concrete walls like a gunshot and then the KGB man said, 'You have caused

125

inconvenience to the Commissioner. Let it be quite clear to you two dog-turds ... there ... are ... no ... political ... parties ... in ... this ... country. Is that clear? They are illegal.'

'But all our work ...'

'What work? A bunch of old women discussing the importance of dialectical materialism ... you call that work ... you're pathetic.' He lowered his voice. 'You have been tried by a People's Court and found guilty of actions against the State. You will serve two years forced labour with the Forestry Commission. You understand?'

'But our families, we ...'

The KGB man's fist crunched into the thin man's face and he staggered back holding his hands to his broken nose as the blood ran down his thin arms. Far away he heard the metal door clang to. Ten minutes later a warder led them back to their cells.


Joe Langley and the two other Trades Union leaders sat listening carefully as the Russian read out the prepared statement that had been issued from London.

'... and all wages will be on the scale laid down in the hand-book. These wage rates are the sterling equivalent of the standard rates at present applied in the Soviet Union. All additional payments are dependent on production norms having been fulfilled.' The Russian looked up from the typed sheet. 'And it is signed by Commissioner Smetana, countersigned by your own Prime Minister, Frederick Cooper. Any questions?'

It was Charlie Harris who seized the nettle. 'What about our own unions?'

'This *is* your own union. The only authorised union in Great Britain.'

'You don't understand ... we're a craft union. All our men are qualified men, tradesmen.'

'That is reflected in your rates of pay, comrade.'

'But we can't negotiate at the level of unskilled men or men of different skills.'

'Negotiate about what?'

'All sorts of things ... differentials, sick-pay ... everything.' He ended limply.

'Differentials are already established in the rates of pay. Sick-pay is the same for all workers.'

'So what does the Union do for us?'

'It represents the workers' interests with the Commissioner.'

'And what about foundrymen in particular?'

'What about them?'

'Fifteen percent of our members are members of the Communist Party of GB. We've always supported your policies.'

The Russian sighed. 'There are no longer any political parties in this country. What you did in the past is in the past, comrade.'

'You're gonna have strikes on your hands, mate. Wait and see what the miners, the power engineers and the railwaymen have to say. They won't stand for it.'

'Won't stand for what?'

'Having no negotiations.'

The Russian stood up. 'Any worker who disobeys a Commission law would be severely punished.'

'You mean you'd put Arthur Scargill and Mick McGahey in jail?'

'Who are they?'

'Trades Union leaders. The mineworkers union.'

'There is no mineworkers union, comrade, and no trades union leaders. The State represents all workers. You're living in the past.'

He nodded at the three men, his contempt for them all too obvious as he swept from the room.

As Joe Langley ate his sausage and mash that evening his wife sat knitting, watching the TV. There was a programme on the building of a new dam on the Chinese-Soviet border. She leaned forward and turned down the sound.

'I don't understand why they don't have the Communist Party. It's their lot after all.'

'It's not, my old love. They're no more communists in the Soviet Union than they were here.'

'But they're all communists, Joe. Aren't they?'

'No way. They're Bolsheviks. Dictators. As Fascist as Hitler. Always were. Always will be. The last thing they want is equality. They want power and that's what they've got. They run their dictatorship in the names of Marx and Lenin but it's phoney.'

'I've never heard you go on like this before, Joe. I used to think at one time that you'd joined the Party.'

'When I was 18 or 19 I did think of it. But in the union I saw it all at work. The fiddles and the manoeuvring. The packed meetings. The rigged ballots and the rigged management committees. And in the end they did the same to the Labour Party. Like grubs in an apple. Those so-called left-wingers and militants didn't give a damn about working men. What they wanted was power. Power for themselves.

'You saw them, love. Preening themselves on TV chat shows, dodging the questions, mouthing the same old rubbish. Desperate to get on "Any Questions", they'd have gone on bloody "Gardeners Question Time" if they'd been given the chance.'

'Did you say anything at the meeting?'

'Not a word, love. Not a word.'

'Why not?'

'There's a time for talking and there's a time for thinking and doing. Now's not the time for talking. I'm sick of talkers.'

'But you think they're doing some good . . . the Russians?'

128

'I'll tell you in five years time, kid. Let's wait and see.'

'There's no custard, Joe. There's a shortage.' She laughed to herself. 'Who'd have thought we'd ever have a shortage of custard powder.'

# 11

President Wheeler was being less than Presidential. His day, like any President's day, was always a long litany of complaints, criticisms, reports of failure of US diplomacy, intelligence, counter-intelligence and economic policy in the 50 States and most of South America, the Middle East, Africa from Cairo to the Cape, and at least two of the United States' allies in Europe and Scandinavia. But for two weeks it had been disasters rather than complaints or mere failure.

No scenario that had ever been created by the Pentagon or the CIA had even vaguely contemplated what had actually happened. No sooner was he faced with one momentous decision than there was not only another, but the old scenario changed again and again. Three to four hours sleep a night had been the most he had managed for the last ten days. Not because he couldn't sleep, but because there was just no time to do so. Everywhere but Europe had to go on the back burner, while they watched Europe boiling over.

'Tell me ...' the President glared at Brodsky, ' ... tell me just one goddamn thing we can do, short of actual fighting.'

The Secretary of State had had no more sleep than the President. But he wasn't the President, so he took a deep breath and went over the ground again.

'We can expose what we've found out about Becque and what he's done, in the UN. We can call a meeting of Heads of State of what's left of NATO. Or we can take some retaliatory action against the Soviets away from Europe.'

'Where, for instance?'

'Cuba, Angola, Mozambique, Ethiopia.'

'My God, am I sick to death of hearing about those goddam countries. Ours and theirs.'

'We don't *have* to do anything, Mr President. We can let them get on with it.'

The President looked pained. 'Britain virtually occupied by the Russians. France and West Germany sweethearting Moscow. NATO a shambles. Our own troops pulled out of Britain, and those in Europe already packed, waiting for us to give the word to come home. How can we sit by and do nothing. They've taken the pants off us, we don't need to hand 'em our shirts for God's sake.'

'There's a difference between acting and re-acting, Mr President.'

'Don't philosophise, Joe. I've had enough of listening to professorial lectures. What are you suggesting?'

'I suggest that we don't throw good dollars after bad. We've temporarily lost our influence in Europe. We've lost our bases in Britain and that means that the Russians control the North Atlantic. We needed that control to ensure that we could defend Europe. We played our part right to the bitter end. The French have never pretended. From de Gaulle to Giscard they've hated our guts. They surrendered to the Germans and we rescued them. So they hate us.

'The West Germans are scared of the Soviets attacking them and making West Germany the battle-ground. And the rest of Europe plays its own little games, country by country. All those parades and rioters in West Berlin, Bonn, Paris, London, Madrid were shouting "Americans go home". So let's do just that. Let Europe take what it asked for. Our boys stay home and we save God knows how many billion dollars that can be better used right here.'

131

Wheeler stared at the silver-framed photograph of his family on his desk. He was silent for several minutes. Then he looked at Brodsky.

'You know you're right, Joe. I wish you weren't.' He sighed. 'I guess it's lesson learning time all round. The British can learn what it costs if you let the mob take over. The rest of Europe can learn what it's like when you've got Moscow as your ally. And I guess we can learn what it's like to get back behind the stockade again.' He sat upright in his chair. 'Let's show 'em, Joe.' He rapped his knuckles on his desk impatiently. 'I want a Bill drafted in forty-eight hours. No more aid to the so-called "Third World". If the bastards want international airports let them find the cash themselves. Stop all our funding to the United Nations. Withdraw our finance from the IMF.' He nodded. 'You know what I want, Joe. Put a special team on it. Turn off the taps. All of them. And get our troops in Europe back home. Fix with the TV companies for me to do a talk on ... let's see ... make it Friday evening so that people can think about it over the weekend.' He grinned. 'Why should we have long faces, Joe. They're gonna love it. Like I said, it's lesson learning time. And lesson number one is gonna be ... "Charity begins at home".'

The reaction of the other EEC countries to the French attempts to get their governments to approve the Soviet takeover in London had varied from cold to luke-warm.

The Netherlands had roundly condemned the occupation as an act of aggression, and brushed aside the argument that it was done at the request of the British government as a throw-back to 'Hitler propaganda'. (The more scathing Dutch editorials pointed out that the Soviet Union and Hitler Germany had been allies when the Germans occupied Holland.) The Belgian government announced that it was a matter for the Security Council of the United Nations, until the opposition pointed out that in fact a member of the Security Council itself had violated the frontiers of another Council member.

The West German government also insisted that it was a matter for the United Nations, and the West German media had gone as near to the edge of open criticism as it dared. The editorial attitudes ranging from 'if it was in fact at the invitation of the legal government of Great Britain then other countries should not interfere', to veiled references to Hitler's meetings with the Czechs. A sub-editor had wisely deleted the word *'Anschluss'* from a paragraph despite its correct use in the context.

The French government fulsomely approved the wisdom of the British government in seeking help from outside. It made the point that if such help was needed it was better to seek it away from the old rivalries of Europe. The French media followed the Presidential lead with the exception of *Le Canard Enchaîné*, which printed what purported to be a photograph of the President walking in the grounds of a Moscow mansion with a group of officials including President Orlov, and hinted that he was the originator of the betrayal of a former ally. There were threats from the Elyseé Palace, but *Le Canard* was used to that, and the following week it printed the photograph of a pretty girl named as Natasha Kuznetsova, a ballet dancer, alongside a photograph of President Becque. The two were linked by a caption which said 'Some like diamonds, some prefer Natasha.'

For weeks there were committee meetings, and sub-committee meetings, at the United Nations, until the US Ambassador to the UN angrily denounced the Russian move as a 'virtual act of war, a brutal indifference to the UN and the free nations of the world'. But the world noticed the use of the word 'virtual', and sighed with relief. The US press referred to Afghanistan and the Soviet press to El Salvador. Both countries claimed inter-government treaties as their excuses for keeping their own backyards clear of weeds.

But as the dust of rhetoric swirled and, as always, clouded both the facts and the issues – which is what it was intended to do – the world settled back on its haunches, its lack of action excused on the basis that what the British people apparently wanted must be given its chance to succeed. Interference in another country's affairs was indefensible. Nobody, neither governments nor nations, wanted to dwell on what had happened. They had been to the dentist, a rotten tooth had been extracted, and the bloody empty socket was best ignored. And there were few who didn't enjoy seeing the Americans get a bloody nose.

The TV camera held the mid-shot of the President at his desk, the flag just in picture on the right-hand side. Then the lens came in close and tight on the President's face. Make-up had emphasised the tan, and the tan emphasised the blue of his eyes. He spoke more slowly than he spoke in private or in small meetings.

'Good evening. I thought it was time to tell the nation of some of the problems that we have been facing recently, and how the United States government is dealing with them.

'The British government's decision to pull out of the Trident programme was only the start of a series of problems in Europe. But in many ways it was typical of what followed. There was a firm and binding commitment between the two governments; a contract. That contract was unilaterally broken by the British government. We were considering what financial help we could offer them when we were suddenly faced with the situation that our long-standing allies had signed a so-called Treaty of Cooperation with the Soviet Union.

'It then became clear that the remaining members of the

North Atlantic Treaty Organisation were no longer willing to maintain their rôle in that organisation.

'In view of these events I have given orders for all our forces in Europe and their equipment to be returned forthwith to the United States. Half of them have already arrived back. In addition, I have notified the appropriate Heads of State that America is no longer a party to the NATO agreements, a treaty that they themselves have abrogated and destroyed.

'Many commentators in political circles and the media, both in America and abroad, have claimed that these events represent a diplomatic defeat, or series of defeats, for the United States. As on many previous occasions, I beg to differ with the experts. If your neighbour turns down your offer to help him when his house catches fire or he is attacked by hoodlums, that is hardly a defeat. It may lead you to think that your neighbour is unwilling to defend his own family and property, but in a democracy that is his privilege. And his responsibility.

'In our dealings with other nations diplomacy sometimes requires us not to speak our minds. To turn the other cheek. To remain silent when we are rebuffed or insulted by the very people who are clamouring for us to lend them more millions of dollars, more fruits of our research and technology. Many ordinary citizens, not used to the ways of so-called diplomacy, wonder why we ship thousands of tons of our farm produce to other countries, only to see it sold on the black market. They may wonder too why we pay millions of dollars to the United Nations only to be pilloried by those nations who ask for and receive our help in cash and kind. I could go on. The list of anomalies is long and depressing. For too long the world of international diplomacy as seen from Washington has looked like a fantasy world where generosity is rewarded by insults, protection by assassination, and good-will by treachery.

'My fellow Americans ... that ... all ... ends ... tonight. No longer are we prepared to be blackguarded by our enemies and exploited by our allies. Tonight marks the start of a new ball-game. I have given orders to the Treasury, to the Secretary of State, and other responsible ministers, that from midnight tonight no Federal funds shall be used for any purpose outside the United States. Our over-burdened Federal budget will no longer have to take the strain of half the world's problems. These countries have so often complained that in taking our cash they have lost their independence. As of today they have no need to complain, their independence is total. We have had enough, my friends. Our tax-payers can breathe again and our boys will stay where they belong. Right here at home. The United States has learned its lesson. In the words of the song, "It's time to call it a day". The President smiled and it was a confident, faintly cheeky smile. 'Goodnight to you all.'

The switchboards at the White House, the TV and radio stations were inundated with calls. In places there were spontaneous celebrations in the streets. There was no doubt that President Wheeler had hit the jack-pot. If there were doubters they kept their doubts to themselves.

With only one newspaper, the *British News* and only one radio and TV network, the New British Broadcasting Company, the public received little news of what was happening outside their own immediate area. People went cautiously about their business, avoiding comment even to old friends.

Factories and commercial offices had their quotas of Soviet advisers but they moved quite slowly in making changes.

The Festival of New Britain was held in Hyde Park, and a wide variety of British products and designs was displayed. The attendance was disappointing despite free entry, but there was considerable competition to get tickets for the Soviet gymnastics team and the Bolshoi Ballet. Moscow Dynamo and Tbilisi Dynamo played several friendly games against local teams in most of the big cities and there were long queues at Portsmouth to go on board the Soviet aircraft-carrier *Minsk*.

Most of the luxury hotels and many public buildings were taken over as offices and living accommodation for Russian administrators. Red Army soldiers were mainly confined to their barracks but were polite and friendly when they were allowed a few hours leave in the cities. But they remained aloof from the public, and contact with individual civilians was forbidden.

By the end of the summer most businesses had been absorbed into the nationalised organisations controlled solely by Soviet personnel. The unemployed young were deployed to farm-work, forestry and road building in the case of males, to nursing and light engineering for females. A few early non-cooperators were tried at local People's Courts and given long prison sentences. They got little sympathy from the public and there were few subsequent offenders.

There was no longer any violence on the streets and all forms of hooliganism were dealt with severely. Petty crime was almost entirely committed by habitual criminals and the police were very much in control. Most police officers had remained at their posts and only at regional and city level were police chiefs under the control of Russian administrators.

It was autumn before the shortages became noticeable. At first it was petty items like ball-points, knitting wool, cutlery and buttons. They caused some irritation and a few jokes in working-men's clubs. But by mid-November there were shortages of food and the shelves of most shops were half-empty. Some staples like bread, butter and flour went on ration but were seldom available. It was then the stories started circulating of the queues of Soviet merchant ships at all the ports as they waited to be loaded with grain and massive containers of British products.

A comedian on a TV show had made a joke reference to the ships and the shortages and had been arrested as he left the studios. Charged as an 'enemy of the State', he had been given a severe warning and the case had been featured on the front page of the *British News*.

The first week in December the 60-foot Christmas tree, a gift from the Red Army, had been hoisted in Trafalgar Square and as if to underline the change of donor it snowed the same night.

The food ration had been doubled for the Christmas week but there were no turkeys or geese available in the shops. There were daily broadcasts about the dietary bene-fits of potatoes, swedes and green vegetables.

Even Harrods, which was now called Vyentorg after its namesake in Moscow, had little to offer the Soviet military and naval officers who were privileged to shop there. Rumour had it that Moscow had been concerned in the early days that its servicemen were overly impressed by such freely available goods in the shops and were intent on making scarce much that was not obtainable in Moscow, even for the privileged.

Tourists from the Soviet Union were to be allowed in the spring and their reactions too had to be borne in mind.

Nobody knew where the rumour started that the Queen would be broadcasting as usual at 2 pm on Christmas Day, but from Ottawa not London. There were people who criti-cised the Royals for deserting the country, but the mass of ordinary working people took it that the Royals had had no choice. Nobody wanted another Ekaterinburg in 1984. But few people took the rumour of the broadcast seriously.

Joe and Mary Langley were just two of the millions who tuned their radio slowly around the old Radio 4 wavelength from 1.55 onwards. The New British Broadcasting station had taken over the wave-length but the dish aerials that everybody had bought in 1983 to get the satellite programmes were still in use by many households despite the ban imposed on them. There were so many new regulations and prohibitions that neither the police nor the Russians had time to enforce them all. There had been a few token prosecutions that had led to heavy fines but no jail sentences.

At exactly 1.58 Joe picked up a carrier wave half-way between the National Service and the old Radio 3 wave-length and at 2.00 pm they heard the faint strains of 'God Save the Queen'. The strength of the signal fluctuated but even at its weakest the Queen's voice was identifiable. She spoke slowly and clearly, much as she always did.

'I wanted to talk to you on this special day, and the Canadian government have cooperated in making this possible.

'When my family and I were told that we must leave our homeland to avoid falling into the hands of the occupying power, our lives changed dramatically. But that has been the fate of us all. Your families as well as mine. The last few years have seen changes that most of us had never thought possible in a democratic country, particularly our own. Men of evil intent exploited our traditional tolerance and freedom for their own ends. When violence and anarchy became the order of the day we were ill-equipped both morally and politically to deal with the situation. Old friends deserted us, some went so far as to hasten our downfall.

'Today a proud nation is occupied by the forces of the Soviet Union and you are suffering the same cruel dictatorship that the people of the Soviet Union have suffered for nearly seventy years. A handful of men, a self-appointed and self-perpetuating élite, in the Kremlin, decide what millions of people shall be allowed to know and think. Controlled by secret police whose actions are a by-word for brutality and indifference to the tenets of humanity.

'I wish that I could bring you a message of salvation but alas, I cannot. Hope, I can offer, not for next month or even next year, but hope in the future, because your future will set the pattern for the whole of mankind.

'Sir Winston Churchill made a radio broadcast in 1941 in which he recognised, as he always did, the strong thread of history. He said – "When great causes are on the move in the world, stirring all men's souls, drawing them from their firesides, casting aside comfort, wealth and the pursuit of happiness in response to impulses at once awe-inspiring and irresistible, we learn that we are spirits, not animals."

'It would be hypocritical of me to wish you a Merry Christmas or a Happy New Year but my heart is with you all, even if present events force me to remain here ... May God Bless you all.'

As the strains of the old National Anthem came up Joe Langley switched off the set. For several minutes they both sat in silence.

Mary Langley wiped a tear from her eye and bent down to pick up her knitting needle from beside her chair.

'The poor soul, she must be wondering where the next blow will be coming from.'

'She's safe enough in Canada.'

'There's been all those demonstrations against them though. The French Canadians or whatever you call them. I saw it on the telly.'

'That film had been edited by the Russians. There wasn't more than a couple of hundred people all told. They just took the same people with several cameras from different directions.'

140

Mary Langley put down her knitting and looked at her husband.

'Can I ask you a question, Joe?'

He smiled. 'Knowing you, I shouldn't think I could stop you, anyway.'

'When you were away that last time why did you tell me to say you were ill when the Russian chap came from the works?'

'I didn't want him to know I was away.'

'I know that. But it's not like you to deceive people. To tell lies.'

'Times have changed, love. I've had to change with them. Like a good many other people I don't count lying to the Russians as lying. Not when it's in a just cause.'

She said softly, 'Tell me about the just cause, Joe.'

'No. It's better you don't know anything. But it's nothing to be ashamed of, I'll swear to that.'

'I'm afraid, Joe. Afraid for you. You're all I've got.'

'Don't be afraid, love. I can look after myself.' He stood up from his armchair. 'Have we got enough milk for some cocoa?'

'Yes, but we need it for your porridge. And we don't have any cocoa left. There was a bit came in to Lamperts but they ran out almost as soon as the queue had formed. Have some tea, we've still got some left. Mrs Wilson gave me a bit after you fixed her water tank for her.'

'Let's go to kip, love. I've got a long day tomorrow.'

# 12

The helicopter settled gently into the churchyard of St Philip's Cathedral in the centre of Birmingham and the Red Army men saluted as Savalev and Cooper came down the metal steps. The British Town Commissioner and his Russian opposite number were introduced and the car took them to the Town Hall and what had once been the Lord Mayor's Parlour but whose door now bore the legend – Town Commissioner (Soviet).

Waiting for them were the Chief Constable, the city representative of the National Trades Union, and the Town Clerk. After a few banalities they sat round the table. Cooper started the proceedings.

'I've come here for two reasons. First of all to hear how things are going, and secondly I understand you've got some problems. I'd like to hear them. Perhaps we should start with the problems first.'

The Town Commissioner (British) nodded towards the Chief Constable. Like most policemen, senior or constables, he had stayed in his job. Somebody had to do it and he reckoned that it was better if it was done by an experienced man. And the Russians had given them powers that they had never had before. They had an authority too, a status in society, that they had not had for sixty years. But the Russian attitude to criminals caused unnecessary problems with the local population.

The Chief Constable looked straight ahead as he spoke, intent on catching nobody's eye.

'We are having to waste hundreds of man hours on dealing with enquiries about convicted men's whereabouts. We seldom know ourselves so we can't give any sort of answer. There are rumours that many of them are in forced labour camps in the Soviet Union and that causes a lot of hostility to my men. Is there anything we can do about it?'

It was Savalev who replied. 'How many queries do you get in a week?'

'Three or four hundred. We can give satisfactory answers to about five per cent.'

'What answer do you give the others?'

'We tell them that we don't know.'

'Nothing more than that?'

'There's nothing more we can say. We don't know where they are.'

'And what's their reaction?'

'Abuse and hostility.'

'What kind of abuse?'

'The usual rubbish. They say we're the British KGB. Arse-lickers to the Russians. That sort of thing.'

'And how would it help if you were to tell them that the criminals had been transported to the Soviet Union to serve their sentences?'

'It would take the heat off my men. They would know that your people were responsible, not us.'

'You don't want to share the responsibility.'

The Chief Constable's face flushed, not with embarrassment. Not even anger, but indignation.

'I don't intend sharing the responsibility for anything I'm not consulted about and that I don't agree with.'

Savalev raised his eyebrows. 'What don't you agree with and why?'

'That men should be imprisoned outside their own country. Where they can't speak the language and their relatives can have no access.'

'You put in a report five years ago to the old Home Office, advocating short, sharp punishments. You've changed your mind since then?'

'No.'

'They only have to serve a third of their sentences if they are transported to a labour camp in the Soviet Union.'

'Makes no odds, Mister Savalev. The sentences are far too long anyway.'

'You think British criminals should have shorter sentences than Soviet citizens?'

'Maybe they both should.'

Savalev wasn't amused. 'Have you been on a conversion course?'

'No. There's been no time.'

'I'll make arrangements for your deputy to take over next week.' Savalev turned to the National Trades Union man. 'And you, my friend. What's your problem?'

'It's kind of hard to explain, commissar. Maybe if . . .'

Savalev interrupted angrily. 'I'm not a commissar. We have no commissars in this country. My name is Savalev.'

'Yes. OK.' The man looked even more uneasy.

'Your problem, comrade.'

'The men complain that the Union doesn't help them.'

'In what way?'

The man shrugged. 'We don't negotiate higher wages or better conditions.'

'Those are laid down by the State. They're not Union responsibilities.'

'I know. I've told them but they still complain.'

'Who does the complaining?'

'There's half a dozen who really keep on at me.'

'Give the names to my colleague here.' Savalev pointed

144

at the Town Commissioner (Soviet) and said something to him in Russian and the man nodded in agreement.

Cooper said to the British Town Commissioner. 'How is the city settling down?'

The man shrugged, smiling. 'Remarkably well, bearing in mind the changes. It takes time for people to get used to new ways of thinking, new attitudes, but in general people have taken it all very well. There's no violence in the streets anymore. Hardly any crime and what there is is dealt with quickly. Somebody said to me a few weeks back that every day in Birmingham is like Swansea on a Sunday night.' He smiled. 'I know what he means and most people like it that way.'

'What about the skinheads and punks?'

'They're all helping build the new roads. They're working. No more Social Security to fall back on so they work. They don't have time for all that self-pity and complaining. They're no problem.'

On the plane back to Heathrow Cooper sat drinking a whisky with Savalev. Despite everything he had grown rather to like the Russian. Cooper could see Savalev's influence in many of the attitudes of the Russians towards the British. Savalev seemed to understand them quite well.

'You seemed rather tough today, Lev.'

'Did I? Maybe I was. I guess it angers me that the British always complain. You put right the real things that were wrong but they've always got something. They're never satisfied. All our Town Commissioners say the same. I warned them on the instruction courses what it would be like but it's worse than I expected. Much worse.'

Cooper smiled. 'If you'd been in any of the last few governments, Lev, you'd consider their attitude now as unbelievable. It was much worse then. Whatever we did they complained. The media added fuel to the fire. You couldn't win. What you're getting is nothing.'

Savalev sat looking out of the window. Without turning his head he said, 'Why didn't you ever marry again, Freddie, after your wife died?'

'Never found anybody I'd care to depend on the same way. I wouldn't have been satisfied with second best.'

'Maybe you should try a nice Russian girl.' He smiled. 'I'll have to sort one out for you to try.'

Cooper smiled. 'Yours are a bit young for me.'

Savalev laughed softly. 'They're a bit young for me. But I like 'em young.'

'I heard you were going strong with a member of the upper bourgeoisie.'

'You mean Daphne, the Honourable Daphne Mather?'

'That's the one.'

Savalev shifted in his seat. 'You know, I looked at her the first time. She's 19. And all that cool blonde beauty, and I was sure she'd be a real iceberg.' He smiled. 'The first time I took her to bed she said I was just an animal. But she loved every minute of it, believe me. Wants it all the time.'

'But it's not more than bed on your side?'

'I don't want to marry anyone, Freddie. Ever.'

'Why not?'

'There's no point unless you're going to have kids, and I decided long ago I'd never have kids.'

'Why? You always get on well with my grandchildren.'

'Oh, I like kids. But they make you vulnerable. It's hard for you people to grasp why we Russians go on about our 20 million dead in the war. I had two sisters and two brothers. And God knows how many aunts and uncles and nephews and nieces. And my mother and father, of course. My mother survived. She lives in Moscow in her one room. Talks to herself and her two cats. Sometimes she recognises me, sometimes she thinks I'm my father or one of my brothers. She and I are all that are left.

'I can remember western commentators saying that they couldn't understand why the BBC's *Forsyte Saga* was so popular in Russia. I can tell you why. It was seeing a family going on year after year, decade after decade. Only dying when old age caught up with them. It was like a dream for us Russians. You westerners say that we don't even realise that we are short of goods and services because we blindly accept what the Politburo dish out. You think we should protest that maybe 25 per cent of our national product goes on the armed forces and weapons. We don't mind all this, Freddie. Just so long as the system lets us have our turn at being the Forsytes. Big families all staying together for decades. Only dying of old age.'

'So why no family for Lev Savalev?'

Savalev's brown eyes looked back at Cooper's face, then, sighing, the Russian turned to look out of the window as he said softly, 'Because, I can't believe it's going to stay that way.'

Nobody really knew why they had taken on Tommy Pardoe. Not even Pardoe himself. He had been a staff reporter with the *Daily Mail* when the Russians came. Not specialising in any area, just covering general news stories with the odd feature now and again. But the new head of the Tass bureau at Gough Square had offered him a job when all the newspapers were closed down. He was taken on as a consultant and it became quite clear in the first few weeks that he would not be asked to write for the *British News*. But he had been given a small office to himself and was asked, for the first two months, to read every word in each day's issue and put in his comments to Petrov the following day. They particularly wanted his comments on any aspect of their general approach that could particularly cause offence to the British public.

Petrov would come in every morning and perch on his

desk with the previous day's report in his hand. At the end of the first two weeks Petrov had stayed longer, making himself comfortable on the only other chair in the small office.

'Why your comment on our reference to the Royal Family?'

'People will resent it. It doesn't work.'

'In what way doesn't it work?'

'Truth or diplomacy?'

Petrov smiled. 'We employ you for the truth, comrade. If we don't get that we are both wasting our time.'

'Easy to say, Mr Petrov, but I don't want to end up in a psychiatric hospital or a Moscow jail.'

'Just tell us your experienced views and there is no danger of punishment of any kind.'

'OK. The Royals. First of all the great mass of people like them. Secondly they can't answer back, and the public don't like that. And thirdly every school-kid knows that the Royal Family were figureheads. They didn't run the country, and to blame them for what went on is just obvious propaganda. Too obvious, and demonstrably untrue. Put in something that the whole population knows is rubbish and they'll think you're either ignorant of well-known facts or making phoney propaganda. Either way they won't believe anything else you print.'

'Do they believe what we print anyway?'

'Some of it. The revelations about corruption among the politicians they believe. The pieces about bringing law and order back they not only believe but approve. They have seen it working. The pieces about full employment they believe for the same reason. But some of the figures comparing British pay-rates and Soviet pay-rates don't square up. They talk to Russians over here and they get the impression that you've exaggerated what Soviet workers get. Used

Moscow figures at phoney rouble rates instead of overall figures.'

'And what else don't they believe?'

'The crap you write about the Americans. They know more about the United States than you do and they're not going to believe it's all changed in a few weeks.'

Petrov shrugged. 'A lot has changed there. They've abandoned Europe. All they care about now is their own preservation.'

'Maybe. But you put it over the wrong way. You write as if they were ignorant about the outside world, like you do in *Pravda* and *Izvestia*. Your people in the Soviet Union don't believe half of what you say. If you go on writing like that here they won't believe anything you print. Not even if it's true.'

'So you think we should say nice things about the Americans?'

'I don't think that, and I didn't suggest that. There was always plenty of criticism of the Americans about their foreign policy, their way of life, all sorts of things long before your people came here. But they were related to hard facts. If you want to have a dig at the Americans just report facts. You can find enough material in any American newspaper that you can quote direct. Just don't tag any editorial on the end. Let the facts speak for themselves. You can editorialise all you like when they're used to you all. And when you've delivered the goods.'

'Delivered what goods?'

'When you've done what you've said you'll do. Peace and prosperity.'

Petrov looked at Pardoe. 'You must have been a very good reporter, comrade Pardoe.'

'I wasn't. I was average. It's just that this is my country and my people. And it isn't yours.'

Petrov looked annoyed but he stood up without further comment. At the door he turned. 'Are you really scared of us, comrade Pardoe?'

Pardoe nodded. 'Shit scared, comrade. And I mean it.'

The small village of Headcorn in Kent had housed the refugee Flemish weavers in the 17th century and there are houses that they had built still standing. It was a village concerned almost exclusively with farming until a small airfield had grown from the original flying school. The airfield was used mainly for private flying and crop-spraying aircraft, and there had, for years, been a running battle between the owners of the airfield and most of the locals who were against its extension.

But there had been no protests when the Russians trebled its size in a matter of months. Two locals who had been leaders of the original protests had been caught nailing a poster to an old oak on the perimeter. The poster just said – 'Genghis Khan rules OK'. They had been sentenced the next day to five years' imprisonment and nobody knew where they were serving their sentences. A few of the original protesters changed their minds because the Russians brought business in their wake. The others said nothing because they were afraid of the consequences.

The airfield was now a site for five SS16 missiles and was defended by a squadron of Sukhoi SU-15s. A battalion from a Red Army motor-rifle regiment was responsible for its security. There was a local curfew from 10 pm to 6 am with special passes for farm-workers needed for early milking.

Cameron Davies sat in the farm kitchen with the other two men, checking the pencil fuses, the timers and the plastic explosives. He wore a pair of surgeon's plastic gloves so that the almond smell of the grey plastic wouldn't leave traces on his hands. There was a bag made from a piece of foam-backed carpet on the table, and alongside it two pairs of wire-cutters and half a dozen egg-shaped insulators with joining plastic-covered wire. And a small meter with a digital read-out that glowed with a red plus sign.

Beside the table on the floor was a matt black grenade-launcher and four grenades. Their markings showed that they had been made in Czechoslovakia. Davies looked at his watch and then at the older of the two men.

'You don't wait to hear what happens. You fire it and then you go to the place. If we make it we'll join you, if we don't, you carry out your orders and stay down there for four days. Then the others will come for you. They'll give the sign. You don't come up for anything else. Understood?'

The man nodded but didn't speak. Davies turned to look at the other man. 'You just stay put on the perimeter wire. You give me three minutes exactly. If I'm not back in three minutes you leave. You take the route we've been over, and back to the field to Jacko here. OK?'

'OK, Chief.'

'If either of you want a crap or a pee do it now.'

Neither man moved and Davies grinned. 'We're the lucky ones. The first ones. Nobody's lifted a finger against the buggers so far and they're not expecting anything. After tonight they'll be hopping up and down and it'll be harder. Tonight's a doddle. It'll go as smooth as a baby's bum.'

Neither man looked convinced, but neither of them gave the tell-tale yawn or swallow that he was watching for.

'OK, Jacko. Put your torch out and open the curtains, and we'll be on our way.'

There was a reception that night at the Soviet embassy. The first anniversary of the signing of the Treaty. A lot had happened in that time but it didn't seem like a year since that ghastly night in the Kremlin. Maybe it was because the Russians had planned it all so well. They'd been both efficient and shrewd. It had been more like the commercial take-over of one big multinational company by another. Some winners, some losers. Some liked it, some didn't. Of course it was not all that difficult when there was no discussion, no argument, no consensus. You just said what you wanted and that was it. But the sheer weight of numbers. Those thousands of 'specialists' already available, already trained. All smoothly put into place in a matter of days. That was frightening. To know that the men in the Kremlin had long ago given the orders that made it possible to take over Britain if it became feasible and desirable. By invasion or treachery. It didn't matter too much how it happened. They probably had similar planning for every country in Europe. Maybe the world. Which country could have resisted. Which country actually *would* have resisted. The United States certainly, and China, but he could think of no others.

As Cooper stood alone, whisky in hand, he realised how few Britishers were there. Nobody who you would have expected to be a favourite son had been accepted by the Russians. All those rabid left-wingers, the Benns, the Scargills, the McGaheys and their ilk, had been cold-shouldered. They were just little men out for power in the Russians' eyes. They had been useful but were so no longer. Men who had worked so hard to bring down governments could try it again. Most of them were in the long-term camp on the Isle of Wight.

And there were no gossip columnists or media men in the crowd, for the simple reason that there was no free media. The New British Broadcasting Company had its TV network and the national and seven regional radio stations. Wales and Scotland had its own TV and radio. All of them were state-owned. There was no commercial TV or radio. They had been stopped in the first week.

152

Cooper had seen Savalev's hand in the fact that all the favourite ITV serials had been transferred to the new company. The *British News* and translations of several Russian magazines were the only publications as yet available.

A long list of proscribed books had been issued to Public Libraries, publishers and bookshops. The list was available in Public Libraries for public reference. Possessing a book on the proscribed list was a serious offence against the State. The list had become the intellectuals' equivalent of Rubik's Cube. However you analysed it it didn't make sense. Why were Graham Greene and his spy stories acceptable but ancient copies of Gollancz's Left Book Club proscribed. The women had come out best. Barbara Cartland and Catherine Cookson had both received the accolade of being read enthusiastically in translation by President Orlov's wife. And Mills & Boon's romance series was publicly praised and given virtually open-ended paper quotas. New writers had sprung up, and publishers had rushed into print with solid volumes on the New Society, while, 'How to live with the Reds' books and articles had become a virtual industry in itself. Just as 'How to live with recession' and 'How to live with yourself' had been so rewarding in pre-Treaty days.

Russian had become the second language in all State schools. There were no other schools. Eton, Winchester and Harrow had become conversion training centres for teachers and civil servants, and the other public schools were now general adult education establishments using the Open University courses as their basis. The Open University was much admired by the Russians, and teams from Milton Keynes were already in the Soviet Union assisting with the setting up of a Soviet version of the OU.

Then Cooper saw Savalev dancing with the girl who had, until the Russians came, been the Honourable Daphne Mather. He smiled to himself as he recalled what Savalev had told him on the plane. No couple could have danced more sedately than those two. Savalev didn't conceal his liking for pretty girls but he didn't flaunt it either. It was hard to tell what Savalev really thought. The Russians called the real hard-line believers 'Soviets', and it was the height of official approval. Savalev was always referred to as a Soviet, but Cooper wondered sometimes if they were not mistaken. There were things he said from time to time, an odd smile that implied a disbelief in what he was propounding. He occasionally said things to, or in front of Smetana, that were a bit near the bone. Maybe they were shrewd enough to realise that Savalev's genuine knowledge of the British had served them well. If he thought like a true Soviet that couldn't have been possible.

He saw Savalev pushing his way through the crowd, the girl in tow. Savalev bowed briefly, smiling.

'Good evening, Prime Minister. Can I introduce you to my friend? Daphne, the Prime Minister.'

The girl held out her hand. 'Good evening, Sir Frederick.'

'Good evening. I'm afraid it's Sir no longer. Just plain mister.'

The girl shrugged. 'To hell with what these creeps want. To me you're still Sir Frederick. But I won't say it out loud. Dear Lev can turn very nasty.' She turned and smiled at the Russian. Cooper realised how attractive Savalev must be to a 19-year-old girl. He was not only very handsome by any standards but, despite his elegance and charm, he was the second most powerful man in the country. She turned back to look at Cooper. 'He says he's got to take you off to some meeting with the great man himself.'

Savalev nodded. 'Smetana wondered if you could spare us a few minutes.'

Cooper shrugged. 'Your humble servant, comrade.'

The girl said, 'I'm going then, Lev.'

'OK. Take my car. I'll get a pool car. See you later.'

Then the two of them were walking down the short corridor to the ambassador's room. Smetana was on the phone talking heatedly and urgently in Russian. Shaking his head as he looked across at Savalev. Finally with a series of *'Das'* he hung up.

'Well that's it, Lev. That's it.'

'What did they say?'

'Phase Two. They've already given the orders. There was no point in arguing.'

Smetana turned to look at Cooper, his face flushed, his eyes angry. 'Maybe you already know what we're talking about, Cooper.' It was the first time that the Russian hadn't observed the niceties of calling him Prime Minister.

'I'm afraid I don't, Commissioner.'

'Have you ever heard of a place called Headcorn?'

'No. It sounds faintly American.'

'American my arse. It sounds bloody English, because it is bloody English.'

Cooper sat silently because there was nothing he could say. He didn't know what Smetana was on about. But he heard Savalev's heavy sigh and guessed that whatever it was it was bad. Savalev wasn't given to sighing.

Then Smetana's harsh voice interrupted his thoughts. 'You'll remember today, Cooper, as long as you live. Those bastards have changed everything. All my work, all our efforts . . . my God I want those men.'

Smetana stood up, lurching clumsily in his rage, and then his big hand swept a pile of files from the desk. Papers flying in all directions to flutter to the ground.

'Perhaps you'd better tell me what's happened, Commissioner.'

Smetana looked at him, teeth bared. 'Don't come that cool calm British shit with me, you bastard. You're part of them one way or another.'

Savalev spoke quietly in the silence. 'For Christ's sake

keep clam, Yuri. We need the Prime Minister's cooperation now as never before.'

But Smetana still burned. 'Cooperation,' he shouted. 'What cooperation. This man has just stood around. Agreeing with everything. Doing what we told him to do. Biding his time.'

Cooper stood up. 'I think it's better if I leave.'

Smetana's fists were crashing on the desk and then his right hand jabbed out, pointing at Cooper.

'You just stay where you are. But I warn you. Give me the chance. Just half a chance, and I'll have your hide. You mother-fucking British crap. I'll have ...'

And the whole room shook as Smetana stormed out, the door slamming behind him.

Savalev was sitting with his arms on his thighs, his head bowed. Slowly he looked up at Cooper's face and said quietly, '*Did* you know anything about tonight's business?'

'I've not the faintest idea what you're talking about.'

'This place ... Headcorn ... it was used as a rocket base. Five SS16s. Four of them were destroyed tonight. Along with two interceptor fighters, about ten thousand gallons of fuel and twelve Red Army men killed.'

'What happened? Who did it?'

'God knows. They're combing the whole area for them right now. We didn't get any details.'

'Is it all that serious? They will be caught and punished eventually.'

'You don't understand, Freddie.' He sighed. 'There's no reason why you should. You were never told.' Savalev stood up, loosening his tie as he paced slowly around the room. Eventually he stood still and turned to look at Cooper. 'I shouldn't be telling you this, Freddie, but we're going to need your help so you'd better know what's behind it.

'There were two schools of thought in Moscow about how we should tackle the British problem. One side, the generals, were adamant about a full-scale invasion. Occupation pure and simple. The other side, I was one of them, said it was a chance in a million to show the world that in an advanced, sophisticated country Communism could not only work, but work well, and the population would like it once it was used to the new thinking. The argument went on for days. It became a full-scale internal row. Resignations threatened on both sides. Finally it came down to a vote. The generals won by two votes. It was to be a conquest. And then ... and then Yevgeni Orlov took his political fate into his hands and vetoed the invasion.

'Doing that meant putting his career on the line. He trusted my advice and Smetana's advice that we could make it work. Tonight's attack puts him in jeopardy. Not right now, but there's no more room for playing it our way.' Savalev sighed again. 'He's ordered a full-scale occupation. Troops are already on their way. A large force so that there's no chance of resistance in future.'

'How large, Lev?'

'Eighty thousand was the figure he gave Smetana.'

'What about you and Smetana?'

'We'll carry on as before but the atmosphere will be a hell of a lot different. It will be treated as an occupation of an enemy country not cooperation between friends.'

'Was it ever cooperation between friends, Lev?'

'What does that mean?'

'I didn't sign the treaty voluntarily. I signed it to save something worse. You came mainly to cut the Americans out of Europe. The dreams you dreamed were never really going to happen.'

'Why not?'

'Even your own people don't share those dreams, Lev. The Soviet Union is a dictatorship, a dictatorship without mercy. Your people are as much an occupied country as we are. You've made some improvements in Russia since 1917.

But in 68 years that's not surprising. Every country has made improvements. Most have done better than the Soviet Union. Either way, your own people are treated so badly if they dislike what they're getting, that they are scared to speak out. You've got camps in the Gulag where your own citizens are treated worse than animals.

'Our people like the end of the violence on our streets. And I guess they've learned the lesson from you people. If the hooligans step out of line you hit them real hard instead of sending them to a psychologist. They like full employment because they haven't yet worked out how it's obtained. If you don't work where you're told to work you starve. Not just go hungry, but starve. And you don't have a roof over your head. Neither does your family. Sooner or later they'll work it all out. They'll work out what it cost.'

'What did it cost, my friend?'

'It cost them their freedom.'

'Sounds like you're on their side.'

'I'm not on anybody's side, Lev. I'm just telling you the truth. You're bright enough to recognise that it's the truth now I've told you. You were bright enough before, but nobody explained about the freedom bit. You Russians never had freedom. First the Tsars and then the Bolsheviks. You came to us too late. King John was our last dictator. The Barons and Magna Carta put an end to our dictators. Your people came too late, Lev.' Cooper smiled. 'You should have got a bright Englishman on your team when you were thinking it all out.'

Savalev looked as angry as Smetana had looked. 'When I hear you talk, Freddie, I begin to think I was wrong. But eighty thousand Red Army soldiers are going to make it right.'

'Can I go now?'

'Sure.'

As Cooper stood at the door. 'You were very nearly right,

158

Lev. You just forgot about people. It's people who are the problem. They always were, since Adam and Eve. Give them paradise, and a year later they'll be complaining. Christianity ... even Communism ... could work if it wasn't for people. If you want my advice it's there when you want it. You only need ask.'

'I hope you're wrong. My God I hope you're wrong. For all our sakes.'

*'Do svidanya.'*

And Savalev half-smiled at Cooper's Russian.

*'Ciao,'* he said.

All through the night and the early hours of the morning the planes droned overhead. Aircraft carriers and troop carriers were already several hours out from their bases at Murmansk.

The morning news broadcasts and the newspaper made the attack on the missile site their headline news. There had been heated argument inside Tass and Novosty on how to treat the attack. There were many who felt it should be played down. Moscow settled the issue just on midnight. It would be played up big. Emphasis on the innocent Soviet soldiers who had been murdered. The damage, not to Soviet missiles, but to the defences of Britain. And a strong suggestion of American involvement.

There were thick black borders round the front page of the *British News* and doleful music on the radio. On page two there was a panel announcing that Moscow had reluctantly decided to send more troops to defend the British. Mention of the reception at Kensington Gardens to celebrate the Treaty anniversary was subdued.

As the day wore on and the planes still droned overhead the people realised that life was going to change. With this many Soviet troops it meant that they were considered a security risk from now on. Many cursed whoever had attacked the missile site. Some even hoped they would soon be caught. A few, but very few, were delighted that the Russians had been given a bloody nose. But they kept their views to themselves. There was a man in Headcorn who felt that way. And it was that man in Headcorn, a farm-worker, who had noticed the patch in a field that was turning brown.

Tommy Couchman was born and bred in Kent. The first five years in Chatham, the remaining twenty-three in Headcorn. For six months he had tried to contain his burning anger. He and his girl had been waiting for a labourer's cottage on the farm to fall vacant. But when the Russians had moved in to the airfield one of the officers had seen her in the shop. A week later Tommy Couchman had heard that she was living in a cottage that had been commandeered by the Russians. She was no longer working in the village. He had gone to the cottage early one morning after milking, thinking he might surprise her enough to persuade her to come back.

A Red Army soldier had been standing guard at the cottage. He couldn't speak English but his lifted rifle made clear what would happen if he opened the garden gate. When his hand reached forward to open the gate the butt of the rifle missed his mouth but smashed his nose.

It was almost eight weeks later when he noticed the brown lines that made up a rectangle of about three feet square in lower Ten Acre field. The brown lines marked where the grass at the edges of cut turf had died and turned brown. He slid his paring knife into the ground and felt it jar as it struck something harder than earth or stones. When he had prised up the plastic board that held the turves he looked into the hole in the ground then closed the board quickly and carefully, brushing loose earth into the joins between the turves. He kept his find to himself.

Two days after the attack on the airfield he walked back from the early milking across Lower Ten Acre. The whole square of turves was beginning to turn brown. He watered the square using a pail, and water from the stream, in his mid-morning break. Whoever had dug the hole wasn't a country man or he would have known that a two inch layer of turf wouldn't hold enough water to keep the grass roots alive. But whoever it was, Tommy Couchman guessed he was on his side.

# 13

She was twenty and very pretty, tall and slim, with long legs, and she wore a white, silk, summer dress that was decorated with poppies. A black belt emphasised her narrow waist and rounded hips. The breeze across Tsentralnaya Square gently lifted the wispy hair at one side of her face.

'What's the statue, Josef. Or is it *who's* the statue?'

'His name was Yanka Kupola. He is our most famous White Russian poet.'

'When did he die?'

'In 1942 I think.'

'What sort of poems did he write?'

He turned and looked at her lovely face. 'He would have written a poem about you and your red poppy dress sitting in the park on a spring day.'

She smiled without looking at him. 'You're getting to be a flatterer Josef Andreyevich. A typical Moscow flatterer.'

'It's your bad influence, bringing your big city ways to the quiet city of Minsk.'

She reached for his hand on the park bench between them. 'Did your friend agree to do your shift tonight?'

'Yes. I'm doing his tomorrow night.' He turned to look at her face. 'I shall miss you so much, Anna.'

'I shall miss you too, Josef.'

'Do you mean that, or is it just . . . you know, politeness?'

'I meant it, Jojo. But if you get your leave in three weeks we can have a whole week together in Moscow.'

'Do you really think you can get me a Moscow permit?'

'I'm sure I can.' She shivered for a moment and then stood up, still holding his hand. 'Let's go back to your room.'

'Will you stay with me tonight again?'

She nodded, looking away towards the Minsk Palace of Culture. 'That's a really ghastly building, Jojo, what is it?'

'The Trades Union Palace of Culture. Stalin style.'

'He must have been a real monster that Stalin.'

'What makes you say that?'

'I read Khrushchev's speech denouncing him. It was in the library at work. He seemed worse than the Tsars.'

'Not an angel like Khrushchev, Brezhnev and Orlov?' There was a smile on his face as he said it, but she saw from his eyes that he was at least partly serious.

'Don't talk about them, Jojo. It's dangerous.'

'They are just men, not gods.'

'Let's go, Josef. I'm getting cold.'

He smiled. 'I'll warm you up, little girl.'

She lay on the bed looking up at him as he reached over for the black and white packet of cigarettes and the lighter on the small table beside the bed. The gesture annoyed her. Why did they always do that when they had made love to her. As if, now they had had their pleasure, they were getting back to the real world of cigarettes and Moscow Dynamo's new goalkeeper and ... Five minutes before he had wanted her so desperately but now she lay naked and available and all he wanted was a cigarette. Just like the others in Moscow.

'It takes time, sweetheart,' he said.

'What does?'

'What you were thinking about.'

'What *was* I thinking about?'

'That you're young and beautiful and naked and you're lying with your legs open but the fool is lighting a cigarette.'

'How did you know I was thinking that?'

He smiled and ignored her question. 'It's just biology, my love. Time has to pass, before I can do it again.'

'You didn't answer me. How did you know?'

'I didn't *know*. But that is what I would have thought if I was a girl on a bed.'

She leaned up on one elbow and she saw his eyes go to her breasts. 'You're a strange man, Josef. I think you must be very very clever at making your films.'

He laughed, kissed her gently and said softly, 'I don't *make* films, I just write scripts for films.'

'But you obviously know so much about people.'

'In this country that is a curse, not a blessing.'

'Why?'

He smiled. 'This afternoon you said it was dangerous to talk about Brezhnev and Orlov. You're right of course. It's dangerous because people might start thinking about what goes on in Moscow, and what Moscow makes happen in Minsk and Kiev and all the other big cities.'

'Why should we care about all that?'

He laughed softly. 'You really are a little goose, my Anna. How can I write good film scripts about how people really live when our masters in Moscow say we live in paradise and I know that most of us live in hell. Only the top people live in a paradise and they hide that from the rest of us. You know that because you help them have their paradise by working in that goddam place in Moscow.'

'But I like the job, Josef.'

'Of course you do. And you get seats for the Bolshoi which you pass to the dentist who fixes your pretty teeth and you phone some man in the Ministry of Transport to let him know that the new Japanese car radios have come in and he lets you have *nachalstvo* petrol ration cards so that your girl-friend's boy-friend can take her to Peredelkino on his motor-bike at the weekend and when you want a chicken she brings you one from her father's backyard. You call it *blat*, the old-boy network, but it's not, it's just part of the whole deception.'

'You think I shouldn't do those things, Jojo?'

'Of course you should. You have to survive, my love. But I don't like a way of life that makes people selfish and dishonest for the sake of a bloody chicken.'

She smiled up at him. 'You called me "my love".'

And he knew enough about girls to know that political philosophy had taken a back seat. He kissed her and she spread her long legs as he rolled on top of her.


Number Two Granovsky Street is a drab brown building with no architectural merit of any kind. It bears a plaque which states that Lenin made a speech to the Red Army leaders in that very building before they went off to continue the civil war. But even that didn't explain the long rows of big official cars outside. Indifferent to the regulations, the chauffeurs parked them half-way onto the pavement and waited for their passengers. The reason for the long, continuous line of cars was a much smaller plaque alongside the entrance that said 'Bureau of Passes'. And the licence-plates of the marked cars provided another clue. They all had the prefix MOC.

Anna Simenova worked in the Bureau of Passes, spending her days doling out to the Soviet Communist nobility the special food allowances for unobtainable fruit, meat and vegetables. She liked the job. It meant serving important people. Top scientists, Lenin Prize winners, men from *Pravda* and *Izvestia* and, from time to time, even cosmonauts. Most of the time of course the customers were unknown, but senior, civil servants.

On Fridays and Saturdays she was transferred to another building next to the cinema on Bersenevsky Embankment Road. Those who regularly worked there always referred to it as Government House, and the customers were even more important than her usual ones. These were the people from the Supreme Soviet itself. People whose faces were familiar from the newspapers and TV.

Anna especially liked working at Government House because her girl-friend Yevgenia worked there too. The first Friday after her holiday in Minsk, as they walked back together to her room, she told her friend about the young man she had met. She didn't mention his name but it was obvious to Yevgenia that it meant more to her than just a holiday romance.

Anna talked about him all the time they were preparing their evening meal and long into the night. Yevgenia was both amused and concerned. Anna had got their room when she was Lev Savalev's mistress. Or one of them, to be exact. And even when Savalev had been around there had been other men. Customers from one or other of the two government shops who fancied the pretty Anna. It was still the same. They had sex with important men and in return they got their Moscow residence permits renewed and a dozen other bureaucratic favours. If true love was going to rear its head it could mean problems for both of them.

The Russian patrol boat turned slowly and came up along-side the fishing-boat. The young Red Navy lieutenant boarded it after they had put down the fenders and tied up. It was a manoeuvre that the patrol boat had done many times, but the young man still prided himself on its neatness. His boat was a *Pchela* class hydrofoil with Pot Drum search radar and other electronic knick-knacks that they seldom needed in their patrolling of the Welsh Coast off Conwy.

The lieutenant checked the fishing-boat's permit and before he went back claimed his ship's usual tribute of half a dozen lobsters. He knew all the fishing-boat captains and his patrols had become more or less routine. From time to time they did a random check and rummaged through a boat from stem to stern but they never found anything to worry them. Sometimes a carton or two of cigarettes that the crew had got from an Irish boat fishing the same waters, but nothing of real importance.

The fishing boat carried on its way to the harbour at Conwy and eventually tied up at the quay and unloaded the slippery open crates of mixed catch. It was poor for three days at sea, but they would make good money from the third that they were allowed to sell on the open market. The locals were eating fish that they once would have thrown to the cats roaming the stone quay walls. The *Gwynedd Princess* lay at her moorings all day, with only her skipper and his corgi on board.

Just before dark a horse and cart went slowly down Rose Hill Street, past the castle, down onto the quay and along to the three fishing boats moored alongside the quay wall. From the first two boats the man with the cart took off a few lobster pots that needed re-binding. At the *Gwynedd Princess* he called out to her skipper and, getting no reply, he climbed down from the cart and scrambled on board.

As he clambered down the companion-way he looked anxious until he saw the man sitting at the table in the small saloon. He had a half empty bottle of vodka and a glass beside him on the table and he was grinning.

His visitor said softly, 'How'd it go for God's sake?'

'Smooth as cream, Johnny. The sub was waiting and we've got four tons of goodies down below. The old man has really done it.'

'What have you got?'

'SAM missiles, launchers, electronic gear, explosives and fuses and there's plenty more where that came from.'

'Did you meet the CIA man?'

'Yes. But it had to be short and sweet. They've changed their minds. No doubt about that. They want to see Andrews soonest. If he convinces them, we could get everything we need. An open budget. Cash, weapons, specialists, you name it, we could have it.'

'Is it official, or unofficial?'

The skipper shrugged and smiled. 'Unofficial but straight from the White House. It's a complete change around on their part. Harry Andrews is their boy.'

'When can we start unloading?'

'Tonight. I'm going out again the day after tomorrow.'

'How many men can you raise?'

'Five. How about you?'

'As many as we need. Thirty if necessary. Let's get started.'

'Have a drink to celebrate.'

The visitor shook his head. 'Let's get weaving.'


Jamie Boyle still wasn't sure about Macgregor. The stocky Clydebank Trades Union leader had always been classed as a rip-roaring Red by all the media. But when Boyle had been the union's legal adviser he had found the rough Scot almost indifferent to politics of any kind, and solely concerned about the working conditions and pay of his men. Like a good many working-class lads from the Glasgow tenements Macgregor had seen Moscow in the aftermath of the Revolution as only just this side of Paradise. But as a union delegate to the Leningrad shipyards he had seen what life was really like for workers in the Soviet Union. The idea of a Trades Union in a country where strikes were illegal and punishable by 10–15 years hard labour, taking its orders from the government bureaucrats, their sole employers was, to Macgregor, a cruel farce. But like a good many others who had seen the light he found it impossible to denounce the Soviet system in public and his reputation as a die-hard communist had stuck with him.

It had always seemed strange to Boyle that the Tories had never understood the real attitudes of working men.

He always found their views to be almost extreme right-wing. It was dockers and labourers and factory workers in general who saw eye to eye with Enoch Powell and the Tory ladies. They would have thrown out all blacks, brought back capital punishment and the birch, and formed vigilante groups to pursue rapists, muggers and young hooligans.

At no time in their operations against the Russians in Scotland had Macgregor or his group leaders shown any lack of enthusiasm for harassing them, but what they were planning now depended for its success on their all having read correctly the mood of the general population.

Boyle shivered as he looked at his watch. He had had the fever for five days and couldn't throw it off. The conditions under which he had existed for months were not conducive to combating disease. Debilitated by poor diet, constantly wet clothes, and sleeping wherever he could find a place, he went from one feverish cold to another. In the early months he had sometimes crept back to the house on the coast and Jeanie, but he found the few days of peace and safety too compelling. He became loath to leave. He found that there was a vast difference between operating inside a formal organisation like the SAS, and working in what seemed like a total and unrewarding vacuum. Like most SAS men he was a natural loner, and the SAS training and experience had made him a highly efficient loner. But behind it all was a structure. The troop, the squadron, the regiment. And behind all that the Army itself, and the government that paid for the country's defence. There was encouragement, sometimes praise, even promotion. And there was the abiding knowledge that whatever he was doing was part of a plan, it all had a purpose. Big or small. Temporary or long-term; knowledgeable, thinking, experienced men had decided that it had to be done.

When Harry Andrews had first discussed his thoughts with him they were still both inside that framework of authority and purpose. But right from the beginning, once it was reality, it seemed too diffuse, too vague. Andrews had said that there were 300 to 400 people in his groups. Each group commanded by an ex-SAS man. He now claimed that there were 4000 active members and at least 30,000 people who could be called on for information or non-violent help. As Andrews so often reminded them all, the odds were not really in the Russians' favour; there was an activist for every 12 or 13 Russian troops. Troops who were in a strange and alien environment, who couldn't speak or read the language. Some couldn't even speak or read Russian. But Boyle knew that behind the optimistic statements that Andrews made was the knowledge that the Russians could pour in twice or three times as many troops in a few days if they felt it was necessary.

He had asked Andrews every time they met what his objectives were. The answer had always been the same – 'Get the bastards out'. Yet Boyle realised that Andrews must know in his heart that you could kill hundreds of Russians, blow up their armouries and destroy their camps, but if the men in the Kremlin wanted their troops to stay they would stay, no matter how heavy the losses. Their revenge would just be stepped up. More brutal and indiscriminate month by month, incident after incident. Andrews' men were just fleas nipping at an elephant's hide.

The light was beginning to go and Boyle crouched just back from the window of the wooden hut looking out over the golf course wondering which direction Macgregor would come from. And then he spotted him, his collar up against the wind, and he flushed with anger as he saw that Macgregor was not alone. There was another man with him despite his strict instructions about security.

Boyle stood back in the shadows and waited until Macgregor opened the door. Then he said, 'Whoever that is, tell him to wait outside.'

He saw Macgregor hesitate and then say quietly, 'It's no' a man, it's a lassie. She's come from the colonel with a message for you.'

Without waiting for a response, Macgregor pushed his companion inside. She had a silk scarf across her face which she pulled down to her shoulders. She said softly, 'Harry sent me to you. I brought an order to Mr Macgregor to bring me to see you.'

Boyle could just see her face in the closing light. She was incredibly beautiful. And she was coloured. He guessed she was Indian or Pakistani.

'Who are you?'

'My name is Indira Singh. Daughter of Sanjiva Singh. You met me once, two years ago at Pen-y-Fan with my father.'

'What was the message.' Boyle's voice was more relaxed.

'My father heard that the Asians and blacks in Glasgow were not willing to cooperate with Mr Macgregor without my father coming himself. They will accept me as his representative so I am sent here to help you and Mr Macgregor.'

'Have you spoken to the Asians?'

'Not until you say that I should.'

For several moments Boyle was silent, then he said, 'You know what your father wants you to say?'

'Yes.'

'OK. You go ahead, but there's very little time left.'

'It will take very little time. There are only four men to persuade. There will be no problem I assure you.'

'Where did you learn such perfect English?'

He heard her soft laugh. 'At London University. I was born in this country.'

'I'm afraid I can't offer you food or hospitality.' He shrugged. 'There is nothing to offer.'

Macgregor interposed. 'I want you to come back with

me, laddie. My place is hundred per cent secure. I've a few things to talk about with you tonight.'

For a moment Boyle hesitated, and then he said, 'OK. Mac. You lead the way.'

The girl was back half an hour before curfew. Boyle wondered whether her obvious self-confidence came from her looks or some other factor.

'How did you get on?'

She smiled. 'No problem. All settled.' She looked at Macgregor. 'They do exactly what you say, Mr Mac.'

Then Lily Macgregor came bustling in. It was time for them all to eat. Boyle hadn't eaten a cooked meal for seven weeks and the two Scots had seen the obvious deterioration of the man who led them. There was shepherd's pie, and stewed apple and custard, and when that was finished Boyle, still hungry, ate round after round of grey bread. When the meal was finally over they sat around the table talking.

'What was the problem with the Asians, Mac?'

'They weren't convinced that it was in their best interest to antagonise the Russians.'

'Why not?'

Macgregor shrugged. 'Why should they? They never got an even break in the old days. The Russians have spent time and money on their propaganda to all the coloured people. They don't deliver, of course, they just make promises. They don't give a damn for the coloureds but they don't give them any worse time than they give the whites. That can look pretty good after our performance.'

Boyle looked at the girl. 'How did you persuade them?'

She smiled. 'My father told me what to say. He is a very shrewd man.'

'Tell us what you said.'

'My father said that I should ask why they came here in the first place and not Moscow. He asked them why nobody had ever hi-jacked a plane because he wanted to go to the Soviet Union. Why the poor desperate boat-people from South-east Asia had not headed their boats to the Soviet Union. He asked if they had ever heard of any Soviet embassy anywhere in the world besieged by people desperate to go there. And he asked if they think that the Berlin Wall is to keep West Germans out or East Germans in.'

'What did they say to that?'

She smiled. 'Nothing. There is nothing to say.'

'But surely they knew this already?'

'Don't you dream dreams, Mr Boyle? Father Christmas, Jesus Christ, the Buddha, Mahomet, Brahma. So why not Karl Marx. We say our prayers to ask help from our Gods. They give us back their dusty answers. But we go on believing because without our God there is nothing. We are all scared to be that much alone in a world that we can't understand.'

Lily Macgregor had had enough philosophising. 'Come on, my girl. It's time you were asleep. I've made up your bed. Say goodnight to the men.'

The girl laughed and put her arms round the stout Scotswoman. 'You sound just like my mother when I was very young.' She turned smiling. 'Goodnight to you both.'

When the two men were alone Macgregor said, 'You know who she is, Jamie?'

'She's Sanjiva Singh's daughter.'

'She's more than that. I should have thought you knew.'

'I don't understand?'

'She's the colonel's girl.'

'You mean Harry?'

'Yes.'

'I can hardly believe it, Harry Andrews with a young mistress?'

'She's more than that, laddie. A lot more.'

'What does that mean?'

'I don't rightly know, Jamie. But it's not just bed. He relies on her. It's kind of weird. He knows exactly what he wants to do, that guy. Always has done, and I guess he always will. But she inspires him some way. Like he's a chess-player can work things out six moves ahead instead of two.'

'How can she do that? What does she do?'

'She's the reason ... no, not the reason ... I don't know how to explain it. Before, he was doing all this because it was the right thing to do. He'd decided that it had to happen and he was the guy to make it happen. No reward. Just his duty. Now she's the reward. She's the prize if he gets it right. Before that cow of a wife disappeared his life was just the SAS and his plan. A duty, and a rather dull duty. She's kinda put a shine on it all.'

Boyle, despite his tiredness, smiled. 'Maybe Robbie Burns could have put it better but you didn't do too badly, describing a loner who's just fallen in love and found he likes it.'

Macgregor grinned sheepishly. 'It's more than that, Jamie. Wait till you see them together ... Let's go to bed, you look knackered.'

'I am, Mac. Almost too tired to sleep.'

'Come on, get moving, skipper.'


Four days later the cities of Glasgow and Edinburgh came to a stop at midnight. They didn't grind to a halt they just stopped. No shops opened, no workers went to work. There were no trains, no buses, no electricity and no phones. No newspapers, no letters, no communications of any kind. The streets were empty and quiet. It was inconvenient for their citizens, but much worse for the Russian Commander and his staff. Nobody spoke to them and when they sent cars to collect key officials they sat calmly and doggedly mute. A dozen or so were arrested by KGB men but there were no police to take them over and the prison staff didn't respond to the ringing and banging on the big entrance doors.

It lasted for a week and was entirely peaceful but it made the point. Without the cooperation of the people nothing worked, the Russians were a small impotent island unless the people cooperated. Some Russians dismissed the whole thing as pointless, a temporary inconvenience. But the Russians in London recognised the significance. Despite all their genuine efforts. Despite bringing back law and order and full employment they had no support from the general public. What had happened in Glasgow and Edinburgh was no more than a nuisance, but if it happened all over the country at the same time there was nothing, short of arrests and violence, that could stop it.

# 14

The pilot of the Yak-36 came in over the Norfolk coast south of Great Yarmouth at just over 650 mph, well below his top speed, banked around the lights of Bungay and headed back over the sea.

He had been sent up from the *Kiev* to escort the big transport plane that was having problems with its navigation gear. Making a wide circle round the Antonov-12, he contacted the pilot to check his flight path and then radioed back to the *Kiev* which gave him clearance to take over control of the transport as it turned slowly onto its descent path to the airfield near Diss.

As the big plane approached the coast the Yak pilot came down until they were about 1500 feet apart and dropped a flare at the correct coastal crossing point, zooming back up through the moonlit cumulus and turning slowly to come in again overhead on the landing line to Diss.

He was back over the land when he saw the blip on his radar. He flicked the switch off and on and the blip was, unbelievably, still there. As he switched channels back to *Kiev* control there was a blinding flash as the missile exploded and the plane disintegrated. The pilot of the transport saw it and his navigator saw it on the big radar screen. As the pilot turned to the navigator the second missile took them right on the nose where all the electronics were housed. The plane rolled slowly over onto its back, the two rear ramp doors drifted away as it plunged earthwards, and the paratroopers inside were sucked out into the airstream. It came down just after midnight on the main road, the A143. The remnants of the Yak were spread over five miles•of beetfields each side of the River Yare.

To the south a big Tupolev carrying 420 passengers and crew disintegrated when it was struck as it left London Outward Control Zone over Brookman's Park. A routine Aeroflot flight carrying a Russian trade delegation and twenty-five Moscow Dynamo footballers was brought down over Warwick.

As Soviet Defence Control in Whitehall took the various reports they were hindered in issuing orders to airfields and military commanders by high-powered jamming across the whole band of frequencies used by the Red Army. There was a twenty-minute delay before they could route their signals through the satellite frequencies. When reports started coming back that the areas concerned were hampered by power-cuts from the grid and at local sub-stations, the Red Army commanders finally realised that it was organised trouble they were dealing with.

Smetana had been at a Polish Embassy reception when the first news came in about the Tupolev disaster but nobody then had realised that it had been the target of a missile. It was nearly two o'clock when the facts became clearer. He received the news as he was undressing in his rooms at the Savoy, which had been taken over for the Commissioner's staff. Minutes later he was in the back seat of the big black Zil with the Soviet flag fluttering on the bonnet. He could barely contain his anger. The streets were empty because of the curfew, but already there were armoured vehicles rolling into place: two BMD fire support vehicles blocking the entrance to Charing Cross Station and four or five big T-64 battle tanks in Trafalgar Square.

At Admiralty Arch Red Army troops and personnel carriers had assembled. A captain was screaming orders as he pointed towards the park. Smetana knew exactly how the man felt but it was a sign of weakness not of strength. He was glad he had seen it. It helped him avoid doing the same. It was a time to be the cool, calm leader.

As they swept onto Horse Guards he could see hundreds of troops and a squadron of self-propelled howitzers supported by several AM-21 rocket launchers. He sighed as he got out of the car and walked across to the Control Centre in what had once been the War Office.

In the conference room the faces were grim. Savalev had already told him that Moscow was waiting for his call. The military commanders had said their say, and it looked as if Moscow had already decided that it was time to show the British that the party was over.

The cool, calm leader image disintegrated during his long call in the annexe, to Moscow. Orlov had reverted to his peasant background. Lacing his diatribe with obscenities, he accused Smetana of deceiving him and the whole of the Politburo. Even the word treason was used. Smetana was informed that his family were already in protective custody. His actual orders were straightforward. He would stay as Commissioner so that the Politburo would not lose face, but General Maljutin would now be in charge. The population were no longer to be considered as neutral, let alone friendly. They were the nationals of an occupied enemy State and would be treated with the utmost severity. The action to be taken against him would depend on his success or otherwise in helping control the British.

For an hour Smetana levelled his score with the Generals, screaming insults about their incompetence and threatening revelations to Moscow of their corruption and anti-Soviet behaviour until his venom was exhausted. Only then was he in a calm enough state to listen to their actual reports of what had happened.

'What have your people done so far, General?'

'We've transported the Mongolian infantry to the Heathrow area with orders to search all houses. They've been given orders to put the fear of God into every man, woman and child. The same applies in the other areas. The KGB are checking on where the missiles could have been but they're awaiting calculations from the airforce.'

'And after the search is done and we've found nothing?'

'We tighten controls on the whole population, levy a national fine of five or six million roubles to be paid in kind. A day of national mourning for our dead, and hostages taken, four for one.'

'How many people have we lost tonight?'

'Just over eight hundred dead. There were no survivors anywhere.'

'Why do you think they did this?'

'Because you were too soft on them.'

'But it was our chance to show the world that communism can work in an advanced country.'

'Don't feed me that shit, Smetana. It wouldn't work back home if we didn't control their every thought and move. Why do you think we spend all that money and resources if we don't have to? People are people all the world over, my friend. Give 'em an inch and they'll take a mile. From now on this country is going to be part of the Soviet Union and run the same way, not like a home for old maids.'

Smetana shook his head. 'And the world sees us failing again. Poland, Afghanistan, Egypt, Vietnam, Somalia, Eritrea and all South-east Asia. We are called in as friends and allies to help, and we end up as occupiers fighting the local guerrillas supported by a population that hates our guts. Billions of roubles down the drain, thousands of our people killed, and all for nothing.'

Maljutin smiled. A grim smile that didn't include his eyes. 'You've been reading too much Moscow propaganda from the politicians, Smetana. The military leaders have the power now. What we want we shall take. We don't need it handed to us on a silver platter by foreigners. And we don't give a shit what the rest of the world thinks. If they raise a little finger we'll bury them just like Khrushchev said we would. He was bluffing then. We hadn't the power to take on the world. We have now, and by God we're going to use it.' He took a deep breath. 'All I want of you, Smetana, is that you don't get in the way. They want to save their faces in the Kremlin. That's OK with me but you've had your turn. It's ours now. Just play your little games quietly on the side-lines and if you behave you'll survive.' He pointed a stubby finger at Smetana. 'But put one foot out of step, my friend, and you and your family will have a one-way ticket to the Gulag. And I mean that.'

The general stood up slowly, looking defiantly at his fellow generals, at Savalev, and the two others of Smetana's entourage.

When only Smetana and Savalev were still sitting there Savalev said quietly, 'Another charming alumnus of the Frunze Military Academy.'

Smetana was not in the mood to be amused. 'I think I'd better go to Moscow and talk to them.'

'Whatever you do, don't do that.'

'Why not?'

'They'll skin you alive right now. Let the dust settle. Let the bloody military take the load for a bit.'

'And let all that thinking, all that planning, come to nothing? Worse than nothing.'

'Yes. And you missed out a word ... hoping. We did a lot of hoping, you and I. Old Maljutin may be a bloody dinosaur but he's more of a realist than we were. Like he said, it's fatal to let people decide how things are going to be. Whatever they get, they want something else. The only way is to give them no choice. Tell them how it's going to be and make the buggers do it. No ifs and buts. You toe the line or the chopper comes down. It's the only way.'

Smetana turned slowly and looked at Savalev. 'That's Moscow's philosophy.'

'So?'

'Have you seen the KGB files on dissidents? There's rooms stacked full of them.'

Savalev shrugged. 'It still works, Smetana. You just need more and more choppers.'

'And bigger Gulags.'

'No. In the end you give up playing games. You finish them off because it's cheaper and easier to administer.'

The workshop was typical of hundreds that had once helped to maintain Birmingham's proud boast that the city produced everything from a locomotive to a pin. A ramshackle two-storeyed building alongside the canal where it crosses Fazeley Street, its ground floor held half a dozen fly-presses, two bending machines, an old German lathe, several vertical drills and a modern Swedish borer. The whole place reeked of decades of spilled oil and machinery suds.

There were twenty-two men sitting on the floor of the upstairs section of the building that was used partly as a store and partly as an office. Andrews sat on an upturned wooden box at the back where he could look through the small circle he had cleared in the grime encrusted window. The window looked out on the canal and towpath, which was overgrown with thistles, plantain and willowherb. The canal itself was green with algae. A rusting cycle frame lay half out of the water on the far bank where a young man and a girl sat with their arms around each other. No wonder keeping lookout was a popular duty.

Andrews brought his mind back to the meeting and Joe Langley, who stood beside the rickety table with the rifle held easily in his big hands. Despite his natural reticence he could talk for ever about weapons. He had always had the great advantage that he not only knew how to use them but he knew how they were made. His Birmingham accent gave an air of sincerity, even poetry to his words.

'. . . so we won't refer to it ever again as a Kalashnikov. It's an AK-47 Assault rifle. Not because we don't like using Russian names, or even because we don't want to admit to using a Russian designed weapon. Because the AK-47 is just a weapon. And as it happens it was a crib of a rifle designed to use the German M-43 cartridge. It was a Kraut design improved by the Russians. Now let's strip it down and see what . . .'

Andrews could remember Sergeant Langley standing under the big oak tree saying those same words, only then Langley was no older than the young men he was talking to. It always seemed to be summer when he thought of those days, and there were arguments in the mess about whether knowing how a gun was made really turned out better marksmen. It was Malins who always insisted that the Kalashnikov wasn't a marksman's weapon anyway.

'. . . a good question. The Germans like us had a big bullet. 200 grains, a velocity of 2500 feet per second and accurate to ranges of a thousand yards. There were several snags to all that. First of all, a thousand yards is well over half a mile, and infantry combat seldom calls for ranges of over four hundred yards, and most men couldn't hit what they were aiming at even at four hundred, so we were wasting fire power. The Germans produced the M-43 round and that meant a cheaper, lighter more reliable weapon could fire it. That led to . . .'

Andrews had been best-man at Langley's wedding because he had no relatives and no close friends. It had seemed odd to see the tough self-assured soldier with the plump, smiling girl who so obviously was going to have to be mother as well as wife to the man who stood beside her in his number one uniform. A man who knew all about how to get the

182

best out of men, but who treated his young bride as gingerly as a grenade with the pin out.

'. . . and several snags. The bolt does not remain open after the last round in the magazine has been fired. So it pays to count or you could find yourselves pulling the trigger on an empty chamber. Then there's . . .'

Way back Andrews had tried to persuade Langley to sign on with the SAS for at least another four years but he had had his instructions from the girl in the rented council house in Birmingham, and those over-rode everything including officers, Queen's Regulations and the new promotion to Warrant Officer II.

'. . . yes we've got Dragunovs but you lads won't be seeing them. They're sniper's weapons. I'll be happy if you can hit your targets firing hose-pipe let alone single shots. Right. Have a smoke for ten minutes then we'll go over small unit attacks in urban conditions.'

Langley walked over to stand leaning against the wall alongside Andrews.

'How many would have survived the SAS, Joe?'

'None, sir. But they're keen and motivated. Plenty of guts. They'll do what we want them to do. All the others have come up to scratch.'

'How many have gone through the instruction courses?'

'Nigh on two hundred. Seven have been taken out to train recruits.'

'How many can you call on now, who would turn out and have a go?'

'Well over two and a half thousand in the city and about three thousand more if you include Stafford, Coventry, the Black Country and Worcester.'

'Any defectors?'

'Five so far.'

'What did you do?'

'Except for one, let's just say I dealt with them.'

'Why the exception?'

'He'd got cancer. Only got a few months to live. Wanted to be with his family. He died a couple of months back.'

'What about his family?'

'We're looking after them. We promised him we would. I'd like you to pop round and see her if you can spare the time. She lives in Aston, by the park.'

'We'll go after you've finished here.'

'I'll see if I can lay hands on a spare bike.'

The two troop-carrying trucks ground their way up Gravelly Hill from Spaghetti Junction and stopped where the main road swept on towards Erdington. The trucks turned off and halted a few yards into Kingsbury Road. It was a long road of Victorian lower middle-class semi-detached houses. Every pair outwardly identical. Blunt bay windows up and down, small front gardens, and concrete or quarry-tiled paths to small porches and glass panelled doors.

The NCO in charge of the column clambered down from the cab of the leading truck and stood looking along the road. It was nearly midnight and there were only a few oil-lights and candles on in the houses. Taking out the small portable transceiver he pressed the 'send' button and the channel button that would link him with the other squads as they got into place at Six Ways, Tyburn Road, Stockland Green and Sutton Coldfield. He spoke in Khalka, the official language of the Mongolian People's Republic. Most of his men spoke Buryat but orders had to be given in the officially approved language.

He signalled to the drivers to douse the headlights and switch off the engines. He laughed at something that came over his radio, muttered an obscenity and switched off, pushing the aerial back into its socket and slipping the radio back into his pocket. Looking at his watch, the whistle raised to his lips, he watched the seconds go by and then blew two long blasts.

As the men scrambled down from the trucks the NCO stood by the cab of the leading truck. There were sixty-three men, armed with light machine pistols, and they ran in threes to the houses. He heard the noise of glass breaking and wood splitting, shouts and screams. A few minutes later a girl ran naked from one of the houses and was grabbed by her long black hair and dragged back into the house. There were two or three bursts of shots and more screaming, then an eerie silence. He smiled to himself. It was a pity they didn't get to do this every time a Moscow plane fell out of the sky. His orders had been to give them thirty minutes and he looked at his watch. Another nine minutes. Time enough to have another woman if they didn't waste time.

Then as the minute hand on his watch moved he nodded to the two drivers and blew two blasts on the whistle. The drivers had started lifting down the jerry-cans and as his men came running they carried the jerry-cans hurriedly back to the houses. Ten minutes later the houses were all well alight, the occupants running screaming up the road. Some naked, some half-dressed, some being carried. A similar operation was being executed by the other squads in the area. In Ilford, Shepherd's Bush, Finchley and Croydon the houses were not burnt down but the troops were allowed to loot what they wanted after the raping was over. There were empty trucks to take away the TVs, radios, furniture, refrigerators, cookers and carpets. A lesson was being given. Moscow-style. There were people still living in Berlin who would have recognised the scenario.

It was getting light by five o'clock, and at the foot of the cliffs at Hastings a man with a Boston accent read from the sheets on a clip-board, holding the pages down to stop them fluttering in the wind. The 3 metre high aerial was fully extended and the microphone was close to his lips. He spoke slowly, spelling out names of people and places and the serial numbers of the trucks and descriptions of the insignia of the 4th Mongolian Border Regiment. It took over half an hour and then he changed channel and pressed the 'receive' button. A voice with only a faint Dutch accent confirmed that all his message had been received.

Half an hour later UPA were passing the news item to their thousands of subscribing newspaper, TV and radio stations around the world.


Two days after the Red Army had taken its revenge on the civilian population Tommy Pardoe sat at his desk. The portable typewriter in front of him held a piece of paper. The paper was blank. It had been blank for two hours.

An hour later Petrov walked in, glanced briefly at the card on the wall, read it, and then looked at Pardoe.

'Why no report on yesterday's paper?'

Pardoe looked up at the Russian. 'Maybe I agreed with everything you printed.'

Petrov nodded towards the card on the wall. 'You'd better remove that, my friend, or you could find yourself in real trouble.'

Pardoe turned to look at the card. Printed in Rockwell Bold typeface it said: 'The censored press has a demoralising effect ... censorship kills civic spirit.'

Pardoe looked back at the Russian. 'How can that get me into trouble?'

'Don't be bloody stupid, Pardoe. You know the rules of the game as well as I do.'

'Maybe I know them *better* than you do.'

'What does that mean?'

'Those words on the card are not my words, they're a quotation from the man who made the rules.'

186

'Don't play games, Pardoe.' Petrov reached forward and ripped the card from the wall, tearing it in half and then quarters, tossing the fragments towards the waste-paper basket.

Pardoe sighed and smiled grimly. 'It's a good job there are none of your experts around, Petrov, or you'd have some explaining to do.'

'What's got into you, Pardoe? Why the aggression?'

'Do you know who said those words?'

'I don't give a shit who said them.'

'A pity. Karl Marx said them.'

'You're joking.'

'I'll bet my month's money against yours that I'm not, my friend. Find one of your Karl Marx experts, he'll tell you I'm not joking. It just proves what they always said about you people.'

'And what *did* they always say?'

Pardoe took a deep, sad breath, and wondered if the Rubicon was a real river or just a myth. 'They always said you people in the Kremlin were neither Marxists nor communists. Just a new set of hooligans having your turn at power.'

For a few moments Petrov was silent, then, his voice soft, he said, 'Has something happened to you, Pardoe? Are you sick?'

Pardoe stood up, his hands trembling as he pulled the blank sheet from the typewriter. Then he turned to look at the Russian.

'Two nights ago your gallant Red Army soldiers raped my mother and my sister. Not in the same house. Not even in the same district. My mother died of a heart attack early this morning. From what I've heard it happened to hundreds of women all over the country. You set them loose on our women, Petrov, and by God you're going to regret it.' There were tears rolling slowly down Pardoe's face. 'It may take years, Petrov, but we'll have our revenge. We surely will. You people are finished now. Exposed for what you really are. Savages, barbarians, animals.'

And as the Russian stood there Pardoe clumsily swept the typewriter off the table and sent it crashing to the floor before he walked out of the room. Petrov reached for the internal telephone, hesitated, and then drew back his hand.

When power was switched on at 2 a.m. half a dozen light sleepers in Alma Street, Chiswick were awakened. In most cases it was lights going on that disturbed them but a radio left switched on had woken one family and a man living alone had been aroused by a vacuum cleaner that had been left switched on when, as usual, power was cut off at 11 p.m. With a little grumbling all of them were back in bed ten minutes later.

At 2.30 a black Fiat turned into Alma Street. There were four men inside, and as the car moved slowly along the street of terraced houses one of them told the driver to stop when he saw number 27.

All four of them got out of the car when it stopped. They all wore dark raincoats and trilby hats and the tallest man led the way up the short path to the doorway. He pressed the bell button and they stood waiting in the small porch. After a few moments he pressed the bell again. Several minutes later they saw the light of a paraffin lamp as somebody shuffled to the door. Two bolts were slid back, a big brass chain was released and the catch moved up on the lock before the door opened.

The man who stood there was wearing his trousers, a pair of slippers and a towel round his shoulders. As he peered at the men in the darkness of the porch he said, 'Who is it?'

The tallest man pushed him to one side and the others followed him into the small hallway. One of them switched on the light and the man who had let them in looked surprised. And then scared. There was only one kind of man who could have the power switched on and pay visits in the early hours of the morning. A KGB man.

The tall man said, 'Where's Joseph Ash?'

'I'm Joseph Ash.'

'You have son named Joseph?'

'Yes.'

'He is living here?'

'Yes. He's in bed asleep.'

The tall man nodded at one of the other men and they made for the stairs.

'Hey. You can't go up there. This is my house, mister. You got no right coming in here like this. You got no ...'

As the hard-knuckled fist took him in the mouth, dislodging his dentures, the old man fought for breath and they left him gasping in the hall.

In the first bedroom they entered a middle-aged woman with her hair in curlers was sitting up in bed, her mouth agape, as they switched on the light.

'Where your son his bedroom?'

The woman, confused, shook her head and started to tremble as she saw the pistols in their hands. The tall Russian turned and walked into the bedroom opposite. A man in his thirties already had the light on and was putting on his trousers. He looked up as the Russian stood in the doorway.

'You Joseph Ash?'

'Yes. What of it?'

'You work at Harvey Engineering?'

'Yes.'

'In machine-shop?'

'Yes. I'm the foreman. What's wrong?'

'You are under arrest.'

'Me? What the hell for?'

189

'Sabotage. You are speaking against the State to your men.'

'That's rubbish. I never talk politics to anyone.'

'You say Soviet engineers are incompetent.'

'You're crazy. I don't know any Soviet engineers.'

'You know Grabowski the Soviet inspector at your works, yes?'

'So what?'

'You make criticisms of him to the workpeople.'

'What criticisms?'

'We have signed statement of witness. He hear your words.'

'Who is he?'

'Is no matter. He is loyal citizen who is not approving.'

'What does he say I said?'

'Is no matter. We have statement. You come now.'

'Where to? I want to see a lawyer.'

The tall man grinned. 'You put on shirt and shoes, comrade.'

For only a moment Joe Ash hesitated, but it was a moment too long and the foresight of the pistol carved open his cheek. For a moment there was just the gash, and Joe Ash stood there in disbelief until the warm blood flowed down to his chin and ran down his pale neck. Without thinking he lunged forward, his arm lifted until the Russian's boot slammed into his knee-cap and he fainted with the pain.

Two of them manacled his hands and carried his limp body down to the car. The tall Russian said to his man, 'I'll search his room. You do the others.'

The fishing limits in the Irish Sea and the Fastnet area had been laid down by the Russians without consultation with Dublin, but they had observed the old arrangements. The Red Navy actively and aggressively patrolled the north-east coast off Belfast Lough where their warships were based, but the patrolling in the Fastnet area was more relaxed. Ships that could make a transatlantic voyage had either been transferred to the Baltic or were immobilised and under guard. If the odd fishing boat from Wales or Cornwall crept over into Irish fishing waters the Irish patrols would see them off.

It was getting dark when they saw the Fastnet Rock light with its five second intervals between flashes, and after that they crept round the coast just outside Irish coastal waters, and shortly before midnight they lay off the tip of Dursey Island. The Met report forecast nothing worse than Force 3 for Fastnet and Shannon, and no fog until early morning.

Owen Phillips let the tide and current take her stem round as she lay to anchor and then wound out the Danforth to hold her loosely. The three crew watched, two on one off, although it was almost an hour before their rendezvous time at 0100 hours.

Right on time they saw the Aldiss blinking from seaward. There were four repetitions of G709 and Phillips acknowledged twice with the same group. Then the winches brought up the anchors and they headed slowly for where the light had been. Ten minutes later they saw the hull. Smooth and glistening like the back of a whale. Except for the huge conning tower with its wide stabilising fins.

Phillips lowered the inflatable and Andrews jumped down awkwardly as they held the nylon warp, paying it out slowly until the rubber dinghy was slowly taken by the current across the gap between the fishing boat and the submarine where a rating in oilskins was reaching out with a boathook.

In the darkness of the night Andrews was aware of the complete silence except for the slapping of the waves and his own breathing. The fishing boat was at least twenty feet away and he was still ten feet from the hull of the submarine that seemed to tower above him. It was nearly another ten minutes before he was hooking the boathook into the rope loop at the stem of the dinghy. As the dinghy touched the steel hull the rating pointed at a rope ladder curving over the submarine's outer shell. As Andrews' fingers scrabbled at one of the wooden struts on the ladder a hand grabbed and held him, and his foot found the first of the wooden rungs. Awkwardly he climbed the ladder on all fours and then he was standing, the rating holding him round his waist, pointing to the thin pillar of light that came from the hatch in the massive tower.

Two men in naval uniform were standing just inside the tower. They were young and tanned and the fair-haired one saluted him.

'Welcome aboard, sir.'

The American captain introduced him to the Royal Navy lieutenant-commander whose name was Harris. They took him to a cabin that was surprisingly bright and cheerful. As he glanced around, the submarine captain said, 'Make yourself at home, sir. I'll leave Commander Harris with you to make you as comfortable as possible.'

Harris took him on a tour of the submarine. He was surprised at its size and comforts. With a crew continuously at sea for three months the US Navy had made the quarters and facilities as comfortable as possible.

He was shown round the computerised control system that monitored continuously the sub's position and the missile control system itself, and he couldn't make up his mind whether he was scared or consoled by this high technology. What seemed particularly eerie was the red lighting in the control room until Harris smiled and explained that when night fell in the outside world the control room was 'rigged for red' and the lighting dimmed in the rest of the ship to mark the difference between night

192

and day. It suddenly made the kind of war he was waging seem hopelessly amateur. He said as much to Harris and the US Navy Captain when they ate together in the wardroom. The American looked across at him as he waited for his soup to cool.

'It's the other way around, colonel, as we found to our cost in Vietnam. We had battleships, every kind of plane and chopper you could want, artillery, all the weapons, tanks and ammunition they asked for. And where did it get us? They ripped our pants off. It was like killing ants with a fifty ton steam hammer.

'I've got a hundred and twenty-seven crew on this ship, and there's another crew on shore ready to take over at the end of our three months' patrol. There's sixteen Polaris A-3 missiles sitting there ready to go. Just name a Russian city and any one of 'em can flatten it. All I do is press the button.' He paused. 'And the moral of my story is that it ain't ever gonna be used. Neither Moscow nor Washington are going to press that button because when you do you know that you're pressing a two way button. The same birds will be heading your way eleven minutes later. We had all this ...' he waved his arm around, '... when we were fighting in Vietnam ...' he laughed, '... if we had used it the whole world would have torn us apart ...' He pointed his spoon at Andrews. '... You and your people are the Vietnamese ... the Russians are us in Vietnam ... in a strange country, not speaking the language, not knowing one village from another. You'll win my friend. It's just a question of time and guts.'

When they had finished eating Andrews said, 'When do we contact the carrier?'

'About twenty-four hours from now. And we're breaking all our regulations to do that, I can tell you.'

'What regulations?'

'My number one instruction . . . I know the exact words . . . "Under no repeat no circumstances will submarine Robert E. Lee SSBN 601 surface during patrol." '

'So how is it you broke regulations?'

The captain grinned. 'Because the counter-instruction came from the Commander-in-Chief himself. They must think a lot of you in Washington, my friend.'

The next day seemed interminable. Harris stayed with him but Andrews had nothing to say to him. They came from two different worlds and he found it impossible to converse with a man whose background was Boston Naval Yard, whose life could be considered normal.

Andrews was transferred to the carrier at 0300 hours, and thirty hours later he was flown to the Naval Airfield on Long Island. An official car took him to La Guardia where he was put on a plane for Washington.

# 15

She sent him the train coupon and the Moscow pass and met him in at Leningradski Station. When she saw him walking down the platform towards the barrier she realised again how handsome he was. Fair, almost white hair, blue eyes, broad shoulders and very tall. She was glad that she had been able to persuade Yevgenia to lend her her car for the week.

It had all been very complicated. Yevgenia's father's TV had broken down – it needed parts that were unobtainable. Unless, of course, you knew a senior civil servant in the Energy Ministry who lusted after a pair of black, soft-leather Italian shoes, which could be made available by Yevgenia's boss, who would like to sleep with her pretty friend Anna. When the music stopped Anna was in bed with Vladimir Zagorsky in his neat two room apartment behind the Central Office of Statistics. And the next morning she had a Moscow driving permit, coupons for 20 litres of petrol and ten days' insurance with *Ingosstrakh*.

But as she watched him come through the ticket barrier she reckoned that Josef Andreyevich Andreyev, film-script writer, was well worth the trouble. They kissed heartily but not passionately, it was too public for that, and then she led him off to the car. And he was satisfactorily impressed.

In her small apartment he looked around and admired everything as any Russian guest should.

'Where'd you like to eat tonight, Anna?'

'It's up to you. You're the boss.'

195

'In that case the boy from Minsk will take his girl to the Minsk Hotel and let her taste what real Minsk mushrooms are like.'

'Where is it?'

'You mean you don't know? In Gorky Street of course. You Muscovites are real peasants.'

He smiled and pulled her down onto the bed.

There were lights blazing in the *Izvestia* building as they came out of the Minsk Hotel and strolled down Ulitsa Gorkovo. They were not drunk, but they were tipsy.

When they were standing across the road from the Mossovet building that housed the Moscow town administration the young man put back his head and looked up at the moon, and with slightly slurred speech he started reciting.

Our strength's ebbing more every moment,
Although our guilt isn't guilt.
Over system-built Russia the moon's out –
Number patch on a prisoner's suit.

And all those government buildings
Blood-blistered by snow and rain
Blind-eye cataracts at their windows –
For ages alone and friendless
Faceless faces of leaders of men.

These wolves in their smoke-filled chambers
Lash at people as if they were dogs,
Then these wolves reach the end of their labours
Into black limousines they clamber
And ...

'Jesus God,' he said, 'I hate this bloody place.'

She hurried him away and they didn't speak until they were back in her rooms and he was lying fully-clothed on her bed.

'Why do you say such things in the street, Josef? We could go to prison.'

He smiled and closed his eyes. 'You don't like poetry then, my beautiful Anna.'

'That wasn't poetry, it was anti-State propaganda. You're crazy if you make up poems like that.'

'I didn't make it up, sweetie. I wish to God I had.'

'What poet writes words like those?'

'What poet? Aleksander Arkadevich Galich ... born October 1919 ... front-line soldier in the People's War ... wrote scripts for *To the Seven Winds* ... *Faithful Friends* ... expelled from the Writers Union and the Union of Cinematographers December 1971 ... hounded by his fellow writers until he had to leave the Soviet Union ... lives in Norway.'

'Was he the man who did those songs on tapes?'

'That's the one.'

'But everybody raved about them.'

He belched as he nodded. 'Sure they did. But when the Kremlin says you're out then you're out, sweetie. And their stooges do their dirty work for them. A nod and a wink are enough.'

She saw the tears on his cheeks. 'Why are you crying?' There was real concern in her voice.

He shook his head impatiently, wiping away the tears with his hands. 'I'm not crying, Anna. Not really. I'm just angry and frustrated.'

'About what?'

'Everything. The way we all live. With those bastards in the Kremlin who can decide whether a writer, a painter, a musician or even a bloody film-maker is good or not ... those Philistines can ruin a man or make him, and they couldn't paint a door let alone a picture. And it's not just the arts. You put one foot out of place and you're in prison and then the Gulag.'

'But there are courts which decide those things.'

'Oh honey. What's the good of talking . . . you don't think a court will find a man innocent if somebody above them wants him in a camp? The laws, the constitution, all of it, are just bits of paper. Nobody takes any notice of them. We do as we're told because we're afraid of them. We daren't say what we think; nobody can criticise the system and survive.'

'But you and I can't do anything about all that. It's just the way it is.'

'That's how they get away with it, because people think like that.'

'What else can people do?' She shrugged. 'We're just ordinary people.'

He swung his legs down to the floor and sat up. 'Forget it, kid. I'm getting sober. Let's have some more fun.'

On the Tuesday Anna got off early from work and hurried back to her flat.

As she entered the building, the old *dezhurnaya* in her thick sweaters and baggy skirt gave her a long look and, as she headed for the stairs, said, 'It's about time you got me some more of that ham. Especially with two of 'em waiting for you.'

She nodded without thinking, so she was surprised when she opened her flat door and saw the man sitting at the table with Josef. He was in his fifties, with a dark complexion, black hair and the most penetrating eyes she had ever seen.

Josef introduced the man as 'Oktyabr', which she thought was silly, calling a man after a month of the year. But she shook hands, smiling, and sat down with them. The man named Oktyabr poured out half a tumbler of whisky and she wondered who he knew that allowed him to get hold of something so rare. He lifted his glass.

'*Za zdorovye.*'

'*Za zdorovye.*'

'Josef tells me you work in the Bureau of Passes.'

'Except Fridays and Saturdays.'

'D'you like it?'

She shrugged. 'It's OK. It's a job.'

'What do you think of the customers. Important people, yes?'

'I never think about them.'

'Do you know a guy named Litovkin? Anatoli Litovkin?'

'He doesn't come in often. His chauffeur collects his things.'

'Where were you born?'

'Tbilisi.'

The man smiled. 'Ah, the town of warm springs they called it. When did you come to Moscow?'

'Four years ago.'

'How did you manage that?'

'A visitor from Moscow got me the job here.'

The man smiled. A knowing smile. 'Ah yes, of course. Where did you live in Tbilisi?'

'Ordzhonikidze Street, between the Railway Station and the Dynamo Stadium.'

'Just remind me, what street is the Stadium in? The entrance.'

She smiled. 'Brdzola Street. Why are you asking all this? Do you know Tbilisi?'

'I know it well, my love. I know it well.' He stood up. 'I must get on my way.' He smiled. 'You seem to have turned this young man's head.' He nodded, smiling. 'I think you could turn most men's heads. Take good care of him. We need him.'

When he had gone she looked at Josef. 'Who is he, Jojo?'

Josef smiled. 'Just a man. He was an army instructor, a major, when I did my service.'

'And now?'

'He teaches history and philosophy.'

'Where?'

'Here, at the University.'

'What did he mean about taking care of you?'

Josef smiled. 'He meant let me make love to you whenever I can do it.'

She laughed softly. 'You're a fool. A nice fool. And who is "we"?'

'I don't understand.'

'He said "we" need him. Who's "we"?'

Josef shrugged. 'Just a turn of phrase. Putting a good word in for me with you.'

She leaned forward and kissed him. 'You don't need anybody to do that for you. Why did he ask me about Litovkin?'

'I don't know. Maybe he knows him.'

'He's nothing to do with Education, he's Defence.'

'Maybe he's just a friend. How is it you got home early?'

'I got another girl to take over and said I didn't feel well. We'll have to eat here tonight in case anyone should see me out.'

He grinned. 'That's fine with me. Anyway I'm not hungry yet.'


When she got home on the Thursday evening the man Oktyabr was sitting there. Waiting for her. And there was no sign of Josef.

'Where's Josef?'

'He'll be back, Anna. He won't be long. I want to talk to you. Sit down.'

For just a moment she hesitated. She didn't like being given orders in her own home, but those eyes were on her face and she pulled out a chair and sat down.

'I've got a problem, my dear. He wants to marry you.'

For a few seconds she was silent. Surprised but suspicious. 'He hasn't told me that.'

'He will. I want you to say no.'

'Why should I? I like him. He'd make a good husband.'

'You wouldn't make him a good wife, though.'

'Why not? You don't know anything about me. Who are you to judge? It's none of your business.'

He took a folded piece of paper from his inside pocket.

'I've got a list of men you've been screwing in the last six months.' He half-smiled. 'There may be some missing but there are twenty-nine names in all.'

'Does Josef know about this?' she said softly.

'I haven't told him. I shouldn't imagine he knows.'

'But if he asks me to marry him and I say "yes" then you'll tell him?'

'Of course.'

'What's it got to do with you who I marry or who he marries for that matter?'

'Have you got a Party card?'

'No.'

'Komsomol card?'

'No.'

'Do you want to marry him?

'I like him a lot.'

'Don't give me that rubbish. I said do you want to marry him or just have sex with him?'

'You get out of my room, mister, or I'll call the police.'

He smiled. 'You won't call anybody, my sweet. This list would get you a stretch in the KGB camp for immoral girls. Five years at least. So just answer me. Do you want to marry him?'

She shrugged. 'Not if you don't want me to.'

He smiled. 'Good girl. Now we understand one another. Let's go right back to the beginning, forgetting everything we've said. He wants to marry you. Understood?'

She nodded.

'You think he could make you a good husband, yes?'

'Yes. I think he would.'

'I think he would too, so we make a deal, you and I. You say yes, and you marry him. On one condition. There are things I shall want you to do. Small favours. Permits, passes and the like. You get them for me, and we keep our little secret, yes?'

'Yes.'

He looked at his watch, and stood up. 'I'll expect an invitation.'

She smiled as he stood at the door before he let himself out. She was used to recognising the signs of real power and the man with the penetrating milky-blue eyes had power. He stank of it.


Josef was given special leave to marry his Anna and found that he had been given a new job that would mean spending three weeks of the month in Moscow and one week in Minsk.

During the next four months Anna provided a continuous flow of permits, passes and documents to the man called Oktyabr. He didn't ask her how she got them, and she volunteered no information. Neither did she give a moment's thought as to why anybody should need so many permits.

She never discussed any of it with her husband. Because she had grown to rather more than like him she hated keeping a secret from him, and regretted the means she had to use to obtain the material. But if he found out, that would be the end of it all for the two of them.

# 16

There was a strong wind blowing from the sea and flurries of snow in the air as Jamie Boyle pedalled, head-down, along the coast road. When, eventually, he turned into the short curving drive of the house he walked as quietly as possible across the gravel and hid his cycle in the massive clumps of rhododendrons flanking the garage.

It was a grey dawn, ominous with heavy black clouds that promised real snow unless the winds moved them on inland, but there were no lights on in the house. He walked slowly across the wet lawn to the bench under the bare branches of the magnolia tree where he had sat with his father when they first came there.

As he sat looking at the house he was depressed at the thought of the wasted months away from Jeanie. He had passed messages through to her but had heard nothing. She had no address to write to. They had no permit for any level of telephone service and the money he had been able to send her had been pitifully little. And what was it all for? To organise and train the leaders of groups of men who believed it was possible to harass the Russians to the point of ending their occupation. Although he had said nothing to the others he saw it all now as a fantasy. A pipe-dream from those long-ago summer evenings when they had planned it all. But the plans had been for putting down unorganised mobs, not thousands of well-armed, trained soldiers of an enemy country. He sometimes heard his own words echoing in his head as he gave them his pep talk about loyalty, courage and patriotism. Did he really believe himself what he was persuading others to believe? And even if he did was it his responsibility? Most of the population had carried on with their lives as best they could. They didn't find it necessary to spend their lives sleeping in barns and basements, hedges and attics. And then he saw a light go on in one of the bedrooms.

He stood waiting in the porch as he pressed the brass bell-push a second time. A few minutes later the door was opened, the heavy chain still in place. Jock MacKay stood there, in an old-fashioned dressing-gown and carpet slippers, peering through the narrow gap.

'What do you want?' The old man's voice was faintly aggressive.

'It's me, Jock. Jamie,' he said softly.

'Who?'

'It's Jamie. Jamie Boyle.'

The old man lifted his head, peering through half-closed eyes. Then he nodded his head slowly. 'Ah yes, Jamie. Of course. Of course.'

The chains rattled and the door opened. MacKay put on his glasses, then held out his hand. As Boyle took it MacKay said, 'So you're back after all. That's fine. That's better. I was just going to make a cup of tea in the kitchen. Come and join me.'

As they sat at the wooden kitchen table Boyle was shocked at how much the old man had aged. The old perkiness had gone, his speech was slow, and his mind pre-occupied.

'How's Jeanie?'

'Fine. Fine. And how are you?'

'I'll be glad for a good sleep and a bath. How have things been, Jock. Any worries?'

MacKay shrugged. 'We've all got worries. One kind or another.' Boyle saw the tears at the edge of the old man's eyes.

'Anything special?'

The old man stood up, his cup rattling in its saucer as he walked over to the sink. Boyle sat silent waiting for an answer but the old man busied himself washing the cup and saucer.

'I'll go up and see if Jeanie's awake, Jock.'

'You do that, laddie.'

Boyle made his way up the broad stairs and turned left to the second bedroom. As he opened the door she rolled over to look at him drowsily, her hand pushing back the hair from her eyes.

'Jamie. My God, I didn't recognise you.' She sat up, patting the bed beside her. 'When did you get here? It's lovely to see you.'

Then their arms were around each other, her soft hair against his cheek, her head on his shoulder. She drew back her head to look at his face.

'When did you get here?'

'I've been having a cup of tea with Jock.'

She raised her eyebrows as if Jock was no longer a favourite.

'You look worn-out, Jamie. Let me run you a bath. It'll only be warm but it will help you relax.'

'What's wrong with Jock?'

'Oh, nothing. Just getting a bit pernickety in his old age. Come on, get those ghastly clothes off and I'll do your bath.'

He went to sleep in the bath and Jeanie had to rouse him, wrap him in a bath-towel and help him over to the bed. to the bed.

He slept for the rest of the day, through the night,

205

until the following mid-day. He awoke feeling good, back on form, the depression lifted.

There was a light sprinkling of snow in the garden but the main fall was well inland and a log fire was burning in the fire-place in the sitting room. They had had tea and toast, all three of them, sitting round the fire.

'Tell me how you've both been surviving.'

MacKay said nothing although Jeanie waited for him to speak. When he didn't respond she said, 'We've been all right, Jamie. There are shortages of everything but we get by one way or another. How about you?'

'I can't say much, kid. It's moving, slowly but surely.'

Jock MacKay stood up. 'I'll leave you two to talk. There's more logs outside the kitchen door, Jamie, if you need them.'

When they were alone Boyle said, 'I've got the feeling that he isn't too pleased to see me, for some reason. He seems a bit distant.'

'Oh, don't take any notice, Jamie. He's getting on and he hasn't settled to the new conditions. It's just age.'

'Tell me how you've been.'

She shrugged. 'Lonely of course. It's isolated here. But don't worry about me.' She paused. 'You haven't changed your mind about what you're doing?'

'I have my doubts sometimes. When I'm low. When I'm missing you.'

'Why not call it a day, Jamie. We could get by one way or another.'

'What makes you say that?'

She sighed. 'Is it worth it? They're here. Nothing's going to shift them. Most people have got used to them. Some even prefer what we've got now to what we had before.'

Boyle shrugged. 'You might be right about is it worth it. But the rest of what you said is based on a fallacy.

Of course people are glad that law and order prevail again. That there's a job for everybody. But that doesn't mean that they are happy to have a Russian occupation army sitting on top of us.'

'Does it really matter? There's always some lot sitting on top of us. Our lot didn't give us law and order and full employment. They didn't deliver.'

'It's a logical way to look at things, honey. But surely we've lost our freedom. Is it worth that?'

She smiled. 'Which particular freedom have we lost?'

'Most of every freedom there is.'

'Tell me.'

He smiled. 'I'd better say that I didn't want to wake you or Jock when I got here yesterday so I sat on the bench on the lawn and my thoughts were very like yours. But that was because I was tired and down. So ... freedoms gone. Well, you've got full employment because there are no Trades Unions anymore. Wages are poor, technology has taken a back seat and you can't pick and choose your job. You go where you're told to go. And yes, we've got law and order back again because if you break a law, no matter how minor, you don't get a trial. It's just a rubber-stamp. If a policeman or a Russian says you did it, that's it. It works I'll admit. But it's totally unjust.

'You can't say what you think. You can't read what you want to read. You can't live where you want to live. You can't bring up your children the way you want to. It's a kind of slavery.'

She laughed. 'Five out of ten for effort, Jamie. Maybe six. But does it matter about ignoring technology if it finds men work. Surely it's better for everyone to have a job. And if you've got laws, surely it's better to make people keep them. And *I* don't want to talk about politics. I don't give a damn about what ideology I live under.'

'You go along with "better Red than dead"?'

'But I'm not "Red". I'm nothing. Better alive than dead, the colour doesn't matter.'

'You seem to have thought an awful lot about it, Jeanie, for someone who doesn't care one way or another.'

She blushed. 'Maybe I'm just argumentative.'

Later, after they had made love, she turned to look at his face. 'How long are you staying?'

'I'll be leaving mid-day tomorrow.'

'Is there anything I could get you that you need?'

'Like what?'

'Like anything.'

'No thanks, honey. I'll get by.'

'How long before you come again?'

'About the same as usual. Two months give or take a week. Depends on where I am and what's going on.'

She kissed him gently. 'Make love to me again.'

He left at noon, waving back at her as he wobbled down the drive on the cycle. Macgregor was waiting for him with the van at Kirkcaldy and dropped him near his father's house just after eight o'clock.

The door opened at the first ring and his father took his hand, leading him into the small hallway. 'Lovely to see you, Jamie. A real treat.'

Boyle frowned. 'Were you expecting me?'

His father winked. 'A little bird told me I might be lucky.'

'What little bird?'

'Don't worry your head about that, laddie. Take your jacket off and come and sit down.'

Jamie Boyle shook his head. 'You don't understand, father. If somebody told you they could have told other people. I need to know.'

His father shrugged. 'Macgregor gave me just a wee hint, that's all. Wanted to make sure I was here when you came. Now come on in and get warm.'

They chatted for a couple of hours. Generalities about the Russians and the occupation, and a little about distant relatives. It was about ten o'clock when the phone rang and his father went into the hall to answer it. He had a telephone permit because he served on the local petrol allocation committee.

When his father came back he said, 'How did you find Jock MacKay?'

'He seems to have deteriorated a lot. Seemed very strange, very old and doddery. I almost got the feeling that I wasn't welcome.'

'How long since you were last there?'

'Just over a couple of months.'

'And before that?'

'Oh it must have been roughly the same.'

'How was he last time?'

'Much as usual I thought. I didn't notice anything different.'

His father looked at him and said softly, 'Son, I've got something I have to tell you. I've had many sleepless nights about it these last few weeks. One of those terrible choices. Whatever you do is bad. Just a choice of evils. I'm terribly sorry about all this.'

'What is it, father? What's happened?'

'It wasn't Macgregor who told me you were coming to see me. It was Jeanie. And that was Jeanie on the phone just now to ask if you'd arrived and if . . .'

'But they haven't got a phone permit, and why on earth didn't she speak to me as well?'

'Jamie. Please, Jamie. Let me get it done with.' He sighed deeply. 'For just over three months Jeanie has had a relationship with a Russian. He lives here in Edinburgh but they have seen one another regularly. She told me about it four or five weeks ago. She brought him here last week. I met him. I think it's a very real relationship. I told her I might decide to tell you. She was torn in two, poor girl. I pointed out how dangerous it was for you but she begged me not to tell you in case it upset you too much, and in case the relationship didn't last. I feel it *will* last, and I feel it *is* a danger. Questions were being asked about you and where you were. I was worried. Jock MacKay has been terribly worried. All his instincts were to send her packing but he realised that that could make things worse. Endanger you, and throw her into the arms of this fellow. I'm terribly sorry, boy. I'm terribly sorry to have to say all this.'

Jamie Boyle sat there. Looking at his father but not seeing him. Trying not to shiver as the cold spread over his body. It explained so much, but he couldn't believe it. She had asked him to make love to her and had responded avidly. No wonder she and MacKay had seemed on edge and almost disturbed at seeing him. And no wonder she knew all the pro-Russian answers. It all fitted. It was all true. But he couldn't believe it. He wanted to walk away and pretend that he hadn't heard it and that it hadn't happened. He wanted to scream.

'Who is he, the man?' he said quietly.

'His name is Borowski. Igor Borowski. He's with the Bolshoi reserve ballet company based here in Edinburgh.'

'How did she meet him?'

'Dr Fox and his wife took her to a performance at the Usher Hall. They're patrons of the Bolshoi company. He's their official doctor. Nothing political. They just like ballet. She met the fellow after the performance.'

'Is he a dancer?'

'No. He's called an adviser. I'd guess he's a KGB man who watches what they're up to.'

'What's he like?'

'A bit younger than Jeanie or you. Pleasant. Attractive, and I'd surmise that his feelings for her are genuine.'

'Does he sleep with her?'

His father shrugged. 'I couldn't know, Jamie. It would be conjecture.'

'So conjecture.'

'I should think so, Jamie. It must be likely. He seems straightforward enough but he's certainly KGB so he's not likely to be your "gentle parfit knight".'

'Where does he live?'

'I've no idea. Somewhere in Edinburgh. They commandeered a lot of houses for the Commissioner's staff. Mainly up by George Heriots.'

'What shall I do, father?'

'I've thought about it ever since I knew that I'd have to tell you. I really don't know, boy. It's so personal. My instinct is that you should do nothing. But maybe that wouldn't suit your temperament.'

'What time's curfew up here?'

'It's the same in Scotland as anywhere else. We're past curfew now.'

And suddenly Jamie Boyle was calm. He knew now what he was going to do.

'Tell me what you've been up to, father.'

'They've paid ex-MPs a reasonable pension. To keep us quiet, I suppose. I serve on a committee that helps them decide petrol coupon priorities, and another committee that advises people who have problems with the authorities on how to go about presenting their complaints. That and the garden, and a few old friends, seems to keep me busy.'

'D'you know what I fancy?'

'Tell me.'

'A plate of porridge.'

'Ah now. Porridge is only available for families with children under fifteen. However...' he held up his hand smiling '... I have influence, my boy. The Lennoxes next door have three under-fifteens and they all hate porridge. I'll see what I can do.'

The depression had come back when his father went next door. He had eaten his plate of porridge and gone up to his old room, the room that had been his until he left university and joined the army. It seemed much smaller than he remembered. There were photographs of rugby teams, his face always looking the youngest. Press cuttings on a cork board, reviews of the two matches he had played for Scotland. A row of paperbacks and law books. A photograph of Jeanie and himself sitting on the rocks at Arthur's Seat in Edinburgh. And in the corner wardrobe was his old evening dress suit and a pair of worn patent shoes with black bows. It all seemed a long time ago.

He slept fitfully and left early the next morning, his father close to tears as he went into his bedroom to say goodbye. And he was fleetingly aware that his father must be lonely too.

He took a bus to Princes Street and walked to Leith. Macgregor didn't seem surprised to see him. As he told him the story he had the feeling that it might not be news to Macgregor.

'And what are ye gonna do about that little lot, Jamie?'

'Will you do it for me?'

Macgregor half-smiled. 'I will that.'

'D'you know where he lives?'

'Aye. Just leave it to me and get on your way over the border.'

A postman had discovered the body of Igor Borowski at the base of the Scott Monument. There was a steel crossbow bolt through his chest and he had been crudely castrated. They found his genitals in his jacket pocket.

# 17

Once upon a time Chelyuskintsev Park had been a pine forest, so the two stations of the children's railway were named Pine Wood and Park. The park itself spread over almost 250 acres and on its northern edge were the buildings of the *Belarusfilm* studio. People were used to seeing the lights on in the buildings all night long, because it produced most of the commercial films distributed through the Soviet Union.

There was no filming that night and only the film processors who checked the automatic machinery were on duty, apart from the group of script-writers and consultants discussing the film on regional agriculture that was scheduled to start when the winter wheat was being sown. The meeting was held in the shack that the free-lance script-writers had slowly acquired as their own personal domain.

Seated around the long table that had been a throw-out from the nearby botanical section of the Academy of Sciences were men from most of the Soviet States: Georgia, Lithuania, Armenia, Estonia, Uzbekistan, Azerbaijan, Moldavia and the Ukraine. The other two were Josef Andreyevich Andreyev and the man who called himself Oktyabr.

'You've all seen the treatment, are you satisfied now with the alterations?' He paused and a few of them nodded. He went on briskly. 'I want it out of the way. But that's our reason for being here. That's what we are discussing if we are interrupted.'

213

'Can't you put a guard outside. Trade secrets and all that.'

The man smiled. 'We've taken some precautions. We could be interrupted, but we won't be taken by surprise.' He smiled. 'But keep the shooting script and the treatment in front of you.' He leaned forward and looked round the table at the different faces. Slowly and intently, like a general inspecting a passing-out parade, looking for future Napoleons or Timoshenkos. His voice was low when he spoke again.

'Have any of you got problems I don't yet know about?'

A man put up his hand.

'Go on, Georgi. Tell me.'

'How can we be so sure that we haven't been infiltrated by the KGB?'

'Are you asking this because you think your group has been penetrated?'

'No. I just want to know how *you* can be so sure.'

'Why do *you* think I can be so sure?'

'No idea, comrade. If you said you *thought* we hadn't been penetrated I could understand. But to say you *know* seems impossible to me.'

Another man nodded. 'I wonder too, comrade.'

'Right then,' Oktyabr went on, 'if I told you how I know, I should be endangering people who are already taking greater risks than any of us here are yet taking. I'm not prepared to do that. You'll just have to take my word for it.' He raised his eyebrows. 'Other problems?'

A man whose Russian was halting and whose accent was obviously Armenian raised his hand.

'When it's dark, comrade, I feel that what we are planning, what we are doing, and what we aim to do, are both sensible and achievable.' He paused and half-smiled. 'In the daytime, when the sun is shining, it seems crazy. How crazy is it? How crazy are we?'

'A good question, my friend. A fundamental question. The root of our problem. Let's go over it again together.' Oktyabr closed his eyes as he spoke. And he spoke slowly as he went on.

'The difficulty is to know where to begin. How far to go back. Let us go all the way back. In the time of the Tsars we had two societies. The rich and aristocratic and the rest of us. Serfs and slaves. Not all the aristocrats were monsters. A few cared about the starvation and poverty. But it was a question of luck. Whose estate you were born on. That decided whether you would be starving rather than just hungry. The Revolution was a dozen revolutions. The Bolsheviks, the Mensheviks and all the rest of them. You know the history of those times as well as I do. The Bolsheviks took over. The workers were to be Tsars of their own fates. Freedom for all. Prosperity for all.

'So the question is – did they do what they promised – the Bolsheviks who call themselves communists?' He paused and looked at the faces round the table. 'I think that the answer is yes. There is more to eat, more goods to buy, more money to spend, full employment, medical services – many, many things. There are people still alive today who once saw owning two cooking pots as wealth, who today have two rooms, an electric stove, a radio, even a TV.' He paused again, smiling quizzically. 'So what are we all complaining about?

'I'll tell you. We're complaining about the price. And we are complaining about exchanging one élite for another. Because to give us the frying pans they took away our freedom. They gave us freedom on paper. The laws of the Supreme Soviet guarantee our freedom. But there is an old Latin tag I learned at High School: *quis custodiet ipsos custodes* – who is to control the keepers. Our laws are meaningless. They are ignored, twisted and abused. The men who administer the law do what the State tells them

215

to do. To make free comment makes you an enemy of the State. The Tsars in the Kremlin, the Politburo and the rest of them, have the power. The power to decide not just every aspect of our lives, but whether we shall live or die.

'What our people produce in the factories – our wealth, is spent on battleships costing billions of roubles, missiles that can wipe out the population of the world six times over. Why? Because the men in the Kremlin are hungry for power, hungry for conquest. Soviet troops under the label of advisers or experts are serving in every goddamn country that will have them. What are we doing there? They say it is to defend the Soviet Union. How are our men in Angola, Mozambique, Libya, Vietnam, Laos, Thailand defending us? They are there to expand the Politburo's influence and control. And to do that, my friends, every worker in the Soviet Union works two days a week to provide the cash, and a third day to provide a billion a day for the Cubans, the PLO, and God knows who.

'But those are only the secondary evils. The real evil is that a Soviet citizen cannot say what he thinks, write what he thinks or even paint what he thinks. Those prehistoric men in the Kremlin can decide that a symphony is not truly communist. A concerto for violin can be subversive. We live in a madhouse, comrades. And it can't go on.

'Our friend there asks if we are crazy.' He paused. 'If we are crazy then most of the world is crazy. No country in the world, no matter how desperate or how poor, has ever voluntarily modelled its system on the Soviet Union. They won't have it. So why do we put up with it?

'I'll tell you why, my friends. Fear. Fear of the Gulag. Fear of the State prisons. Fear of injustice in our courts. Fear of the secret police. Fear of the State's revenge, not just on us, but on our families. Small fears as well as big fears. Fears that our children may not be allowed into university. Fear that our children may be stopped from the careers they want to follow.' He paused. 'Do I need to go on? Is this what the sacrifices were for? The millions murdered in the Stalin purges. The twenty million dead in the People's War.' He looked from one to another. 'We, my friends, live in a country that no foreigner demands to live in. We are envied by none and despised by many. The whole world laughs at our propaganda even if it quakes at our missiles. The whole world pities our people who lack every freedom worthwhile having. We are not crazy, my friend who asked the question. We should be crazy if we were prepared to go on as we have done for so long.'

There were many nods of approval but nothing more. He had not expected more. He was preaching to the converted. He was only the catalyst who had brought them together. All he had done was try to assemble the complaints, the frustrations, the arguments that had been going on below the surface for over a decade.

When he met them individually on their home-ground they talked openly and freely, but in a meeting like this they stayed silent. The instinctive, protective caution of years of censorship was not overcome in a few months. They would need time and some signs of success before they could bring themselves to talk freely in front of others.

'Now. Let us get down to our work. You have built up your teams in the last few months, you have taken the precautions that I laid down in my instructions, and the time has now come to use the machinery that you have created.' He paused to let the words sink in. 'Before you leave I shall be talking with each one of you individually about the supplies that are now available for your use. You will do nothing at any time until you have specific instructions from me.

'But more important even than the actions I shall want you to take, is your understanding of our objectives. They are nothing to do with more roubles in a pay-packet, more TVs and refrigerators, or even more food in our bellies. We don't even demand a new political party. What we do demand is the end of all élite groups and the abuse of State laws against the people. Neither Karl Marx nor the Soviet Constitution calls for such abuses as being necessary. We want a human face on our society. What the Czechs wanted before our tanks rolled into their streets. A society where a man can say what he thinks without being sent to the Gulag as an enemy of the State. A society where courts administer the law according to the law not to the whim of some ape in the Kremlin. Where sentences and prisons are not intended to break a man's spirit or starve him into submission.

'Outside the Soviet Union the things we want are not considered as great concessions, but are taken for granted. We don't need to become capitalists to want these changes. True communism can take them in its stride. We live in a prison, comrades. It's time to escape.'

He looked around the silent group and nodded towards one of them. 'Georgi. I'll see you first. Josef has things to say to the rest of you and he's got the maps and compasses we promised you.'

He stood up and, followed by the other man, he went into the small room that had been partitioned off at the end of the hut.

The man who was waiting for Andrews at Dulles International was about his own age, but taller, and tanned, with eyes that looked as if they were used to far-away horizons. The man held out his hand.

'O'Malley. Pleased to meet you. I've got a car waiting for you. How are you feeling?'

'I'd like a bath and shave before I meet people if that can be arranged.'

'You betcha. You're staying at my house for a couple of nights. We'll fix you up. Don't worry. You're a pretty unusual sort of guest.'

Andrews smiled. 'How's that?'

'Made welcome by both the Pentagon and the CIA and, believe me, that's very unusual.'

'Which are you?'

'CIA. I'm the guy who's been getting your traffic and dealing with it as helpfully as I can. How'd the navy boys look after you?'

'Fine.'

'Here's the car. Jump in, the door's open.'

O'Malley tried to keep a conversation going as he drove down the highway but it was heavy going. His guest was no conversationalist and seemed neither interested in the gossip of Washington nor in responding to even the most mundane questions about his own circumstances. Langley were going to be very disappointed with the man they had slowly come to see as something of a hero. He didn't look like a hero and he didn't sound like one either. Maybe Grace would be able to thaw him out.

'Have you been to Washington before, Mr Andrews?'

'No. I'm afraid not.'

'You been anywhere in the States?'

'Just one visit. Some years ago.'

'Did you enjoy it?'

'It wasn't a pleasure visit.'

O'Malley gave up the unequal combat and concentrated on his driving. His passenger didn't even look at the scenery. Just sat there with his eyes closed. Maybe the guy was just tired. Two days on a US sub, three days on a carrier and a flight to the Navy field before coming to Washington could slow anybody down.

It wasn't reasonable to expect an American to realise that his guest was half-starved, battered by months of solitary responsibility, of being constantly on the move, constantly haunted by the possibility that what he was doing was pointless, or worse.

Andrews opened his eyes half an hour later as they slowed up in front of a row of shops and houses that could well have been in Paris. The car stopped outside an antiques shop that seemed to specialise in china.

'Our apartment's over the top. Let's go on up.'

The woman who opened the door to them was much younger than O'Malley, dark-haired, good looking, with high Slav cheek bones, and a wide sensuous mouth. She held out her hand, smiling. 'My, you look tired. You're going to have a warm bath and a good sleep before you guys start work. Let me show you your room.'

It was a light airy room, its chintz curtains flapping lazily at the open windows. As Andrews stood there she looked at him. 'Where are your things?'

Without thinking he reached in his jacket pocket and pulled out a razor and a worn shaving brush. For a moment she just looked at his face and then she said quietly, 'Have that bath later. Just get into bed and sleep. I'll keep the wolves away.'

He nodded and began to take off his jacket. For a moment she was tempted to help him but then she turned and left, closing the door quietly behind her.

Downstairs her husband had poured himself a whisky.

'Is he all right, honey?'

'You must be out of your mind if you think that.'

'Why? What d'you mean?'

'That guy's ill. He needs a doctor. Call Gibbons and tell him to come over right now.'

'Let's wait until he's had his sleep.'

'No way. Not if you want him to wake up, honey. He's going to die on you if he doesn't get attention.'

An hour later Dr Francis Gibbon had come into the sitting room and, dumping his medical case, had demanded a drink.

'Tell me about him, Charlie. I couldn't get anything out of him.'

'Is he seriously ill, Frankie?'

'He's half-starved, exhausted physically and mentally, but he'll be OK in a few days.' Gibbons looked at Grace O'Malley affectionately. 'You exaggerated a bit, my dear, but you were right to get me over. I've left some instructions on the table in his room and four bottles of pills. I've given him a hefty dose of vitamins and something to calm those jangling nerves. But he'll be fine in a couple of days. He's a tough fellow. I'd say that he's used to roughing it, and basically as strong and fit as a gorilla. Who is he?'

O'Malley shrugged. 'Don't ask, Doc. But thanks for the speedy aid. We'll take good care of him.'

President Wheeler set great store by his weekends back home in Texas. He managed to make it at least once a month, and even if it meant arriving in the early hours of Saturday morning he reckoned the trip was well worthwhile. He swore that there was something in the Texas air that did him good, and was not amused at jibes suggesting that the only thing different about Texas air was dust and the smell of crude-oil.

The helicopter had brought him over from Air Force One as soon as it landed and he was in an amiable mood. He had beaten the odds. It was mid-afternoon and it was still Friday.

He moved the carefully placed folding chair out of the discreet shade into the sunlight, his shirt discarded, wearing only a pair of well-cut trousers and open, leather sandals. The extra time had been bought at the expense of one

221

last business session with the Secretary of State. And doing business in the sun, and shirtless, was his idea of how most business should be done.

'So tell me, Joe, is he any use?'

'He's better than that, Mr President. He's just what we need.'

'In what way?'

'He's not political. He's the undoubted leader of the guerrillas. No rivals. No opposition, and he's making it work. And our people in Europe rate him highly. He's experienced, he knows exactly what he's doing, and he's got lots of guts.'

'Doesn't sound too good to me, Joe.'

'Why not, Mr President?'

'What happens if the Russians get him? What happens if he gets killed?'

'He's agreed to take an American as his second-in-command if we give him more support, and back-up from Amsterdam and Washington.'

'What does Bob Klein think of him?'

'Total approval. No doubts. No reservations.'

'And now you want me to see him?'

'If you can spare the time, Mr President.'

'Is he down here?'

'Yes, Bob Klein has brought him down with O'Malley, the man we've agreed as second-in-command.'

'Is O'Malley acceptable to the Pentagon? It's not just a CIA affair, you know.'

'Yes. They've agreed. There was some discussion about his age.' Brodsky smiled. 'They couldn't pursue it openly because he's four years younger than Andrews, the Englishman.'

Wheeler grinned. 'And probably fifteen years younger than me.'

'Or me, for that matter.'

'And you haven't mentioned our other card?'

'No.'

'Not even a hint?'

'Not a word of any kind.'

'Let's keep it that way.'

'Yes, Mr President.'

'Anything else?'

'No, sir.'

'Wheel your people in for a snack at six. We'll have it out here.'


Brodsky made the introductions and Wheeler tried not to stare at Andrews, but he was interested in this man for whom everyone had nothing but praise. It was the man's eyes that intrigued him. They were light brown, almost yellow, like the eyes of a bird of prey. An eagle's eyes. Watchful, alert, and strangely disturbing. The man was more or less relaxed now, but he wondered what those eyes were like when he was angry.

'Help yourself to food, Mr Andrews, let's not stand on ceremony.'

'Thank you, sir.'

'What prompted you to start your campaign, Mr Andrews?'

'I planned it quite a long time before the Russians came in.'

Wheeler smiled. 'You must have had a pretty good crystal ball to have seen that coming. We could do with one of those ourselves.'

Andrews smiled. 'I didn't see that particular thing coming. I imagined there was going to be a civil war, started by either the extreme left or the extreme right. I made plans to stop them if it was possible.'

'Have my people helped you in the ways you wanted to be helped?'

'Yes, thank you, sir. They've cooperated in every way. Generously and effectively.'

'And you don't mind Mr O'Malley joining you?'

'I welcome it.'

'You've been put in the picture about our plans in Europe?'

'Yes, sir.'

'Do you think they'll work?'

'They've *got* to work, sir. There's no other way.'

'And you see the Russians getting back behind their own frontiers as the result?'

'Not from what we shall do.'

'So what will happen?'

'Europe has learnt its lesson from the occupation of Britain. All those slogans about "Better Red than dead" have gone by the board. All the rosy dreams about communism died in Birmingham and London. There's no illusions left in Europe about the Soviet Union now. But our efforts won't shove them back. What they *will* do is grease the skid-pad so that when Europe together with the United States says "get back inside your own frontiers and stay there", they'll go.'

'Any politicians in your family, Mr Andrews?'

'None, sir. Thank God.'

'Why "thank God"?'

'Nobody in Britain will ever trust politicians again. They let us drift into the mess. They were interested in power. Not to rule the country either wisely or strongly, but just simple power for the class or group who supported them. The House of Commons had become a farce: liars and hypocrites.'

'No honest men?'

'An honest man wouldn't have stood for Parliament. And if he had he would never have been elected.' He paused.

'You know, sir, hundreds of people, all sorts of people, have said to me how wonderful it is not to see those crafty faces on TV any more. The Trades Union leaders and their internal rivals, the politicians, the tycoons, all mouthing their lies, knowing they were lies, even aware that the public knew they were lying, and not giving a damn.'

'So what will you have instead? Who will govern if not politicians – the armed forces?'

'No. A group of men, a forum, maybe twenty men and women who have no axe to grind. They will run the country with their decisions based on a written constitution.'

Wheeler smiled wryly. 'Maybe we can help you there. I've often had a hankering to tinker with ours.' He stood up and looked at Klein. 'You'll look after Mr Andrews, Bob.' He turned to Andrews and held out his hand. 'I'm glad you could spare the time to come and see me. I wish you the best of luck, and if you have problems that can't be settled on the ground you may contact me personally and directly. Bob Klein will tell you how to do that.'

As Wheeler stood on the lawns with Brodsky later that evening waiting for the helicopter to land he turned casually to him and said, 'What did you make of Andrews?'

'I think he'll do a great job. We could do with a lot more like him.'

'I'm not so sure, Joe. I'm not so sure. What does a guy like that do when things are running smoothly? No big causes. Just hard work and play.'

'They probably grow roses, Mr President.'

Wheeler looked unconvinced. 'It's gonna be a long, long haul, Joe. And it's got to work. By God it's got to work. Especially in Britain. I put us behind the stockade and the country likes it. Those who don't know the facts of life. They'll have my scalp if we get involved in Europe all over again and we come up with just the same old scenario we said we wouldn't go along with. There's got to be a prize, Joe.' He paused. 'What *is* the prize?'

Brodsky was well aware that Wheeler knew what the prize was. Just as well as he knew himself.

'I guess there's two prizes, Mr President. Both done up in the same wrapping paper. When you told the people that we'd had enough, the timing was right and the spirit was right. You said exactly what they wanted to hear. At that moment any attempt at counting the cost of that policy would have been given short shrift. But from the administration's point of view we *have* to count the cost. Farmers, industry and commerce, the banks, the unions and even the arts, are already aware that isolation costs jobs and dollars. They haven't complained – as yet, but another couple of years and the problems will be greater. We need trade, Mr President and that's the main prize.'

'And the other?'

Brodsky sighed deeply before he spoke again. 'I guess we just don't belong behind a stockade, Mr President. Not permanently. The second part of our reward is the chance to be Americans again.' He smiled wanly and said softly, 'We've had time to reflect. Time to draw breath. We've taught the rest of the world some lessons, especially the Europeans. And we've taught ourselves some lessons too.'

'What lessons, Joe?'

'That we don't belong behind a stockade, Mr President.'

Wheeler drew a deep breath and looking towards the helicopter he said, 'They're calling you, Joe. Love to the family. Have a nice weekend.'

'You too, Mr President.'


The hood was down on the MG and Savalev sat reading the paragraph that she had marked. He read it several times and then looked at her, shaking his head.

'I don't understand it. What does it mean?'

'It's about you and me, dear boy.'

'But why should they say we are talking about Uganda? I've never been there, nor anywhere in Africa.'

'It's a joky way of saying that you're screwing me.'

He looked again at the paragraph, reading it out slowly. 'Among the élite of Moscow the bouncy Lev (the Lech) Savalev is reported to be deeply involved in discussions pertaining to Ugandan affairs with a member of our own former élite, The Hon. Daphne Mather. "Daffers" is said to have previously been Ugandan adviser to a long line of deb's delights before she fell for the oily charm of the Soviet Number Two in beautiful down-town Baker Street, where Holywell Mansions have become the latest Soviet love-nest.' He looked at her frowning. 'Where did you buy this?'

'You don't buy it, sweetie. It's passed from hand to sweaty hand. Like your *samizdat* in Moscow.'

'Where did you get it? Who passed it to you?'

'Oh Lev, dear. What do you expect me to say?'

'The truth.'

'OK. I found it in the ladies' toilets at Victoria Station.' She laughed at the look on his face. 'Smile, Lev. It's funny. It's only *Private Eye*. Nobody believes it. They always get it wrong. But it was fun to read.'

'Maybe we should stop meeting for a couple of weeks or so.'

'Let's do that, my sweet. Your friend Barakov has been trying to get me in a corner for weeks. He says he's loaded with coupons for everything.'

'You mean Leonid Barakov?'

'Of course.'

'He tries to sleep with you?'

'Why not? Free love and all that.'

Savalev shook his head slowly in amazement and disgust.

'You know there's something about London that corrupts people.'

'Of course there is. That's why they used to flock here from all over the world. And now it's your turn. Relax and enjoy it.'

Savalev forced a wan smile. He preferred even his *Private Eye* image to that of the country bumpkin. He wondered if Smetana ever saw *Private Eye*. Smetana's girl was Russian, hand-picked by the KGB. Weekly medical check-up, very pretty and didn't cost a *kopek*. Maybe that was the safer way. Those old bald heads in the Politburo were not always as stupid as they seemed. He must look up Uganda on a map.

He drove her back to town and took her for a meal at the newly opened *Aragvi* in Sloane Street, which was modelled on the original in Ulitsa Gorkovo in Moscow. It served the same Georgian dishes – *kharcho* and roast mutton and chicken cooked on hot stones. The girl ate heartily, and it seemed strange to him that it was only the upper-classes who had taken to Russian food. The general population still stuck grimly to those terrible chips.

By the time they got to the coffee he had mellowed. 'I apologise for the piece in the magazine. It must be embarrassing.'

'Not for me, sweetie. But Daddy went berserk.'

'Maybe I should explain to him about us.'

'God, no. He knows all about that. But some oaf smashed his car windows in. Thought it was mine.'

'I'll get them fixed for him.'

She smiled. 'Don't worry, he's had them done. Your friend Barakov fixed them. He's a bit of an arse-licker. Thinks if he pleases Daddy he'll get to screw little old me.'

There are times in the history of all occupying forces when the problems are homely and domestic, and this was one of those times. Savalev felt angry and frustrated that night, but there were not many days left for him when life would be so tranquil.

# 18

As far as the eye could see to the west was the lush green pastureland, while away to the north lay the long snow-capped range of the Celestial Mountains. The grass was an exceptionally rich green, and the pale wash of blue-green sky almost cloudless.

The man on the rough grey pony rode with his long legs loose and slack, his boots little more than three feet from the ground. The coarse white coat of sheepskin hung on him carelessly. The smaller man on the pony just in front of him had his head bowed against the wind, which was biting despite the sunshine.

For centuries the long wide valley had been a main link in the silk route, but now it led to Urumqi, the capital of China's largest autonomous region of Xinjiang.

Six hours later they were inside the city whose name had once been Dihua – the City of Enlightenment. It was a strange city, entirely devoid of beauty, style or dignity, with not even a single building of any architectural worth. Under Chinese Communist rule it boasted now a People's Park with a lake, a bridge or two, and a handful of traditional style pavilions. Thirteen different nationalities lived within the grim confines that housed half a million people. Most of them were Uighurs of Turkish origin. Once renowned for the manufacture of musical instruments and carpets, Urumqi now appears in Five Year Plans as producing iron and steel, tractors and chemicals, coal and petrochemicals. It could have fitted without being noticed into Birmingham's Black Country at the turn of the century or one of Pittsburgh's outlying mining areas. In an effort to find some vague recommendation for the city, it could be said that its seedless grapes are sweet, and its ginseng sells well in China's capital, Beijing, which westerners call Peking.

The two men slept that night under untrimmed fox furs in the back-room of a second-hand carpet shop. The shorter man had eaten a lamb kebab; the tall man ate nothing and drank nothing.

It was barely light when they rode out of the town the following morning and it was mid-afternoon before they came to the first of the circular flat tents called *yurts* and the tethered groups of horses. It was in one of the larger tents that they ate and slept that evening.

The man they ate with wore the blue tunic and trousers that had become the traditional modest uniform of high officials of the People's Republic of China. Their meal was elaborate, lasting over four hours. Starting with steamed meatballs, they ate on slowly and with careful protocol through curried chicken, spiced hot beef, steamed buns sweetened with a black bean filling, egg custard cubes and tomatoes, clear soup, white rice and finally, fresh watermelon.

The man from Beijing listened as the tall man talked. Asking a question from time to time but at no time looking at the two men sitting opposite him in the tent. His name was Hsin Qi and he was one of seven people who had discussed for a year after Mao's death whether the Party should maintain that Mao was infallible. And it had been five years before their consensus that he was fallible had been announced publicly. His instructions from the Party Chairman two days before the meeting at the horse-breeding farm had made clear that his mission was the penultimate

231

step in the chain of decisions that could decide his country's rôle in the world for the next hundred years.

The questions he asked as they ate, sometimes seemed away from the thread of their discussion. Simple irrelevant questions such as a peasant might ask when bargaining with a city merchant about his produce. But the tall man's face was impassive as he answered them carefully and at length. He was used to that sort of question in his own country.

It was past midnight in the smoky tent when Hsin Qi looked at the tall man's face. He looked for a long time and then he nodded. That nod was his agreement and commitment, and its only manifestation. There were no papers, no signatures, no shaking of hands. But the tall man reached into his saddle-bag, took out a small packet and handed it to Hsin Qi. When it was opened there was a small disc of yellow gold engraved with two *pin yin* Chinese characters. One for the figure ten and one for the word 'month'. Hsin Qi duly reached into his jacket pocket and handed the tall man something wrapped in silk. It was an irregularly shaped piece of white nephrite jade inscribed with the Cyrillic characters that make up the word *Oktyabr*.

Hsin Qi left by helicopter the next morning and the tall dark man and his companion saddled their ponies for the long journey back to the frontier and the Soviet Socialist Republic of Kazakhstan.

# 19

There was a back entrance to the house down an alleyway of old-fashioned blue bricks that had been there since the house was built in 1901. The left hand house of a pair. On each side of the back alley were tall wooden fences about six feet high, the right hand the higher of the two, with long trails of bright red and yellow Virginia Creeper.

In one of the high-ceilinged upstairs rooms the window had been boarded up except for one of those small spy-lenses used on hotel bedroom doors to inspect callers. The view from the lens covered the back garden of the house and a bowling green that had been part of the local Working-men's Club until it had been taken over as a Red Army Club.

Joe Langley sat with the three other men around the table, the paraffin pressure lamp in the centre. On the bare wooden floor beside the table lay three weapons. RPG–7Vs. Their projectiles lay together on a piece of worn carpet. Two of the warheads were High Explosive and one was a heat-seeking round.

A stop-watch and an electronic wrist-watch lay on the table in front of Joe Langley. There was half an hour to go but there was no talking. Joe Langley was a poor conversationalist unless he had something specific to say. And for almost 18 months he had spent most of his time alone, moving from group to group, accepted as their leader because of his leadership, experience and his success.

Those years before when Langley had faced his third SAS interview in six months it was only Andrews' judgement and influence that had got him through, although Andrews had only been a lieutenant in those days. Langley had excelled in every area except one: he was marked down as having poor leadership qualities. This, despite the fact that the group he led came first in every group activity. They changed his group-mix three times, in case it was the individuals who were responsible for the success. It had made no difference to the results of the man who they considered lacked leadership qualities. When they asked him questions, trying to draw him out, to read his mind, he answered just 'yes' or 'no', whenever that was possible. When it wasn't, his replies were as brief as possible. A telegram, not a letter. The answer always provided sufficient information but nothing more. He was patently honest, and it became obvious that his laconic replies were not a sign of deviousness but basic to the man's character. He was a natural leader, but not a communicator. He didn't have even an average man's instinct to impress. He was never commissioned but he turned out to be one of the best CSMs the SAS ever had. And it would be fair to say that any man who made CSM in the SAS would have been a captain in any other regiment.

For a week Langley had cycled around the area of that night's target. Timing, calculating angles and measurements, planning every detail. Then for ten days the others had been shown the terrain and coached in their roles. They had had dummy runs again and again in Brookvale Park until Langley was satisfied that the three could carry out the operation almost without thinking.

At precisely nine minutes past midnight the four men walked silently down the back alley, their faces and shoulders collecting dew from the hanging creeper. There were no street lights, and no lights on in the houses in Mere

Road. All electric power for civilians was still being cut off at 10 pm every night, and was not switched on until 5.00 am except in rural areas, where farmers had always been given power and light at 4 am.

As they crossed Anchorage Road they could hear the shouts and general noises from drunken Russians at the club. At the foot of the hill where it met Slade Road, Langley stopped them and went ahead alone. There were sometimes Red Army motor patrols along Slade Road from the heavily guarded Spaghetti Junction to the Red Army camp at Witton Lakes, but they were visible for almost a mile in both directions as they rumbled through with their headlights and searchlights blazing. As he expected, Slade Road was empty of vehicles. For a few moments he stared across the road to the rising ground where the group of grim red-bricked buildings stood in silhouette. They had once been called, truthfully but disparagingly, the 'Work 'us'. They were now called, more euphemistically, Highcroft Hospital. In fact, they were the administrative amd communications HQ of Number 1 Guards Group of the Red Army, recently transferred from their regular HQ in Dresden, East Germany.

Back with the others Langley led them past the row of houses facing the old workhouse grounds, crossing Slade Road crouching, over into Fentham Road.

Fentham Road is a steepish hill with the buildings and their grounds on the left-hand side at its crest. There were tall iron railings and a high privet hedge around the grounds and a row of terraced houses on the other side of the road. The four men made their way cautiously on the side with the houses. Langley pressed the light button on his watch and the digital display lit up. There were two minutes and fifteen seconds to go.

Exactly on time a light flashed quickly on and off in the downstairs front window of the furthest house in the row and Langley squeezed the arm of the first man to go. When all three had disappeared into the darkness Langley made his way slowly to the furthest house, moving into the entry between the two houses that led to the outside coal-house and a shared backyard. Silently and slowly he wheeled the four bicycles down the entry to the front of the house, propping them along the low brick garden wall. All of them facing the way they had come. Finally, he opened the cast-iron access plate that led to the main drains, and lodged it open with a wooden block.

The first rocket hit the main communications building as Langley got back to the front of the house. He felt the earth shake and then, after a moment's silence, a huge orange flame surged upwards, expanding slowly as it rose, like a flower blooming in a slow-motion film. Then Langley saw the sudden glow of the internal rocket on the second projectile and the heat-seeking device took it to the heat of the fire and pieces of the building went up, silhouetted in the glow of the flames. They had timed the third projectile for a delay of a minute so that when it hit the vehicle park it would take out the helicopter, the armoured vehicles, and the troops rushing for the pursuit trucks. Then with a menacing roar thousands of gallons of petrol and diesel went up in flames as the third rocket landed.

The first two men came back together. Panting, only eyes visible in their blacked-up faces as he sent them on their way. When the third man had handed over his launcher Langley wrapped all three in black plastic sheeting and lowered them into the drain access. Removing the block and closing the cover plate.

They were back in the house in Mere Road in seven minutes, and there had been no sounds of pursuit. The bicycles had been put in the shed in the garden of the empty house next door. Then they climbed the knotted rope to the attic and lowered the trap door after them.

The attic itself was neat and clean, the floor insulated, boarded over and then covered with a 2 inch foam thickness of carpet underlay. The furniture was light and modern, and spread along a chipboard shelf was a transceiver, two 12 volt car batteries, a trickle-charger and five pairs of hand-held CB radios. A tall refrigerator stood in one corner alongside a small table with a toaster, an electric cooker and a boiler ring. Crockery was on shelves above the table, and a mini-TV set with its aerial extended was on the bottom shelf of a set of bookshelves. There were very few books apart from technical manuals, maps and guide books.

Langley took the first four hours of the watch but none of the lights or microphones gave any indication of people entering the house.

On the evening TV newscast the first item showed President Orlov opening a new hydro-electric dam in Siberia, the second covered a football match between Dynamo Tbilisi and a Red Army team. The third item followed Commissioner Smetana on a tour of a reopened textile mill in Bradford which had just been awarded a five year order for supplying cloth for Red Army uniforms. The selection of short items covered a Soviet vet and the new baby panda at London Zoo, a group of workers from Clydeside visiting Lenin's tomb in Red Square, and a brief snatch of the Bolshoi ballet rehearsing for a performance in Manchester. There was no mention of the sabotage in Birmingham, nor of the similar operations that had been carried out in Glasgow, Portsmouth and Chatham.

Andrews had taken a risk in spreading his best men over so many targets at the same time but O'Malley had been told that the propaganda effect in the outside world would be enormous if it could show how extensive British resistance had become.

President Wheeler had a predilection for hot chocolate that

his wife had desperately tried to cover up when they first moved to Washington. Those who liked him counted it as a typical but tolerable vulgarity, and those who disliked him said that it was either proof of his juvenile character or a contrivance. All part of the rags to riches image that he liked to project. In fact both views were correct. He genuinely loved hot chocolate and had firm connoisseur's views on how it should be concocted, and he didn't give a damn whether it was vulgar or not. And it *was* part of his image that he didn't give too much of a damn what the media or Washington hostesses thought on hot chocolate, rags to riches, or the problem of finding servants in Georgetown. His middle daughter had once said that he was definitely 'non-Preppy', and when he had asked her to explain what that meant he had grinned, patting her neat bottom saying, 'You keep telling them that's me, honey. I love it.'

Joe Brodsky noticed the large chrome-plated Thermos labelled 'Chocolate' and assumed that it was going to be a long, late session. He poured himself a neat whisky and as he leaned back in his chair the door opened and a man stood half-in half-out of the room, talking sharply to someone in the corridor outside. When he eventually closed the door he apologised as he walked towards them.

'My apologies, Mr President, there was a truck across the highway on the bridge.'

Wheeler nodded without comment. 'Sit down, Bob. Do you want to make this formal or can we swing around a bit?'

'Whatever you wish, Mr President.'

'You've seen the DIA's report on the state of the game in the Soviet Union?'

'Yes.' He smiled. 'They've used quite a lot of our material so I'm familiar with the data and the arguments.'

Wheeler neither smiled nor frowned at the comment.

The sniping that went on between the CIA and the Pentagon was normal and traditional, but he found it boring and annoying when he was the audience.

'Have there been any dissenting views of any significance?'

'Not really, Mr President. We had a comment from Ottawa that according to their figures we've underestimated the expenditure on research and development covering satellites. Otherwise they agreed with both our figures and our evaluation.'

'So give me the CIA run-down. As briefly as you can.'

'The Russians are spending between twenty and twenty-three per cent of their GNP on defence and intelligence and a further three to four per cent on sustaining the Cubans, the North Koreans and a mixed bunch of terrorists and guerrillas all over the globe. Their production of almost all domestic products has been falling year by year for the last seven years. The whole economy is crumbling because of bad management and bureaucratic inertia. The people are complaining more openly than we've ever seen before. The last two harvests were actually quite good but we estimate that ten per cent just rotted because the machinery wasn't available to gather it in.

'We've had reports of seven strikes. Strikes are illegal but they've had them all the same. Miners and heavy engineering workers who claim that their meat rations are less than half of what the Poles and East Germans are getting. But it's probably the figures in Appendix E that are the real problem. A worker in Moscow has to work three times as long for his food as a German, or a Frenchman does. For a small colour TV or a car a Russian works ten times as long as an American. At one time the complaint was that they had money but there was nothing in the shops to buy. There's still no goods, but now there's no roubles either. Their workers are totally disillusioned, they work as little as possible and the black-market's growing fast. What happened in Poland in '80, '81 was a lesson the Soviet worker hasn't forgotten.

'If we continue the arms-race they can't match us or even hold level unless they sacrifice even more on the domestic front. The whole country is slowly coming apart at the seams.'

'Tell me what we could be doing if some of the restrictions were lifted. We'll discuss the DIA report as a focus point.'

'I'd like to give some thought to that, Mr President. Can I come back to you?'

'Yes, of course. Come and have breakfast with Joe and me tomorrow morning. It's Saturday so we can take it easy. I'll expect you at eight.'

Robert Klein stood up. 'Right, Mr President.'

As he walked down the corridor Bob Klein wondered if Julie hadn't been right when she was against him leaving the law practice to take over as the Director of the CIA. She had said that he was wrong for it on two counts. Firstly his age, he was neither old enough nor young enough. According to her, 52 was exactly the wrong age to be making a change. The second reason she gave against it was that Mike Wheeler had always been his hero-figure. With considerable insight his much younger wife had said that if you worked for a hero he either ended up with feet of clay or you lost your independence. You went along with his thinking, not because you agreed, but because you liked the man. And his liking for Mike Wheeler had started way back.

The *Washington Post* had wondered editorially if the White House shouldn't be renamed Dom Polski because President Wheeler had appointed Poles as Secretary of State and Director of CIA and the First Lady came from a Polish family from Chicago. Mike Wheeler had been Governor of Texas and he had not lost touch with his boyhood friend who now sold tractors, and when the friend's son had earned the chance of a place at Austin it had been Mike Wheeler who persuaded them to let him go, and had given him a spare-time job in the Republican organisation that provided the cash. Bob Klein had made his own way since then, but for him, Mike Wheeler would always be the man in the white hat.

Bob Klein had had his office cleared for the meeting and a longer table moved in with half a dozen straight-backed chairs. He had stood looking at the TV set as the others came in one by one and took their places round the table. The NBC newsreel showed pictures from a US Navy aircraft carrier about 40 miles off the west coast of Ireland. Three Soviet fighters were buzzing it one after the other, so low that you could see the insignia on their swept back wings. The commentator was saying '... typical of the harassment of our ships in international waters ... President Wheeler has instructed our ambassador in Moscow to lodge ...' Klein switched off the set and moved to his place at the head of the table.

'Good morning, gentlemen. Before I start, let me remind you that notes will not be taken at this meeting. If anyone asks you what you were here for refer them to me. Whoever they are.' He closed his eyes for a moment to collect his thoughts then looked around the table. 'The White House has agreed to our proposals covering Poland, East and West Germany, Belgium and Holland. As you know, the Dutch never went along with the French plan right from the start. They've been sympathetic to the British all through the occupation and are willing to support us in the new operations. So our new phase will be controlled from Amsterdam. For your ears only, the Dutch Royal Family and the Dutch government have both been made aware of what we plan and have unofficially given it their approval

241

provided that the only Dutch nationals used are those already involved, and that there is no attempt to use Dutch cooperation as a recruiting or propaganda lever. OK?'

There were nods of agreement and Klein went on. 'Just give me an outline each one of you of the present state of play and what you need to step things up. You go first Steve. Your people are going to carry most of the supply load in the beginning.'

The big blond man pursed his lips, looked down at the table and then at the others. He had a surprisingly quiet voice.

'OK. Here goes. My group is six Americans, all CIA or ex-CIA. Eight Dutchmen. We can call on well over a hundred Dutch nationals in strategic positions any time we want. We've got a limited supply of weapons and explosives. Five transceivers and a base transceiver that can get us back here to Langley. We have no contact with the embassy or the consulates, and they have not been informed of our group.

'So far we have limited our activities to information-gathering on Russian planes at Dutch airports, their embassy staff and consulate and trade mission staffs. We pass all our stuff direct to the UK.' He looked at Klein. 'Can I mention the UK set-up at all?'

Klein shook his head. 'Nope.'

The blond man shrugged. 'We also pass our stuff back here. We've got our own printing facility with IBM setting, and contacts with Dutch nationals at the airport, at the telephone exchange that covers the Soviet Embassy, at the TV and radio stations, on the newspapers, in the police, and the army. And . . .' he smiled, '. . . with their intelligence organisation. Our cover is a tour operator for travel to the States, and a small import-export company. They both function apart from being a cover.'

As the man leaned back, relieved that his piece was done,

242

Klein said, 'OK. Tell us what you'll be doing now we've had the green light.'

'We shall be producing an underground sheet. A four-pager called *Vrij England* and we shall cover all the abuses, corruption and inefficiency of the Soviet bureaucracy in Britain. We shall try to prevent goods and money moving from the Netherlands to any Warsaw Pact country. We shall feed information to all the media and the politicians and when we get clearance we shall physically harass all official Russians we can identify, both diplomatic and trade people. We shall destroy Soviet aircraft whenever we can, and ships of course.

'Finally we want to arouse the public and keep the row going in the United Nations.'

Klein looked at the others. 'Any questions?'

A man in a blue denim shirt and jeans said, 'You say all this as if it was just a sales drive with no dangers, no opposition. How come it's all so easy?'

The blond man shrugged. 'Maybe I've explained it badly. Not easy, but the vast majority of the population are on our side. Well – on the side of the British.'

'Why are they so pro-British?'

'I don't know. Maybe it's because they are both monarchies. Or were. They're a bit like one another. Easy going, tolerant, but real bastards when they get going. I think they've always taken one another for granted. No great flag waving or treaties but they like one another and respect one another. There's no doubt that they'll go a long way to help get the Russians out of England short of actual fighting.'

Klein nodded to the man in the blue denim shirt.

'Give us the German picture.'

The man cleared his throat and leaned forward with his arms on the table.

'We've got a very mixed bag of opportunities. In West

243

Germany we've got fewer resources to call on than in East Germany. It sounds crazy, but it's easier for us to recruit and operate in East Germany than West. It's the old old story, the East Germans don't need telling about what the Russians are like, they experience it every day. And apart from that they're used to foxing the Russians, manipulating them. But the West Germans have become like the British were, turning a blind eye to the obvious, just hoping the worst doesn't happen and when, inevitably, it does they put a bright face on it and console themselves that it could have been even worse.

'In West Germany the support is working-class and middle-class. The upper class as usual are feathering their own nests and devil take the rest. I can call on nearly four hundred strategically placed people and activists, and maybe fifteen hundred others who would pass on information but not do anything active.

'In East Germany my first-hand contacts are fewer but very influential and there are thousands who would co-operate with these people. Real cooperation, sabotage, violence, the lot. So we shall have a programme that covers the same things as Amsterdam but we shall harass and sabotage Soviet troops and lines of communication. I see that as our main rôle. We don't need anti-Soviet propaganda. They know more about the Russians than we do.'

Klein said, 'What are their feelings about the British?'

'In West Germany mainly favourable but anxious not to be contaminated by the "English disease". They're a bit out of date on that of course. In East Germany I don't think there's any feeling one way or another. The British have long been out of their picture. We don't need any pro-British feeling there anyway. They hate the Soviets on their own account and that's enough. We're going to need big arms and explosives drops and a lot of cash.'

Klein nodded. 'We'll be having separate meetings. We'll

go into that in detail. There'll be no problems.' He nodded towards an older man who looked, and was dressed, more like a diplomat than a CIA man. Which was reasonable enough as that was what he was. Ex-CIA and now a bureaucrat.

'Give us a brief picture on Belgium.'

The older man smiled. 'Nothing dramatic I'm afraid from Brussels. There's an amazing residue of goodwill towards the British, left over from two world wars. But the Belgians aren't given to uprisings and resistance. They are used to being over-run and occupied. They don't lick arses but they cooperate so that life can go on as normally as possible.' He shrugged. 'History's taught them that that's the way to do it. Sensible, civilised, and very discouraging for our type of effort. And with the permanent dogfight going on between the Flemings and the Walloons it's even more difficult to put much emphasis on the British.

'However, I have been able to recruit a large number of Belgian businessmen and diplomats. Maybe recruit is an exaggeration. Let's say I've got a large panel of spokesmen who will take a strong pro-British anti-Soviet stance at EEC and UN meetings. From bureaucrat level right up to the top. More than that I can't provide.'

Klein interposed. 'Let me say that more than that we didn't expect or ask for. We want to have Belgium as a sanctuary area. We're going to need that when our people come up against their own authorities.' Klein turned to the young man with the pale moonlike face and blue eyes. Despite his youth he was almost bald, the pale red hair like a priest's tonsure, only the moustache growing vigorously. 'Now Poland.'

The young man took a slow, deep breath, hesitated and then slowly shook his head.

'I don't want to discuss the Polish operation here. Let me just say that what *we* want and what *they* want coincide completely. They are pro anyone who wants the Russians back behind their own frontiers and are very pro-British. What I am doing is support them in every way I can. There is no chance of me recruiting a separate network. They don't need any propaganda or encouragement from me to be anti-Soviet. They hate their guts and have done all through history. They are all patriots, men, women and kids, and brave to the point of stupidity.

'Now we've had the go-ahead and they begin to see anti-Soviet moves in other countries my problem will be to provide them with what they need and still restrain them from launching a full-scale attack instead of keeping to sabotage.'

The man in the denim shirt said, 'If they started anything like a military attack on the Russians they could ruin everything. The Russians would just use it as an excuse to start a war in Europe. We want them back in their own bailiwick, not roaring around Europe.'

'I'm well aware of that, and things are being done to warn them too. But it's not easy when they see what the Russians do in their daily lives.'

'We've got enough Poles in the White House, can't they exercise some influence?'

The young man glanced at Klein who nodded briefly.

'That's being done. And Voice of America are bearing it in mind in their reporting.'

'Any more questions?' Klein looked around the table and a man who hadn't spoken put up his hand.

'Go on, Leonard.'

'I've sat in on a lot of meetings like this. From the Bay of Pigs cock-up to . . . well I won't go over old ground . . . all I want to say is that we wanted all those other operations to succeed. Some did, some didn't. But this time there's going to be no choice. This operation has *got* to succeed. It may not look like it, or feel like it, but you fellows are making history. If we lost out on this one the clocks would go back a thousand years. We didn't pick this fight, it was started by those motherfuckers in Paris, and the Russians made their move on the back of it. They must be bitterly regretting it right now, but the whole world is balanced on a knife-edge. If Moscow gets away with this you'd better start digging that hole in your backyards. And I'm not bluffing or exaggerating. If we don't drive those bastards back to their own frontiers then we've had it. All of us. This isn't an exercise in diplomacy, or even a trial of strength. It's the last chance. The very last chance.'

There was silence round the table. A silence of embarrassment, and uneasy recognition that maybe, for once, it was truth not rhetoric that they had heard.

Then Klein said, 'Let's eat, and then I'll see you all separately. Those who need personal cash or travel arrangements can see Facilities after lunch.'

# 20

In the second year of the occupation there had been a genuine attempt on the Russians' part to relax their attitudes to British institutions that they saw as non-political. They allowed the Cup Final to be played at Wembley despite their rooted aversion to large crowds gathering in confined areas. There had been a sadly depleted Wimbledon where most of the players had been invited rather than qualified in competition. Most of the foreign competitors were from the Warsaw Pact countries, India and South-east Asia.

The Indians had sent a strong cricket team for what had been officially called the European Test Series, and the Anglophiles among the administration had taken tuition on the rules of the game and eventually given up in despair.

So many of his British contacts had sung the praises of the Promenade Concert season that Smetana had given permission for the New British Broadcasting Company to revive them provided the music programme was cleared first with him. Not being musically inclined himself he had delegated the task to Savalev whose musical knowledge was both all-Russian and limited mainly to the ballet music to which his girl-friends at the Bolshoi had danced and he had witnessed from time to time. He had insisted on including a few items of Russian music that were not familiar to the British concertgoer, but he had done little more than scan the programmes for music by composers who had been banned or were refugees from the Soviet Union.

The same restriction applied to performers. Not that any of them were now available in Britain.

Having heard of the great sentiment attached to the last night of the Proms he had arranged for several top Soviet officials to make up parties for the occasion. The programme had made a small gesture to its Russian sponsors and the first item was an orchestral arrangement of Rachmaninov's 'Vocalise'. It was followed by Vaughan Williams' 'The lark ascending' and Walton's 'Belshazzar's Feast' before the interval. The Russians were delighted with the obvious enthusiasm of the audience despite being slightly concerned at the effusiveness of the young promenaders.

The second half had been an ever increasing nightmare for Savalev. It had all looked so innocuous on the programme. Elgar: Pomp and Circumstance No. 1 and Henry Wood: Fantasia on British Sea Songs. Then suddenly, as the tempo of the music changed and the drum rolled, those thousands of Union Jacks appearing and the whole audience singing. Despite his fluent English he hadn't been able to make out the words except for the first line, which seemed to be repeated again and again. 'Land of Hope and Glory...' But it was the ghastly song afterwards that had really done the damage. The second time round the whole audience had turned to face the Soviet dignitaries in their boxes and, flags waving defiantly, they had sung it again and again. 'Britons never, never, never, shall be slaves... Rule Britannia, Britannia rules the waves...' It still made him go cold when he thought about it.

The next day he had raised hell with the British staff, but, as if they were prepared for his onslaught, they had shown him video recordings of the last night of the Proms of six previous years. Every one was exactly the same except that they didn't turn towards the boxes and there weren't tears running down their faces. Smetana and several others had walked out as the crowds sang but he was not unduly incensed by Savalev's gaffe. He said it might help to defuse the underlying tensions they obviously still had.

What had first been anger by the men in the Kremlin at the start of the week had turned to virtual disbelief by the weekend.

In Amsterdam an Aeroflot Ilyushin had been completely destroyed in a service bay. Despite obvious evidence that its destruction was deliberate Moscow had been prepared to treat the incident outwardly as an accident. But when a second Ilyushin had been blown up at Schipol there was no hiding the fact that it was sabotage.

In the United States the Teamsters Union had declared that no cargoes from any Warsaw Pact country would be handled, and the announcement made clear that the ban was permanent. The Seaman's Union had warned that ships owned by, or chartered to, Warsaw Pact countries would be refused facilities and picketed if they tried to enter United States ports.

Mid-week came the assassination of the Soviet City Commissioner for Glasgow and an unsuccessful but violent attack on two KGB officers in Cardiff. In Paris a crowd estimated at over 20,000 had assembled at the Arc de Triomphe to protest against the Soviet occupation of Great Britain. The Soviet Ambassador in Paris reported that the French police had stood by, taking no action despite a Ministerial order to clear the area.

By the Friday the scale and implications of what was happening became obvious. An early morning street cleaning-team in Paris had discovered a body hanging by its neck from one of the trees in the Champs Elysée. The body was male and naked, and taped across the chest was a white card that said: *Traître de sa patrie et de l'humanité*. It was not until four hours later that the corpse was recognised as that of Charles Alphonse Becque, President of the Republic.

The final straw was the distribution of a four-page underground news sheet. On the front page was a photograph of President Orlov addressing the 1983 Congress with a banner-headline quoting words from his speech. 'THE SOVIET PEOPLE MUST GIVE THEIR ENERGIES IN SERVICE TO THE STATE, NOT LOOK FOR REWARDS TODAY BUT REWARDS FOR THEIR CHILDREN AND GRANDCHILDREN...' The rest of the front page contained quotations from recent exhortations by other members of the Politburo and several leading Ministers. The front page looked exactly like the front page of a normal *Pravda*. The title, the mast-head, the type-face and format were exactly like any issue of *Pravda*. But the following three pages were political dynamite. There was a separate piece about each of fourteen different top functionaries including President Orlov and seven other members of the Politburo. Each piece gave details including names, addresses and sometimes telephone numbers, of girls who were their mistresses or casual sexual partners, and details of the privileged rations of food drawn by the individual concerned in the previous six months. This was followed by lists of privileged purchases of rare imported items obtained in the same period, a photograph of the man's house, his country house and his private and official cars. In several cases there were photographs of the man concerned with a named concubine. In the case of President Orlov the list of his private cars showed 25 rare and expensive cars from Rolls Royces to Ferraris, and the list of his sexual partners was long and varied. It included the wives of several senior officials.

The first copies of the fake *Pravda* had been discovered by the police at Kuznecki Most underground station of the Moscow Metro system, and in the next two hours there were reported findings all over Moscow. As the day wore on reports came in of findings in every major Soviet city and hundreds of towns. A meeting was called in the Kremlin where anger was used as a cloak for personal embarrassment. But apart from giving instructions to the police and the KGB to investigate with vigour and urgency, nobody had any constructive suggestions to make. Only after the meeting had broken up did the news start coming in from all over the world that the scurrilous news sheet had been distributed in 25 other countries, carefully and accurately translated into the appropriate language. By midevening the Voice of America was quoting extracts in its broadcasts and was adding those first sly jokes that keep any corruption scandal on the boil.

The following day the world's press was front-paging the revelations and the cartoonists were having a field-day. Editorial comment was either deadly serious in its approach or amused, according to its readership, but the outcome was damaging to Moscow whatever approach was used. It's not easy to decide whether you would rather be seen by your fellow-countrymen and the world as a hypocritical crook or as a poltroon caught with his trousers down.

As the KGB and *Izvestia* evaluation team examined copies of the *samizdat Pravda* they realised that the fake was too good to have been produced in the Soviet Union. The paper, ink, format, type-faces were exact. It had been professionally produced. But the most serious aspect was its distribution in the Soviet Union. As the days went by it was estimated that at least 3 million copies had been distributed in the Soviet Union alone. That represented not only a massive printing operation but a huge transport problem. Hundreds of Soviet citizens would have had to be involved in the distribution for it to have been so effective. They decided that the physical distribution must have been over a period of weeks to be able to have them passed around in the same two-day period.

Local Party leaders were being harassed by their communities as to why the allegations had not been denied, and their own local peccadilloes were being brought out into the open. Hot-headed local Party leaders had had people arrested but the public protests were getting back to Moscow and the victims had mostly been released with a caution.

In a stately home in Maryland a man crossed through seven separate lines of type at right angles to a thick black line. Vertical lines ran from top to bottom of the chart marking off the days of eight consecutive months. The whole thing looked rather like a fishbone and a small legend in the top left-hand corner said simply, 'G709 Critical Path Analysis'.

The area of Rynek Starego Miasta in Warsaw still looks much the same as it did in the 18th century except that the old Town Hall has gone, and the square is now given over to open-air cafés, and artists and tourists. But despite the romantic flood-lights across the cobbled streets the man had insisted that they met downstairs in Fukier's old wine cellar.

The smoke-filled atmosphere and the hubbub of voices provided some kind of security and O'Malley had recognised that the Russian knew his way around Warsaw far better than he did.

It hadn't been difficult. He had come in on a French passport and the man who called himself Oktyabr had met him at the airport and taken him to the house in the Old Town. This was their third meeting in two days.

The pale blue eyes looked at him casually as the man lit a cigarette. 'How much is promises and how much is fact?'

'Anything I say we will do will be done. What about your part?'

The man half-smiled, a self-confident, knowing smile. 'You know already that I can do my part or you wouldn't be here my friend. Tell us what we can have.'

'Tell me what you want and I'll tell you if we can supply it.'

The man reached in his jacket pocket and pulled out a theatre ticket. 'There's a microdot on the full-stop after the producer's name. It's a list of what we want.'

'I haven't got a reader with me.'

'So read it when you get back.'

'How do you get access to microdot equipment?'

'You don't imagine I would tell you, do you?'

'Maybe not. Give me some idea of what you want.'

'Money. In gold or silver. Krugerrands or Maria Teresa dollars. Rocket launchers. Surface to surface missiles. Surface to air missiles. Sub-machine guns, ammunition. Transceivers that are simple to operate, and forged documents.'

'What sort of quantities are we talking about. Missiles for instance?'

'Genuinely no limit. Whatever you provide I can put to good use. Less than two hundred ground to ground wouldn't be worth having, but I could put a hundred SAMs to very good use.'

'Would you agree to coordinate with us on timing?'

'Timing of delivery or timing of use?'

'Both.'

'On delivery almost certainly. On using, maybe.'

'Can you provide genuine documents for us to copy for the forgeries?'

'Yes. No problem.'

'How can I get in touch with you again?'

'The same as this time.'

'I mean in a hurry.'

Oktyabr looked for long moments at O'Malley's face. Then he said softly, 'I assume you are CIA?'

'Yes I am.'

'Married?'

'Yes.'

'Children?'

'Two.'

'Would you risk one of your children's lives for the sake of the freedom of the United States?'

'No. Definitely not. But I'd risk my own.'

Oktyabr smiled and put his hand on O'Malley's hand as it rested on the table. 'A good answer. I believe you. OK. When we leave here I'll give you a name and a code-word. The contact is at our mission to the United Nations in New York. Shall we go?'

'OK.'

The weather was still warm enough to walk across to one of the cafés and sit outside and drink a coffee. When the coffee had been brought and they were alone at the table the Russian said, 'Why did your people take so long to get in touch with me?'

'They had to be sure you weren't a plant. When we were reasonably certain we contacted you.'

'What made you reasonably certain?'

'Oh, several things. We heard on the grape-vine some of the things your people had done in the Soviet Union. And we heard about the help you had given to the Englishman.'

Oktyabr smiled. 'Don't call him an Englishman. He's very touchy about it. He's a Scot. But what does that prove.'

'I guess if you were a plant the man would be in jail

or dead by now. You know who he is and you know how to contact him. You've known that for five months but he's still alive.'

Oktyabr smiled. 'You are like children in many ways you Americans. Nice children but inclined to be clumsy.'

'Why do you say that?'

'You underrate the Russians. The KGB.'

'How?'

'If I had betrayed our Scottish friend they wouldn't necessarily have picked him up. They could put him under twenty-four hour surveillance and build a beautiful long list of all his contacts.'

'And meantime he blows up Soviet camps and sabotages communications and kills Russian troops.'

Oktyabr smiled, shaking his head slowly. 'You imagine that would worry the KGB if they were getting information they wanted? Not on your life, my friend.'

'Why has it taken so long for the Russian people to protest against the Kremlin?'

'You'd need to *be* a Russian to understand that. First of all fear. Stalin had half a million Russians murdered without trial during the purges. Not dissidents or trouble-makers, but party members.' He smiled. 'That makes people very cautious. Stalin may be dead but the machinery he used is still there. And secondly, although nobody believes the rubbish put out by the Politburo's propaganda machine there have been improvements in the system since Stalin. The USSR is an incomplete socialist state. But there are democratic aspects to the regime in the industrial and economic areas even though there is no democracy in political terms. But the ruling élite have learned the wisdom of voluntary self-restraint in how they rule us. Unfortunately for them, in political terms there is no such thing as an incomplete democracy. The door is either shut tight or wide open. They thought they could open the door just a little way. That was a mistake. That's why they cannot survive.'

'How long *will* they survive?'

'Who knows? Ten years. Less with your help. Less still if Europe and America use their strength.'

'And what will take its place?'

'Democracy in some shape. That has to be argued and decided. My people just want to genuinely control their own lives.'

'Shall we meet again before I leave tomorrow?'

'No. The name of the person you should contact is Simenov. Gregor Illyich Simenov. You phone him at the UN, not at his home. The password is my name. Oktyabr.'

They had arranged to meet together on the Thursday, at the farm at Pen-y-Fan. Joe Langley had arrived first, followed two hours later by Jamie Boyle and Macgregor. Indira Singh was already there. She had been staying with Glyn Thomas and Meg while Harry Andrews was away. They were waiting for Sanjiva Singh.

Andrews had been back for two days and they had all been elated by his news. There were things he hadn't told them, but they were pleased enough with what he had been able to tell them. O'Malley was seen as positive proof that the help and supplies from Washington would really be continuous. He had also brought a breath of American self-confidence. He was tanned and well-fed, a messenger from a world that was still free. A world where there were still new films and hamburgers, a world that knew what you meant when you spoke of 'Dallas' and Kojak, and all the other TV things that they had once dismissed as rubbish but watched avidly. A world where the evening news was put together but not manufactured.

There were people who still had video recorders that worked who gave discreet parties on Saturday nights showing cassettes of old TV programmes. The Russian-controlled TV network provided excellent material. Nature and travel films, Soviet documentaries and magnificent feature films of the Russian classics. Savalev's influence had allowed an extended life for Coronation Street and Crossroads although the scripts were heavily censored. But it was like a diet of nothing but porridge and people found that they missed the rubbishy quiz shows. A Morecambe and Wise series had been passed until after the first show when the Russians realised that there were subtle ways of poking fun at the new authorities that the mere reading of the script didn't show up. Even cassettes of old black and white films like *Casablanca* and Laurel and Hardy had a high black-market price.

Perhaps what cheered them most was seeing the effect on Andrews when he came back, of ten days sleep and good food. He was back to his old energetic, almost arrogant self.

There was no sign of Sanji by ten o'clock in the evening and it was unlikely that he would risk trying to get through the continuous Russian road-blocks in the dark. But Glyn Thomas had stayed up all night in case he got through.

When Sanji hadn't arrived by nine the next morning Glyn had taken the risk of trying to raise him on that day's frequency, but there was no response so they guessed that he was at least on his way.

Andrews had taken Indira for a walk up the hill and they sat in the sunshine at the edge of the grassline, the steep rocks rearing up behind them another six or seven hundred feet.

She was wearing a faded blue denim shirt and a matching skirt, sitting with her legs bent, her head resting on her knees, looking at him.

'It's great to see you looking so fit, Harry. Did you enjoy it apart from the journey?'

'I missed you. I knew I would, but I didn't realise how much. I dreamed about you once.'

'Nice dream or nightmare?'

'A nice dream.'

'What happened?'

'I'd better not say. You'd be shocked.'

She smiled. 'Now you *have* to tell me, you stinker. Was it sex?'

'I'm afraid it was.'

'Anything you've not done to me in reality?'

'A couple of things.'

'Tell me, you idiot.'

He reached out and closed his hand round a dry stalk of sorrel, drawing his closed hand upwards until it was full of the dry reddish petals. He turned back towards her smiling.

'Open your hand.'

She spread out her hand, her long slim fingers apart.

'Close your fingers. That's right.'

He filtered the dry seeds into her palm. 'Some people call that Idiot's Gold, some call it Fairy Gold.'

'What is it?'

'It's called sorrel. It used to be a highly prized plant.'

'Why?'

'It removes stains, it quenches thirst and you can eat the boiled leaves.'

'How do you know these things?'

'I used to learn about plants and berries for survival courses.'

'Let's go back to sex and me being shocked.'

But Andrews' eyes were half-closed against the sun as he stared down towards the farmhouse.

'Glyn's waving to us. We'd better get down.'

The girl raised her head and looked down to the farm.

'I can't see him. Yes I can. I thought you were just copping-out.' She stretched out her hand as he stood up and he pulled her to her feet.

Despite the rough ground he kept his arm round her slim warm waist as they walked down.

259

Glyn was waiting for them in the cobbled yard. He looked tired, and Andrews remembered that the Welshman had had no sleep. 'Get some sleep, Glyn. I'll be around now.'

'OK. I'd like a word with you first.'

'Sure, what is it?'

Glyn hesitated and then turned to the girl. 'Meg's looking for you, love.'

As the girl walked away slowly, and obviously reluctantly, Andrews said quietly, 'Why upset her, Glyn. She's just as much one of us as anybody else.'

'I've just had some bad news, Harry. Real bad news. I didn't want her to hear it.'

'What is it?'

'I've just had a radio call from Moraji Patel in Manchester. They've got Sanji's group. All except a handful. They got them three days ago.'

'Where were they?'

'At their number four place over the fish and chip shop in Brixton.'

'Did they get Sanji?'

'Yes. There were five of them there. They got them all.'

'What happened? Where are they now?'

'Sanji's dead. They tried to make him talk. Tortured him. Broke his fingers and his ankles and then put a gun to his head and said they'd shoot him if he didn't start talking. He didn't, and they shot him.'

'And the others?'

'They were taken away for interrogation. A couple of hours later they were raiding all Sanji's places. They picked up about fifty people including Sanji's wife. They took them in trucks to the camp on the coast near Rye. An old holiday camp and hotel at Camber Sands. They've got the radios, the code-pads, the lot.'

'The code-pads don't matter. They're all different and there were no contact records of any kind.'

'Somebody's talked, Harry, we don't know *what* they've given away.'

Andrews shrugged. 'Nothing that could affect any other group. But we'd better warn the others.'

'I've done that already by radio. I didn't give any details. I've asked Crowther down on Romney Marshes to get us details of the camp.'

'I don't think we can do anything for them, Glyn. We're too near the last stages. We couldn't risk any more lives.'

'What about Indi's mother?'

'I'll see if we can get some outside help. We can't do anything. You're quite sure that Sanji's dead?'

'Yes. They left his body there, and two of his boys went back after they'd gone and took him away. He's being cremated.'

Andrews turned to look at Glyn Thomas's face. 'It's our first real set-back, Glyn. We've been very lucky so far. Somebody must have talked or they'd never have got onto Sanji. I'd better do the rounds and grind into them about security again.'

'Are you going to tell Indi?'

'Yes. I'll tell her.'

When he saw that look of tension back on Andrews' face the Welshman said quietly, 'Let me tell her. You can comfort her afterwards. It'll be easier if I do it. Less emotional.'

Andrews shook his head. 'Thanks. But I'll do it myself. Does Meg know?'

'No. Just you and me.'

As they got to the farmhouse door she was there with a cup of tea, smiling. 'Every hour on the hour.'

He took the mug and reached for her other hand. 'Come and sit on the bench with me.'

'OK.'

When they were seated he put the mug on the cobbles and

slid his arm round her shoulders. 'Look up at the top of the mountain, Indi.'

When she was looking up towards the clouds that wreathed the top of the mountain in their cotton-wool base he said, 'I've got some bad news, sweetie. The Russians picked up a lot of people in your father's group. They shot your father and have taken a lot of prisoners including your mother.'

There was a long pause and then she said softly, 'Are you sure? There's no chance that there's a mistake?'

'No. It's true, love. I'm terribly sorry.'

'Tell me what happened.'

He gave her the barest details, and after a few moments silence she said. 'Why did you tell me to look at the top of the mountain before you told me.'

'Whenever I was unhappy in the old days I would go for a walk and look at a big tree to give me some sort of perspective about time and proportion. My problem measured against nature. Hundreds of years against my few. Rain, sunshine, storms and winds and generations of people who had looked at that same tree. It calmed me down more often than not.'

'It makes me think of something my father often said to me because I wasn't interested in religion. He said, "All your university learning, all your convictions that there is no such thing as God, will change one day. Not from logic or reasoning, but because that day you need a God." She turned her face to look at him. 'I think today's that day for me, my love.' And she put her long elegant hands to her face and sobbed, her head bowed.

Andrews saw the slender neck and the curls of rich black hair and realised again how beautiful she was. And how young. He wished that he could bear the pain and sadness for her. She was too gentle, too generous, too innocent to have to bear such burdens. And for a fleeting, ghastly moment he wondered if the death of her father could spoil their relationship. It was a thought that he dare not harbour. What he was doing had taken the whole of his time and the whole of his mind. He had thought of nothing else for years and the advent of a totally different set of opponents had made little difference to his thinking. But his relationship with the girl had changed all that. Before, he had been physically and mentally involved, but now he was emotionally involved as well, and he was aware of his vulnerability. More than aware, afraid. He had a personal stake in the outcome now and the girl had become his hostage to fortune. His Achilles' heel. Love wasn't a word he liked or used. To him it was one of those weasel words that mean anything and nothing. A word that was used too freely. And all too often used by men and women to dodge rather than confirm. But love was a word that was much in his mind as he looked at the girl.

At last she lifted her head, turning to look at his face. She shook her head slowly. 'It seems terrible, Harry, not to belong anywhere.'

'You do belong somewhere. You belong with me.'

She put her hand in his. 'Remember your Scottish poem. "He travels the fastest who travels alone." '

'I'm not aiming to travel fast, sweetie. And you've belonged with me for a long time now.'

'A few months, Harry, that's all.'

'Seven months and eight days.'

The melting brown eyes looked at his face. 'I love you, Harry Andrews. I swore to myself I'd never say it. But I do.'

'I love you too, Indi.'

'That's not one of your words, Harry. What does it mean to you?'

He thought for a moment. 'The nearest I can get is that I love you more than myself. If only one of us could be happy I would rather it was you.'

'My father worshipped you. You were his hero.'

263

'Why was that?'

'Oh, largely the wrong reasons. You were brave but not selfish, you were devoted to a cause. You didn't drink much alcohol and you didn't chase women.' She smiled warmly. 'There were other things too I'm sure, but those were the things he said aloud.'

'Did he mind about you and me?'

'He never said, one way or another. We never discussed it. But he never changed his opinion of you, I know that.'

'Would you consider marrying me?'

'No.'

'Why not?'

She half-smiled. 'It doesn't need considering. Of course I'll marry you.'

'Straight away?'

'Today if it's possible, and you want.'

'I'll have to be here for two days then we'll go to a place in Cambridge. We'll get married there.'

'Have they looked after my father's body?'

'Yes. He was cremated. Some of his men who weren't caught saw to it. I'm sure they will have done the right things.'

'Dare I ask about my mother?'

'I'll see what I can do. I'll send a message to her meantime. Just to let her know you're OK.'

They had a small celebration that evening with a bottle of Glyn Thomas's dandelion wine. Indi had been with Meg all day as Andrews outlined the latest position to the men. It was good news that he had for them despite Sanji's death. They had all left in the early hours of the morning. Langley back to the Midlands, Jamie Boyle to Scotland and the border counties, and Andrews to London.

# 21

Cameron Davies sat at the trestle table in the attic at Pen-y-Fan checking over the blue-prints of the pylon sites covering an area south of a line that ran from the Wash to the Midlands between Birmingham and Stafford. Joe Langley and he had already calculated where the charges would have to be placed for maximum damage but the choice of pylon depended on achieving the maximum disruption with the limited explosive available.

O'Malley had made six trips to take explosives and detonators to Jamie Boyle and his men in Scotland and the North, and Joe Langley had carried out the distribution in the South. The problem was to choose the pylons that would cause the maximum disruption for the Russians. Most of their military installations had emergency generators and Andrews had asked for minimum disturbance to the public where this was possible, so the choosing of each site was an individual problem. There was material enough to cover 300 pylons.

For the first time in their campaign Andrews, Langley and Boyle had travelled around the country together covering 22 strategic towns and cities, bringing in local group leaders to go over the strike plans in detail. They had warned of the possible consequences but the group leaders had sworn that their own people would accept whatever happened in their areas. They were sure that the majority of the public would support them.

The anniversary date of the signing of the Moscow Treaty fell on a Sunday and in major cities the Russians put on open-air military band concerts, gymnastic displays, exhibitions of Soviet arts and crafts and parades of armed vehicles and troops in their best uniforms. Few adults had attended and their audiences were mainly silent children who were rewarded with small bags of boiled sweets. After dark there had been firework displays but the only watchers were the usual handful of local cooperators and people directly employed by the Russians. Their names had been noted by local resistance men and women.

Shortly after midnight the leaflets had been distributed street by street to every household and they were still being distributed when the first distant thuds of the explosives were clearly audible. The leaflets had, for the first time, given the names of the resistance leaders. The text was short but explicit.

## TO EVERY CITIZEN OF GREAT BRITAIN

1. You will not attend your place of work until you are told to do so by a broadcast on 330 metres. This is the old Radio 2 wavelength on your radio. A voice you will recognise is the only voice you will obey. The broadcast will be made on the day concerned at 6 p.m.

2. The illegal occupying forces will attempt to intimidate you into breaking this strike. If you value your freedom and your children's future you will not give in to their pressures. They will make arrests and take revenge on the civil population but they cannot arrest the whole population.

3. Any man or woman cooperating voluntarily with the occupying power will be severely dealt with by the resistance.

4. Our country has been turned into a vast slave camp where men and women have no choice, no freedom and are daily humiliated. This will only cease when the occupying power realises that we shall never cooperate with them.

5. There are tens of thousands of brave men and women in the

266

resistance who daily risk their lives to defend your freedoms, do not let them down. Your courage, your loyalty, your spirit can and will end our enslavement. You are not alone and your sacrifices are not unnoticed. There is no street in Britain that does not have its resistance man or woman. They miss nothing and they have long memories.

6. If you are still not convinced that the occupying powers are both ruthless and merciless you will see them in action in the next few weeks. Let those actions speak for themselves.

7. In World War II Sir Winston Churchill said he could offer only 'Blood, sweat and tears'. Not even in those grim days when the Soviet Union and Nazi Germany were ALLIES did we have to add 'Torture, slavery, murder' to his list. Only the brutal forces of Moscow have made that necessary.

8. Be strong. Not just for today but tomorrow and all our tomorrows.

Harold Andrews
James Boyle
Joseph Langley
Cameron Davies
Glyn Thomas

All through the early hours of the morning people were roused from their sleep by the Red Army vehicles roaring through the night to the sites of twisted and shattered electricity pylons lying in remote valleys and along hillsides and farmlands difficult of access and difficult to identify in total darkness.

As the reports from all over the country came in to Red Army HQ in Whitehall and Field HQ at Caterham it became clear that not only was this by far the largest and most determined act of defiance they had experienced but that it was going to take weeks, even months, for the damage to be repaired.

Several copies of the resistance leaflet were handed in by cooperators as soon as curfew ended and Smetana was torn between immediate retaliation and holding off for a few days to avoid proving the document's charges of brutality well-founded. Moscow had solved his problem in a matter of minutes. The generals were now in charge and martial law would be declared. Workers would be taken forcibly to their places of work and if they refused to work hostages would be taken and executed on the spot.

A Red Army officer had been allocated to major works or groups of smaller plants and the army lorries had been sent to round up the workers on the payrolls. Even the slightest reluctance to board the lorries was met with clubbing and rough handling.

But the problem of making unwilling workers work was virtually insurmountable at large plants. A handful of men refusing to carry out their duties could leave whole production lines stagnant.

Officers called together groups of fifty at a time and in halting English read them the declaration of martial law and the consequences of disobedience.

It wasn't until 3 p.m. that the first executions took place, but by 5 p.m. several hundred men and 40 women had been shot in front of their workmates. But the hostages taken were the openly defiant ones whose noncooperation was the cause of the hold-ups and when their bodies lay in pools of blood there was no one available with the skill or experience to take their places. The sullen, angry faces of the remaining workers led to officers calling for reinforcements and in some cases to dismissing the workers until the following day's morning shift.

The following day the chaos was worse. The brutal killing, the insistence that it was watched by the workers themselves had had its effect. Even what was almost three years of Soviet occupation had not bred the fear that had subdued Soviet workers after decades of merciless brutality.

Soviet technicians had been brought in to get production going at major plants but it was pointless. Men and women simply made gestures of working and lines halted from minor sabotage every ten minutes or so.

After four days of turmoil Maljutin had broadcast in Russian on TV and radio with his words translated sentence by sentence. It was a mixture of appeal to workers for cooperation for their own good and the threat of deportation in large numbers if the cooperation was not forthcoming.

After two further days had passed with no improvement Red Army units took random hostages. Not only workers but people just walking in the streets. Soldiers with submachine guns bundled their victims onto army and civilian lorries and drove them away.

The hostages were taken to Portsmouth where four Soviet troopships were waiting for them. Even at that late stage there were hostages who were shocked at the brutality and indifference of the Red Army soldiers. But the Red Army had carried out similar functions in a dozen countries around the world. And they had carried out similar tasks in the Soviet Union against their own citizens. The Red Army carried out the orders of its masters in the Kremlin, knowing full well that they would be executed or sent to a slave-labour camp themselves if they showed even the slightest compassion for their victims.

The night the three transports sailed ground-to-ground missiles destroyed completely the Red Army HQ in the old War Ministry buildings. Smetana's HQ at the Savoy Hotel blazed all night and in Birmingham, Glasgow, Manchester, Newcastle, Cardiff and London individual Red Army units were fired on by single missiles. There were over 2000 Soviet deaths and many more severely injured. And all night and the following day Red Air Force troop-carriers droned in to every airstrip and airport in the country bringing more and more re-inforcements.

As on every day of the General Strike every household tuned in to the two wavelengths of the old Radio 2, switching from one to the other. On the tenth day on 909 kHz listeners picked up the hum of a carrier wave at 5.58 p.m.

There had been much speculation as to whose voice it would be. At 6 p.m. precisely the music started and even before the cries of seagulls people smiled, and then they heard that familiar voice. 'I hope that most of you will remember the signature tune of "Desert Island Discs". It used to be on the wavelength of Radio 4 and I wish that I was about to introduce another guest and his eight records. Sadly that cannot be, for the moment. I have been asked to tell you that the General Strike is now over. You can go back to your work tomorrow morning if you so wish. You have seen the brutality of the Soviet Army. The same brutality experienced by ordinary people in East Berlin, Poland, Hungary, Czechoslovakia, Afghanistan and many other countries. You have also seen that the Soviet occupying power cannot run this country without your cooperation.

'The resistance will be continued vigorously by the resistance forces themselves. You have played your part and they have taken new strength from your courage and your cooperation. Rest assured that the brutality will be avenged day by day as the forces of freedom gather against these aggressors.

'I am speaking to you from outside Britain which is itself a sign that we are not forgotten or abandoned by the rest of the world. The world may seem very dark to you at the moment but it will not stay that way ... like our resistance leaders said ... tomorrow will come. This is Roy Plomley speaking. Goodnight and God bless.'

All over the free world detailed reports of the Russian brutalities had been front-page news and the main item in radio and TV news broadcasts. Moscow had fallen into the trap and issued an angry denial of beatings and deportations, claiming that the stories were complete fabrications by Washington.

The following day Washington had released a mass of still photographs that showed only too clearly what had been happening. Moscow responded that the photographs were posed and faked, and then the special media section that had been set up in New York released film and tape to the TV stations with translations of the sound tracks that indicated painfully clearly the distress and pain of the civilians being brutalised and the Russian ships loading their prisoners and casting off. None of it could have been faked, the names on the hulls of the Soviet ships were clear enough and four days later sound tapes were made available of tapped phone calls between Soviet officials and Red Army officers and the units they controlled. There were interviews with eye-witnesses that were sadly and patently authentic.

Questions were raised angrily in every European parliament and assembly. Even governments that were not pro-Western had sent official protests to Moscow. Latin America, the Arab countries, India, China and Japan included.

The governments of all the Scandinavian countries other than Finland introduced bans on trade with the Soviet Union and its satellites and were followed by the Netherlands, Belgium, Italy, Greece, Spain and Saudi Arabia. Portugal, Ireland, Turkey, Canada, Australia and New Zealand closed their own embassies in Moscow and sent the Soviet Embassies in their own countries packing.

A week later France and Germany withdrew their Ambassadors from Moscow and finally made clear the anger of their own people.

Lights burned in the Kremlin all through the night as accusations of incompetence and mismanagement were angrily made or refuted. The Kremlin seemed to have lost its magic touch. For years it had got away with every adventure it had tried. In Africa, the Gulf States, South America, Afghanistan, Poland, it had flouted international opinion and got away with it. Not just succeeded beyond the Kremlin's wildest hopes but with virtually no hand lifted against them apart from the Americans. And the Americans with their export bans on grain shipments and high-technology had been undermined without a second thought by their so-called friends or allies. The grain had come from Argentina, the technology from France and Germany. And to cap it all the Soviet Union had once more made its point. The capitalists would trade with anyone. Money and trade were more important than freedom, especially other people's freedom.

They not only traded but their governments and bankers offered cheap and extended credit into the bargain. The Soviet bloc owed the West so much money that their creditors daren't call their bluff anywhere in the world. All the theories about the inevitable collapse of capitalism were being fulfilled. The men in the Kremlin could afford to ignore the parlous state of its own industrial and agricultural economics. The West were obligingly ready to plug the holes, not only with their own products but virtually with their own money too. And meantime the Soviet economy could be geared to a war machine that made war unnecessary. An overwhelming superiority that made war pointless. The dominoes would just fall one by one. A gentle push, a frown or a snarl from the Kremlin, and they came into line, whether it was abandoning their nuclear missiles or ignoring the Americans' efforts to control Soviet aggression around the world. Who cared after the first few months what was happening in Afghanistan? Who cared who was being deposed or murdered in Massawa or Addis Ababa even if they did control the Red Sea and part of the Indian Ocean? Who could even point out on a map which country was Cambodia, or Vietnam, or Kampuchea?

Nobody in the Kremlin had said that it was all too good to be true. It *was* true and it was just a question of time before the rest of the world called it a day and gave up the grinding, exasperating, fruitless struggle.

And now, suddenly, everything had changed. Even in

the Soviet Union itself there were strikes, protests against living conditions, protests against the Gulag even, and a subtle upgrading of the standards of the protests against the State. But it was the reaction to the situation in Britain that amazed and shocked them. They had done nothing there that they hadn't done in a dozen different countries. Why the uproar about the British? No government in Europe had had a good word to say for Britain and the British three or four years ago. Why the furore now? What was so special about the British?

Despite all the internal arguments they were determined to continue to control the British. The people didn't matter, they had nothing to offer anyone, but that small group of islands sat in command of the North Atlantic, barring the American way to Europe and the Baltic. If it was necessary they would wipe the British out. Transport the remnants to east of the Urals and colonise with Soviet families.

Day after day and night after night the arguments raged but no final decisions were made. There was a missing piece in the jigsaw. Like ancient philosophers they waited for a sign. A sign that would tell them which way to go. Not even vaguely did the thought enter the mind of any member of the Politburo that what they had done and were doing in Britain had destroyed a myth that they themselves had planted and cultivated for decades. The myth of 'It couldn't happen here'. It had been promulgated cleverly and remorselessly by Soviet sympathisers in Europe for decades. What happened in Warsaw, Prague and Kabul were special and different. It couldn't happen to you. Poles, Czechs and Afghans knew that it could, but they were used to that sort of thing. It was part of their history. And they were a bit like pretty girls who wore tight sweaters and got raped. They'd asked for it. French, Germans, Italians, Dutchmen and Britons were in a different league. Or had been, once upon a time.

# 22

Lev Savalev stood looking through the gap in the curtains. He was naked. The false dawn was beginning to darken as he looked out towards the gardens of Buckingham Palace. He had taken the penthouse suite at the top of the Rossiya Hotel. A couple of years back they had taken down the London Hilton signs when they took over the hotel as apartments for senior Soviet advisers.

The Hon. Daphne Mather was naked too on the ornate circular bed, her long legs apart. But Savalev had had enough. He was due at Heathrow in five hours time and it was going to be a one way journey. He walked over to the bed and lit a cigarette from her packet.

'When did he tell you, Lev?'

'Three days ago.'

'What reason did he give?'

Savalev shrugged. 'He doesn't have to give reasons. If he says go then I go.'

'Why do you think he's sending you back?'

'I'm bloody sure why. The military are making a worse cock-up than we did. Smetana hopes that when I get back I can convince them that he should be in charge again, or at least that any black marks he got before will be rubbed out.'

'What will you do in Moscow?'

'God knows. They'll probably send me back to that ghastly training camp again.'

274

'They won't send you to the Gulag or anything frightful like that?'

'I shouldn't think so. But I'm too out of touch to know what the bastards are thinking.'

'What does Gulag mean in Russian? Is it a place or what?'

Savalev smiled. 'It's a lot of places. It's the initials of an organisation – *Glavnoe Upravlenie Ispravi-telno-trudovikh lagerei*. It means the Main Administration of Corrective Labour Camps. And it's administered by the KGB.'

'Where is it?'

'Gulag camps are all over the Soviet Union. There's over fifty. Maybe sixty by now.'

'How many people are in the camps?'

'Only a top man in the Gulag organisation could give an accurate figure but it'll be about two and a half million actual criminals and around ten million politicals.'

'Ten million! Christ Almighty. What the hell have they done?'

'They're enemies of the State.'

'What does that mean?'

'They have criticised the regime or the system.'

She looked at his face. 'Poor old Lev. It's terrible.'

'Why do you say that?'

'You're worse off than we are. It's unbelievable. Why do people stand for it? Why don't they complain?'

'Because they don't want to go to the Gulag themselves.'

'Is Smetana still out of favour?'

Savalev gave a short laugh. 'Honey, *he's* out of favour, the generals are out of favour. Everybody's out of favour. According to Smetana, being posted to this country is reckoned to be only one step better than being sent to Siberia. You can't win in this dump.'

'Why don't you just do a bunk?'

'What's that mean ... do a bunk?'

'Run away. Go into hiding. Just don't go back.'

'And do what for Christ's sake?'

'You know I can never understand why you Russians are always saying "For God's sake" and "For Christ's sake". You don't believe in God so why go on about him?'

'I guess we're being absorbed by you bastards.'

'Oh come off it, Lev. You've had a good time here. Living like a millionaire – screwing every girl you fancied. What more could a guy want?'

Savalev stubbed out his cigarette. 'You wouldn't understand, honey.'

She took his hand and slid it up between her legs. 'Are you going to do it again? Just for Auld Lang Syne.'

And Savalev was enough of a gentleman, or a lecher, to stretch out alongside her on the bed and pull her to him.


There was an official letter waiting for Savalev at Sheremetyevo. His old rooms were available and he would report as soon as possible to Dzerzhinski Square. He was relieved. It didn't look as if it was going to be as bad as he feared.

The following day at KGB HQ there was no red carpet but no recriminations either. He was given a few days leave and then was to join the team investigating the mounting subversion inside the Soviet Union.

He had gone to draw his rations from the Bureau of Passes and it had been Anna who came for his coupons. She smiled. 'I heard you were coming back, Lev. How did you like it in London?'

'Just needed you there to make it perfect, sweetheart.'

She laughed. 'That wasn't what I heard.'

'Never listen to Foreign Ministry gossip, it's always unreliable.'

'It wasn't Foreign Ministry. Anyway. We've got fresh supplies of all fruit except strawberries and raspberries. Beef, chicken, geese. Both grades of caviar and plenty of cheeses.'

'You choose for me, Anna. And choose things you like too.'

She smiled up at him. A knowing smile. 'I'm married, Lev. Didn't you know?'

'So what? Who is he anyway?'

'He's a film-script writer and he's very nice.'

'You still in your same room?'

'Yes. We're trying to do an exchange to get an extra room.'

'When can I see you?'

'I told you, I'm married.'

'Don't be silly. Come to my place.'

'Have you still got your old apartment?'

'Yes. I moved in last night. Tell old Lemontev that you don't feel well and come back with me.'

'I couldn't risk it, Lev.'

'Come off it, kid. You wouldn't be still working here if you weren't being screwed.'

She hesitated. 'I'll come when the place closes. My husband's in Minsk for a few days. But it can't be a regular thing.'

Savalev smiled. 'Of course not, honey. Two or three times a week'll be fine.'

She laughed. 'You are a bastard, Lev. You've got plenty of single girls you can screw.'

'See you later, kid.'

She nodded and he leaned forward over the wooden counter and kissed her before he walked out.

A plate with triangles of Georgian cheese, two plums and a spoonful of black caviar lay tilted to one side on the bed between them.

As Savalev scraped caviar onto the corner of a *blini* he said, 'Tell me about your fellow. What's his name?'

'Josef. And he's handsome and young, and he's very talented.'

Savalev grinned. 'He'd have to be to keep you satisfied, madame.'

'I don't mean like that, you idiot, although ...'

Savalev reached out and cupped one of her breasts. 'Don't get huffy, it was only a joke between old friends. Did you miss me?'

'No. There's always plenty of offers to do what you want to do.'

'What's he doing in Minsk?'

'That's where the film company is. He's there for a week or ten days every month. Why are you taking the plate away ...'

But her complaint was stifled by his mouth on hers and her lithe young body responded eagerly to his.

When it was over he lay back looking up at the ceiling, his hand stroking her thigh. 'Tell me what's been happening in Moscow while I've been away.'

'How long have you been away now?'

'Just over two years. Two years three or four months.'

'What do you want to know? Didn't you get *Izvestia* and *Pravda* in London?'

'I mean the gossip. Who's screwing who, and who's getting stabbed in the back.'

'Your old boss Podgorny is sleeping with the girl who had the lead part in *Tomorrow's Dream*. Old Tkachev is sleeping with one of our delivery boys who is also sleeping with Karov. Tkachev would be furious if he knew but Karov also has a boy who paints scenery for the Bolshoi. Ustinov's son is taking drugs and is screwing Orlov's daughter and is going to end up in the Gulag for sure. Then ...'

'Tell me what else you know about Podgorny.'

'What kind of things?'

'Bad things of course. What else?'

'He's in trouble. Something to do with dissidents, subversion, enemies of the State or whatever you call them.'

'What about them?'

'They've been organising strikes. One lasted a week. And one was at the atomic plant at Chelyabinsk. Somebody sabotaged something important. Turned off a valve.'

'How did you find this out?'

'He sleeps with the film-star and her husband visits me. He's jealous of Podgorny but he daren't do anything about him. Podgorny hinted to Natasha that her husband could end up in the Gulag if he tried to interfere. He's a real bastard but I expect you know that.'

'Do you tell your husband about these things?'

'No. He isn't interested, and if he knew half what goes on he'd be suspicious about me.'

'Will you stay the night?'

'Is that what you want?'

'Yes.'

'Will you do something for me if I stay all night?'

'What do you want?'

'Petrol coupons and a travel permit.'

'How many and where to?'

'As many as you can get, and as wide a permit as you can get.'

'I haven't got coupons yet but you can syphon a tankful out of my car tomorrow morning. You'll have to specify places on the permit. Where do you want to go to?'

'It isn't for me.'

'Who's it for?'

'A guy who gets me dresses and underwear.'

Savalev laughed. 'You cheeky bitch. He'll have to give destinations and stop-over points. And nothing down near the China border. I couldn't get that for myself.'

'I'll give you a list of the places when I come here tomorrow ... oh, Lev ... not again, already.'

Orlov had flown back to Moscow from the official opening

of a new exhibition at the Hermitage. If there was one aspect of Russian art that bored Orlov it was ikons, and opening an exhibition of ikons in Leningrad was his idea of wasted time and a wasted journey. But the French ambassador was to be there and he wanted a word with him in private. But he was going straight from Sheremetyevo to the new *dacha* he had had built near the writers' colony at Peredelkino.

He cursed to himself as he saw Fomenko waiting for him on the tarmac, an elderly woman standing just behind him.

'What is it, Fomenko? My car's waiting. I'm out of circulation for a couple of days.'

'I want a word with you before you leave, Prime Minister. It's important and urgent.'

'Who's that wretched woman with the glasses?'

'She's Professor Piatkova, a specialist historian.'

'What the hell is she doing here?'

'A letter was found on your desk this morning. I thought it was maybe a crank letter. I sent it across to the KGB. They passed it to the professor. She works in their evaluation section. She made an urgent report. They phoned me and sent her over. I think you should have a word with her.'

'Can't you deal with it for God's sake?'

'I can. But I advise you to see it. I've taken over an office here. We could use that.'

Orlov sighed, his face clearly showing his irritation.

'Let's go then. Ten minutes. No longer.'

Fomenko had taken over the VIP reception suite and he had signalled for the woman to wait as he opened the door of the inner room for Orlov to go through.

As Orlov sat heavily in one of the leather armchairs he said, looking at his watch, 'Right now. What's it all about?'

Fomenko took a plastic folder from his case and handed it to Orlov who started reading the letter without even removing it from the folder.

He read it slowly and carefully, then with his thumb and

forefinger he lifted it out by one corner and started to read it again.

When he had finished he slid it back inside the folder and looked across at the mural on the wall facing him. It was a painting of Red Square at dusk with a watery moon and a layer of snow. All blues and greys, the History Museum silhouetted against the smoky sky. He turned to look at Fomenko.

'It's just the work of a crank. Some lunatic who can't get a Moscow residence permit.'

'You'd better hear what the professor has to say. She says there are significant phrases.'

Orlov picked the folder up again and looked it over again. It wasn't typed, it was printed.

## AN OPEN LETTER TO YEVGENI ILYICH ORLOV, PRIME MINISTER OF THE SO-CALLED UNION OF SOVIET SOCIALIST REPUBLICS

As the appointed (not elected) leader of the Communist Party we hold you responsible for the dictatorship of the self-appointed élite who are abusing the toiling masses of Russia.

As leader of the Bolsheviks who gained power by force, and illegally, with the aid of money from our then enemy, the German government, we require you to take urgent steps to rectify the historic wrongs that have been perpetrated on the Russian people.

We require you to implement the following programme:

1. Freedom of Speech and association of all workers in political parties and independent trades unions.

2. Free elections by secret ballot supervised by independent bodies.

3. The liberation of all political prisoners.

4. The immediate abolition of all special privileges seized by Communist Party members at all levels.

5. The abolition of the secret police (KGB – Komitet Gosudarstvennoy Bezopasnosti).

6. Freedom of travel internally and externally for all citizens.

7. Independence for all so-called Soviet Republics and countries in the Warsaw Pact.

8. Publication of this open letter in all national media.

Unless we see immediate evidence that our demands are to be met active steps will be taken to obtain justice for all citizens.

The Second Provisional Revolutionary Committee

Orlov sighed as he looked up from the folder. 'Send her in then. Send the stupid bitch in.'

Fomenko brought the woman into the room and pointed to the chair opposite Orlov.

'Tell the Prime Minister what you told me.'

The woman looked at Orlov as if she wanted his approval so he nodded and folded his arms aggressively.

'Comrade Prime Minister, the description of this organisation ... its name ... the Second Provisional Revolutionary Committee ... has a special significance ... you will recall, I'm sure, that the First Provisional Revolutionary Committee was the name of the counter-revolutionary organisation set up by the naval clerk, Petrichenko, with the insurgents on the battleship *Petrovpavlovsk* in 1921, when the Baltic fleet mutinied against the Communist Party at the naval base at Kronstadt.'

'I wouldn't argue with you, Professor. Go on. What's all this about the party being funded by the Germans?'

'That refers to the old original allegations made in 1917 that Lenin and the party propaganda campaign had been funded by the German government.'

'Did anybody believe it?'

'There were letters produced from Comrade Lenin to two men named Haniecki and Kolovskii acknowledging receipt of the money. And the German Foreign Minister,

Kühlmann, wrote a report to the Kaiser about funding Lenin that is still in the German archives.'

'Anything else?'

'Yes. The wording of the demands is based on the exact words used by the original committee.'

'So what does all that prove? That the lunatic who sent this letter is a historian or what?'

'I think it all adds up to the people concerned wanting you to take it seriously.'

'Nothing more to say?'

'No, Comrade Prime Minister.'

Orlov nodded dismissal and the woman left the room closing the door behind her. Orlov looked at Fomenko and said icily, 'Anything else, my friend? Would the KGB like me to declare a national emergency?'

Fomenko shrugged. 'I thought you should see it as soon as possible.'

Orlov stood up. 'Tell them to bring my car round.'

It was exactly a week later that the first blow fell and Orlov realised that he had misjudged the situation.

In the Saturday issue of *Pravda* the open letter appeared in full. It was in the centre of the football and racing commentaries. An anonymous phone call from an observant paper-seller had first brought it to the KGB's attention. A KGB team had gone straight round to the printing presses and within ten minutes they had traced the names and addresses of the layout man and the proof-reader for that particular page.

One lived near the *Sokolniki* metro station. The proof-reader lived near the second-hand bookshop in *Ulitsa Kachalov*. The layout man's room was empty. No furniture, nothing. They went through the routine of finger printing and took a dozen of his neighbours for questioning. Nobody had seen him for ten days.

The proof-reader was in hospital. He had been knocked down by a hit-and-run car driver four days before and was still in a coma.

The insertion in *Pravda* had not been mentioned by any of the media. It was obvious that tens of thousands of people must have read it but there seemed to be little response. The KGB had logged 40 calls about it and *Izvestia* had received letters and calls, but fewer than a hundred. Of those callers who gave names and addresses some, when interviewed, found the advertisement strange and meaningless, others had wondered why a satirical piece had been put in the sports section.

The blow fell when the letter was discussed in detail on Voice of America and *Deutsche Welle*. Most Western newspapers gave mention, reproducing the text, both as a news item and a feature.

Neither Orlov nor the rest of the Politburo lost much sleep once it had proved to have had little effect on the population.


The old man looked up from the leather-bound copy of *War and Peace*. His eyes were on the young man's face.

'Ten roubles. No more.'

'Ten?'

'Ten.'

'I'll take it.'

The old man reached inside the cash register and took out a ten rouble note, handing it across the untidy piles of books on the wooden counter. As the young man took the money the old man nodded.

Josef walked to the end of the shop through the bead curtains and up the steep narrow stairs. He turned right, along a short corridor and knocked on the door that had a typed card printed alongside it on the wall. The card said

'Dom Knigi Bookshop, 44 Kveshchatik Street, Kiev (Second-hand department).'

For a moment he waited but there was no response from inside the room. He opened the door cautiously and looked inside. Every wall in the room was lined with shelves and every shelf was packed with books. The man called Oktyabr was sitting in the bay of the window in a wicker chair. He was looking out of the window exhaling the blue smoke from a long thin cigar. 'Come in, Josef,' he said, without turning his head.

Josef closed the door, looking round for somewhere to sit. He moved a carton of paperbacks from the end of a worn old-fashioned settee. A cloud of dust rose as he sat down.

The man in the window turned his head, smiling. 'Did you get your work done?'

'Most of it.'

'Did you get the photographs?'

'Yes.'

'Have you got them here?'

Josef unlocked his soft leather brief-case and took out a large brown envelope, handing it to the man as he put out his hand.

One by one Oktyabr looked at the photographs and Josef watched him. He guessed that he was 50 or maybe a little older. His dark black hair was smoothed back over his head like pre-war film stars had it. He was handsome in a strangely forbidding way. The dark tanned skin and the narrow black moustache gave him an old-fashioned look. His fingers were long and his nails well-manicured. His blue shirt was well-cut and modern and his brown trousers were tucked into soft leather cavalry boots. Josef had never met another man like Oktyabr. He knew so little about him but he knew that he would gladly risk his life if the man said it was necessary.

He seemed to have no doubts. Complete self-assurance. On occasions when he had brought bad news the man showed no sign of displeasure or anger and when he brought news of success, no elation. He would give explanations if they were asked for but the explanations were brief and sparse. Enough to convince but no more. There was no element of asking for help, no attempt to persuade. To Josef the man was a hero. But a rather frightening hero. There was a power and a tension inside Oktyabr that seemed only just under control.

As Oktyabr pushed the last of the prints back into the envelope he looked across at the young man.

'D'you know a man named Savalev? Lev Savalev.'

Josef shook his head. 'Afraid not.'

'Ever heard the name?'

'No. What does he do?'

'Will you be able to film at the factory without being seen?'

'If I can have that place at the top of the lift shaft, yes. I can use both cameras on remote control. The pictures won't be perfect.'

'Newsreel standard?'

'Oh yes.'

'Do you know the little passage by the church on Andreevsky Spusk?'

'No. Is that the church on the hill?'

'That's the one.' He took a key from his shirt pocket. 'There's a house in the passage way with a blue door and a geranium in the window. Let yourself in with this key and I'll see you there in an hour.'

'Will anyone be at the house?'

'No.'

They had gone out for a meal at a restaurant and then walked back to the rooms by the church. The man seemed relaxed and Josef plucked up the courage to ask the question that worried him.

'Is the strike a real strike?'

'Yes.'

'But they'll put them down. They'll send in the soldiers.'

'Yes. Of course.' The milky blue eyes were unblinking. When Josef didn't reply the man said, 'But they'll learn some lessons.'

'Who will?'

'The authorities. The Bolsheviks.'

'And the men?'

'They'll learn some lessons too.'

'What lessons?'

'That they can cease to be slaves if they have some courage.'

'Do they have that much courage.'

'They had it against the Germans.'

'But they were our enemies. We were at war with them.'

'Would you like a drink?'

'No thanks. I don't drink.'

'Why not?'

'My father was a drunk.'

The man poured himself a vodka and sat back in his chair. For a moment he glanced towards the window as if he were trying to decide something. Then he turned to look at the young man.

'My father was a general. A Red Army general. He fought for them in the civil war. A great commander and a devoted Party supporter.' He paused. 'Do you know about the purges? Stalin's purges?'

Josef shrugged. 'Only that they happened. As Khrushchev said in his speech to the Presidium whenever that was.'

'Try and remember this. In 1937 and 1938 Stalin had murdered three out of five marshals, 13 out of 15 army commanders, 57 out of 85 corps commanders, 110 out of 195 divisional commanders, 220 out of 406 brigade commanders, and 11 Vice Commissars of War, and 75 out of 80 members of the Supreme Military Council. In percentages that amounted to 90 per cent of all generals and 80 per cent of all colonels. And the purges were still going on when the Germans attacked us. My father was one of the generals.'

'That must have been terrible.'

'That's why a small country like Finland kicked the shit out of us for months in the World War. That's why we lost twenty million dead. Just because one madman was scared of his own nation.'

'And that's why you do all this?'

'Not quite.'

'What other reason?'

'You've heard of Vorkuta?'

'The coal-mining area?'

'Yes. What else do you know about Vorkuta?'

'Nothing.'

'My mother was very much younger than my father. When the NKVD came for him they were in bed. It was two o'clock in the morning. They kicked the door down. There were six of them. They beat him with rubber truncheons in front of my mother. Then they held him. Made him watch while they beat her too. She was twenty. Then they raped her in front of him. All of them. When they had finished with her they shot him. My mother was sent with thousands of others to the slave-camp at Vorkuta.'

There were tears on Josef's pale face and his voice quavered as he spoke. 'It seems like a nightmare. I'm so sorry. So sorry.'

'I was born in that slave-camp eight months later. I grew up there. There were tens of thousands of prisoners there working as slaves and treated like animals by the guards. The guards could do what they liked. Starve you, beat you, kill you. And they did all that.

'But after the war a different kind of prisoner came. The officers from Vlasov's and Krasnov's armies who had been taken prisoner by the Germans. My mother died of a fever and starvation in 1946. One of the officers kind of adopted me. Protected me. Taught me things. Encouraged me to stay alive.

'In 1948 there was an uprising led by the Red Army officers. They took over the guards' weapons and five thousand broke out of the camp. They were intending to start a partisan war in the forests. I was with them. I was 11 then. When we got out onto the tundra Moscow sent in Red Air Force planes. They shot us to pieces. About 50 of us survived. I was one of them.

'We were sent back to Vorkuta. I was beaten and they used me sexually, but I survived. In 1950 the communists were being beaten by the Americans in Korea and Moscow decided to liquidate the slave-workers in the camp at Kolyma. There were over a million in those camps. When they started the killings word got back to Vorkuta and there was another revolt and break-out. Properly organised by a Colonel Antonov.' He paused and then said, 'I escaped.'

Josef sighed. 'What happened to you?'

The man half-smiled. 'I'm here.'

'What do you do? In Moscow.'

'I lecture at the university. You know that.'

'But you spend very little time there. How do you get away with it?'

'There are ways.' The man stood up. 'You'd better get some sleep. So had I.'

# 23

Wheeler stood alone, in the Oval Office, gazing out of the window and seeing nothing. He had been tempted in the early hours of the morning to say a prayer. He wasn't sure whether it was to be a prayer for guidance, or a blessing on a decision already made. As a man he was in no way a believer, but as President he had to attend church services from time to time. His only concern had always been to disperse his favours equitably over both Protestants and Catholics and the rest of them. But despite the solely official and political capacity in which he attended, he was always fleetingly impressed by what went on. He envied people who could believe. It relieved a man of a lot of responsibility. Their way the buck needn't stop on the Oval Office desk, it could be passed on and up.

When his aide showed in Brodsky and Curnow he came back to earth and politics, and there was no longer that uncomfortable feeling of faint indecision. It was back to politics and decision, the things he was good at.

He nodded. 'Morning, Mr Secretary, morning, General. Make yourselves comfortable.'

General Curnow was what a general should look like, bulky, tanned, old-fashioned enough to still have a crew-cut, his uniform bulging with good solid muscle.

When they were settled in the chairs facing his desk Wheeler sat down himself.

'We've been over this so many times. We've heard the

experts' views for and against. On paper we shouldn't have any doubts. I'm not saying I have any doubts, but I want one last look with you two. Maybe it will help if I say that I'm convinced that it's the right thing to do, but I want to make sure that there's no negative aspect that we haven't weighed up. So if either of you has any second thoughts or your advisers have had second thoughts, now's the time to say so. There won't be another chance. When I've pressed the button I can't unpress it.' He leaned back in his chair. 'Mr Secretary, you go first.'

'Well, Mr President, there have been no second thoughts, nothing has changed, neither facts nor opinions. As you know, sir, on paper the sums always come out in our favour. However, I think we have to bear in mind that we are, in the end, dealing with people under extreme pressure, and logic doesn't always apply in those circumstances. We can look at the pressures we propose applying. We can imagine how we should react ourselves under those pressures. We can evaluate how more aggressive leaders would react, but we still end up with men, not professors of logic or historians. And the men we are concerned with are already riven with rivalry and dissent. They are men who already see their power being undermined in their own country. Men whose attitudes to peace and war are not only different from our own but different from one another. That is the only area where we could go wrong.'

Wheeler nodded. 'I agree. Let's come back to that in a moment. General, your views.'

'No change in the Pentagon view, Mr President. Faced ourselves with the pressures we intend applying to Moscow we should have no sane choice but to go along with the scenario. In solely military terms they have no choice. We and our allies are overwhelmingly superior in every aspect. Only a military incompetent could advise them to challenge us. No one military man would be called on to give an opinion on a thing like this, they would have to consult at least twenty or thirty top men. I have no doubt they would not recommend challenging us. Their military people are competent and experienced. They may be belligerent but they would not be asked to offer an opinion on anything other than whether they could guarantee success against us. That they could not do, Mr President. And because they are professionals they would not make any such guarantee.'

Wheeler nodded. 'If you were faced with this scenario in reverse what would you tell me?'

'I would tell you, Mr President, that we should be defeated if we fought.'

'And if I told you to fight?'

'Then I should give the necessary orders immediately.'

'Would they be obeyed?'

'I have no doubt, sir, they would be obeyed.'

Wheeler looked at them both. 'So all we have to do is decide if there is any possibility that the Politburo could defy the facts and tell their generals to fight. What are your views on that?'

'I'm sure that if their military were ordered to fight they'd fight, Mr President. Under protest, maybe. And wanting their orders formally and in writing. And I am sure that they would record their own doubts about the outcome.'

Wheeler turned and looked at Brodsky. 'So, Mr Secretary, will the Politburo give those orders despite their generals' warnings?'

'Let's look at what they will be faced with. The so-called Warsaw Pact countries in ferment. Active discontent and some rebellion in the Soviet Union itself. Then the whole of Europe, except Finland, ready to take action. That is a daunting enough prospect in itself. Then if we had to play our last card their worst fears, their nightmares, would be coming true. Almost the whole of the world against them is too much.

'But let us hypothesise that they are equally divided in the Politburo. Half ready to agree, the other half ready to defy us. What then? The hawks will be required to show what they expect to achieve. What can they offer? Only one thing. That before they go down they will have made the rest of the world, us in particular, pay a terrible price. They can offer nothing more.' Brodsky paused. 'That's not much of a prize, Mr President. What can the other side offer. No destruction. No loss of Soviet territory. Their armies and weapons still intact. The opportunity to work out a real disarmament treaty that will allow them to put their resources to civilian production not armaments. And finally a chance to look like the saviours of peace, the creative thinkers. Kudos all round in the Politburo. And ... not insignificantly ... their own lives.'

'Just one snag, Mr Secretary. They can dodge their own internal problems by starting a war. That would bring the country together. Isn't that one of their options?'

'I don't think so, Mr President, for two reasons. First of all they face the situation I described. Inevitable defeat despite the destruction they cause us. Secondly, even if they ignore that aspect they still have to deal with their internal problems. Our solution means that they have help in doing that and no loss of face. Only a handful of people will know why they backed down. Those people have a strong interest in not revealing what they know. If one of them ever did talk he could bring no evidence to substantiate his case because there is none. Not a scrap of paper, even using a code-name wasn't considered secure.'

'Which way will President Orlov lean?'

'Our way.'

'Why so sure?'

'If he goes the other way he's finished whatever happens. The Russian people don't want war and the man who led them into a war would be finished ... whatever the outcome.

Millions of Russians would die on Day One. He's far too shrewd to be the cat's-paw for the generals.

'Apart from that he can be the man who pulls them back from their present adventure. He'd be President for life. Nobody could ever push him aside.'

'Why have you suggested Vienna as the meeting place?'

'It's only a short journey from Moscow.'

'Is that the only reason?'

Brodsky shifted in his seat. 'I thought it might be a fitting place. It was the place where Khrushchev bullied Kennedy when he was barely in the White House.'

'Forget it. The only people who will remember that will see it for what it is. Petty revenge. Where else?'

'Switzerland?'

'No. It stinks of the United Nations and the old League.'

'Ireland?'

'Fine. But not Dublin. Would the Irish go along with it?'

'They haven't been asked. It would mean extending the "need to know" area again.'

'You go then, Joe. As quietly and unofficially as you can. I'll speak to their Prime Minister today. I'll not tell him what it's about. Just that it's top level and I want him to see you and agree it if possible.'

'Right, Mr President. Can I wait while you call him?'

'Sure.'

Wheeler reached for the phone. 'Get me the Prime Minister of the Republic of Ireland wherever he is ... what ... well ask them to get him out of bed for God's sake.'

An hour later Brodsky was air-borne with a fighter escort out into the Atlantic which would be replaced by carrier-borne fighters from the aircraft-carriers that were strung out right across the North Atlantic.

Colm O'Brien wasn't an expert angler but he loved the calm and tranquillity, and the beauty of rods and reels. The 30 foot Seamaster was the most expensive purchase he had ever made apart from his house in Dublin, and he still owed the bank just over £4,000 on that. His children had given him a new Hardy rod and a Swedish reel for his birthday, and the family were all due to spend the weekend with him on the boat on Lough Derg until the phone call had come through from Washington that spoiled it all. But they had wanted top security and he had insisted that a boat anchored in the Lough was better than most places. Brodsky was due any time now, his plane had already landed at Shannon, and O'Brien was well aware as he cast the spinner out across the water that several dozen pairs of eyes and binoculars were watching him from the woods and bushes on the banks of the Lough.

O'Brien at 55 still had his carroty red hair, but he had never had the quick temper that was supposed to be a characteristic of red-headed men. He was a calm, dogged man with an amiable nature who had risen to the top of Irish politics with an inevitability that had never been satisfactorily explained by the political commentators. He was both typically Irish and demonstrably not Irish. His aloofness made him aware of the foibles, pettiness and greed of many of his contemporaries, and his Irishness made him understand them. He made judgements in his own mind but found no need to pass on his judgements either in public or in private. After dozens of those schisms and feudings that are the feature of most countries' politics there came a day when the battlefield was suddenly empty and there was nobody there among the corpses but Colm O'Brien. Nobody had been surprised, and few had either cheered or protested when he became Prime Minister. But as the years went by he had healed old wounds and smoothed down ruffled feathers and brought a businesslike managerial character to both parties in the Dail. It was his negotiations with London that had come nearer to solving the Belfast problem than any man before him. There had been no inspiration or great originality to his proposals, he merely said out loud the things that most Irish citizens had always thought but never dared to say. There was a sense of justice about the Irish, provided it wasn't related to history, where their memories could be so easily inflamed by the mischievous by both myth and fact. Colm O'Brien was the first Irish Prime Minister who had the courage to make an offer to the Ulster Protestants that they would have been economically and socially foolish to refuse. It was within a year or eighteen months of final acceptance when the Russians had intervened.

The Russians had behaved as if they had never heard of an Irish problem. There had been no consultation or negotiation. Holders of Irish passports were given a week to leave Britain, and in Belfast the records of the police and the Ulster Defence Force had been confiscated and used to root out all those listed as members of the IRA. Ulster was the only area of the United Kingdom where the Russians had behaved with severity and brutality right from the start, against Roman Catholics and Republicans.

There were many who rejoiced at their ruthlessness. They had solved in two months a problem that had been insoluble for sixty years. If you wanted to be Irish all well and good, provided you were in the Republic of Ireland and not in Britain. When the Irish government had protested their protests had been ignored. The aircraft carrier and battleships in Lough Foyle and Belfast Lough were answer enough. The Russians had done, almost overnight, what the Rev. Ian Paisley could never have achieved in decades. There were nods of approval from many British citizens. It had always been a crazy anomalous situation that the Irish could shoot the British in Ulster while their citizens streamed over to

England from the Republic for abortions, divorces, National Health services, jobs and the dole. The euphoria had not lasted long. Like many a quarrelling couple, time lent a perspective to history that made both parties realise that they missed one another. An ignorant outsider had swept history to one side and the rest of the world had long grown weary of both sides' whining and self-righteousness. Not even to the professional Irishmen in Boston and New York was it more than a nine days' wonder. The western world had its own problems to solve, and there was a certain unhappy logic to the Soviet attitude. Apart from which, their command of the North Atlantic was now virtually complete.

Colm O'Brien had recognised that there were no prizes for anyone in clashing with the Russians, and was relieved in a way that he no longer had that Ulster albatross hanging round his neck. The Americans had kept friendly and continuous contact with Dublin, and O'Brien had raised no objection to either party when both the Russian and United States embassies had almost doubled their staffs. The Soviet diplomats were restricted to a five-mile radius around Dublin and they were under constant surveillance, but most of the diplomatic niceties were observed by both sides.

As he unhooked the spinner from the spiny mouth of yet another striped perch he saw the helicopter coming in over Mountshannon, the little village that he used as his angling base. They were used to the to-ing and fro-ing that his presence caused, and took it in their stride, glad of the extra business that it brought but not prepared to be over-awed by well-known faces and large black limousines.

Then he saw the launch leaving the jetty, heading towards him. The lights were going on in the village and he switched on his navigation lights, going down into the saloon to draw the curtains before switching on the main lighting.

The launch came slowly and neatly alongside the fenders, and he held out his hand to help Brodsky across. When the American was on board O'Brien nodded to the two men in the launch.

'I'll radio when I need you.'

'Right, sir.'

O'Brien turned to look at the American. 'Nice to see you, Joe. I thought we could be more private on the boat, and it can look more like a vacation than business. OK?'

'That's fine, sir. Where shall I put my bag?'

'Leave it here. Have you had a meal?'

'Yes. I ate on the plane.'

'Let's go down and have a drink. Mind your head.'

As O'Brien poured the Jameson Ten Year Old into each of the glasses he said, 'I gather you're in a hurry, so you just fire away, Joe.'

Brodsky smiled. 'I've got to go through a bit of a ritual first, Colm. It really is vital that it's kept on a "need to know" basis so forgive the skirmishing.'

'Sure, my friend. Just start the music.'

'We want to arrange a meeting where nobody except the people at that meeting know what was discussed and agreed. That nobody should know who was at that meeting. And finally that nobody, or as few as possible, should even know that the meeting has ever taken place.'

O'Brien shrugged. 'Sounds possible. I assume you want to hold this meeting in the Republic?'

'Yes.'

'Who will be at the meeting?'

'That's problem number one. I'll tell you if you make it a condition, but I don't want to tell you.' He smiled. 'You don't need to know.'

'No skin off my nose, Joe, but our security people need some idea of where trouble might come from.'

'There's no possibility of any trouble from anywhere. The security is only against people knowing where we are and

298

who we are. We don't want to involve the Gardai or the army or your intelligence people.'

'How many people would be involved in the meeting?'

'About thirty. That would include the principals and the staff.'

'People would be bound to notice a crowd like that anywhere in Ireland.'

'We've got a cover story worked out, Colm.'

'Try me.'

'We should be a film crew shooting for a new feature film.'

O'Brien smiled. 'Not bad. And if they recognise anybody you just claim that they're actors.'

'Something like that.'

'So why didn't you just go ahead and do it? Why involve me?'

'For several reasons. Firstly we wanted you to know, and we wanted your blessing. Secondly we shall need some privileges in landing planes and so on.' He grinned. 'We'd even hoped that a hint could be dropped that we were getting special privileges because there was Irish money invested in the film. Thirdly, if the meeting works, the whole world is possibly going to remember where it took place. We should like it to be in Ireland. We thought you might like it too.'

O'Brien looked down at his glass for several moments and then looked up at Brodsky's face. 'This is direct from the President is it?'

'Yes.' Brodsky smiled. 'I'm just the messenger boy.'

'Tell me something, Joe. You say that if this meeting is a success the world will remember where it took place.' He paused. 'What if it's a failure?'

Brodsky shook his head slowly. 'It won't be a failure. Nobody at the meeting could let it be a failure. They couldn't afford to.'

'You haven't answered my question, Joe. What happens if it's a failure?'

Brodsky sighed. 'I guess we all find out if there *is* a life after death. But it ain't gonna happen, my friend.'

'Where would everybody be coming in ... Shannon?'

'Is there any place we could hire for a week or ten days that's not too far from Shannon?'

'Yes. There's a country mansion not far from here. It's government property. We could hire it to your film company.'

'We need it for two weeks from the last day of next month.'

'That's OK. It's seldom in use. Take it that it's available any time from today at two days' notice.'

'We'll remember your cooperation when it's all over, Colm. We shan't forget your help.'

'I'll light a candle for you, Joe. A big one.'

Brodsky smiled and O'Brien said quietly, 'I'm not joking. I mean it.'

Brodsky nodded. 'I'm sure you do, Colm, I'm sure you do.'


President Wheeler had already seen the film an hour before but he sat with Brodsky and the others in his private room to watch the newsreel. All three networks had it as their lead item.

The film was grainy and the colours debased but it showed clearly enough what they wanted to see. They could see the long shot that showed the main block of the works and the noise of the machine guns was emphasised by the flying glass from the office block windows. It was the big tractor plant just outside Kiev.

A BMD armoured personnel carrier edged its way into the foreground and then another. They turned by the main gates and headed down towards the foundry. The film cut to a mid-shot, obviously later in the day. There were flames waving out of the windows and two T-55 tanks lay abandoned with their tracks hanging loose and the bodies of several crewmen on the ground beside them. Three big T-10 heavy tanks were slowly demolishing the outer chain-link fence around the perimeter. As the leading one smashed its way through, the two others closed in, and the camera adjusted to show four more waiting to follow. For a moment the TV screen flickered, salmon pink then orange that became flames before the film cut again. The next shot showed the smoking debris of the tanks. Unrecognisable as anything other than twisted steel where the missile had blown them apart. Only one body was visible, the flap of its combat jacket flapping slowly in the wind. A map with an arrow came up on the screen and Wheeler leaned forward and switched off the set.

As he leaned back he turned to Brodsky. 'They must really mean it, those men.'

'They do, Mr President. Our people's reports have emphasised that again and again.'

'How did it end?'

'Moscow sent in the Red Air Force. They bombed the whole place to the ground.'

'Did anyone survive?'

'About a dozen got out before the bombing started. They had to be ordered out.'

'Has there been any public reaction in the Soviet Union?'

'The whole area has been cordoned off by the army and the KGB. The only reference to it in the media was that there had been an industrial explosion at the Kiev tractor works. But there are over two million people in Kiev who know what really happened. You can't bottle them up for ever. And Voice of America are using it in tonight's newscasts. It's been transmitted overseas to all press agencies.'

Wheeler sighed. 'They must have fantastic guts those people.'

'And desperation, Mr President. The lid was going to blow off sooner or later, even without our help.'

'I know that all the reports have been saying that for years but I never really believed it would happen.'

'There's more to come.'

Wheeler turned his head to look at Brodsky. 'Our people?'

'No. Theirs and ours. Thousands of theirs and a handful of ours.'

'And what do they hope to get out of it?'

'Some freedom. A chance to run their own lives. To say their own thoughts out loud. Honest judges. No secret police thugs.' He paused. 'The things we take too much for granted.'

During the next seven weeks all leave was cancelled for the Red Army and the KGB. For Orlov and the whole of the Politburo it was a long drawn out nightmare. In the early stages troops had been sent in, battalions at a time, to deal with sabotage of industrial plants and communications but it didn't work as it had always worked before. It wasn't the usual walk-over. People were fighting back. Troops were actually being fired on. Being killed and wounded. Loud-hailers were being used to persuade the conscripts not to fire on their fellow countrymen and in isolated cases they were responding.

Cities and towns were being sealed off irrespective of whether there was unrest or not and units were having to be brought back from the Warsaw Pact countries and even the borders of the Soviet Union itself. In a dozen different locations there was real trouble. Sabotage, strikes, sit-ins and demonstrations but trying to forestall new outrages was stretching resources to breaking-point. Even bombing troublesome towns was considered but the implications were too frightening, and despite a total censorship news of the troubles was leaking to the outside world. And the world was watching.

Slowly the problem receded but it was obvious to the men in the Kremlin that it was not because of the success of their repressive measures, but because the dissidents chose to relax their pressures on the State. And the men in the Kremlin got the message. It wasn't the end of the troubles. It was a warning. More could be arranged if it was necessary.

It was after a long meeting of the senior members of the Politburo that the phone call came through for Orlov. A personal call from President Wheeler. Orlov took it alone in his inner office.

# 24

A small piece appeared in the *Irish Times* about an American film-crew hiring a country house to shoot scenes for a major film about multinationals and their influence on world politics.

The Americans came in on two 747s just after midnight and were taken straight to coaches parked on the airport perimeter. The fighter escort had kept clear of Shannon's Air Control so that they could not be picked up on the radar screens, and the US Navy carriers had stood out to sea awaiting instructions.

They deliberately left the unloading of the lights and cameras and the aluminium cases holding the paraphernalia of a large film-crew until mid-morning where the transfer to the trucks could be seen.

Stanhope House was set in over a hundred acres of its own grounds which were mainly parkland, woods and an ornamental lake. Originally Georgian, the main building had been given its two wings much later. Despite the later additions it was still an elegant building and had been kept in first-class condition by its several owners. Inside, it was now almost wholly Adam, the series of apartments fine examples of the superb decoration. The furniture and fittings delicate and graceful, the Gobelin tapestries setting off beautiful examples of rococo furniture, its gilt and marble as pristine as expert care could make it.

The two opposing American intelligence teams had two days of final rehearsal and set to work the moment they arrived. They had worked together for six months, and were now so steeped in their parts that their antagonism was almost real. A team had been assembled whose knowledge of Soviet politics and the Soviet military was uncanny. Fed by all the diplomatic and intelligence sources likely to be available to Moscow they competed daily with their counterparts who represented the United States. Seldom meeting together they had each been given daily situations to which they must respond as if they were the actual Russians or Americans they represented. The evaluation teams worked round the clock checking, comparing and assessing the two opposing sets of reactions to the various scenarios presented to them. After the first two months it was reckoned that their responses were almost a hundred per cent accurate, and gradually the Russian team were reacting to world news as if they were in fact the Russians they represented. The quirks and idiosyncrasies of the actual Soviet leaders were taken into account, and it became uncanny how the team's reactions mirrored and forecast the eventual Soviet response of their counterparts to the actual events.

For two weeks before their arrival at Shannon they had been faced daily with the scenario that was about to be tested in real life. Each day minor alterations were in-built until the fine-tuning had allowed every variation in response to be assessed.

The final scenario had been gone over carefully by Wheeler and Brodsky, and on the two remaining days before the meeting Wheeler, and the man who acted as Orlov, had faced one another with only the two interpreters, until there came a point when Wheeler felt that he was getting too familiar with the data and was losing flexibility in his own approach and reactions. He had had enough. There was more adrenalin than blood flowing through his system.

The two teams continued their realistic play-acting but Wheeler had deliberately relaxed before the ordeal to come.

Manchester airport had been closed for two hours before Orlov's plane landed and the helicopter took off scheduled for Belfast. Nobody, either British or Russian had any idea that the President of the USSR had landed in Britain and taken off immediately. The helicopter had landed on the which circle laid out on the lawn in front of Stanhope House and had been cleared by Shannon Air Control as part of the film company's establishment.

The Soviet support team, twelve in all, had flown into Shannon logged as electricians and technical advisors and had passed through customs and immigration as a party rather than as individuals, on O'Brien's personal instructions.

Wheeler had done the courtesies for Orlov. Taking his hand and leading him back to the wing of the house designated for the Soviet team. Orlov made no attempt to disguise his anger and resentment, his face was grey and pallid, his gestures aggressive. Wheeler found himself ticking off the various reaction predictions of his team against those first few minutes of the encounter. They were uncannily correct even if they had no overall significance. President Orlov had insisted that the meeting should start as early as possible the next day, and that there would be no social or diplomatic contact until then. He had also demanded that his security men should be free to examine the wing occupied by the Americans, and Wheeler had refused.

Brodsky and Fomenko had agreed that the meeting should start at nine sharp, and Wheeler, Orlov and the two interpreters had assembled in the small annexe in the main building as the ormolu clock struck the hour.

The two Presidents sat facing each other, their individual interpreters beside them.

Wheeler started his preamble. 'Mr President. There are

306

sixty-three people on my side who know that you and I are meeting here. There are only seven who know the subject of our meeting. I am assuming that you have taken similar security precautions.' He paused for a sign of agreement. There was none and he continued. 'We have gone to great lengths to convince you of our good-will. We have exposed the locations of our missiles and our armed forces. We have shown you that we have the locations of your country's missiles and war machine too. We have given details of every aspect of our capabilities down to the smallest unit and the most routine of weapons. Where we have weaknesses we have exposed them. Even our research and development plans have been openly provided. My only object in all this is so that we can both appreciate the consequences of any armed conflict. You have had time to study my proposals and I anxiously await your response. I should add that although I have neither informed nor asked the approval of my colleagues apart from the Secretary of State I can give a solemn undertaking that our agreement would be faithfully carried out.'

Wheeler stopped talking to await a reply but Orlov just sat there in silence listening to the translation. Wheeler was well aware that Orlov spoke reasonable English. When the interpreter had finished Orlov looked at Wheeler.

'You have been dreaming dreams, President Wheeler. Children's dreams. Women's dreams, where everyone lives happily ever after. We don't live in such a world.'

Wheeler listened carefully as Orlov's words were translated. The words weren't the exact ones they had imagined, but the sense fitted their analysis.

'President Orlov, if that was all you had to say you wouldn't be here. So tell me what you have to tell me.'

'My generals say your analysis of the outcome is wrong. You would not be able to destroy us.'

Wheeler shook his head slowly. 'Your generals are too

307

experienced, too competent to have told you that.' Wheeler noted that they were no longer using the interpreters. Earlier than the team had expected. 'Your top generals are here with you, Mr President. Maybe it would be helpful if they discussed our analysis openly with my people. I'm sure that they would not succumb to the temptation of kidding you, but they certainly wouldn't risk their reputations trying to kid fellow professionals. Or me. How about it?' Wheeler held his breath as he waited for an answer. If Orlov said yes to the proposition it would be the first bad sign.

Orlov shrugged. 'Is that what you want?'

'I just want to establish with you that the parameters I put to you are correct.'

'You couldn't convince me no matter what your people say. They're paid to say what you want them to say.'

'You know that's not true. Not for my fighting generals and not for yours.'

'Your country would be destroyed, President Wheeler.'

'No, President Orlov. Your country would be finished. There wouldn't be a city left standing. We should be severely wounded but we should survive.'

'So why do you start issuing threats to the Soviet Union?'

Wheeler took a deep breath as he arranged the vital, key answer as he opened his mouth to speak.

'Because I know you have to listen this time, President Orlov. Because for the first time in forty years there is a chance we could end the cold war and spend our time and money on making refrigerators instead of cruise missiles and SS20s.'

'What makes you think I have to listen?'

'Because you've gone too far in too many places. Even if we took no action against you right now you are being eaten away. In Poland, Czechoslovakia, Hungary, East Germany, Rumania the pressures on Moscow for independence are increasing every day. Not just a few dissident poets and writers, but men who are prepared to fight for their independence. You have active dissidents in the Soviet Union, together with food and consumer goods problems directly due to the arms race. You will know, as I know, that your occupation of Britain has turned your friends in Europe into enemies. I am offering you far more than you deserve. You're like a gambler who has put all his money and winnings on the turn of a card and loses. But we are offering you your stake money back.'

'Just one thing wrong with that pretty picture. This gambler's got a gun pointing at your guts.'

Wheeler slid his queen onto the table. 'Tell me why you came here, Orlov.'

'To give you a warning. You lift a finger against me and you'll know you guessed it wrong. It will be too late. But you'll know.'

'You mean you think my calculations on what would happen in a nuclear war are wrong?'

'You bet they're wrong.'

'So do me a favour. What would your reaction have been if I was right and your generals told you I was right. What would you have done?'

'Maybe I would have done a deal.'

'Tell me about the deal you'd have suggested.'

'You stay out of Europe and we'll stay out of the Middle East and South America.'

'You'd ditch the Cubans?'

'If it was necessary.'

'So all we are disagreeing about is Europe?'

'We aren't talking about anywhere, Wheeler. We're speculating. Nothing more.'

'OK. So in our hypothetical deal you're asking us to get out of Europe. What does get out mean?'

'Exactly what it says. Leave it as our sphere of interest.'

'But what if they resist you and fight for their freedom and independence?'

'Then we put them down. That's no problem. Two weeks. It would take no more.'

'We're beginning to talk like gamblers, Orlov. But we're not gamblers we are statesmen. So let's be formal again. Does the Soviet Union want peace or war?'

'Peace. We've always wanted peace. We've said so a thousand times. It was the United States that wouldn't negotiate a peace formula.'

'But you know why just as well as I do.'

'Why?'

'Because you wanted peace so that you could grab one country after another. You did it anyway. Despite SALT One, despite Helsinki, Vienna, Geneva and all the rest.'

'It was always at their request. We just helped stabilise friendly governments.'

'What I am offering is more than you deserve. You know that already.'

'So what are you offering? Spell it out.'

For a moment Wheeler hesitated, then he said, 'Do we need interpreters Mr President?'

'I don't.'

'Can we ask them to leave?'

'Sure.' And Orlov nodded a brusque dismissal to his man. Wheeler's interpreter left with him. When they had left the room Wheeler looked directly at Orlov.

'Let me spell it out then. You withdraw from Britain and the Warsaw Pact countries. You stay inside your own frontiers, and the Soviet Union and the United States sign a Peace Treaty with mutual guarantees. We negotiate a disarmament treaty right down to bows and arrows. You'd go down in the history books as the man who brought real peace, and your resources would go to putting your non-military economy right.'

'They won't buy it, Wheeler. I tried. The generals said they could do more than you knew, or your people knew. They said it was a knife-edge situation. If we went down they could bring the US down. All the way. The Politburo said our forces were evenly balanced and for all I know they could be right.'

'You mean your generals recommended you should fight? And that they could win?'

'No. They said both sides would be finished but they could do you more damage than your people could have calculated.'

'I don't believe that.'

'I'm not sure that I do, but that was the advice they gave the Politburo. That we couldn't win but that you couldn't win either.'

'What did you recommend?'

'I recommended that we compromised.'

Wheeler played his king. 'We wouldn't compromise. It's one way or another, but all the way.'

Orlov's face was grey, and Wheeler could see a pulse beating beside his left eye. He counted out the seconds in his mind before he spoke. And then he said quietly. 'How did the generals suggest they would deal with the southern borders?'

He saw the surprise and horror on Orlov's face as he absorbed the words and their meaning. His voice was almost a whisper when he said, 'You mean the Chinese are in this too?'

'Of course.'

'I can't believe it.'

'He's on one of our carriers, it's lying-to off the bay. I can get him here in a couple of hours.'

'Who? Not Deng himself?'

'Yes.'

Orlov closed his eyes, sitting there silently for long

minutes, his hands clasped together, the knuckles white. And then he opened his eyes and looked at Wheeler.

'Have you got documentation that confirms Peking's attitude?'

'No. But you can talk privately on a closed untapped line to Deng Xiaoping if you wish.'

Orlov nodded and Wheeler stood up, walking across to a mobile communications console, its heavy duty cable leading to a plug in the wall.

Wheeler lifted the red telephone and carefully pressed four heat switches one after the other as he held the receiver to his ear. For several moments he waited, then as the quiet voice spoke at the other end he said what he had rehearsed so many times in the last few weeks. *'Wang shi dzou ... aweile ... ch'ing ... dzedze.'* Then he beckoned to Orlov who walked across. As Wheeler handed him the receiver he said, 'Speak slowly and clearly in English or German.'

Then Wheeler walked away to the far corner of the room, standing, looking unseeing at the books that lined the shelves of the mahogany bookcase. He could hear Orlov speaking slowly and carefully but he couldn't hear what he was saying. Not that Wheeler had any doubt of the outcome. The bastards were in the nutcracker and Orlov knew it. It was tempting to squeeze them all the way but enough was enough.

Orlov was walking slowly back to the chair and he sat down heavily, his hands on his thighs, and Wheeler joined him again.

'Were you satisfied, Orlov?'

'We'd better talk. Find some solution.'

'There's only one solution we would accept.'

'You'd better lay it out.'

'We sign an agreement that will be known as the Soviet–American Shannon Agreement. The preamble will state that the meeting was initiated by you and negotiated with me.

312

That both governments have ratified the agreement. You have initiated these negotiations because of your government's concern for world peace and prosperity. Both governments are prepared to make sacrifices in pursuit of world peace.

'The Soviet Union will withdraw its forces from all territory outside the Soviet Union including the UK, Afghanistan and the Warsaw Pact countries. It will also instruct its Cuban and South-east Asian mercenaries to cease operations wherever they might be. A separate disarmament treaty will be negotiated based not only on a reduction in arms but on a mutual defence treaty between the Soviet Union, the USA and China. The treaty will require public disclosure of all armed forces and weapons, their numbers and their locations, and the reasons why they are necessary. A tripartite satellite programme will be set-up to monitor every country in the world, not just the three leaders. There will be no secret deals, no diplomacy, *all* the facts will be published world-wide and updated monthly. If you shift a missile, or we do, you have to say why. Nobody can stop you but the whole world will know you've done it and can read your explanation. And believe it or not.

'There will be a separate treaty covering trade and aid. The USA will make available to the Soviet Union all its scientific and technological information owned by the government. Private companies will be encouraged to sell information if they wish to do so.

'All this has already been drafted in detail. You can bring over anyone you wish to guide you. Our people or your own. But none of it is negotiable. Not one word.'

Orlov had sat unmoving while Wheeler was talking and it was a long time before he spoke.

'And the Party in the Soviet Union?'

'That's your business, Orlov. The outside world doesn't like what you do to your people but that would be up

313

to them and you. As far as these treaties are concerned
the Soviet Union goes on as now. There will be free and
supervised elections in Poland, Hungary and the rest of
the Warsaw Pact countries and if they choose communism
they can have it. But your troops and advisers are out.'

'The commercial cooperation. Is that real?'

'Absolutely.'

'It's strange reasoning. Hard to understand.'

'It's not hard Orlov. It's very simple. What the Americans
are saying is that all over the world politicians, diplomats,
governments have worked on the basis that the less people
know the easier it will be for their rulers. That's why we
have propaganda. A one-sided version of some shifty move
that makes it look good or tolerable. But at the top of
the heap we all know it's just a game. A game to deceive
our own people as well as outsiders. From now on we're
going to turn it inside out. From now on the people of
every country will know what's going on in every other
country so far as defensive and offensive forces are concerned. They may not care most of the time. But when
something makes them care or they're alerted to something
then they will actually know. Our intelligence organisations
already know about everything they need to know. But
you don't tell your people anything and we hold back
information as well in the name of national security.'

'Is there a deadline?'

'Of course. I want a signature today and an announcement tonight.'

'My signature would not be enough.'

'Orlov. Forget the past. If you announce a peace treaty
between the USA, the Soviet Union and China not even
your bitterest enemy is going to utter a word of criticism.
Just think of what it means for your people. Making the
things they really want, instead of missiles. Security for
all time, guaranteed by the USA and China. And you and

the Politburo will be the ones who made it happen. You'll be there for life if you behave yourselves.'

'Just one more question, Wheeler.'

'Go on.'

'Why do you do all this? What's the pay-off for you? You've nearly finished your two terms.'

'I've been in politics all my life, Orlov, one way or another. But I'm not really a politician. I did the wheeling and dealing to get things done, but to me it was a waste of energy for the others as well as me. It was inefficient. A game. And I'm tired of playing games. And in the end I came to the conclusion that political ideologies aren't universal. Communism may work inside the Soviet Union. As long as your people will put up with it that's their business. Provided ...' and Wheeler jabbed out a monitory finger, '... provided they can pack their bags and leave if they don't like it. What we call western democracy is fine in various forms. Provided the people want it. But I doubt if democracy or communism will cut any ice in any part of Africa. It may sound good but they are based on tribes not nations. Maybe a benevolent dictatorship suits them better.

'We really need to stop the world for a year and have a look at what the hell we're all doing to one another. As that isn't possible this is the next best thing. We can't stop the world but we can stop a lot of what's happening. It's time the people were told what it's all about. It won't stop the Politburo trying to get one up on us but, by God, the whole world will know it. No more of us keeping quiet and letting you get away with it in a fog of propaganda. When you lie, they'll know it. The British have had to find out the hard way what Soviet communism is all about, and the rest of Europe has learned at their expense. You've got yourselves deep in the shit, Orlov, and you know it. So do the rest of your friends and rivals in the Politburo.

They won't like the fact that it's you who's fixed it but, by Christ, they'll go along with it.'

'So why the hurry? Why not work it out together?'

'We're not horse-trading, Orlov, I told you that. We don't want to sit around tables with your po-faced friends arguing about every word and comma. That would take years. If we had made as many blunders as you people have you would have forced us into a corner when we were down. You'd have humiliated us and enjoyed it. And some day we'd have come back and settled the account.

'You're in deep, deep trouble, Orlov. All over the world and in so many ways. Politically, economically you're cracking up, crumbling to pieces. But we're giving you a second chance. A chance to look like a hero instead of the failure you really are. It's our one last act of diplomacy. After this you'll be whatever you really are.'

Orlov sighed deeply. 'What if the Presidium denounce me and the treaty?'

'Do you think that's likely?'

'Is this room bugged?'

'No. Absolutely not. What you and I say to one another is off the record and between the two of us.'

'What assessment of the Politburo reaction did your evaluation team come up with?'

'Two dissenters.'

'Who?'

'Ivanov and Zagorsky.'

'Why Ivanov?'

'He's not very bright and he'll expect the generals to support him.'

'And will they?'

'We're sure they won't. How about you?'

'I think you're right.' He shook his head. 'You've worked it out well, my friend.'

'So what's the problem?'

'The protocol. This is the kind of thing we should discuss in the Kremlin for months and you expect me to decide in a few hours and then make an announcement without consulting the ruling body.'

'I can have full details of the treaty and its appendixes in the hands of your fourteen Vice-Presidents ten minutes before the announcement goes out.'

'The Soviet people won't hear my announcement.'

'They will. We can cut in on all your national and regional radio and TV stations with sound and pictures.'

Orlov half-smiled. 'Is this the same kind of thing as our COSMOS device?'

'It's one step better. It's compatible with PAL and SECAM as well as our own home TV system.'

Wheeler saw Orlov's tension go, his body relaxing, his face less tense, and he turned to look at the American. 'The response from the people would be instant and positive. The Politburo wouldn't dare to denounce it. The mere fact that it was possible would bring overwhelming support.'

'And your own feelings?'

Orlov shrugged. 'It has to be done. It's worth trying and if we fail the world will see that at least we tried.'

'So you agree?'

'Yes. I agree.'

'OK. Then a suggestion. You and I will go over all the material together for the rest of the day and through tonight. Get a few hours sleep in. Prepare our individual speeches tomorrow and make the announcement tomorrow night instead of tonight. Let's make it real good stuff.'

'I'll have to explain it to my people who are here.'

'No you won't. We'll combine our two teams as of now and we'll tell them together how it's gonna be.'

'OK.'

# 25

Wheeler had given the revised instructions to the TV team and they had scheduled the whole operation with Washington. All major TV and radio stations in every country in the world would be given four minutes notice of the televised news conference. No details would be given of its content just that it was a joint US/Soviet/Chinese announcement of major importance. They were to be told that their own programmes would be automatically interrupted for between 30 and 45 minutes but there would be no programming charges.

The US Ambassador in Moscow was given the time when he should open the sealed packet in his safe where he would receive instructions about opening the steel case holding the material to be distributed to the Vice-Presidents of the Politburo.

Wheeler's own team were to be allotted a partner from Orlov's party on a man to man basis with instructions to stick with them every minute of the time until the broadcast was over. Wheeler and Orlov worked through the night to reduce the texts of what they would say to the shortest possible statements that still covered all the vital benefits to all concerned.

They had invited the local Dublin representatives of API, Reuters, Tass and Novosty for an unspecified interview and both Wheeler and Orlov had agreed that there would be no rehearsal. Wheeler would speak in English with sub-titles in Russian, Chinese and French. Orlov would speak in Russian with English, Chinese and French sub-titles.

The big entrance hall had been cleared and a long desk placed in the centre. The press agency men would be brought in later and chairs for them were on the far side of the set. Both Wheeler's and Orlov's men would see the announcement on monitor sets in the main dining hall.

The floor of the entrance hall was covered with a mass of thick cables that led to five mobile consoles that controlled three world regions and the satellite and interruptor systems that would insert the broadcast into all stations broadcasting at the time. There was no possibility of matching the different world time zones and it was decided that Moscow would be the pivot time on their 6 p.m. programmes. The United States system would allow for station announcements to be made of a most important broadcast in the early hours of the morning with the station openly admitting that they had no idea of the programme's content or format.

The broadcast had taken 35 minutes with Orlov speaking first and Wheeler second. The second camera had cut from time to time to Deng Xiaoping's impassive face. China was not a party to the agreement but his presence was significant enough. It indicated approval but not pressure on either side.

The handful of press had seemed both impressed and incredulous and the few questions they put were on the lines of 'Will the Politburo and Congress ratify the agreement?' Both Orlov and Wheeler had smiled and countered by asking if the questioner could imagine any government not ratifying an agreement that meant an 80 per cent cut in defence expenditure, commercial and technical cooperation between the two world powers and peace for the foreseeable future. When Wheeler had been asked why now, not years earlier, he had smiled and pointed at Orlov. 'The man and the hour and a world that needs a long rest from the tensions of the last four or five decades. A chance to build not destroy.'

Only in the case of some of the Pacific islands did the beam not lock into the local TV frequency but medium and short-wave radio coverage had been total.

Wheeler and Orlov waited impatiently for the reactions to come in to the control room from all parts of the world. The first news was discouraging. The US Embassy in Moscow had been surrounded by troops and in Washington two hawkish senators had made statements saying that 'the agreement would never be ratified in a million years'.

Most European capitals reported a cautious response that consisted mainly of requests for confirmation that the broadcast and the agreement were genuine. But an hour later the news changed dramatically. All over the world countries, even those barely concerned with the old East–West clashes, reported that broadcast stations were being flooded with wildly enthusiastic calls from the widest spectrum of the public. Whether it was the early hours of the morning, mid-day or evening in the country concerned thousands of enthusiastic people were celebrating in the streets.

The Soviet troops had been withdrawn from the American embassy and people were dancing and cheering in the streets of all the major Soviet cities.

In a moment of mutual and unexpected euphoria Orlov and Wheeler exchanged planes and crews for the return journeys to their capitals. Air Force One would fly Orlov to Sheremetyevo and an Ilyushin called over from London with its crew would fly Wheeler back to Dulles International.

More than half the members of the Politburo had had the courage or shrewdness to show their hands by meeting

Orlov's plane at Sheremetyevo. If they had had any doubts they were dispelled by the thousands who converged on the airport and lined the route back to the capital. There were some cold hard eyes that looked back at him at the first meeting in the Kremlin, two generals had resigned but Orlov ignored the unspoken opposition and rode triumphantly on the waves of optimism from the public.

Wheeler's piece of showmanship with his Red Air Force plane and crew had gone down well, and this small, spontaneous gesture had, in a way, indicated the benefits to come more than any speech would have done.

From all over the world came messages of congratulation and goodwill to Moscow and Washington. It was as if a bitter, long drawn out divorce case had ended in conciliation and the family were all back together again. Nowhere was there any pay-off for criticising ex-enemies. The world didn't want it and the public weren't going to let it happen. There were no vanquished, no dead, no wounded and few losers. All that ordinary citizens wanted was to show their good-will. If there were doubting Thomases they kept their doubts to themselves as committees, associations, leagues and clubs bent their minds to a thousand and one ways of showing their old enemies the extent of their goodwill. Caviar, vodka, Moscow Dynamo, the Bolshoi and the Moscow Symphony Orchestra flowed one way and Levis, the Cubs, the Mayors of Chicago, Los Angeles and New York, the Boston Pops and pedigree Herefords flowed the other. Not always did they function as expected but always in a golden glow of wild public enthusiasm.

Only in Britain did the situation seem uncertain. The Royal Family had waited for almost a week before they came back. Nobody had invited them back because there was nobody who had the authority either to prevent or invite their presence. Wheeler had made sure that Harry

x

Andrews and his men were acknowledged as national heroes but the population were not in a mood for heroes or villains. Britain was not a party to the Shannon Agreement, as everybody now referred to it. Britain like the rest of the world were just witnesses to something that benefited the country immediately. No war had been won. The Russians had pulled out *en masse* in the first few days. There were no heirs to the good fortune. No rulers to rule, and seemingly no urge on the part of the public to call for leaders. And all the sources of leaders were old. Not tried and trusted but tried and distrusted. Distrusted to a point of loathing bordering on hatred. Particularly for the old institutions of Parliament and politicians, the bureaucracy and all elements of the old establishment.

The Royal family kept a low profile. They were obviously loved but it was an old, rather nostalgic love. Like a much loved wife who'd gone off with another man but who had eventually returned. Everybody glad that she was back but aware of time that had passed. No open accusations of unfaithfulness but an awareness that there were questions that were better not asked.

Units of armed forces who had gone overseas had returned, but their leaders were reluctant to take any sort of initiative. Through no fault of their own their rôle had been exposed before the occupation as being incapable of fulfilment. They had not been used against either the law-breakers who had brought down the country, neither, and again through no fault of their own, had they defended the country against its enemies. They were neither despised nor welcomed. They were vague neutral figures, best ignored for the time being.

Several groups of people, mainly ex-journalists, started local newspapers whose formats and content were more national than local. They encouraged local discussion and their letters columns ended by taking up half their space.

But the views expressed were mainly negative. People might not be sure what they wanted to replace the old gang but they were almost unanimous about what they didn't want. And high on their list were the old political parties and the former politicians.

There were newspaper features about an all-woman government, Plato's Republic, the human face of Anarchy and separate governments for Wales and Scotland and seven regions of England. But nothing aroused positive and universal approval.

At the end of two weeks Andrews could see a re-run of the old scenario happening again. Discussion, disillusion and no control or guidance. Reluctantly he took on a rôle that he had never wanted or considered.

He had long talks with Jamie Boyle and his father. Nothing concrete was decided but the outcome was a tour of all the major cities with mass meetings organised by the members of Harry Andrews' local groups of resistance fighters.

To Andrews' surprise he and his men were given rapturous welcomes everywhere, and it seemed that they had a special position in the public's mind. It was not that they were seen as heroes, the country was in no mood for either heroes or heroics. But they were a group of men with a special virtue. They were not part of the old establishment, and had, in fact, had the foresight to counter the results of its weakness. And they were not part of the humiliation that went with the Russian occupation. They had countered that too. Not decisively, but effectively enough to show that Britain might be worth saving by the nations that had once been her allies and friends. They were the only people who had not been part of the nation's fall and humiliation.

The most important outcome of the mass-meetings was that Harry Andrews was acceptable as a man and leader by every kind of person. Men and women, young and old. His possible detractors from the old establishment had neither the platform nor the courage to express their opposition. And in their heart of hearts those old hands knew that whatever case they put forward for a return to the pre-occupation establishment they would be laughed at or lynched depending on the audience.

Harry Andrews remembered that half-joking remark of President Wheeler when they had met at his Texas home and Wheeler responded immediately with a plane load of non-party advisers. Both he and Andrews realised that the vacuum in British life needed to be filled urgently. Perfection might have to be sacrificed to expediency.

The central case was decided in days. The British should have a Constitution based on the American Constitution but with the benefit of hindsight. There had been many criticisms by the American advisers, particularly the lawyers, of even some basics of the American Constitution but Andrews over-ruled them on the grounds that the men who had drawn up the Constitution had done it in similar circumstances to those now prevailing in Britain. He had reluctantly agreed right from the start that there had to be politicians and perhaps that meant inevitably that there had to be political parties.

But Andrews admired the care and concern with which the original Constitution had been beaten out and he allowed changes to be made only when the original had amendments or conditions that applied solely to the United States. Additional conditions were written in that prevented the funding or control of any party other than from individual members of that party. Representation or sponsorship, overt or covert, by any group representing any outside interest of either labour or capital was prohibited.

For Harry Andrews the saving grace, the one excuse for accepting the rôle of politicians was a Constitution that allowed the courts to over-ride any law passed by Parliament that offended the British Constitution.

The new concept was put to the people at another country-wide series of mass meetings and Andrews asked for an audience with the Queen. The rôle of the monarch was both enhanced and reduced by the British Constitution, and the Queen's advisers had been kept in touch but not consulted in its preparation. The Queen had welcomed both the Constitution itself and the more positive but restricted new rôle for the monarch.

Andrews announced the new structure for the government of the country on the Guildhall steps to cheering crowds and almost overnight the optimism and the energies of all sections of the people seemed to surge and blossom. Commerce and industry that had wallowed in uncertainty, revived. Groups wanting to start newspapers and broadcasting got together to make plans and raise money. Potential congressmen and senators began to form their interested groups and formulate their plans for the forthcoming elections for President, Congress and Senate. The Senate was to be based on the old House of Lords with minimal party affiliation.

A group of independent men of talent had been chosen arbitrarily by Andrews, with the advice of his American consultants, and they ruled the country in the two months prior to the elections, with only a glance at old laws and no concern for old loyalties.

The first President of Great Britain was a woman. A highly qualified academic who had once been a senior civil servant but who had become Vice-Chancellor of Newcastle University just before the occupation. No party had been allowed to use any of the old names but the Congress majority which was held by a party styling itself the Middle Party was recognisably an amalgam of both the two old major parties. The Senate included former members of the aristocracy and middle-class professionals and the majority had stood as independents. Congress contained few lawyers and businessmen because the Constitution precluded both congressmen and senators from holding any other paid position while in office and for five years after ceasing to be in office. During which time they were on full pay according to their serving status and length of service. Elections were to be held every four years on fixed dates.

Scotland and Wales had their own Congresses with a flexible basis for central funding in return for surrendering their defence and foreign policy to the Federal Senate.

Jamie Boyle had not contacted Jeanie since he had heard of her relationship with the Russian and when he eventually made his way back to the house at Cramond it was with no sense of pride that he had been part of the organisation that had been termed 'The Resistance'.

He had bought a second-hand car and motored back to Scotland because apart from walking that would take longer than any other way.

It wasn't a homecoming. It was just going back to a house that had once been a home. An empty house that he had heard had been vandalised. His father had never spoken again of Jeanie or the dead Russian and all that seemed from a different world. A world that had ended a long time ago. He had phoned Macgregor and asked him to fit new locks and keep the keys until he called in to collect them.

When he finally got to the Scot's new address on a small pre-occupation estate of semi-detached houses he felt a brief spasm of relief that the man had at least improved the conditions under which he lived. The motherly Lily had been blinded in one eye in a random attack by Soviet militia on a group of women protesting against the starvation level rations in the last few months of the occupation.

The big tough Scot had become a wild animal, spending far too much of his group's time and resources on a personal vendetta against the militia group, killing nine of them in a period of two months but failing miserably through lack of preparation on some of the sabotage operations Harry Andrews had ordered. Cameron Davies had been sent to Glasgow to report on what was going on. He had said nothing but had taken a grip on them all and got them back into line. Davies reckoned that he had been well-rewarded when he married Mac's daughter, Helen.

It was Helen who answered the door to Jamie Boyle's knock, and the warm arms that went round his neck, and the soft mouth on his, were a welcome that was genuine and unexpected.

'Come on in, Jamie. Lily will be delighted.'

'How is she?'

'It's taking time, Jamie. She was a very active woman and she tends to get annoyed when she collides with the furniture and can't pour the milk in the saucepan properly. If you pretend you haven't noticed her eye she'll be very pleased with herself. And she's a bit of a vain old cat is my mam.'

And Lily had shed a tear. Not a tear of sadness. Not even specially for Jamie Boyle. Just a tear of mixed pleasure, relief and pain for humanity in general.

Mac was his usual quiet self and when Boyle had taken the house keys after the meal he had walked out to the car with him.

'And what are you going to do now, wee man? Back to the law books and the villains?'

'I don't think so, Mac. I think maybe I'll try the States. For a few months anyway.'

'And what about the wee lassie?' Mac said softly.

'You mean Jeanie?'

'Aye, of course.'

'I never think about her.'

'I don't believe that. You've no need to kid me, my bonny boy. That's just pride talking.'

'Why should I think about her?'

'Because you once said you'd love her for a' your days. For better or worse.'

'She said that too.'

'Aye. And like you, she meant it.'

'Not when the chips were on the table and that's when it counts.'

'Just the Russian. Nothing more than that?'

'That's enough for me.'

'Have you no' put your weapon where it didna' belong?'

'Once or twice. But not until after that business.'

'You mean you just screwed a lassie without giving a damn for her?'

'Not necessarily. I liked them and they liked me.'

'Did you ever kiss them as well as screw them?'

'Of course I did.'

'Out of liking and affection?'

'Yes.'

'And that's OK for you but not for Jeanie?'

'I didn't start it, Mac. That's the difference.'

'Ah well. You learn something every day.'

'What's that mean?'

The burly Scot prodded Boyle's chest with a thick hard forefinger. 'It means it'd take more than a bloody Russki sticking his thing in my Lily's belly to make me stop caring for her and we didna' make any fancy vows in a kirk. I'll tell you that.'

'Where is Jeanie? What happened to her?'

'How in hell should I know. You're her man, my boy, not me.'

Boyle sighed. 'I'll see you sometime next week, Mac. I'd better be going.'

'Take care then, Jamie. There's a lot of people love you. More than you think.'

Boyle had stopped the car half-way to Cramond. There was no point in going to the house. It was just a bloody house. A building. Maybe one night only and the next day he'd arrange for it to be sold.

As he stood at the front door he noticed the shiny chrome of the new lock as he put in the key. As he opened the front door it all looked much the same as when he had left it that night. Obviously Helen or Lily had been in to make it less bleak when he came back. And then the door to the sitting-room opened and she was standing there, looking at him, her head to one side, the long hair curling onto her shoulder. And she said, very quietly, 'Long time no see.'

He put down his bag and tried not to look at her. But there was nowhere else to look. And he wanted to look anyway. There was no colour any more in her cheeks and the dark shadows under her eyes didn't come from make-up. He wanted to say something neutral. Or even something nice, but it was easier and more tempting to be unkind.

'What brings you here?'

'Just you,' she said. 'And me.'

'You don't have to worry about me, my dear.'

'D'you know something?'

'No. Tell me.'

'I'd give everything I've got in the world and anything I might have in the future if, when you said "my dear" you'd meant it.'

He stooped for his bag, grasped it and stood up again.

'I'll leave you to it.'

'Leave me to what?'

He shrugged. 'The house. Whatever it is you want.'

'I want you, Jamie. No houses. Nothing else.'

'It's too late for that, Jeanie. That went a long time ago.'

There were tears at the edges of her eyes and she had to take a deep breath before she could speak. And despite the deep breath her voice quavered as she spoke.

'And that's all I ever meant to you? One terrible mistake and I wasn't fit to be spoken to. Not even worth the traditional curse or broken nose.'

'Is that what you would have preferred?'

'By God, yes. When they've cursed her or punched her in the face the anger's gone. Even for the Rangers and Celtic hooligans they speak afterwards.'

'You wouldn't like their words, Jeanie.'

'I'd have gone down on my knees for any profanity, any obscenity, if it had been from your mouth. Just a chance to speak. That chance you so often used for your clients. The things you always said could save a cruel sentence. What did you call it...the plea in mitigation? You said even murderers deserved that plea before they were sentenced.'

'We do what we feel at the time, Jeanie. I'm not a saint. I'm a man. Not even a good man. I acted according to my instincts.'

'So why...'

And as he watched, her face went grey and slowly, terribly slowly, her body slid down the wall and her head bounced as it hit the floor.

For a few moments he stood frozen, then he dropped his bag, lifted her body and carried her into the sitting room, laying her on the couch and loosening the top buttons of her blouse.

As he walked to the door he noticed that there was a fire burning in the grate and a bottle of whisky and two glasses laid out on the glass table. As he soaked a towel in cold water he felt a mixture of sadness and guilt.

Sadness at her obvious preparations for them to talk together and guilt that as he unbuttoned her blouse he wondered how many times the Russian had done the same.

As he came out of the kitchen with the wet towel dripping the telephone rang. He turned and walked to the hall table to answer it.

'Boyle,' he shouted.

'Jamie,' his father said. 'How are you?'

'I'm fine.'

'You don't sound fine. You sound distraught. Have you quarrelled?'

'You knew she was here?'

'Of course. It was my suggestion. She was beside herself with anxiety. I told her not to be. I said ... just talk to one another. I told her to have faith in you. Your good sense. Your kindness. I said that even if it doesn't work out you both cared for one another, loved one another, all that can't be trampled on just because she hasn't the courage to face you ... don't sigh, boy. She's my daughter as well as you being my son. I care very much for you both. Why don't you both come over and talk with me, I'm very lonely.'

'I'll call you later, father.'

'You promise?'

'I promise.'

For a few moments after he had hung up he just stood there his eyes closed, the towel wet against his clothes.

Her eyes were already open as he went back into the room and when she saw him she tried to sit up and failed. He sat on the settee beside her and took her hand.

'I want you to listen very carefully to what I say. Will you do that?'

She nodded.

'I'm sorry for what has happened. Sorry for your part. Sorry for mine. I was shocked and I was angry, and it just swept all other feelings away. If you'll forgive me, I'll forgive you. Maybe we won't forget, and maybe that doesn't matter. We shall forget it in the end. So let me say I'm sorry for my part, today as well as before. Let's try for a year. I'll do my best, you'll do yours. But we never mention any of this ever again. No matter how provoked either of us may be. We start like we left off and the rest never happened. OK?'

She nodded. 'You'll give me a chance, Jamie. A real chance?'

He sighed. 'I'm such a fool, Jeanie. Such a fool. We don't need a year. Just let's get on with it.'

And he sighed again as her arms went round him and she rested her tired head against his shoulder.


Harry Andrews and Joe Langley had been to the inaugural sitting of the first Congress. It had been decided to abandon the old Palace of Westminster as being both too divisive and too redolent of the past failures. A new Congress and Senate building had been designed and approved on the derelict wasteland of the old docks area. But that was due to take two years despite all the promises and contributions from other countries in both cash and kind.

Meantime the Albert Hall had been stripped and fitted out as the temporary home of Congress and with a touch of impartiality the Festival Hall became the temporary home of the Senate. There were no longer the rows of benches in their adversary formation, and none of the ancient historic niceties of the old Commons. No Mace, no Black Rod, no arcane parliamentary procedure. Not even the battered top-hat that used to be required to raise a point of order.

The seats were set in a vast semi-circular segment and congressmen were seated in alphabetical order. A broad dais housed the speaker's place, the duty Justice Commissioner, and slightly below was the podium for speakers. There was no ceremonial. No opening prayer. But the procedures encouraged reflection and consideration with an emphasis on fact and opinion rather than rhetoric. It was a businesslike gathering and, as the Speaker frequently reminded them in its early days, when congressmen produced incorrect facts it would be referred to later, and if such errors persisted the offender would go before the appropriate committee. Abuse of anyone, a member of Congress or the public would be quashed immediately as would speeches couched in inflammatory terms.

As the two of them sat in the Steak House in Kensington High Street Langley said, 'You should have been in one of those seats, Harry.'

'Me. For God's sake. Why me?'

'They wouldn't have been there if it wasn't for you. Organising the resistance and then coming up with the Constitution thing.'

Andrews smiled. 'A lot of people were talking about having a written Constitution long before the Russians moved in.'

'So why didn't they do it, then?'

'It paid most of them not to. Maintained their privileges and gave them power to make the laws to suit themselves and their parties and supporters. Politicians were in the business for power. Nothing else. All the words about the good of the people were so much white-wash. Given a choice or a vote as between the people and the party, they never hesitated. Whatever side they were on. There was nothing to choose between the bastards. The power in the Labour Party didn't lie with its general members.

333

Not even the working-class, whoever they were supposed to be. The leaders of the Labour lot had never done a day's manual work between them.

'And the Tories didn't represent commerce and industry. Most of them couldn't have run a fish and chip shop at a profit.'

'What about the fact that it was your planning and your hard work and leadership made it all possible.'

Andrews shook his head. 'Nice of you to say that, Joe. But it isn't true. Our resistance wouldn't have got rid of one tank or one Red Army soldier. We were just flea-bites. Irritations. All we did was show the Americans and the rest of the world that the occupation wasn't voluntary. Wasn't at our request. They saw us resisting and it stirred a few consciences. And in Washington it showed that we'd still fight on our own. Just like we did in World War II when we fought the Nazis for over a year entirely on our own. And the Russians and the Nazis were allies all that time.' Andrews smiled. 'We mustn't kid ourselves, Joe. We started the slide for the Russians, we greased the slippery slope for them. But alone they would have wiped us out. No doubt about it.'

'What are you going to do now?'

Andrews smiled. 'They've offered me an interesting post at Boston University. Teaching the history of Britain from 1970 to today, 1987. And we've started a baby. Indi will be with me. And you? Why didn't you have a go for Congress? You'd have romped home.'

'They've given me a decent pension. I expect it was you fixed that. I've had enough. We both have, me and the wife. We're moving down to Cornwall. A nice little bungalow and a brand new shed in the back for me. An engineering workshop. I'm going to make scale-models of the old steam locomotives. Duchess of Athol, Sir Nigel Gresley, the Royal Scot. That sort of thing.'

Andrews smiled. 'You look younger even now, just saying it.'

'I feel it, guv'nor. I'm younger than I've been for years.'

Glyn Thomas and Meg had watched the men photographing and sketching their farmhouse loft. Making copious notes before removing the electronics and radios to their new home at the Imperial War Museum. It was to be a permanent exhibit, a complete reconstruction of the loft at Pen-y-Fan. The base HQ of British resistance. Even the old foam carpeting was being carefully pulled up to be relaid at the museum.

Glyn Thomas had cooperated in every way except one. He refused to discuss any of it with anyone. Neither with the museum authorities nor the media, nor the army would he discuss any aspect of the resistance movement. Offers of money were brushed aside with a scathing sentence. Pensions, decorations and a lump sum gratuity were treated as insults, though none of them were offered in anything other than admiration and gratitude.

Of all the original leaders of the small group who had trained and organised the eventual resistance groups he was the only one whose views were harsh and uncompromising.

Meg had sat with him many nights after the Russians had left. Watching her husband process all those names, cover-names and data through the computer. His final figures had shown 10,491 full-time and active members, and 210,000 auxiliaries had provided some sort of service ranging from information to specialised knowledge. To many they were a roll-call of honour, 220,491 men and women who had risked their own and their families' lives in the cause of the resistance. But to Glyn Thomas they were cause for shame. Neither Andrews nor any of the others could persuade him otherwise. He just snarled back angrily that what it all added up to was that despite the brutality, the humiliation, the virtual slavery, fewer than one half of one per cent of the population of Great Britain were prepared to defend their way of life against a tyranny.

To Glyn Thomas your name was on that computer print-out or, so far as he was concerned, you didn't exist. Glyn Thomas was one of the walking wounded that the Russians had left behind them. A sad, bitter man whose only concern was his farm and his wife. And Meg Thomas loved him the more for his mental wound but sometimes wondered if God hadn't after all answered her prayers those years ago when she had prayed for a child. And the answer had been 'No'. Because God knew better than she did what was to happen.

# 26

The girl from the Ministry of Culture pointed through a clump of birch and pine trees to the wooden house.

'That's his house.'

Art Lane told the driver to stop, and the convoy of van and two cars halted on the sandy track.

It could have so easily been any house in New England. Well-made, functional and handsome. With silver birches in the small flat garden and a picket fence.

As the cameraman joined him on the track he pointed to the house.

'I want a long shot from here and then zoom in slowly onto the door of the house. About fifteen seconds maximum.'

'D'you want it softened at all?'

Lane frowned and sighed then said, 'Give it me both ways, Charlie. I'm not sure. Depends on the interview.'

Twenty minutes later Lane and the girl were standing in the sun-filled room at the corner of the house. The room was well heated but Art Lane still wore his sheepskin jacket as if it were some kind of armour against his alien surroundings.

The *dacha* was in Peredelkino just outside Moscow, the artists' and writers' community that was the reward for Party loyalty. Even some who had subsequently fallen from grace were still allowed to stay there.

The room was sparsely but well furnished with a comfortable three-seater settee and several armchairs. A TV and a radio stood on the lowest of a set of bookshelves. A paperback copy of Gibbon's *Decline and Fall of the Roman Empire* lay face down and open on a small marble table at the side of one of the armchairs.

'Is he ready?' Lane asked the girl.

'Yes. Shall I bring him in?'

'Yes. Let's get started.'

The man who came into the room with the girl looked pale but healthy enough and Lane held out his hand.

'Mr Cooper. Art Lane NBC. Head of features. Thanks for seeing me.'

Cooper nodded and waved to one of the chairs. 'Do sit down, Mr Lane.' Cooper sat down himself on the settee and Lane leaned forward.

'Do you want me to use your title in the interview, Sir Frederick? We're happy to go along with whatever you wish.'

Cooper smiled wryly. 'Just Cooper will do nicely. Or my first name. Frederick or Freddie.'

'I'd like to go over some of the questions I had in mind for the interview. And let me make quite clear that we have no intention of making this a hostile interview. As far as NBC are concerned and Time-Life this is an interview of record. Neither for or against anything you may have ... er ... decided to do in the past.'

Cooper nodded and lit a cigarette, his hand trembling slightly.

'Did you always smoke, Mr Cooper?'

Cooper smiled. 'A newly acquired vice I'm afraid.'

'Why did you start?'

Cooper shrugged. 'Why does anybody start? Loneliness. Too much time unfilled. And ...' he smiled ' ... I rather enjoy it.'

'Looking back over the past few years do you see any lessons that could guide our future thinking?'

Cooper sighed and looked at the American. 'D'you really want me to talk on these lines?'

'Sure. Why not?'

'You may not like the answers. Your audience may not like them either.'

'You go right ahead, Mr Cooper. Just say exactly what you feel.'

'I think the last ten years have shown great flaws in our society. Both East and West. But perhaps I'd better keep to my own area. In Britain we prided ourselves on our tolerance, our democracy and our parliamentary system that gave us democracy and maintained it. All over the world newly created nations modelled their institutions on ours. And all over the world they failed. We put it down to the fact that the people were black or brown, to the problems of tribalism or religion. But of course it wasn't like that at all. It was democracy itself that was a failure.'

'In what way did it fail, sir?'

'Oh, in many ways. Or maybe it would be fairer to say that maybe democracy didn't fail but we confused democracy with freedom. Complete freedom. Not just freedom to think what we liked. Or worship as we liked. Or say what we liked. But freedom to do what we liked.' Cooper smiled bleakly. 'There was a song that Frank Sinatra used to sing called "I did it my way" or some such words. It became a kind of national anthem. An excuse for any excess or failing in personality. It said you could not only do what the hell you liked at other people's expense but that you were one hell of a guy for so doing. It was going back to the caveman again. The biggest, toughest caveman gets the most meat and all the girls.'

Lane smiled. 'You don't mean we've got to blame Francis Albert for all the world's problems do you?'

'Of course not. But that song symbolises what went wrong. Tolerance can end up by being no more than weakness, lack of will. And freedom is too big a concept. You end up by tolerating the freedom to commit violence to get money or goods. Violence to gain power and control over people's lives.

'You know there's a prime example in your own field, broadcasting. The BBC was made to provide what was called "balance". If one man on a chat-show was known to be of one political view then there had to be another of the opposite view. If a policeman aired his views then a criminal had to be given equal time. Nobody ever asked if it was right or sane to let liars and power-seekers air their views against honest men. We called it freedom but it wasn't, it was madness. We let people become confused about what was right and what was wrong. They weren't stupid but they saw and heard public men, Trades Union leaders, politicians, on TV and radio blatantly lying. It wasn't their lies that confused the people it was the fact that the media never came back and said that they were liars, never challenged them.

'You saw men who were leading strikes that caused the greatest inconvenience to the public, weeping crocodile tears on TV saying how they had no intention of harming the public. It was just a coincidence that the airport people were striking at peak holiday time and the energy unions were striking in mid-winter. Nobody believed them. They didn't expect to be believed. It was just a great media game and nobody called them liars to their faces. And the public took the point. The Establishment, the powers that be, no longer cared about truth or lies, right or wrong. It was significant in the end that the commercial TV men had a bigger audience. It didn't depend on a government handout for its funds. The BBC did. You have to be pretty courageous to tell your paymaster he's a liar and a cheat.'

340

'You blame the media then?'

'Not at all. They were just the mirrors that reflected the situation. The press were independent. They spoke up often enough but people got tired of it. It didn't affect what was happening.'

'So who or what *was* to blame.'

Cooper sighed deeply. 'I don't know. I really don't. I've thought about it endlessly. One of the root causes as I look back was Parliament itself. You had the two main parties. The Tories and Labour. Totally opposed. Agreeing on nothing. Whatever one party did in office the other ripped to pieces when it came to power. They had majorities in terms of seats but never in terms of votes. Nothing ever got done. It was like children knocking down each other's sand-castles. For the life of me I can't think how the public put up with it for so long.

'Maybe the public didn't care enough. But how would they have expressed their will for a change. They may know they didn't like what they'd got but they weren't capable of saying what should go in its place. Or maybe they knew they'd never get what they wanted because the politicians wouldn't let them have it. Were we all too lazy? I don't think so. Maybe World War II knocked the spirit out of us, but other nations survived much worse conditions.

'Were we too selfish? Too concerned with our own lives and survival? Again I don't think so. Not more than other nations. No. It's a sad thing to say but I'm left with the conclusion that not only democracy doesn't work but that total freedom means total anarchy.'

'What do you think, sir, of the new ideas being put forward by the new men in Britain.'

'It's not for me to comment.'

'An indication perhaps. Are they basically good ideas?'

Cooper shrugged. 'Only time will tell, Mr Lane.'

He was humming, trying to remember the words of the Beatles' song 'Yesterday', as he put the key in the lock. But there was a key in the lock already, on the other side. He opened the door and for a moment he wondered if he'd gone into the wrong room. The bookshelves had gone and the two framed prints. And then he saw the man, the torn books and the splintered shelves and furniture. He was wearing civilian clothes but Josef knew at once that he was KGB.

'Who are you? What do you want?'

'Josef Andreyevich Andreyev?'

'Yes.'

'You are under arrest.'

'What for?'

'Under Articles 2 and 10 of the Code.'

'What's that mean?'

'You can take your brush, soap and razor and one blanket.'

'But what am I supposed to have done.'

The man's fist came so quickly that he had no time to dodge. He heard the cartilage crunch in his nose and then his head was in his hands, rocking with pain, aware of the warm blood streaming through his fingers. As the man's boot took him in the groin he passed out in a mounting wave of pain.

When he came to he was lying on straw on a concrete block in a dark smelling cell. He could see the wire cover over the light in the ceiling. When he went to move he fainted from the pain in his groin and he heard his own groan before he lost consciousness. It seemed only a few minutes before he was being shaken awake. He opened his eyes to look up at the man standing over him.

'Josef Andreyevich Andreyev?'

'Yes,' he whispered.

'Your wife is Anna Andreyeva?'

He nodded, and the pain made him close his eyes. He screamed as the man's hand grabbed his hair pulling up his head.

'Who gave you your orders?'

'Please God . . .' he murmured before he passed out again.

It seemed a long time before he came to again. He was standing. Somebody behind him was holding him up. Big hands under his armpits. A man stood at the open cell door as he was pushed into the corridor. Then they were in an old-fashioned lift and he felt the bile coming up to his mouth as the lift ground upwards. Then another corridor. But this one was different. It was clean and brightly lit and he half closed his eyes as a door swung open and he was shown inside. A chair was shoved roughly against the back of his legs and the man behind him held his shoulders to keep him upright.

A man was sitting behind a modern teak desk and as his eyes focused he could see that the man was well-dressed. More like an American than a Russian. He thought for a moment that he recognised him from somewhere. And then it all started again.

'You are Josef Andreyevich Andreyev?'

'Yes.'

'Film-script writer and assistant producer?'

'Yes.'

'And your wife is Anna Alexandrevna Andreyeva?'

'Yes.'

'Where does she work?'

'At the Bureau of Passes, Granovsky Street.'

'Where is she now?'

'I don't know. She wasn't at the flat. How long have I been here?'

'When did you last see her?'

'This morning before we both left for work.'

The man sighed. 'D'you know where you are, Andreyev?'

'In prison.'

'You're in the Lubyanka, Andreyev. And I am a KGB officer. And you are in deep, deep trouble. You understand that?'

'The man quoted some law. I didn't understand.'

'Your wife gave you petrol coupons and a travel permit the morning of the day you were arrested.'

'No.'

'Don't be stupid, Andreyev. I've got them here.' And the man reached over and lifted the small cluster of papers. 'Do you admit that she gave them to you?'

'She didn't give them to me. I've never seen them before.'

'For God's sake, Andreyev. Don't waste my time. They were found in your pockets. They come from the Ministry of Agriculture. There's the Ministry stamp on every one of them.'

'I don't know anybody in the Ministry of Agriculture. Neither does my wife.'

'Do you really want to play the hero, Andreyev. There's no audience and no applause.'

'I want to see a lawyer.'

The man grinned. 'You must be out of your mind, comrade. You've been seeing too many American films.'

'I've no more to say. Just take me to court. Try me or whatever you people do.'

'You won't be going to any court, my friend. You either talk without help or you'll be helped. You can do it whichever way you like.' He paused. 'Maybe it would help if I told you that your wife has admitted giving you the coupons and the permit. Did she tell you how she got them? Did she?'

Andreyev shivered involuntarily and shook his head. The man smiled. 'I'll tell you, comrade. A very senior man in the Ministry of Agriculture wanted a new colour TV. His official driver said that he could get one for him in exchange for petrol coupons and a travel permit to ... to where ... a nice little trip to Peredelkino maybe ... but no ... to Leningrad perhaps, the Venice of the North. But no. To Kharkov of all places. Dear dirty old Kharkov where they make locomotives and tractors and aircraft. What we call strategic industries. So what does an official chauffeur want with a nice little trip to Kharkov? Well that isn't what he wants at all. There's a pretty girl he wants to screw. But the course of true love is hampered by the fact that the pretty girl is married ... but ... it turns out that there is just something that would overcome her scruples. Roses? No. Chocolates? No. French perfume? No. But she will open her long legs wide for petrol coupons and a travel permit to Kharkov. So. The deputy minister gets his new TV, the pretty girl gets what she wants and the driver screws the brains out of that whore you call your wife.'

'I don't believe it, comrade. It's all lies. She's never given me any petrol coupons or travel permits to anywhere. Never.'

'They were in the drawer with your shirts, my friend.'

'You said you found them in my pockets.'

'Never mind what I said. They're here.'

'Where is my wife?'

'Forget about her, comrade. Just worry about yourself. You're half-way between the Gulag and the grave. If you cooperate you'll get five years in a camp. If you don't cooperate then ...' The man shrugged helplessly as if it would be out of his control '... it's up to you.'

'I want to see my wife.'

The man stood up. 'How about you think about it overnight? Think very carefully, comrade. It could be the last thinking you ever do.'

The card on the door said simply: *Radek P. G. Director*

– *Anti-subversion Directorate*. Savalev knocked and a woman's voice called out for him to go in.

'Is he available?'

She shrugged. 'I'll see.' She picked up the white telephone and said, 'Colonel Savalev is here, comrade Director.' She listened for a moment then hung up looking across at Savalev. 'You can go right in.'

Radek was leaning back in his big black leather chair and he pointed to one of the chairs in front of his big desk and waited for Savalev to sit down.

'What can I do for you, colonel?'

Savalev had never sorted out Radek in his mind. He was smooth and well-educated but there was something odd about him. Once upon a time he thought the strangeness was just that Radek was so obviously a survivor. But it was more than that. He wasn't afraid, and everybody was afraid of somebody. Instinct had always told him to tread very carefully with Radek.

'I've got a problem, comrade Director.'

Radek nodded but said nothing.

'I traced petrol coupons and travel permits to a suspect. A man. He denies all knowledge of them and I think he's telling the truth. At the same time I'm sure he's a dissident. I think he would talk but I'm not making any progress. I thought maybe you should look at him.'

Radek shook his head. 'I haven't got time, Savalev. What's his name?'

'Josef Andreyev. He's in films.'

Radek reached out and broke the ash of his cigar against the side of the blue crystal ash-tray.

'Why is he suspect?'

'We put travel permits for the places where we had the troubles through the computer. Andreyev had been in five trouble areas two weeks before the trouble started.'

'Where was the current travel permit for?'

'Kharkov.'

Radek raised his eyebrows. 'And it's in his name?'

'No. It's a general pass, no specific name and no date restrictions.'

'Where did he get it?'

'His wife got it for him?'

'How?'

'It was a *blat* deal. She screwed for her part.'

'Maybe she's the suspect.'

'I'm sure she isn't.'

'How can you be sure?'

'I happen to know her. She's stupid but she's not capable of doing anything.'

'Apart from obtaining illegal documents you mean?'

'I guess so.'

'Where is she now?'

'In the women's jail.'

Radek looked towards the window for several moments before he turned to look at Savalev.

'D'you speak Polish?'

'No.'

'I want you to go to Warsaw. There's a file. My secretary will give it to you. It's marked Karminski on the front. He's a senior official in Z–2. Look him over for me. Just sniff around. I'll get you transferred on temporary liaison. Don't take more than a couple of weeks.'

'Is he suspect?'

Radek smiled. 'Everybody's suspect, comrade Savalev. You. Me. Everybody.'

'And what about Andreyev?'

'Who?'

'Andreyev. The suspect I was telling you about.'

'Give the files to my secretary. I'll look them over and

347

decide what to do.' Radek stood up. 'As a matter of interest what do you think about the detente with the Americans? Do you think it will work?'

Savalev shrugged. 'It's impossible to tell. Those arrangements always have secret clauses and unwritten agreements. It has great dangers for us.'

'What kind of dangers?'

'It could encourage the dissidents to cause even more trouble than they have already.'

'You don't think that if the people are offered more opportunities to decide their own lives that they might respond?'

'I'm sure they won't respond favourably. It's all very well signing the Shannon Treaty but we know it can't work. As soon as one privilege has been granted they will complain and want more. If they're not controlled completely, every hour of their lives, the country would be in chaos inside ten years.'

'You don't think democracy can work?'

'We know it can't work. It's never worked anywhere. Sooner or later one group or another takes over.' He shrugged. 'That's what politics are all about.'

'Do you think communism works?'

'You want the truth, comrade?'

'Between ourselves.'

'It isn't communism or any other ideology that works. It's power that works. The names are just disguises. Like religions.'

'And you don't mind that?'

'Frankly no.' He smiled. 'As long as I'm part of the power group.'

'Well. Let me have your report about Warsaw when you get back.'

When he was alone the man named Radek walked over to the window that looked over Dzerzhinski Square. He wondered if it was the world that was crazy or just the people. He wondered how best to cover up for Josef Andreyev and that stupid wife of his. Not that she hadn't been useful. Maybe it would be best to have them both transferred to one of the film units attached to the Soviet Trade Missions in London or Washington. He turned and sat for a long time at his desk his chin cupped in the palm of one hand, his washed-out pale blue eyes staring at the picture on the wall. A photograph of a young woman, its pose old-fashioned, its colours so faded that they were barely distinguishable except for the same washed-out blue eyes. It was all going to take a long time. A long long time.